ORPHAN

MONSTER

SPY

ORPHAN MONSTER SPY

MATT KILLEEN

VIKING

VIKING

An imprint of Penguin Random House LLC

375 Hudson Street

New York, New York 10014

First published in the United States of America by Viking,

an imprint of Penguin Random House LLC, 2018

LIBRARY OF CONGRESS CATALOGING-IN-PUBLICATION DATA IS AVAILABLE

ISBN 9780451478733

Printed in the USA   Set in Bembo MT Std and Avenir Book

10   9   8   7   6   5   4   3   2   1

For all the other beaten,
bullied, and abused children.

ORPHAN

MONSTER

SPY

ONE

August 28, 1939

FINALLY, THE CAR came to a stop. With difficulty, Sarah opened her eyes, blinked to clear her vision, and looked up from her hiding place in the footwell. Her mother was slumped in the driver's seat, her head against the top of the steering wheel. She was gazing through the spokes to where Sarah crouched. Her mother's eyes were *almost* the same, wide and pretty. Her pupils were so big Sarah could nearly see herself in them. But now they seemed dull. Her mother was no longer in there.

Sarah reached out, but something hot dripped onto her hand, and she snatched it back. Her palm was bright red next to her white fingers.

Lauf, dumme Schlampe!

Sarah could hear the voice in her head, but her mother's lips weren't moving. Her nose was blocked and her eyes hurt. The pain was a fog across her thinking. Again she heard it. *Lauf! Run!* She looked at her mother's face once more, in time to see her forehead slide off the top of the wheel. The eyes, still staring, now regarded the floor. *Lauf. Just run.* Sarah thought the voice was her own.

The door handle turned, but the door didn't open. She tried again. It opened a crack, but she was pushing against the whole weight of the door, as if up a hill. Her hand was slick with blood, so she rubbed it on her coat and tried again. By sticking her shoulder against the door panel, she managed to heave it wide open, spilling the cold light of evening into the car. She scrambled up and out. The Mercedes had come to a rest in the ditch by the roadside, its nose buried in a warehouse fence.

Sarah looked into the car and saw what the bullet had done to the back of her mother's head. She fought a wave of nausea as the door swung shut, but she felt nothing else. Not yet.

Her heart was beating fast and loud in her ears, the air stinging her nose. Her neck felt hot. Behind her, the soldiers from the checkpoint were just rounding the distant corner that she and her mother had careened around moments ago, just before the shot. There were voices, shouts, running feet on the asphalt. Dogs began to bark. They were closing. Where now? What now?

Lauf.

Sarah flung herself onto the warm hood and crawled across it toward the break the car had made in the warehouse fence. The shards of broken windshield tore at her hands and knees. She slid off into the brambles and then pushed through them on all fours, picking up splinters of wood, thorns, and broken glass.

Don't look back. Keep going. Ignore the pain in your hands and knees. Lauf.

She let the voice run riot in her head as she broke through the fence. Her voice? Her mother's? It didn't matter.

Onto your feet now. That's it. Lauf, lauf, run, run.

She sprinted into an alley between two old buildings, kicking up the sludge deposited by overflowing gutters. Looking up she could see the rusting gutters hanging from the roof edges, the leaf litter that blocked the drains. About two meters high. Too high. Too precarious. But this claustrophobic corridor continued into the distance, and she could hear the dogs closing.

Get up there, dumme Schlampe.

Don't call me that.

Well, you're being one. What kind of a gymnast are you?

A Jewish gymnast. Not permitted to compete.

You're a dead *Jewish gymnast if you don't move. Are you hardy? Pious? Cheerful? Free?*

Sarah found herself laughing at the old saying. What would Jahn, the father of gymnastics, think of a Jew—*Deutschlands Unglück*, Germany's misfortune—using his words as inspiration? So she put a skip into her step, ignoring the tightness in her calves, the pain in her neck, the chance of slipping, repeating, *"Frisch, fromm, fröhlich, frei,* hardy, pious, cheerful, free," with her eyes on the gutter all the way. She launched herself into the air, caught the troughs neatly on either side, and swung herself up and to the right, the metal creaking and complaining as she went. She hit the corrugated iron roof with a crash, slid for a second, and stopped just shy of the roof's edge.

Beat that, Trudi Meyer. I'll have your gold medal now, danke.

She lay unmoving, staring into the vast and darkening silver sky, the sense of triumph slowly ebbing away like the light in the west. It was leaving a cold sensation in her stomach. If she couldn't calm her breathing, they would hear her. She thought about that last look back into the Mercedes, then pushed the memory away. She put it in a special box and closed the lid. She looked at the emptiness above and listened.

Over her heaving chest she could hear the dogs. The shouting grew closer. Then there were muffled footsteps—a soldier was walking between the buildings. The noise was too indistinct to work out how far away he was, and her breathing was too loud, much too loud. She counted two seconds, took one last long breath, and clamped her mouth shut. She realized she could just make out a star where the sky was darkest. She also discovered she couldn't breathe through her nose, so all she had to do was keep her lips together.

Footsteps, right below her.

A star. Or a planet. Was it Venus? The feet stopped. Planet. *Star.*

There was movement, the sound of material scraping against the brickwork. The gutter creaked. Her chest began to throb as the pressure grew. There was loud breathing and the sound of boots against the wall. More pressure, more pain, the urge to spring to her feet and run away. She turned her head very slowly to see thick, dirty fingers gripping the lip of the gutter. Inside her head she started to scream. She wanted to open her mouth and let it out. So, so much.

At that moment there was a snap, a tearing, and a shriek. The gutter, the dirty fingers, and the heavy breathing vanished in a cascading crash. There was swearing. Shouting. Catcalls. Laughter. Footsteps receding. Quiet. Distant barking.

Sarah opened her mouth and let the breath explode out of her lungs. She gulped down the cool air. Her shoulders rose and fell and rose again because she couldn't stop them. She began, quietly, to sob.

Sarah was good at hide-and-seek. In better days, when she could still play with other children, she was always the last one to be found, long after the others had grown bored and moved on.

She lay there watching the stars emerge and brighten, listening to the sounds of the docks. She could still hear the dogs, soldiers, and shouting, far-off but ever present, like the other children running round the house calling out for her.

So, you're just going to lie there? the voice hectored her.

I'm waiting for it to get dark.

No, you just don't know what to do, it crowed.

Sarah turned her head. She could see a crane and the funnel of a ship. In the background, the vast lake, the Bodensee, was vanishing into the coming night. In the other direction, the rooftops of Friedrichshafen spread out below her, and she couldn't be seen from its distant church spires. Beyond her feet, a crumbling, old warehouse regarded her with derelict eyes, dark and deserted. Safe. This was as good a hiding place as any for now.

Then what? A Jew with no papers, stuck in a German port with no money.

Sarah ignored herself. Or her mother, whoever it was. There was no future, just the now. Her mother had driven them here, so she must have had a plan to cross the Bodensee by the ferry or private boat to Switzerland and safety, away from the beatings and starvation and abuse. But all that was gone. That was, if she'd had a plan at all. That level of organization had been beyond her mother for years. It was no wonder that it had ended in disaster, in her death . . .

Sarah pushed the thought away, into her box. It was all too raw, like the aching in her nose.

That special box deep within Sarah had started out tiny, like something her mother would keep expensive jewelry in. There had rarely been time to be frightened or cross in the past six years, since the National Socialists had come to power, so Sarah had locked each humiliation and injustice carefully inside. That way she was free of the dread and anger. But now the box was like a traveling trunk, varnish blistered and swollen, the wood turning green and the brass tarnished. The contents oozed under the lid and dripped down the sides. Worse still, she had begun to imagine herself *becoming* the box, with everything inside, everything she had hidden, free to slosh about inside her, ready to take shape and eat her alive.

Her heart was racing again. She calmed herself by imagining she really was playing hide-and-seek. She was deep in a cupboard under the stairs, covered in a hanging winter coat, the open door inviting the other children to take just a swift and cursory look inside. Invisible, waiting, invulnerable. Exhaustion spotted its chance and wrapped its arms around her. In the twilight, on the mossy metal ridges, Sarah dozed.

She is walking next to her father. He was tall, but now he seems huge. She must be very small. She looks up along her red-coated arm to where his enormous hand cradles hers. The ground is soft underfoot, and the bright sun, too intense to look at, is bathing everything in a golden glow.

"Can you see, Sarahchen?"

"See what, Papa?"

He laughs and stoops to scoop her up into his arms. She is a long way up but feels safe, strapped into position by limbs like tree trunks.

"Can you see it now?"

Sarah screws up her eyes and peers into the dazzling sky. It hurts and she has to shade them with her hand. A low buzzing is beginning to fill the air.

"What is it?"

Another laugh. "Wait and see."

The noise grows, one drone overlapping with another like a beehive, the sound of a million insects at work.

"Daddy, I'm scared."

"Don't be."

The drones become a throbbing that begins to pound at her chest. She clings to her father's black jacket out of fear or excitement, unable to decide which. Then she sees it.

Huge, silver, shining in the sunlight, filling the sky, bigger than the biggest thing she's ever seen. In its shadow, boys are running, pointing, trailing streamers. Sarah cranes her neck back to watch this giant rippled cigar block out the sun and rumble overhead.

She starts to giggle and then laugh. She looks into her father's eyes and he into hers. He starts to laugh, too. Everyone is laughing . . .

Sarah's eyes opened. With a jolt she remembered where she was and understood what was happening. The moon had risen, and everything was illuminated with a rime of silver light. The metal roof was shaking, and the nose of the Zeppelin was already overhead. She had nowhere to hide. Instead she lay there and let the massive airship roll past, a Jewish girl on a rooftop, a glittering outline just a few meters from prying eyes.

They aren't looking for you, they're doing something else, they'll look right at you and it won't mean anything, because they aren't looking for you. *You're just a winter coat in the cupboard.*

She was close enough to see the windows in the Zeppelin's fabric and the dim light from within. She could see the roughly stitched repairs, the name hidden underneath the hastily re-painted dope, and the shafts of yellow light extending along the curve of the balloon from the control car's windows. She gripped her vibrating bed. *I am a winter coat*, she repeated to herself, as the gondola slid past.

Windows covered the whole front end of the observation car, and the electric light was almost blinding. Inside, two figures stood watching. It was impossible to believe that they couldn't see her, and yet, as they drifted past, they remained static. The droning rose in volume until the power cars roared past on their spindly pylons, their propellers a blur. The body started to thin out, leaving only the vast tailfins to pass. They had been painted black, but the swastikas were still visible in their white circles, a wolf in a poorly made set of woolen robes, fooling no one.

Finally, the airship had passed. Sarah exhaled loudly. It was as if the other children had opened the cupboard door and seen nothing out of the ordinary. She sat up, the muscles in her legs and back complaining. The swarm of bees receded as the Zeppelin sailed away and the rooftop settled. As it passed over the deserted warehouse, she spotted a figure on the building's flat roof, visible in the moonlight. Someone was standing and watching the airship through a pair of binoculars, like he was looking for a rare bird.

She watched him follow the curve of the Zeppelin until he was looking at the tail. He was all in black, silhouetted against the bright darkness of the sky, barely visible but absolutely there. So lost in her curiosity was she that she didn't move from her sitting position, even when he lowered his glasses and stared off past the end of the airship into space. Why was he there? The airfield must have been three kilometers away.

He started and pulled the binoculars back to his face. Deep in her belly something dropped away, and she had to suck her next breath in.

She was not invisible, and he was looking right at her.

The man slowly let the glasses fall, and, after a second, he waved.

Go, just go, she ranted at herself as she exploded into life, rolling over toward the edge of the roof and pushing herself off. It was dark down there out of the moonlight, just two little windows of silver at either end of the alley. To one side, the larger warehouse and the man with the binoculars. To her left, the way she'd come: the fence, the ditch, the car. So she pushed herself right, driving her stiff legs forward, her fingers trailing against the brickwork on either side to keep her balance. Through the fog of dull ache in her face, she was conscious of a growing stabbing pain deep in her head. She was desperately thirsty. She ran her tongue over her lips. They were broken and chapped. Her tongue made a noise like a cat's, rough and dry. It had been more than a day since she had drunk anything. Her mother hadn't wanted to stop on the way from Vienna but had brought nothing to eat or drink. A terrifying 630 kilometers under the eyes of the whole Fatherland, through the birthplace of National Socialism itself. It seemed inconceivable that they'd made it so far.

The waterfront to her left was poorly lit but looked small, not vast and anonymous like she had imagined. She pushed straight on into the maze of buildings in front of her.

Just keep moving.

Where?

Always with the why and the where. Concentrate. It's like an accent, a gymnastic routine, a piano piece. Fix your mind on the task at hand.

I'm tired. I don't know what to do.

So now you're going to cry like a little baby?

No.

Indeed not. Did I raise you by myself so you could just give up?

Sarah swallowed down a sob. Had it been her mother's voice all along? *Oh, Mutti*, she murmured to herself, *oh, Mutti.*

Stop it.

I can't. What I saw in the car . . . all too much . . .

No, STOP.

She froze. Over the distant hum and noise, she could hear running water.

She followed the sound to an old and peeling door. It was ajar, revealing a dark interior. Sarah needed to use her shoulder, and as it scraped open she was hit by the smell of ammonia and sewage. She took an uncertain step inside, but the blackness was absolute. Closing her eyes to let her night vision improve and using the slimy wall as a guide, she crept into the room toward the sound of water. She opened her eyes but couldn't pick out any details. The room couldn't have been that big, but it felt like a cavern, or the giant mouth of some stinking beast. *The dark is your friend*, she told herself. *Big arms to hide you. Love the darkness.*

Her fingers brushed up against something that moved. She wanted to snatch her hand back but resisted and reached out again. She touched the thing, and it vanished once more. She waited and it returned to her. It was a thin chain, with a knot at one end, the other disappearing upward. She grasped the knot and pulled down.

There was a click and then a light so blinding that Sarah lost her balance. She was in a squalid bathroom with a broken toilet bowl in the corner behind a rotting wooden partition. A long trough ran the length of the far wall at floor level. Everything was filthy, but next to Sarah a rusting tap spat brown water into a low, long basin.

She grabbed the edge of the sink and thrust her mouth under the tap, opening it up to full. The liquid tasted warm and rusty, but it was wet and it didn't stop. Sarah gulped and swallowed, gulped and swallowed, ignoring the sense of smothering when it went up her nose. After a minute, she stopped and stretched out her back, letting the water drip down her chin, feeling the life seeping back into her body.

"Oh, look, it's the little girl from the roof."

A man's voice. Sarah froze. *Dumme Schlampe! You left the door open.* The man was between her and the doorway. There was nowhere to go and nothing to do. That helplessness took the weight from her shoulders. She felt oddly calm and light. So light that she felt herself rise above the sea of panic. She grunted an affirmative noise and bent down to drink again, trying not to imagine the next few hours.

TWO

"WHAT ARE YOU doing here?" said the man.

"Drinking," she replied between gulps.

"What were you doing on the roof?" His delivery was flat, almost emotionless.

Don't be fooled. That just means you can't read him.

"Looking for someone." She stood up and wiped her chin. It seemed to be covered in brown dirt. She purposely avoided looking straight at him, buying time to think of something without her eyes giving anything away.

"On the roof?"

Trap.

"Yes." She was just delaying the inevitable. It didn't matter what she said, and this made her feel free. Bold. "What were you doing watching the airship?"

"I'm asking the questions." The merest hint of tension. Not anger.

"Yes, you are." She cocked her head to one side and waited. The man was dressed in black, with a woollen hat and a dark knapsack. His face looked dirty. Not what she'd expected. He just stared back at her like he was trying to work something out. Sarah wondered if she really could just brazen this out. "Well, I shouldn't take up any more of your time, so . . ."

The man pushed the door shut behind him. Sarah took a step back. He leaned against the door and folded his arms.

"And you're going where, exactly?" Colder. Almost icy. Sarah wanted to shiver.

"Home, now. I couldn't find . . . my father. He's a dock-worker."

"Why were you looking for him?" She was definitely being interrogated now.

"His dinner was ready."

"At four in the morning?"

"He's working nights."

"On the roof?"

"I was looking everywhere."

"And what happened to your face?"

Sarah reached up and touched her nose. It stung like she'd been slapped. Something flaky peeled off in her fingers, and she looked down to see what it was. It was then she noticed that the front of her light brown dress was stained a dirty red brown. Congealed blood had crumbled off on her fingers.

"I . . . walked into something in the dark," she tried to say, but the words were lost as she choked, then coughed and finally sniffed, wincing with the pain. The man laughed. It was a joyless thing, full of scorn. Sarah found a wellspring of anger and defiance deep inside. She stared into his eyes, a girl on the verge of a change, covered in dried blood, rust, mold, and rotting leaves. *Be the duchess, darling,* said her inner voice, her mother's voice. *You're onstage; they are not. They are yours to command. They are ready to be convinced. So convince.*

"Yes, I got lost and walked into a broken piece of guttering. Shall I show you?" He had watery-blue eyes with dusky edges. *Don't blink,* she told herself.

"What's your name, girl?" he asked more softly. The creases around his eyes seemed to smile. There was something odd about his accent. He was Bavarian, she thought, but odd words seemed different . . .

"Sarah, Sarah Gold . . ." *Think.* "G . . . Elsengrund." *Dumme Schlampe.* Sarah slumped against the sink. The man laughed again, this time not so hollow.

"Oh, oh, oh, you were doing so well. You'll have to do better than that, Sarah Goldberg, Goldstein, Goldschmitt—whatever you are."

Sarah began to wash her face, hoping it would hide the tears that pricked the corners of her eyes. The man came very close, then sat on the edge of the basin. He spoke quickly. "Wash your dress, wash it clean, it can stay wet if need be . . . and wipe your coat down. You're from Elsengrund, right? Right?" Sarah nodded. "That's good, stick with that . . . and use Ursula or something. Sarah—doesn't get more Jewish than that. You have anywhere to go?"

Sarah shook her head. She had been defeated, but now she was uncertain what was happening.

"And no papers? That's good. If they were stamped, they're useless for Switzerland anyway. Ferry is your best bet. Little-girl routine, like you're meant to be there. Wait for dawn, but not here. That roof is as good as any." He paused. "One more thing . . ." He caught her face and grabbed hold of her nose. Sarah managed to seize his wrists, but before she could do anything, he pulled. Sarah squealed despite herself. The pain was all-consuming. Then there was a loud crack and it was over. She staggered backward, too scared to touch her face.

"Don't touch it, it's straight now . . . definitely less noticeable." He wiped his hands on his trousers. "You didn't know it was broken?" Sarah's hands trembled in front of her. She inhaled through her nose: it was sore but clear. The voice in her head was silent. She looked up from the floor to see the man in the open doorway.

"And trust *no one*. Good luck, Sarah of Elsengrund." Then he was gone.

Sarah watched her hands. It took a full minute before they were still.

_____

Dawn was cold and gray. After a clear night, dirty clouds had rolled in from the lake to turn the sunrise into a faded photograph. Sarah stood in the shadows, her damp dress wrapped around her legs like moldy curtains. It rubbed against the cuts on her knees and thighs until it was all she could think about. She let the irritation eat her up as it kept the voice in her head quiet. Right now she didn't need it.

The blood had washed out to leave an ugly stain on her dress, so she had buttoned up her dark coat to hide it. Around her neck was a piece of dark sacking that could be mistaken for a scarf. It smelled of stale milk, but it was dry. It was the only thing she was wearing that was. She had pulled her hair into some kind of order with her last hair clip and braided the rest at the back of her head, tied off with a piece of wire. She would look fine at a distance, but, as with a scarecrow, a close-up view would fool no one.

Sarah hadn't let herself sleep. Every time she closed her eyes, she saw blood and chasing dogs. Conscious, she was able to control them, but when she drifted off, they ran her down and leapt at her. She woke barely able to breathe for sobbing. Awake she could keep her mind on the here and now.

The ferry horn sounded. That was her cue. She stepped into the light and, ignoring the gnawing pain in her legs, began to skip down the road toward the harbor. She might be fifteen but she could pass for eleven, or younger if she acted the part. Sarah had always been small for her age, something that years of poverty had made more pronounced, and this was a role she had played before—staying small, unobtrusive, childlike. The town was starting to make its way to work across the cobbles, staring at its own feet or making a swish-rattle bicycle noise as it passed. Tired and disgruntled and *uninterested*. Sarah kept the rhythm of her movement going, resisting the urge to break into a run. Instead she began to hum a tune she'd heard the *Bund Deutscher Mädel*, the League of German Girls, singing when they marched past her house. She felt the beat in her head, drawing strength from its bounce and thrilled by taking the song over for herself.

"*Uns're Fahne* something something," skip, skip, "*uns're Fahne* something *Zeit!* . . ." She struggled to remember the words. The banner *something*. She was nearly at the entrance. "*Und die Fahne führt uns* something something . . ." What was the next bit? *Yes, yes . . . our banner . . . banner?*

"Our banner means more to us than *death!*" shouted the soldier as he loomed in front of her.

Sarah shrieked as she bumped into his chest and stumbled backward, the smell of sweat and leather thick in her nose. He towered over her, a gray monster with brown straps.

"I mean, what is your youth leader teaching you?" He shook his head, hands on his hips and rifle slung over a shoulder. He was young, maybe twenty, his brow furrowed with theatrical disapproval. Sarah made herself smile, pushing the corners of her mouth up until her cheeks hurt.

". . . more to us than *death* . . . than *death*!" she shouted back and giggled, almost hysterically. "Oh, she's very good really. Sorry!" she called over her shoulder and waved hurriedly. She watched the soldier smile, shaking his head as he turned away. "Death . . . death . . ." she breathed, trying to slow her pounding heart. She waited for strong hands to grab her shoulders, but nothing happened.

They're not looking for you, the voice said.

Then why are they even here?

Keep singing. Keep smiling. The voice changed the subject. *You play the part all the way into the wings, on into the dressing room. You don't stop until the final curtain.*

The ferry was drifting toward the dock, and beyond it was the blurry horizon. Above it Sarah could see the jagged shapes of the mountains across the lake, mountains that meant . . . freedom? Safety? She had only the vaguest notion of what she would do even if she got on board the ferry to Switzerland.

Keep your mind on the show. Everything else—the party, the fame—those are for afterward, not now. *The show is where you earn them.*

On the right, a line of passengers was forming. To the left a horse and cart had been parked, waiting for the boat to dock. Everywhere else, there were soldiers and police, checking, looking, talking, guarding, watching.

Sarah slowed her pace. She would have to time this just right. The ferry stopped, lines were thrown to the dock, a few passengers hopped off the ramp. Wait. The line began to shuffle on, the cart and horse trotted forward. Momentary chaos . . .

Crying, my love, is an art. It's about control. Not keeping it in— any fool can do that. Taking it inside and storing it until you need it, that's the secret. No leaks, just a tap that goes on . . . and goes off.

Crying?

Take the horror and use it.

Sarah recoiled. She had kept the image of her mother in the car at arm's length, until now.

No.

Yes, the voice insisted.

No, it hurts.

That's the point. Look back into the car.

Sarah pleaded. *Mutti, no . . .*

LOOK INTO THE CAR, DUMME SCHLAMPE.

The blood.

Yes, the voice whispered.

So much blood . . .

Tears streamed down Sarah's face as the emptiness wrapped itself round her stomach. She threw up in her mouth but swallowed it down.

Now.

She ran along the waiting passengers, shouting, letting the rage and fear take over.

"Vati! Vati! Daddy! Daaddee! Where are you! Vati!" The people in the line shuffled uncomfortably and looked at one another. Sarah accelerated toward the ramp. "Vati!"

"Whoa, stop, *Fräulein*. Miss, please." The sergeant took a step back, thought about raising his gun, and stopped, uncertain. Sarah skidded to a halt and raised her hands to her face.

"Where's Vati? He said he'd be here!" she wailed, and squeezed her eyes shut. "He must be here . . . Vati!" She looked up at the sergeant's face, opened her stinging eyes, and snorted snot down her face over her open mouth.

"He's on board? Is he? . . . Just . . ." The sergeant looked around helplessly and his troopers looked back dumbly. He shouted to a policeman deep in conversation on the other side of the ramp. "*Wachtmeister*! Some help here!"

"Vati!" howled Sarah. "Is he on board?"

"Yeah, like I'm your slave, *Scharführer*," the policeman called back.

The sergeant turned back to Sarah. "Ticket? Who has your papers?"

"Vati . . ." *Keep going, keep crying, keep screaming.*

"But . . ."

"Excuse me, can we get on board?" Polite voices getting agitated.

"VATI!"

"Just go, okay, go find your father . . ." The sergeant raised his arms and made a shooing motion to Sarah, who ran past him and climbed aboard, taking one look back to see the horse and cart block her view. She waited a moment and then ran for the staircase to the top deck, wiping her nose and mouth with her coat sleeve.

Good girl. I'm sorry. You're not dumb.

Ignoring the voice, she shoved the crash and her mother's absence back down into the dark, regaining control. She went toward the bow and squeezed herself behind a life buoy, out of sight.

She leaned out and looked back at the harbor with a feeling of extreme triumph. This was better than a gymnastics medal, better than a curtain call, better than getting home without being called names. Finally, after all this time of being endlessly starved, harassed, and attacked, the dirty Jewess Sarah was the *Königin*, the queen, the boss. The National Socialists, their marches, their window-breaking, and their vicious hate could go take a giant jump. She felt like screaming to the sky with the gulls and taking off after them.

The sense of victory, of raw howling satisfaction, didn't last long. When that thin seam of passion had been exhausted, Sarah felt oddly hollow, like chocolates raided, eaten, and then the empty box rewrapped.

She looked at buildings, the twin spires of the church off to the west. She was looking at her country. *Her* country. She had been running scared so long, she'd forgotten what she was actually running from. She belonged *here*. She was not a stupid *J* stamped in a passport. She was German. They were making her leave *her* country, like they made her leave the house in

Elsengrund and the apartment in Berlin, and when she and her mother fled to Austria, they made her leave there, too.

The victory was now hollow and filled with bile, ringed by fears and doubt.

She sniffed and spat over the rail. This drew a reproving glance from one of the passengers, but Sarah didn't care. They couldn't get her now.

Could they? She looked back at the dock. The soldiers were busy, disorganized, distracted. Two of them had drifted to a corner for a smoke. The sergeant was arguing with the policeman. Nobody was in charge, like they didn't know what they were looking for.

Didn't they know what they were looking for? A girl, an escaping Jew, a blonde Jew at that, whose mother had panicked and plowed through a roadblock, because everything she did was a disaster. Why hadn't they caught her? Unless . . . they weren't really looking for her in the first place?

She watched the last few stragglers coming on board and a man running along the quay. He had a long black coat and a carpetbag trailing behind him. The sergeant moved to head him off, arm outstretched. The smokers finished their cigarettes and approached the ramp.

The roadblock that her mother had driven into: it was *unexpected*. Everything else had gone according to plan. Was there a plan? They'd gotten to a border in a car they shouldn't have had, but after that?

Her mother might have described the plan in detail, but Sarah hadn't been listening. She was angry at the National Socialists, even the other Jews for whatever they'd done to bring this on them all, but she reserved her deepest, seething, suppressed resentment for her mother, for her drinking, her failures, and her hopelessness. Worse still was the endless line of fantasy and optimistic delusion. Crashing the barriers and getting herself shot, that was *typical*.

But if the roadblock hadn't been for them, if they *hadn't* been the target, what were these soldiers here for? Maybe there were checkpoints everywhere now . . .

They wouldn't let the man on board. Sarah leaned out for a clearer look. The policeman was now taking an interest. The man took off his hat and ran his fingers through his blond hair. The ferrymen began to untie the lines, impatiently coiling the wires and watching. The man now had soldiers on three sides. He retreated a step and gestured back into town. He tried to reclaim his papers, but the sergeant pulled them away. Sarah watched the shoulders of one of the onlooking soldiers, the coarse material of his uniform stretching as he shifted his gun into his right hand.

Sarah looked out over the lake to the mountains. To safety, maybe. No visa, no friends, no money, no mother—Switzerland didn't want Jewish refugees, so she'd have to be careful on the other side, but she had no choice . . .

Then she looked back to the harbor. This man, she realized, was the reason for the roadblocks and soldiers. *Hunted.* She knew what it was to be hunted.

The policeman circled behind the man and waited about ten meters back, blocking his retreat. The ferrymen started to shout at the soldiers. Late. The sergeant turned to them and shouted back, just as the man looked up toward the ferry. Sarah saw his watery-blue eyes and recognized him. He had the look of a cornered animal, so different from the face he had used the night before. A man without friends. Without a choice.

The departure horn sounded above her.

Sarah was at the top of the stairs before the sound finished. She slid down the banisters on either side on her hands and hit the deck running, her palms burning. The ramp was now up, so she took a half step and leapt over it. She saw the sliver of dirty water beneath her, and then it was gone.

"Vati! Vati! Daaa-ddiee!" she screamed as she landed and charged into the group of soldiers. She saw the tiny flicker of recognition in those blue eyes and bounced into his arms. He staggered from the unexpected weight and then hefted her up to his hip with difficulty as she wrapped her legs around him. "Oh, Vati, Vati!" she cried.

"Oh, Ursula. There you are. There, there. Safe now," he muttered. He looked up at the soldiers. "Look, can I just . . ."

"Vati! Home now!" wailed Sarah.

"Look, can I just take my daughter home now?" He reached out for his papers. "Please? It's been a horrible morning."

Sarah stared into the man's shoulder and told herself not to look up. Expensive soap. No cologne. The ferry horn sounded again.

"Bring the right papers when you're going *anywhere*. Wastes everybody's bloody time. Even when you're looking for your snotty children, which, by the way, you forgot to mention."

"Thank you, thank you. Sorry." The man took the papers and turned.

"And remember your ticket, you cheap git," one of the soldiers spat. The others laughed.

"Of course, thank you. Excuse me." He walked away. "And where were you, young lady? I said wait at the train station."

"Sorry, Vati."

He walked on in silence until they passed the harbor entrance and were halfway up the hill.

"That was incredibly stupid." He exhaled.

"A simple thank-you will do," Sarah murmured.

THREE

―――――――――
―――――――――

"YOU WERE SAFE, Sarah of Elsengrund. On the bloody ferry. What were you thinking?" he whispered with a deliberate intensity.

Sarah wondered this herself. One reason stood out.

"They weren't going to let you go, were they? I know what they do to you when they get you."

"I told you to trust no one."

"Yes, you did."

"This is like carrying an ox."

"You're doing fine."

"You're far too big. No one carries a ten-year-old like this."

Sarah slipped off his hip. After an awkward moment, she took his hand.

"Like this," she said. His hand was soft. Not a workman's hands.

"Why?" he asked after a pause. Sarah looked at her shoes, scuffed, scratched, and muddy. She wasn't sure why. She had acted without thinking about it. A part of her had spotted something hunted, someone lost like her. He was right, she had been safe. But she hadn't felt safe at all. She wondered how she felt now.

"My father had an old book, written a long time ago, that said if your kingdom is being threatened by another . . . you need to . . . find out who threatens them."

The man snorted.

"'The enemy of my enemy is my friend.' Yes, the Arabs say that as well." Sarah could feel him tugging on her hand as he walked faster. "You've read the *Arthashastra*? An ancient manual on being a king? What does your father do?"

"I don't know. He left lots of books like that when he went." Sarah suddenly felt very vulnerable. "Where are we going?"

"The Stadtbahnhof, the railway station. It's crawling with the SS, but since I can't get out of town by ferry, that's the best option. Now. Again." His voice was steady, but Sarah felt the nervous tug on her hand again. They were taking the backstreets, crossing and recrossing the road so he could glance behind them.

Feed off your leading man. Make his emotions trigger yours. If he's good, he'll be doing the same. Sarah looked up at the man, his face a mask pulled too tight at the corners, his blue eyes now glacial between movements. *If he's not, you have to be twice as powerful, twice as good, twice as beautiful. You have to be a distraction.* Sarah began to swing her arms and hum to herself. The man stopped.

"What are you doing?" He looked down at her.

"I'm *being* a little girl. Why, who are you being?" After a moment he snorted and walked on, allowing his arm to be rocked from side to side.

They rounded a corner and emerged into a wide, open space where the railway station waited, an imposing building decorated in lurid yellow and white.

"Looks like an *Apfelkuchen* covered in lines of cream." She sighed.

"That's what you see? Apple cake? Not the military trucks and staff cars? The SS guards?"

"I haven't eaten in a long time."

Sarah stared at the tabletop and ran her fingers along the patterns. She couldn't trust herself not to watch the black-uniformed figures walking about outside the glass. Their smudgy reflections drifted from one side of the table to the other, like storm clouds gathering over the countryside on a close summer evening.

A cup and saucer slid in front of her. She looked down at white froth and frowned before leaning in to sniff. There was a glorious golden coffee smell cradled in the aroma of hot milk.

"Oh," she chirped. "Melange?"

He shook his head. "No, not Viennese. Italian. Try it."

She put her hands around the scalding cup and raised it to her lips, letting the warm updraft touch her face. Her nose brushed through the froth, but it gave like soap suds and vanished, popping in a million tiny crackles. The rich, dark liquid flowed through it and cooled as it tore the bubbles apart and slid into her mouth. Both sweet and bitter, sharp and comforting, invigorating and calming like strong arms carrying you through a storm. Electric lights flickered into life in the rooms of her mind. Her aches and pains vanished as if the bruises and the scratches had just melted away.

"Oh my God." She chuckled, tapping her chest with both hands. "That's . . . that's . . . amazing." The man leaned in and made a quieting motion with his fingers. "Oh, sorry," she gasped, covering her mouth, eyes smiling wide. One last hiccupped squeak escaped before she whispered, "Sorry, sorry, sorry . . ." The plump bald man behind the counter laughed as he polished a glass and smiled beatifically at Sarah.

"You can add sugar, of course, but I rather dread to think what that might lead to," said the man as he stirred his coffee. "*Espresso* is coffee brewed under intense pressure. Then you add the heated milk and foam to make *cappuccino*. It's a true art form."

"I want another one of these," she babbled, and jerked the empty cup from side to side. He shook his head as he passed a plate across the table.

"Let's see how that one works first. Here, eat the train station."

She fell upon the apple cake and began stuffing the flaky pastry into her mouth with warm applesauce fingers. The barman laughed again from behind his shiny brass pipes and went to serve a customer. Behind him was a painting of a bald man in a funny hat thrusting his jaw and dimpled chin into the air, like a clown imitating someone powerful. Men who wanted to look like that, Sarah thought distractedly, were probably trouble.

"*Scho*," she mumbled, mouth full, crumbs escaping from the corners. "You haff a planf?"

Sarah felt . . . not safe, exactly, but she didn't feel alone. The café's steamy warmth had enveloped her, and the coffee, the cappuccino, was happily tingling down her arms and making her heart feel strong. Right now, when deep down she knew she had nothing to lose, nowhere to go, nothing to hope for, she felt strangely liberated. It was as if she had stayed on the ferry after all.

"*I'm* taking a train to Stuttgart. You, you've no papers, you look like you slept in a bush, and you smell like vomit." He hid his mouth with his cup, and his eyes were unreadable.

"Then again—" Sarah swallowed the cake. "They aren't actually looking for *me*, are they? So, like I said, you have a plan?"

"How old are you?"

"Fifteen," she said with great emphasis. He gave his snort.

"That explains a lot. You look eleven at best."

"What's your name?"

"Keep calling me Vati."

"Plan," she repeated. The café hissed and clinked around them. The distant trains rasped and rumbled under the muttered conversation. The barman began to sing, a basso tuneless growl of lost love. A seagull squawked from outside as if in answer. The man's eyes, so beautiful, so blue, would have been cold had their intent not been so obviously shuttered, like a summerhouse in winter.

He downed the dregs of his coffee and lit a cigarette in one swift motion. He held his matches up between his first and second fingers.

"What is this?" he said.

"A book of matches," Sarah replied, avoiding the acrid smoke.

"Yes and no." He opened the book and bent the cardboard back away from the flat, wooden matches. He then slid the cigarette, filter first, between the two so the lit end stuck out. He then closed the matchbook and dropped it into an ashtray. "Okay, now what is it?"

To Sarah, it was just a square of colored card with a long white tube emerging from one end.

"It's a very small gun?" she ventured with a smile. He tutted and stood up.

"You think about it." He walked over to the bar and began to order something. Sarah watched the lit end of the cigarette slowly consume itself. The gray curling smoke looped upward and seemed to follow her as she moved away from it. The white tube got shorter. The glowing embers crept closer to the card.

"So?" He stooped over the table and gathered his things.

"It's a firecracker. It burns down, lights the card, the matches catch fire." She smiled up at him, but he didn't look at her.

"Very good. Let's go."

"What's the *plan*?"

"Just do what you do." He was already halfway to the door. Sarah stood and followed, brushing flakes of cake onto the floor.

"*Grazie mille!*" She smiled at the man behind the counter, who smiled broadly.

"*Prego.* Hey, beautiful, what happened to your pretty face?" he continued in Italian.

"Oh, I'm such a klutz." She laughed, touching her bruised nose as she walked through the doorway. Her companion let the door close behind her.

"You know, as a Jewish fugitive, you might want to avoid using Yiddish words. Just a thought." The scorn dripped through every word. *Dumme Schlampe,* thought Sarah. She looked back through the glass. Nobody seemed to have noticed. *Get on with the show. Nobody notices anything. Sometimes you wonder why you're even up there.* She skipped after the man and began to hum.

"And as you're supposed to be from Bavaria, you might want to ah-void that Parisian lilt that your accent acquires every time you think you're being funny. Just . . . a . . . th—"

"Yes, thank you, Fräulein Akzentpolizei."

"Oh, I like that, I like being the accent police. You did it again, by the way."

He stopped next to a litter bin and began to drop things from his bag into it. "So tell me what you see."

Sarah turned toward the platform.

"Soldiers checking everyone's papers. No ordinary *Bahnschutzpolizei,* these. They think a lot of themselves, like the man in the painting. That's the *Schutzstaffel,* the SS?" The man gave a positive grunt as he busied himself behind her. "But they aren't in charge. There are two men in long coats by the ticket office, and the soldiers keep looking at them like they need to be told what to do."

"Gestapo. Secret police. Very good," he said next to her. "You going to see me off, then?"

"See you off?" She trailed after him. "What does that mean?" He did not slow his pace.

"Keep up, I'm late," he called over his shoulder. Confusion gave way to concern, and something unpleasant awoke in Sarah's stomach. She sped up and tried to get in front of him. Was he intending to leave her here after all that? Sarah looked at the last few hours and saw how shallow this link between them really was.

"What are we doing?" She began to feel cheated.

"Come along."

"What . . ."

"Papers, please." The guards were on top of them. There was a tall officer in an immaculate dark uniform, his fox-like features topped by a spotless peaked cap and a shining death's-head badge. It made his skin look too pale, like he himself was close to death. He was flanked by soldiers affecting a bored arrogance but with machine guns gripped tightly in both hands. Sarah looked up at the man at her side as the SS officer looked at his papers. His face was impassive, even irritated. The shutters were closed. He was going to be fine. He *knew* it.

"What are we doing?" she whispered.

"Not now, Ursula, be a good girl." He didn't even look at her.

"Herr Neuberger. You work at the Zeppelin plant?" The officer's accent wasn't local.

"Yes."

"And what do you do there?"

"As you well know, I'm not allowed to talk about it." Authority. Arrogance.

"Is that so?" The officer swallowed. It was like a snake passing a bird. He pushed the pages of the booklet back and forth, not really reading them. "And where are you going? If, of course, you can talk about *that*?" He smiled. It was a sickly thing, like a stillborn kitten. He put it away again.

"Stuttgart for a meeting, and no, I can't talk about that, either." He was going without her. After everything she did, he was going without her. The misery welled up inside her, and she didn't even try to stop it.

"Stuttgart! Stuttgart? Without me?" she shouted, her foot involuntarily stamping.

Everybody looked at her. The SS officer. The guards. The other passengers. Her companion, a look of injured innocence on his face.

A train whistle punctuated the illusion of silence, and the noise of the engine rose behind it. For an instant, Sarah saw in his eyes just the tiniest flicker of recognition, the slightest flash of a message. *Go on.*

"Again? Stuttgart again? Oh, Vati, how long will you be gone this time? It's just not *fair!*"

"Now, Ursula, behave. It's not for long and then I won't have to go again . . ."

"That's what you said *last* time." Sarah raised her voice over the incoming train and folded her arms.

"Now stop. We have one ticket, you aren't coming and that's final."

"Herr . . ." the officer tried to interject.

"Vati, no. Vati, don't go. You *promised.* No more trips." Her arms swung petulantly.

"That's enough, Ursula. There's the train, now are you coming to see me off or not?" He held out his hand to the officer. "My papers, please." The carriages ground to a halt in a fizzle of noisy steam. The officer had to shout over it.

"Where are *her* papers?"

"What?" Exasperated disbelief.

"Vati . . ."

"*Her* papers?" A queue had formed behind them.

"She doesn't need papers. She's a *child*."

"For the *train*," the officer said.

"She's not going *anywhere*. Look, that's my train. Papers?" He reached out his hand and stepped toward the platform. Sarah grabbed his outstretched hand and pulled back on it.

"No, Vati, don't go . . ." Sarah began to cry. *Think about the car . . . No, think about being left behind.*

"Ursula, *stop*. Do as you're told." He snatched his hand clear and grabbed his ID out of the officer's hand, before seizing Sarah's arm.

"Please, Herr Neuberger . . ." The officer found himself stepping back to avoid being pushed over. He gestured to the guards. "Bäcker, go with him."

They walked onto the platform. Sarah allowed herself to be half dragged toward the train, sobbing loudly, before they stopped next to the carriage door. One of the guards gingerly followed the scene. The man stooped and wrapped his arms around Sarah.

"Wait for it," he whispered. "Any second now."

"Wait for what?" Sarah tightened her grip on him, utterly lost.

The train whistle went, deafeningly close. He stood and climbed into the carriage. He turned and leaned through the open door.

"Home to Mutti now. Go on." The train shivered and rocked gently. Sarah looked up into his eyes. The stern irritation vanished and the cool blue pools smiled at her. *Now*, they said.

The train started to move. Sarah took a half step to her left. Then another. She could see the guard reflected in the metal and glass, standing about three meters away. She looked back up into his eyes. *What?* She stared. He rolled his eyes and looked at his watch.

The flash lit up the side of the carriage, silhouetting Sarah and the guard for an instant before the scalding wind pushed her forward. She fell, then two hands grabbed the lapels of her coat and lifted her in one clean motion in through the moving door.

Behind her the fireball burned itself out in the rafters of the ticket hall, having set light to everything within five meters of the litter bin. There was smoke, screaming, chaos. The platform receded as the train accelerated and the guard picked himself up off the ground.

Sarah was lowered carefully to the floor, and the train door closed behind her.

"I obviously need to work on my timing," he said, smiling, "but I thought that went pretty well."

FOUR

SARAH STOOD ON the road, surrounded by splintered glass and wreathed in fog. Her mother's sweet and powerful singing voice sounded dry and close. The noise of dogs began to claw at the mist behind her.

The girl in the song was a mistreated servant, a slave . . . but she knew something that her owners did not.

Sarah broke into a run as the distant dogs began to yelp in time with the beat.

Something horrible was coming.

Sarah found her mother standing on the bank above the crashed Mercedes. She glistened in her fur and feathered hat, smiling eyes wide and bright as she sang.

The girl was a pirate princess . . .

There was howling, screaming, hot breath on the air, rising in volume and growing closer.

So when the pirates came and destroyed everything . . .

Her mother hissed the last lines over the noise of paws scratching through the glass.

The pirates asked the girl . . . should they show anyone mercy?

Sarah glanced at the shapes looming though the fog. By the time she looked back, her mother's hat had slid off her head to reveal the horror underneath.

The girl said, No mercy.

That'll teach you.

The first dog, all muscles and teeth, broke into view and launched itself at Sarah.

Sarah jerked and banged her head against the window of the train. Every time. Every time she closed her eyes now. She looked at her traveling companion, apparently sleeping opposite her.

"Stay awake," he said, without opening his eyes. "They can't get you if you stay awake."

"Who can't?"

"Your demons."

"What do you see when you close your eyes?" she asked, part curiosity, part jab. He snorted and folded his arms.

"Brecht."

"I'm sorry, what?" Sarah replied.

"You were mumbling Brecht. All very Jewish-Bolshevik. You have to stop that."

"It was a song that my—" Sarah stopped as a surge of loss rose like vomit. She waited for it to fade and continued. "My mother sang it onstage a few times."

"Your mother wouldn't be welcome in the new Deutsches Theater. Neither would you, singing that song."

The journey seemed to last forever. Four trains. No, five. A long and dreary play in a narrow theater powered by strong coffee and apple cake. The drama was punctuated by brief snatches of activity, tickets and checkpoints, stations and inspectors, with Sarah playing her part when needed but mostly waiting in the wings for her cue. She remained silent, as she had always been taught by her mother, in case the audience hears you. In between, the gentle rocking of the carriages marked the slow turn of the clock.

Her fear, the desire to run from everyone they met and to check the corridors outside their compartment constantly, had washed away slowly, like the tide, to be replaced by a throbbing tension, cloying boredom, furry teeth, and itchy grubbiness. Her limbs ached and her eyes threatened to close, but the threat of the dogs in the mist was greater. The journey was every-thing, the only show in town. Sarah didn't want to think about the final curtain.

At the start they *couldn't* talk. There were passengers and guards on the trains, customers in the cafés, prying eyes and open ears everywhere. Now they were alone, but Sarah felt that if she started asking questions it would break the *kischef*, the spell, and everything would fall apart. Everyone, their eyes thus opened, would turn around and wonder why the dirty Jew was sitting on the train.

That had to change, though. The deeper they got into Germany, the farther from real safety she was. Back to the smashed windows, the abuse, the fear, the hunger, the midnight arrests—and now she had no papers, with no excuses. The voices that she had resisted were whispering again. *You are running right back to the start, back to the place you escaped in '36.*

She stretched. She felt her cheek twitch, and the skin under her eye seemed to flutter. She wondered if it was visible to anyone else, so she tried to see her reflection in the window. Germany at its grayest slid past, blurred by grime. Breathing on the glass, she dragged a fingertip through the condensation. She was about to draw an *S* but stopped herself. She sighed loudly.

"I take it back. Go to sleep," he said shortly.

"What about my demons?"

"I no longer care." The carriage darkened as the train overtook another traveling at a slower speed. Sarah watched dark, squat, frog-like shapes rolling past.

"More tanks," she thought out loud. Their progress across Germany had been unhindered, but they were not traveling alone. The stations, trains, roads, bars, and cafés were packed with soldiers, sitting, waiting, walking, laughing. An army was on the move. "Do you want to see?"

"Not anymore." His eyes stayed closed. "I think we all know what it means."

The shapes drifted by the window, light, dark, light, dark.

"Do you have a plan?" she murmured.

He was quiet. Light, dark, light, dark. Just when Sarah began to think she hadn't actually said anything, he sighed noisily. "Yes." He put his head to one side and resettled his body.

"Does it involve me?"

"You want to discuss this now? Here?"

Sarah waved her hand at the empty carriage in frustration and opened her mouth to speak. She slammed her jaw shut and inhaled slowly.

"Yes. I want to talk about it now," she whispered carefully. "Where are we going?"

"Eventually? Berlin."

"Why?" This seemed absurd to Sarah.

"We're going home."

"I don't have a home," Sarah muttered witheringly.

"You're from Berlin, from Elsengrund."

"We left for Vienna in nineteen thirty-six because of the Nuremberg Laws."

"Family? Friends?" he asked testily.

"No family. The rest will be gone, or they'll have their own problems to deal with."

"Don't you have any . . . *Christian* friends?" He sighed.

"I'm talking about *Christian* friends." She snorted in an imitation of what seemed to be his usual exclamation. "We didn't run a"—she wrestled for a suitable example—"bagel factory."

They fell silent as somebody bustled past the compartment.

"Herr Neuberger. Is that your name?" she asked.

"If you like." The shutters lowered.

"What do you do, Herr Neuberger?"

"This conversation is over."

His folded arms tightened. Sarah sat on the sudden spurt of anger and squashed it. It was getting harder each time to do so. Down where the voice came from, she was seething.

The tanks vanished. The carriage filled with dull light and quiet.

"Do you not have anything to read?" she complained. After a moment, he made a gruff noise and fished into the carpetbag at his feet. "You do? Wonderful." He tossed her something and promptly closed his eyes.

The cover had been torn from the book to make it lighter, and the binding was beginning to come apart in a spiderweb of white thread. She looked at the title page.

"*Achtung—Panzer!* by Heinz Guderian," she read. "Is this a story?"

"In a way. We're all going to be hearing it."

Berlin seemed bigger, brighter, grander under floodlights and full moon than it had three years earlier. It was more imposing, more severe, and more frightening than she remembered, unrecognizable as the city where she grew up. Columns stretched into the air as if the sky were a vaulted ceiling.

Sarah slipped in and out of sleep. The dogs ran through its streets chasing the taxi, and her mother bled on every corner. She was carried from train to rattling cab to green marble mansion block, head buried in the overcoat shoulder. She could have been carried into hell itself for all she knew.

The foyer was brightly lit and smelled of leather and polish, all straight lines and green lamps. His feet made no sound on the thick carpet that ran down the center of the hall.

"*Guten Abend*, Ulrich," he said without stopping.

"And good evening to you, Herr Haller . . . and who have we here?" The concierge hurried to his feet and attempted to make it to the lift before him.

"My sister's child. Will you get the elevator, please?"

"Certainly. A good trip?"

"Not at all. The work of the Reich had to wait for family concerns. Most disagreeable."

The lift gate slid open on well-oiled rails. They passed Ulrich, who smelled of stale tobacco.

"Good night, Herr Haller. Sleep well."

The gate slid shut with an expensive *thunk*. Sarah felt the floor shake gently, and with a distant whine, the lift rose.

"Herr Haller?" Sarah murmured.

"If you like."

"Onkel . . ." She snickered slowly.

Plush carpets, delicate light fittings, and smooth walls that were a fan of shadows. The jingle of keys and the whispering noise of an opening door. They traveled into a large cool space, dim but for the shafts of moonlight, more right angles, thick rugs, and luminous marble.

They passed into a smaller space, and she was lowered onto something soft and white. It yielded to her shoulders, scratches, and bruises. She stretched out an arm, but the softness went on forever. There were receding footsteps, and then a voice spoke from the doorway.

"Sleep well, Sarah of Elsengrund. And welcome home."

The door closed. Sarah turned her face into the clean smell of soap powder and gave in to it, not caring if the dogs were waiting for her.

Sarah was sitting on the hall carpet facing the front doors. She was waiting.

What was she waiting for?

Nearby someone was crying. Playing minor chords on a piano and sobbing. Crying and singing. A high, beautiful, but cracked voice stumbled through a song, missing words here and there, between sniffs.

Nice while it lasted, an' now it is over . . .

Sarah picked herself up and went looking for the voice.

What's the use o' grievin', when the mother that bore you

(Mary, pity women!) knew it all before you?

Her mother was leaning over the edge of the piano keyboard. In the jet-black gloss surface before her, Sarah saw her own small, confused, and worried face. It was smeared at the edges by the curving side of the grand piano, her golden hair escaping the red ribbons, making a halo like a Christian angel.

"Ha! Sarahchen. Pity us women, yes?"

Her mother hammered a huge dark chord with the sustain pedal down. Then she laughed. It wasn't a happy sound.

"He's not coming, my princess. No, not today . . . or tomorrow . . ." She picked up a glass of amber liquid and poured it down her throat. "No, maybe not ever again. You know why?" She raised her eyebrows.

Sarah shook her head slowly.

Her mother was beautiful. There was porcelain skin framed by curls of fiery red escaping from a mane of shining locks piled with studied and meticulous carelessness on her head. There were the greenest of dusky green eyes, like liquid knife-points of polished marble. There was a mouth of perfect shape below high cheekbones, and to this was added a thick diamond-studded choker and glinting earrings that turned and flashed in the candlelight. Her forest-green velvet dress susurrated as she spun on the piano stool.

She stuck a gloved fingertip into her nostril and

pulled her face violently into profile. "This. *Genetics.* The perpetuation of the international Jewish conspiracy." She let go and rolled her head back to face Sarah. "We are the *World Plague* and your father's dirty little secret." She swallowed down the rest of the glass and reached for the bottle.

Sarah took an uncertain step toward the piano. Her mother swung back and pointed at her with sudden venom in her eyes.

"And you know what, *princess*? That's you, too, Rapunzel with her golden hair . . . Doesn't matter what you look like. Out there, they're still going to *hate you.*"

She spat the final words with such disdain and fury that Sarah felt it in her cheekbones and her eyelids, all the way to her groin. Tears began to run down her hot face and she couldn't stop them, even as she closed her eyes. When she opened them again, her mother was at her side and coiling velvet arms around her shoulders.

"Oh, baby, I'm sorry, oh, Sarahchen, Mutti's sorry, oh, I'm such a dumme Schlampe . . ." Sarah looked into her mother's face, which was also streaked with tears. She watched her eyeliner dissolve in muddy rapids. She smelled of musk, alcohol, and hopeless emptiness. "We'll be okay, baby. You and me. We don't need anyone. Who's my princess?"

"Me," Sarah squeaked between breaths.

"Yes, my Sarahchen."

The red hair and green velvet closed over her head.

Sarah woke in the dark, her face wet. Her mother was gone. The absence, the *hole* that this left, was a wound, like the back of her mother's head. Sarah's existence felt dominated by that void. But this emptiness also meant her mother could make no more demands on her, could no longer control or endanger her. Sarah struggled with this sense of relief as it was swamped by guilt and ingratitude, before capsizing under the bitter weight of the nothingness.

She shuffled out of her clothes and fought her way into the sheets, tearing at the hospital corners in frustration. Eventually, they came loose, and she wrapped herself by rolling over and over, before curling into a ball. Once still, she began to cry all over again.

Tearful, fitful sleep followed, but it was soft and clean.

Finally, her eyes opened to a dazzling silver light that flooded the room, washing out the edges and details to leave a blurred white coating to everything. She rose unsteadily and propped herself on an elbow. Past the foot of the bed, where the radiance was at its most intense, almost lost in the glow, stood a figure, arms outstretched. It looked for all the world like giant feathery wings had sprung from its shoulders and stretched off into the distance. Sarah was enthralled at the magnificence of the image, one torn from the halls of an art gallery.

The figure shook its arms out with a flourish, and the wings flew away. It turned away from the curtains and spoke. "Get in the bath. You smell disgusting."

FIVE

SARAH SHUFFLED DOWN the hall, the sound of running water recalling her thirst and panic near the docks. This time there was just a steamy fog and mirrors bejeweled with drops of water, a comforting heat and the gentle scent of soap. She locked the bathroom door.

He had taken her photo against a white wall, a head-and-shoulders shot in her stained dress. Now Sarah pushed the grimy material into a sink of warm water, but after a perfunctory rub she realized it was hopeless. The blacker the water, the worse the dress looked. She gave up and climbed into the huge, filling tub. It was scalding hot, so she stood on one foot and then the other, waiting for the pain to ebb away as the cold tap spat into life. Facing her was a giant mirror that filled the wall, and between water-drop trails Sarah could see her whole body.

Her legs and arms were crisscrossed with scratches, scabs, and livid bruises turning black. Her knees were swollen out of shape. Underneath somewhere was her mother's porcelain skin, but it was lost from view. The contusions couldn't hide the muscles, though, the taut wire and whipcord that Sarah was pleased to see hadn't faded in the years since she was banned from gymnastics class. She hadn't wasted the time spent hanging from the banisters of their Vienna apartment or flipping down its halls after all. She had wanted to be ready for the call, to hear it had all been a dreadful mistake and she had to come back immediately.

Yet the Fatherland managed quite well without you, didn't it? No shortage of winners at the Olympics in '36, were there? Didn't miss the mongrels and Mischlinge *at all . . .*

What about Owens? Jesse Owens the American Negro. She'd watched him. Faster and better and longer than all the blond-haired, blue-eyed, statuesque supermen.

The voice fell silent. Sarah could now drop both feet into the water, and she slowly crouched into the steam. The rest of her body was flat and uninteresting to her, which was fine for now. Her head spun with grown-up problems and injustices, but she still looked like a little girl. Getting unwieldy body parts, getting confused and angry, getting tall and heavy . . . it could all wait. She needed to be light and lithe.

The water burned her knees, and she hissed into it. She looked up one last time to see her face. Her nose was now black, fading to yellow at the edges. Given time to stare, she realized that she looked different, almost unrecognizable from certain angles. The eyes were the same, pale blue but fierce and deep and alive like her mother's. Her hair was long and knotted and greasy, but unmistakably golden blonde, like a crown of precious metal that had been dropped on the floor. She teased out the braids and shook it out over her back into the water.

With that familiar mixture of shock, pain, and tremendous comfort, Sarah sank into the water, submerging herself entirely before settling on the surface. She dissolved into the soapy liquid and risked letting her mind off its leash. She found herself thinking of Owens.

Going to the Olympic Stadium had been hugely risky for a Jew, even back in '36. There had been so many trains and buses and public places that were forbidden to her where she could have been recognized or stopped or hassled, but in the end, she was just another little blonde girl swept up into the crowd. In an audience of a hundred thousand, she was invisible.

It was clear in the early seconds of the 100-meter final that Jesse Owens was the strongest. There was no ignoring it. He accelerated away from the Aryan field with ease, challenged only by Ralph Metcalfe, another black American. The crowd stuttered momentarily as Nazi Party members and worried faces looked around for direction. How were they supposed to react to the defeat of the supposedly superior race?

But the excitement was too much, and soon no one could help themselves. Owens shot through the tape, and Sarah screamed herself hoarse along with everyone else.

However, as Owens and his teammate stood on their podium giving a simple military salute, surrounded by white faces and Heil-Hitler arms, Sarah saw the danger they represented. Not just for the National Socialists and their delusions, but for her and those like her. This humiliation of the hosts was a potent counterargument that had been missing from Germany for many long years, and Sarah could almost feel the coming backlash, their need for revenge.

She became scared and slipped away early on half-empty buses. But Owens's wins, all four of his gold medals, thrilled her in a way she couldn't quite grasp. Until now. She realized he was the enemy of her enemy. He had embarrassed the Nazi Party and the nation in its own backyard. He cowed the people until they couldn't help but follow him. She yearned for a fraction of that power.

She shut off the gold taps with her feet and floated. She could hear voices, muffled but just about distinct enough to make out.

". . . worth it. What were you thinking?" Tense. Agitated.

"Just do it . . . and as quick as you can." The familiar voice, dismissive.

"You're getting soft. That's dangerous." The accent was thick and difficult to pin down. "Now we're a bloody *Underground Railroad*." English. Two words of English.

"Shut up." Voice like a slap. Reproving. Warning. In charge. They moved away. A door slammed.

English . . . or American? No, English. Sarah had been sure that he'd be French. She trawled through remembered conversations. He was good. Very good.

You haven't a clue who he is. Not the slightest idea.

Doesn't matter. Not at all. I'm . . .

Safe? Is that the word you want to use?

Fine for now, is what I was going to say.

Sarah slid a sponge down a leg, removing some of the most superficial scabbing and leaving lines of new pink skin in its place. She could hear his voice again.

". . . yes, I'll hold."

She nudged a larger scab into the water, and the skin welled up bright red, dripping blood into the suds. She scowled at herself.

"Yes, thank you . . . this is Herr Haller, yes, good morning. My sister has sent her child to the city in totally unsuitable clothing. I'll need a whole new wardrobe sent out to me immediately . . . Some travel clothes, a formal outfit . . . oh, yes, a *Jungmädel* uniform would be excellent . . . about twelve years old . . . an average twelve . . . If I wanted to trail down to Schöneberg with a poorly dressed niece, I wouldn't be speaking to you, would I? You have experts in this area? Make some judgments, *Fräulein* . . . yes, yes, yes . . ." Sarah listened to him bully and overrule, cajole and manage, from a position of total ignorance. *Just carry on, stand up there like you're meant to be there and people will believe it.* He was very, very good—her mother's acting lessons made flesh. She couldn't help but be impressed.

So all the information you have about him is automatically suspect.

Yes, it is.

"Ursula!" Sarah jumped at the closeness of the voice, just outside the door and too loud. "I have to leave. There's food in the kitchen, I assume your mother got that far in your education?" A question not expecting an answer.

Footsteps. Door. Silence.

Sarah was alone. Again.

Sarah had grown up in some luxury, even if it had been fading, slipping away in pieces her whole life. That meant everything had been *thick*. Thick carpets, thick curtains, thick doors, thick gowns. This apartment was expensive in every way, more expensive than anything Sarah had seen in some time, but it was different. This was about the *absence* of things. Polished marble and white walls, untouched. A barely used leather sofa and an armchair made of chrome pipes. The low glass table had a small pile of magazines that seemed to float in midair, and there were no curtains, just white fabric covering one giant window through which a directionless sunlight flooded the room. Even the decoration, where it existed, consisted of right angles, lines, and angular birds.

And dominating one wall, as if appearing next to her, a huge portrait of the Führer.

At least the bathrobe was thick. She huddled inside it against the sudden chill.

The kitchen was of similar design but showed signs of habitation. There were fresh bread, meats, and cheese, which she pushed hungrily into her mouth without assembling the components into a meal. The bread was warm and fluffy, the sausage spicy, and the cheese unbearably creamy on her tongue. An icebox revealed milk, clean and cold and topped with cream. She gulped it down, letting it trickle from the corners of her lips and down her neck.

Further investigation revealed empty cupboards, the kind she'd come to associate with slow hunger and shortages. *He isn't here much, is he?*

She took the remaining bread to gnaw on and went in search of closed doors.

The main bedroom where she had slept had one closet with mirrored doors. Inside were four suits, shirts, and ties, all identical. A row of shoes gleamed black. *No dust, someone cleans. That means that nothing truly revealing will be found in the open.*

There was a box room, with no boxes, or windows, just a poorly assembled camp-bed. It didn't look slept in, so he must have folded the sheets. *Soldiers do that.*

One door was locked. Sarah knelt and peered through the empty keyhole and saw a small room lit by daylight, maybe a desk and chair. She cocked her head to one side and examined the lock itself. The brass gleamed like it had never been used, so she looked down and examined the paintwork below it. There were no telltale scratches where a bunch of keys would have left a mark. *A long key, on its own, that he wouldn't risk losing outside. Somewhere easy to get to from here, but somewhere safe from the cleaner.*

Sarah had played this game endlessly as a child. Left alone and bored in the big house in Elsengrund as her mother slept the afternoons away, she had explored, figuring out where things were and why, where there were keys and why there were locks. She uncovered the puzzle pieces and wove stories from things she found. It didn't matter that she didn't always understand the secrets. It was enough that they were there to be discovered.

By the time she was breaking into houses in search of food, she was not just a formidable thief but an insatiable voyeur.

The armchair was on the other side of the room, and the sofa was too far to be convenient, but there wasn't really anything else in the room. She looked back at the lock, which read *Chubb of Wolverhampton*. Well-made and tough to pick, even if she'd had anything to do it with. Chubb locks were a challenge she relished, and she delighted outthinking them. She leaned her head against the door. Maybe behind the painting? Too easily discovered, bound to pique interest if it was found by whoever cleaned.

She looked along the surface of the wall stretching away to the window. She realized that the column shape in the middle was merely decorative. The rather severe bird shape attached to it stood a few centimeters from the rest of the plaster. She shuffled over to it with a chuckle. She slid her small hand underneath and found what she was looking for halfway up. The key was on a rubber hook and rested on soft bumpers. It couldn't have been dislodged by accident.

It slid into the lock silently, and the well-oiled barrels rolled inside with an irresistible elegance. British locks were excellent, she thought, not like most of her mother's German knockoffs that barely opened even with the right key. She covered her hand with the end of the robe and turned the polished door handle. No telltale smudges to give her away.

What if you don't like what you find?

She looked back to the painting. *You mean, what if he really is a Nazi, but one who rescues Jews?*

He hasn't rescued you. You rescued him.

Shhhhhh . . . thought Sarah.

The door opened to reveal a small office. It was lit by a skylight high above, with a bookcase that covered most of the back wall, a green metal filing cabinet, and a walnut desk. It was a mess of papers, files, magazines, and open books. A small and ugly rug lay wonkily in a corner. One revolving chair sat facing the door.

Another girl would have been disappointed, but Sarah knew better.

The desk was scattered with maps and magazines, or rather dull tomes with titles in several languages like *Physikalische Zeitschrift, Physical Review,* and *Die Naturwissenschaften.* There were no identifying papers or keys, no notepads to investigate, and even the blueprint for an airship that she found underneath it all told her nothing new.

The only personal item was a letter, sitting on top of a blank envelope. A quick shuffle revealed it was from a Lise Meitner, "with thanks." It contained some drawings that Sarah couldn't make sense of, something about drips of water, bunches of grapes, zigzag arrows, and numbered letters, but in the absence of anything else she turned to the front page and skimmed through it.

Dear Helmut,

Uh–huh, thought Sarah.

I am writing this letter "in the clear" as I think they call it and entrusting it to Otto to deliver to you in person, as time is short. First, thank you for your help getting to the Dutch border. Your plan was a good one and now I'm safely in Sweden.

The phrase *Underground Railroad* drifted again through Sarah's mind. So she was not the first.

It was these events that have made up my mind to entrust you with this. I have been denied the resources, lab time, money, and access required to prove the following beyond doubt, as I always have been denied these

things, first as a woman, then being classed as
a Jew

Bull's-eye.

and now a refugee. So rather than attempt
to persuade the governments of France, Britain,
or the United States without the appropriate
proof, I am hoping that you will see the danger
and act.

Sarah glanced at the clock. Plenty of time.

We have talked about "nuclear" physics,
Fermi, Otto Hahn, and my work in some detail
before, so you know the background

Sarah kept reading, but the words grew more technical and
more complex until it seemed she was reading a new and unfa-
miliar foreign language. She skipped farther and farther ahead
and was about to put the letter down when she spotted a phrase
in capital letters and underlined.

a bomb, about the size of a GRAPEFRUIT,
with ENOUGH DESTRUCTIVE POWER TO
FLATTEN A CITY.

She read back, but the preceding paragraph was impenetrable. She read on.

Trust me when I say that the construction of such a device will be possible, along the lines I've described. When the war comes and sides will finally be chosen, my conscience will not let me build such a thing, but I am only too aware that human nature will happily demand such a thing of others less inclined to refuse.

One such is Hans Schäfer, of whom I have talked before. Not only does he know all this, but now he has access to the notes and materials I had to leave with Otto. He has no respect for academia, and he has the personal fortune to follow this up in his own time and to his own agenda. Worst of all, he has the connections within the new order to turn research into production under conditions impossible elsewhere.

I have little fear . . . That said, he scares me, like I am a little girl with a monster under my cot. He has scent of a weapon the likes of which God himself would hesitate to use in all his vengeance. He will build it if he's allowed to.

Helmut, DO SOMETHING. Stop him, or at
least slow him down in some way.

With thanks,

Lise Meitner.

PS: BURN THIS.

Sarah carefully replaced the letter, struggling to control a prickling excitement. Evil scientists and shadowy experiments. It read like a cheap paperback. But when she thought about bombs, she pictured the cannonball and burning fuse from the cartoons. How would one throw a bomb that powerful? She delved into her head for more and unearthed a memory of a man talking about the *Weltkrieg*, the World War, of endless mud and giant holes.

She gazed up to the skylight as the light brightened momentarily. The sun had escaped the cloud, and now tiny motes danced in the golden column. She tried to grab them, delighting in their ability to escape her.

Escape. The skylight was too far for her, but within the reach of a grown man, standing on the desk. The people who had started hiding communists and others preferred attic spaces, because there was always a way out onto the roof. Cellars were coffins.

Her hair got in her face as she shook it again. She needed a brush. So he had an escape route. Did he move into the top-floor flat deliberately, or was it a coincidence?

She wandered over to the bookshelves. When she had visited other houses, she had always sought out their books. Like the contents of a desk, a library tells you about the person. There are books passed on in the family. That's who they were. Then there are the books they think they should have. That's who they want to be. There are the books they want *you* to see. That's who they want *you* to think they are. There are books they want to believe they like and then the books they really like, the dirty little secrets. If they're old and dusty enough, that tells you all you need to know about that person's mind. Everything was there if you only troubled to look. Sarah read everything, voraciously and indiscriminately.

Her desire for the written word was insatiable. When she had lost everything, there were still a few precious books for her to escape into. Even these small shelves were a feast for her eyes.

She recognized a few names. *Mein Kampf*; Guderian the dull tank man; books from her father's library, *The Thousand and One Nights*, *The Wonderful Wizard of Oz*, *Ben-Hur: A Tale of the Christ*; books in German, French, English, Russian, Arabic . . . Japanese? She ran a casual finger from right to left. Steinbeck, Shakespeare, Scholem, Sartre, Sade . . . *Scholem*? *That's a compromising possession*, she thought. *Doesn't get more Jewish than that*, just as Herr Haller had said to her in that filthy toilet so long ago . . . yesterday? No, the day before. H. G. Wells—she pulled *The Time Machine* off the shelf. Most copies of this had been burned when the Nazis came to power. *The World Set Free?* She hadn't read that.

It was a confused picture. The letter was incriminating, but that was new. Ordinarily, was there enough here to warrant an escape route? *Only if he was hiding something else.* On a whim, she tapped the wood behind the books.

Nothing. Just a wall. Sarah laughed out loud at herself, and with a little skip she shoved the book back into place with the others. This time the wood made an unmistakable hollow bump.

SIX

"WAKE UP."

Sarah's hair had fixed itself down over her eyes with sweat. Her face was stuck to the leather of the sofa and made a noise like an opening honey jar as she jerked up her head. She breathed heavily, like she had been running, and pushed herself into a sitting position with stiff arms.

"Demons again?"

"Dogs," she croaked.

The room was dim but lit from the walls somehow. He was a dark shape sitting in the armchair opposite her. The table in between had something on it.

The lamp was unfairly bright when it came on, the bulb

too vivid to stare into. She shielded her eyes and pulled the robe around her shoulders with her spare hand. A cloud of irritating smoke billowed from behind the shade and passed over her. She coughed.

"So, what did you find?"

Her mind was muddled from sleep, and she couldn't think. Her head hurt. She had locked the door and replaced the key. She'd left the bread outside the office. She had spun the chair to face the door, again. What had she forgotten?

"What. Did. You. Find?"

She gave her head the tiniest shake and pulled her hair back from her face. She looked right past the burning light and glared defiantly at the darkness.

"You dress the same every day, in freshly laundered duplicates. You're rich. You're rarely here and eat out. You're used to getting your own way. Someone cleans, so you keep your life in perfect order and pretend to want nothing, lest something give you away." There was a pause.

"Go on." Another cloud of smoke drifted past the lamp.

"You haven't read *Das Schwarze Korps, Die Wehrmacht,* or *Der Stürmer,* even though you keep them on your coffee table and up-to-date when you're here. Like that painting, it's a bluff. You're no Nazi. You have . . . British friends . . ." She was guessing now but plowed on. "They're not happy about my presence."

"And . . . ?" More smoke.

Sarah swallowed. She needed some water. "And . . . what?" she asked, attempting to sound jolly and unconcerned.

"What else did you learn?"

She was about to lie, but thought better of it. "How did you know?"

A hand emerged from the gloom into the light. Between a well-kept finger and thumb was something very long, gossamer-like and golden in the electric light.

"Just the one, but enough."

Oh, dumme Schlampe, Sarah thought, to a chorus of agreement in her head.

"Well . . ." she began with renewed brightness. "You go to serious effort to deny access to your office, where you have various banned and politically dubious books. You study airships, science journals, military history, and technology. You read at least five languages at a high level. You have a Jewish friend called Meitner whom you smuggled over the border to the Netherlands. She wants you to do her another favor. Is she pretty?"

"Is she what?" He couldn't keep the surprise out of his voice.

"Is she pretty? Beautiful? Why would you take the risk of helping her if you aren't . . . what are the words? An *Underground Railroad*?" She finished in English. He almost laughed.

"Professor Meitner is a formidable woman. Go on."

"She thinks you can make her problem go away. She thinks it's everyone's problem and that this is . . . 'your area of interest.'"

"Indeed? What else?" His voice was again flat and noncommittal.

"No, that's it." She stopped, waited two beats of her heart, and then added, "Except for the secret compartment behind the dangerous bookshelf, where you have two guns, dark clothes, knives, tools, papers for five different people all with your face, stacks of high-value Reichsmarks, French francs, US dollars, and a stack of Krugur . . . Kruga . . . gold coins. You've a radio with an aerial you run up to the skylight, which is also your escape route."

"That all?" He couldn't keep the amusement out of his voice.

"Some things, I don't know what they are. But you're a spy."

"That so?"

"If those things weren't locked up, I wouldn't have been sure, but they were hidden, so they're secret. That makes you a spy."

There was a long pause. Then the lamp was redirected to light the table, leaving Sarah blinking dancing stars away.

"Very good. A professional would have struggled to do better. And you didn't try to lie. Never lie when you can tell the truth. Lies have to be worked out in advance, or they will tie you up and eat you." He reached down and stubbed out his cigarette. On the table was a small suitcase and some papers, which he scooped up and tossed gently to Sarah. "New identity card and passport, money to get to the border. Then find a synagogue and start crying. Get as far as you can from Germany."

Sarah opened the card. There she was, standing against the hall wall, with the name Ursula Bettina Haller. Most miraculously of all, the papers were unstamped. There was no red *J,* no police station attendance stamps. Ursula was German and she wasn't Jewish.

"Why are you doing this?" Sarah felt something—an itch in the corner of her eyes, and it left her breathless. It took her a few seconds to recognize the emotion, so long had it been since she'd been *grateful*. It made her feel vulnerable, and she was immediately suspicious of it.

"You saved my life, in all probability. I once lived with a people who like to think they take all that very seriously. Consider the debt repaid."

She closed the papers. A deal. That made sense to her, but there were too many loose ends here.

"What had gone wrong in Friedrichshafen?"

"I outstayed my welcome at the Zeppelin factory. I neglected to bring a passport, which was foolish, making my emergency exit impossible. Always have another way out."

"They were looking for you." With an inward *thunk*, something obvious dropped into place in Sarah's head, something she realized she already knew.

"Yes."

She couldn't read his face. At all. It was like a clay mask. "Roadblocks? That kind of thing?" A yawning abyss opened deep inside Sarah.

"Yes."

"Like the one my mother drove into?" She paused to form the words. "My mother was shot *because of you*."

He looked down and didn't say anything. Preparing another mask.

Her mother's failure had not been self-inflicted.

Oh, Mutti, I'm sorry.

The guilt opened a wound in Sarah's defenses, and a single tear ran down her cheek. She swatted it away angrily like it was a fly. She had gone months without crying, and now it was happening all the time. She had to re-establish some control.

"I get it now. This is *Wergeld*. Blood money. You aren't giving me this because I saved you. You're giving this to me because you murdered my mother."

He had still not raised his head. "If you like."

"What is your name? Your real name, and don't lie to me. 'Lies will tie you up and eat you,'" she repeated without humor. He met her gaze.

"I am Helmut Haller."

"Your *real name*," she screamed in an explosion of suppressed fury. Her voice echoed through the carpetless apartment.

In a voice she had not heard before, more human, more vulnerable, and in an English accent, he finally answered. "Captain Jeremy Floyd."

"*Captain Jeremy Floyd*, we are *not* even. I don't think we will *ever* be even." She delivered the last sentence with exquisite calm. She channeled the rage, mopping up the excess and ladling it into her box for later. She had a measure of control. She could think. "This"—she threw the papers and money onto the suitcase—"it's not enough."

He was just another *thing* to happen to her, to happen to her mother. She wanted to hurt him, as she had wanted to hurt everyone, but she had accepted a long time ago that she couldn't. *It would be like trying to hurt the rain to stop the storm*, Sarah thought.

"What do you want?"

"I don't know."

But she began to realize that she did know. It didn't make sense, but at the same time it did.

"Very well." His voice was Haller's again. "When do you want to leave? The suitcase has clothes for a week or more. I've destroyed your old ones."

Disappointment. It should have surprised her, but it didn't. She knew what she wanted, what the *Wergeld* needed to be. Somewhere in the distance a piano began to play. *But we're not done*, thought Sarah. She cocked her head to one side and stared at him, so he had to go on.

"Of course, you can stay and work for me."

Unexpectedly, Sarah's stomach danced, a happy little ripple of tingles like the night before a birthday. She felt she was betraying her mother, yet there it was. Excitement. The chance to do things. A place to be.

She squashed the feeling.

"For you? As a . . . spy?"

"If that's what you want to call it." He shrugged.

"Against Germany, against my homeland? Become a traitor?" She allowed her voice to take a hard edge. He made a dismissive noise.

"Sarah of Elsengrund, this is not your country anymore. Not while the Nazis are in power." He pointed at her. "You are a Jew. You have no rights here, and there is no place for you."

"But I'm not a Jew," she huffed in exasperation. "Not really. I've never been to synagogue, I don't know the prayers, I don't eat the food, I don't observe the Sabbath. I'm as Jewish as pork sausage." Sarah was bored with this endless self-justification. It was futile.

"That doesn't matter to them—it's all about blood. Look, you've seen what they've done with the communists and their religious opponents." He was more animated, more emotional than she had ever seen him. "How long before you all end up in Sachsenhausen as slave workers?"

"*All* of us?" She laughed. "Where would they put all of us?"

"A few short years ago, the Nazi Party was some angry men in one beer hall. Germany had no army, wasn't *allowed* an army. Don't underestimate them. That's been everyone's mistake."

Sarah shook her head. "France hasn't, has it? They've got that Maginot Line. I saw in the cinema, there's big guns and walls and everything . . . They're ready."

"Well, let's see how that works out, shall we?" he sneered. "The fact is, you have no value here. Ursula Haller does. What was it you said, from the *Arthashastra*? 'The enemy of my enemy is my friend'?"

"Who is my enemy?" Sarah sat forward.

"The Nazis are your enemy. Germany is just . . . caught in the crossfire."

"And who is their enemy?"

"I am . . . or my country is. Or it will be when those tanks roll into Poland in a few weeks' time."

"No." She sat back. "Poland will have to take care of itself."

He bought her a balloon. She was about to protest and then suddenly grinned as a child would. *Stay in character. You can be at the back, stuck in the chorus, but there will be one person staring right at you if you drop your mask. It's inevitable.* It was big and red, constantly tugging to be free, so Sarah had to wrap the string twice round her hand. It danced on the warm breeze but couldn't get away. "Thank you, Onkel." She meant it as a joke, but the illusion felt natural and right.

They drifted along the cinder path and through the old trees by the wall of the zoo. The deck chairs were full of dozing adults. Around them children ran with a boundless energy in the heat, the distant monkey noises mixing with the yelps of joy and mock terror. Couples passed them, arm in arm. The happy hum of thousands of Berliners basking in the midday sun lapped over Sarah and her concerns.

She shook her head. She had become very conscious of the sedative effect the festive atmosphere was having. Could she be Ursula Haller, for real? Could she just walk around the Tiergarten?

"What if someone recognizes me?" she mused, although it was difficult to believe that such a bad thing could happen on a beautiful day like this.

"Dressed like that?" Sarah was wearing the *Jungmädel* uniform of white shirt, black neckerchief, and long navy skirt. "People only see what they expect to see. You look like a blonde, blue-eyed, little Aryan monster, so that's what you are."

"So . . . who *am* I now?" In or out, she could no longer be Sarah. It felt like closing a door.

"Ursula Haller, my niece. Your mother has developed a . . . mental feebleness. We are ashamed. We will not talk about it."

"Where is my—Ursula's father supposed to be, then?"

"He was killed in Spain. We have just returned from there."

"Why don't I have his name?"

"I changed it to mine when I became your guardian. I didn't like the awkward questions about it."

Sarah loved secrets, or rather the structure of them. She tugged at the Captain's fiction, but no loose end appeared. There was no way in.

"What was he doing in Spain?"

"Bombing communists. If anyone tells you that the Luftwaffe had no casualties, then look them in the eye and say, 'If the Führer says that, then I must be mistaken,' and change the subject." His tone changed. "Do I need to repeat any of this?"

"No, not at all." Sarah realized she was the secret. She felt . . . thought about. Considered. Part of something. It was intoxicating. They walked a little farther. "So, uncle, what do you do?"

"You do not really know. My factories make wireless sets, but they also do vital but mostly secret work for the Reich. I travel often. I have important friends and have become rich in the Führer's economic miracle."

Sarah stopped and she watched him walk on. "Mmm . . . and what, Captain Floyd, do *you* do?" she said, eyebrows raised.

He took her arm firmly and guided her away from the deck chairs, toward a tree with huge roots that sprawled across the turf. He sat in a nook in the bark, like it was an armchair, and pointed to a smaller limb next to it. Sarah sat, letting the balloon flutter from side to side with the flexing of her fingers.

"Look." He gestured.

"At what?"

"Just look."

The gardens spread out in front of them, curving down until they reached the wall of the zoo. Some boys were pushing around a leather football, arguing about who would be Hanne Sobek. Farther down, a man and woman inched toward each other on a blanket while pretending to reach for the picnic. Below them, the outdoor restaurant served tea and gossip among the trees and the modern streetlamps, bathed in a yellow-green dappled light. An accordion started up to muted applause, and a few enthusiastic souls got up and headed hand in hand for an unseen dance floor.

"Berlin at play," said Sarah. "So?"

"What's wrong with this picture?"

Sarah looked again and, with the suddenness of seeing a duck where there had been a rabbit, knew the answer.

Every adult man seemed to be in uniform. Brown, gray, and jet-black like dark shadows on the surface of the day.

"The army."

"Not just the army," he said.

"The army. The police. The SS . . . the fire brigade, the doctors, the train drivers. The zookeepers." She laughed without humor. She pulled her legs up and wrapped her arms around them. She laid her head on her knees and watched the world sideways. "I see."

He turned to her and put his elbow on his knee. His accent became unmistakably British.

"I didn't fight Germany in the Great War, I fought the Turk. I've lived in this country off and on for ten years. I have nothing against your *Vaterland*. But him . . ." He pointed at a distant SS officer in his black uniform. "Him—him—him—" His finger snapped from side to side. The world grew darker with each movement, and his voice took on a hard edge. "They're like mold. They've grown and now they're everywhere." Sarah followed his finger as it moved. They *were* everywhere. "And like mold they're all the way through, not just on top. They're eating everything from the inside out. If you love your country, you'll serve it best by helping me."

She looked at the man who had gotten her mother killed and then raised her own finger. "If I'm to consider this, you must always tell me the truth." She waggled the finger to emphasize the point. "Starting now. That doesn't just mean not lying, I mean you have to tell me everything. Don't leave anything out."

"Okay." He sat back.

There was something she had to know.

"You went to Friedrichshafen to look at Zeppelins. So when you found me in the toilet at the docks, why were you there?"

"To kill you. You were a loose end."

"But you didn't."

"No."

"Why?"

"I . . . reconsidered."

"Maybe we're more even than I thought." She sighed. In a way he had killed Sarah, or rather she had by jumping off the ferry. That was the moment of decision, and it was long gone.

The boys' ball bounced up and slapped into Sarah's knees. She yelped and nearly lost her balance, having to fling her arms out to stay on the tree root. Then she smiled as she watched it roll away.

"*Entschuldigung!*" shouted one of the boys.

Only then did she notice the balloon had come loose and was escaping the leaves above, making for open sky. Sarah let it take her fight away with it. She found herself happy and free.

She wasn't hunted, hungry, or hated, and now she had a house the size of a country to root around in.

She put being a traitor in her box, along with her mother's death, for a chance to stand on that podium with Jesse Owens, telling the rulers of her country that they were wrong. The box was overflowing, but it closed.

"So, how do we start?" she said.

SEVEN

THE WAR STARTED the next day.

The Poles had attacked a German radio station on the border. The Wehrmacht responded to this aggression by pouring into Poland. Their tanks had pushed aside the ragged Polish forces on horses and bicycles, and soon the German peoples of Danzig and East Prussia, torn from Germany after the last war, would be reunited with the Reich.

The French and the British failed to see that the Fatherland was just defending itself and declared war on Germany two days later, using the agreement they had tricked the Führer into signing at Munich as a justification.

Everyone was delighted.

Sarah struggled to wear the right face among all the jollity. She was thinking about the massing German army, the hundreds of tanks she'd passed on the way to Berlin. Why would the Poles, with an army of horsemen and old men on bikes, provoke a war with a massively superior enemy? It was an inexplicable piece of hostility that gave the waiting Wehrmacht all the excuse they needed. The whole thing sounded like the *Flunkerei* of a child playing on the street, a tall tale where each question about it was met with another even more fabulous statement.

But what were the Poles to her? Everyone knew they were easy to dislike, and it was true that they were cutting off a piece of Germany from the rest. What did it matter? She had enough to worry about.

Her concerns were like wearing a coat in a stuffy room. Sarah knew she only had to take it off to be more comfortable.

But Sarah didn't know any Poles, so how did she know they were unlikable? Because she had been told so. Because people said that if something was dirty or old, it was Polish. Because she had swallowed that story whole, without checking the ingredients.

With the stomach-turning sensation of having forgotten something really important, Sarah realized that she was thinking like the little Aryan monster she appeared to be. *This is how it happens*, she thought. This is how the people turned their backs on the Jews, why no one helped on *Kristallnacht*. People had enough to worry about.

Poland is packed with Jews, dumme Schlampe. They suddenly have a lot to worry about.

Preparations. Photographs and maps. Diagrams and plans. Nights on a camp bed in a box room. Meals of juicy sausage and warm, crisp bread rolls. Strong, bitter coffee; thick, creamy milk; and fat bags of brown sugar.

Sarah squinted at the grainy image. The figure was barely distinguishable from the background, his face obscured by distance. The Captain straightened it against the grid of the map.

"Hans Schäfer is a gifted scientist. Brilliant, but suspicious and paranoid. His arrogance makes him unpopular, so he's struggled for academic recognition. However, he's rich and powerful. He's moved all his work on uranium to his estate near Nuremberg. Huge amounts of machinery and materials have been arriving for the past two years, but it's locked up tight. Walls, military guards. I'd need a battalion of troops to break in."

"So I'm your battalion?" She smirked.

"Yes. A very special unit."

The Captain pinned a new photograph to the map. This photo was a little clearer. A blonde girl, with a very serious face, in a *Bund Deutscher Mädel* uniform and coat. He tapped the image with a fingernail.

"Schäfer has a daughter about your age—your real age, I mean—who has had friends stay on the estate. She attends a local *Nationalpolitische Erziehungsanstalt.*"

"A *Napola*? A National Socialist school? You're sending me to a *Nazi Party* school? A *Jew*?" Sarah laughed. It was too ridiculous, but one look at his face showed her he was completely serious.

"You've said it yourself. You're *not* a Jew, not *really*. It's just acting. You *can* act, can't you?"

"'All the world's a stage, and all the men and women merely players,'" Sarah said in English, holding her hands up in surrender.

The Captain smiled despite himself. "How do you do that?"

"Do what?"

"Shakespeare. English. Accent recognition. Any of it."

"When the laws changed in nineteen thirty-four, my mother wasn't allowed onstage anymore and couldn't work. We'd lost all our money in the crash, so she schooled me herself. Languages, accents, acting, listening to records of speeches, nothing really useful . . . but she was the truly gifted one. Polish, Czech, English, French, Dutch, even *Russian*. She was amazing. I was eight or nine before I realized that most people only speak one or two languages. In the end, it was all she could do to . . ." Sarah stopped, feeling hot behind the eyes, like she had just given something away. She plowed on. "I didn't have friends. I had books. We had a library in the house in Berlin and nothing else to do."

"What about your father?"

"I don't know anything about my father," she said hurriedly. "He left a lot of military books. Different eras, the Chinese, the

Hindus . . . every culture seems to love killing. Do you believe you can know people from their library, Captain Floyd?"

"I don't know. Who am I?"

"A liar and a trickster."

"Correct." He nodded and slowly smiled.

Preparations.

Sarah woke as the box room door flew open. By the time she had opened her eyes, rough hands had pulled her by the arms from the cot and thrown her into a corner. She hit the walls, a jumble of arms and legs, collapsing onto the carpet.

A powerful light shone in her face, and it stung her eyes. She covered them, but flashes of red still danced in the darkness of her fingers.

"What is your name?" The voice dripped with menace.

"What . . ." she mumbled, disorientated.

"Your name," screamed the intruder.

"S . . . sula. Ursula Haller," Sarah managed.

The light went out, and before she could open her eyes again, the door closed, leaving her alone in the darkness.

Diagrams and plans.

"I don't really understand." Sarah shook her head at the notes and arrows.

"You don't really need to."

Sarah sucked at her teeth and tried a different tack. "All right, this bomb . . . Lise Meitner's *Pampelmusebombe*, the Grapefruit Bomb that Schäfer is making. Why are you—why are *we*—why is it important for Germany? There have always been bigger and bigger bombs."

"Not like this," the Captain said with great intensity, gesturing to emphasize his words. "One little bomb could destroy a city. Instantly. Can you imagine that?"

She still couldn't. She couldn't envisage any bomb, for that matter. Then she remembered the flash and heat of the Captain's improvised explosion at the station. Something about the memory made her want to recoil from it. "No. Not really."

"Look at it this way. If you flattened half of London, or Paris, and you forget about the dead," the Captain continued, seemingly pulling the ideas together as he spoke, "there'd be, what? A million injured people? How would you treat them? There aren't enough hospitals. How would you put out the fires of *thousands* of homes? The country would collapse in a day."

Sarah thought about this, the lines for the doctor after *Kristallnacht*, when the storm troopers wrecked the Jewish neighborhoods. Still, the idea was too fantastic, like something from an H. G. Wells novel—Martians tramping over shattered London in their three-legged machines.

"But a whole city? All at once? With the buildings, the people, the women and children . . . No one would do that. How could anyone?"

The Captain seemed as if he was trying to remember what he was saying. Then he stood. "Let me show you something."

From his secret office and shelves of incriminating books, he brought out a French magazine, *Cahiers d'Art*. He stood in front of Sarah and flicked through it as he spoke. "I was in Spain, two years ago, during their civil war. On the one side, the Republicans—"

"The communists?"

"The elected government," replied the Captain with irritation. "On the other, the Nationalists. A fascist military rebellion. Just a year in, things were not going well for the Republicans. The Nationalists could call on the Luftwaffe, the German air force, and that was decisive."

"Why?" Sarah didn't look up. He was leaving things out as usual.

"Why what?"

"Why were you in Spain? What were you doing, exactly?"

The Captain rolled his eyes. "I was there on business. I found myself in a town in the Basque Country, about thirty kilometers behind the front lines. There were no Republican troops stationed there, so it was a safe place to hole up for a while."

He found what he was looking for and handed the open journal to Sarah. She didn't recognize the painting on the pages, but the strange, angular, chopped-up style reminded her of

Picasso. Unlike the jumbled, colorful, and cheerful musicians and dancers from her mother's books, though, this piece was painfully monochrome—gray, black, dirty white—and flat, like bits of newspaper pasted onto a board. It could have been drawn by a child, but that made the images more unsettling. Order had broken down, and chaos had torn the canvas into stark pieces. The screaming horses were people, the people were bulls, crying or dying, crushed under hoof and foot. A building burned, a crying mother cradled a dead child, twisted, shrieking. Panic, pain, fear, and grief. As her eyes moved from terrible image to terrible image, the Captain talked, his voice emotionless at first.

"It was Monday. Because of the war, it wasn't officially market day, but the farmers had to sell their produce and the townspeople needed to buy food, so the main square was full anyway. Refugees from the fighting resting, gathered around their few belongings. A few soldiers, who were probably deserters. Late that afternoon, the church bells rang, signaling an air raid. Everyone crowded into the *refugios*, little more than cellars, but no one was worried. Why would the Nationalists attack a town of civilians?

"But they did." He grew less objective, more involved, more moved. "One plane came over and dropped its bomb load right in the center of town. Everybody scrambled out of their shelters and ran to help. People under rubble, trapped in burning buildings, no one knew what to do. Farmers and priests pulling at the bricks with bare hands . . . So, after a few minutes of this, a whole squadron of the Luftwaffe—Italians, Condor Legion, whatever—flew over and emptied everything they had onto the town. Chaos. People tried to get back into the shelters, but the refuges were destroyed by the first attack. Flames, dust, noise. With nowhere to go, the people ran for the fields. A stampede, the small and the weak were trodden on . . ."

The Captain's voice sounded strained. After a moment he continued. "As they ran away, waves of fighter planes swooped down and strafed them with bullets and grenades. Men, women, children . . . chased into the crops and slaughtered like grouse on a hunt."

"That's . . . horrible," Sarah murmured, conscious of how inadequate the words were.

"That's *nothing*." His voice was full of derision. "The planes had hardly gone, just ten or twenty minutes of crying and screaming and trying to stop the blood with your hands, staring at the jagged shapes of smoking buildings, when we heard the low hum. Bombers, moving across the sky in threes, carving lines across the town for two and a half hours. Explosives shattered and flattened the buildings. Firebombs rained down like confetti, setting everything they touched alight. Animals ran burning and screaming through the streets. Men lit up like torches staggered among the wreckage, beyond help. When they were done, the town was gone. A skeleton was all that remained, filled with sixteen hundred corpses and nine hundred maimed, ruined people."

"Why did they do that?" Sarah felt sick. "Why would anyone do that?"

"To terrorize the Basques by destroying their capital. To block the Republican retreat. To test out their new bombing technique. Maybe they were trying to hit the bridge outside town and got lost. It doesn't matter why. What matters is they *wanted to do it, so they did*. It's that simple. If it fits their purpose, they will do it." He tapped the painting. "That was just twenty-two tons of explosive. Professor Meitner thinks Schäfer's bomb would be more powerful than five hundred tons of dynamite. One bomb. The people who did this, who murdered these people, wiped this town from the map. If they could destroy Paris or London with one bomb? They wouldn't hesitate."

There was silence. Sarah looked at the painting one last time and closed the magazine, sealed the horrors away inside. Something else bothered her.

"Twenty-two tons of explosive. Exactly twenty-two tons. How do you know that?"

The Captain had his back turned to her. His shoulders twitched and then were still. "I sold them the bombs," he said.

Preparations.

It was 4:00 a.m. when the Captain kicked the door open and shone a powerful flashlight on the camp bed.

It was empty.

From a dark corner behind him came a voice. "I'm bored now. I think we're ready."

The Captain nodded. "Good night, Ursula," he said as he closed the door.

"Good night, Onkel."

EIGHT

October 4, 1939

"BUT I DON'T *like* other children," she complained. "They don't like me. That's the flaw in your little plan."

"Then be someone who does like children. Be someone who is *likable*."

"I might as well wish I could fly."

"Just concentrate on snotty self-confidence. *That* you can do."

She pulled a face.

"It's just school," he added in a more conciliatory tone.

Sarah hadn't gone to school. At the start it was a choice. Her mother thought she was too good, too special, too important to mix with children of *die Arbeiterklasse*. It was only later that she wasn't allowed to mix with other children. The irony of this was not lost on Sarah. First she had tutors and a governess, then as the money started to run out, her mother taught Sarah herself. This began as an occasional treat and in well-organized and thoughtful sessions, but as her mother's own work seeped away, Sarah's education became incessant and frustratingly random. History came from thick Moroccan-bound and dusty tomes on ancient battles, geography from maps of lost empires, and the many, many languages from her mother's acidic tongue.

And acting. Endless, day and night, unceasing. How to deceive, convince, emote, and project. How to focus attention and lose it on demand. How to be someone else until she didn't know where she ended and the performance began. Sarah began to realize that she was being trained for a career on the stage that she would never have, to play roles in countries she wouldn't travel to, for people who would never see her. A sense of absence had pricked at the skin under her eyes and at the bridge of her nose. She knew that being with others would make it go away.

She had loathed her loneliness and loathed it now. It was a sign of weakness.

NPEA Rothenstadt was a gothic monstrosity: part castle, part mansion, the diseased imagining of Count Dracula and Dr. Frankenstein in the depths of the forest. It would have been comical in the sunshine without the massive flag of the Third Reich draped over the entrance. It dripped genuine menace. As the Captain's car approached it down the tree-lined avenue, the towers seemed to reach up into the sky like claws, the red flag a tongue. Sarah's impression that she was walking into the jaws of a sleeping beast was unshakable.

Use the fear. Fear is an energy. Break it up and build something new.

The car purred into position outside the door. "You get in. You ingratiate yourself"—Sarah opened her mouth, but the Captain silenced her by holding up a hand—"with the target by whatever means necessary. Other than that, enjoy yourself."

"I don't enjoy myself," she said coldly.

"Then *pretend* to enjoy yourself." He gestured to the school. "Shall we?"

After the brightness of the day, the entrance hall was a gloomy cave of dark wood paneling and grand staircases, murky portraits and unlit candles. The ceiling stretched up and vanished into darkness that hung like a low rain cloud. Despite the veneer of splendor, the prevailing smell was carbolic soap and boiled cabbage. In the center of this hallway stood a single tall girl of about sixteen in the uniform of the BDM. She was lit by one shaft of bright sunlight that fell from an unseen window far above, and her braided blonde hair shone. Her polished shoes stood exactly within a white square, Sarah noticed, like the work of a meticulous chess player.

"Heil Hitler." She saluted, and after Sarah raised a cursory arm, she looked at the Captain and waited.

A clock tocked in the silence. After what seemed like too long, he replied, "Indeed. Heil."

"Herr Haller?"

"Yes."

"You will follow me, please." She marched away. The Captain turned to Sarah. The corners of his mouth flickered, and a fire danced in his eyes for just a moment. "Shall we?"

Sarah raised her eyebrows in admonition and waited for him to move. She made a small gesture with her hand, and he strode quickly after the girl. Their footsteps clacked and reverberated in the brown darkness.

"Herr Bauer wishes to apologize for the lighting. Preparations for tonight's vigil require it." Hers was a voice accustomed to being obeyed.

"Then why is he apologizing?" the Captain replied. The girl took a misstep but recovered quickly, her cold expression reasserting itself over the sudden fluster.

"Herr Bauer is obligated on occasion to make allowances for *outsiders*."

The Captain pulled a face like he had been slapped and flashed a grin at Sarah. *Stop it,* she thought. *No,* she reconsidered. *He's being Herr Haller.*

Who are you being?

A shocked and nervous little girl.

You stop it.

"Wait, please," said the girl, and she walked the last few meters to a large oak door alone.

The Captain placed a finger on the small of Sarah's back and tapped gently. "Curtain. Break a leg."

Sarah knew better than to judge by appearances. Young and old, tall and short, ugly and beautiful, fit and crippled—Sarah knew them to be equally capable of goodness, or in her experience, equally vicious and horrible. The headmaster, Bauer, was fat. But despite herself, Sarah found him unbearably so.

He was not comfortably plump or slightly overfed, not jolly, round, nor chubby as some people can be, but excruciatingly bulbous. It was a fatness that looked like it came from a deliberate, sustained, and highly disciplined overconsumption that had no hint of pleasure in it. The unceasing sense of hunger that had been a feature of the last few years yawned to life inside Sarah, and she knew instantly that she loathed this man. She tried to picture the quantities of food necessary for such an experiment, but here her imagination failed her. The tiny little girl inside her howled and stamped her feet at the injustice, at the waste.

A line of sweat was gathering on Herr Bauer's top lip as he glared at Sarah over his steepled fingers. She had no desire to make eye contact and instead watched the uniformed officer behind him. He, in turn, was absurdly thin, little more than a skeleton covered in skin. The contrast couldn't have been more pronounced. He was staring straight ahead with such conviction that Sarah was tempted to glance around to see what she was missing. The silence dragged on, and she became intensely aware of her hands. Should they be together? No, they should be loose to indicate calm. *Don't move them, dumme Schlampe.* The headmaster sighed heavily.

"Herr Haller. We appreciate and respect your desire to have your . . . niece . . . admitted to this school. We acknowledge the implied compliment. However, I cannot see any reason why we should accommodate you."

Sarah frowned. This was supposed to be the easy bit. It hadn't occurred to her that they might simply not want her.

Don't let it show, remember who you're supposed to be.

"Herr Bauer, this is . . . awkward." The Captain sat back and looked away as if collecting himself. "Your school came recommended at the highest level. I was only yesterday talking to Herr Bormann—"

The headmaster raised a hand and interrupted. "Herr Haller, spare me your party connections, your wife's salon guest list, and family connections to the Führer. Everyone who wants to send his daughter here claims special status in the new order on the flimsiest of evidence. Do you know how many brothers Hermann Göring must have if everything I've heard in this room is true?"

"He has nine siblings. I imagine that makes for quite an extended family, Herr Bauer," the Captain answered.

Herr Bauer opened his hands and made a dismissive gesture. "My point remains, I invite everyone to make that angry telephone call to his powerful friends, should those friends actually exist. This school is exclusively for the cream of the next generation of German women. Your niece's provenance is basic at best." He fingered the papers on his desk with indifference. "Your importance to the Reich is equally nebulous. I'm sure"—he rolled his eyes theatrically—"that you have been blessed financially and your munificence would be boundless, but it isn't about that, is it? It's about purity, intelligence and brilliance, strength and power. Exactly what does your frankly undersized niece have to offer us?"

"I can play that piano."

Everyone looked at Sarah. She'd had enough of being talked about like she wasn't there. She pointed at the grand piano in the corner of the office.

Herr Bauer snorted. "*I* can play the piano."

"Not like me." She stared right into his tiny eyes and wanted to retch.

Herr Bauer licked his lips slowly, then clicked a pudgy index finger toward the piano. "Be my guest."

Sarah got up from her chair slowly, remembering to smooth her skirt as she did so, and then clasped her hands demurely in front of her. She'd felt goaded by the man's disdain and was now unsure of herself. She felt her legs moving heavily as if through syrup, and the air seemed stale and close. She could see now that there was no music on the stand, nothing to suggest what might be acceptable. What did she know by heart? She went through her repertoire, rejecting each piece as unsuitable, an endless string of cabaret numbers penned by Jews and undesirables. Wagner, wasn't it the Führer's favorite? *Something you know, idiot.* She arrived at the piano without an idea in her head.

It was a beautiful Grotrian-Steinweg just like her mother's—polished, dusted, and untouched. Sarah could almost see the golden-haired toddler looking back at her from its flawless curves.

She reached out and let her fingers brush across it as she passed. Little cloudy trails blossomed and evaporated in their wake. *Think.* She lifted the front top board and slid the music shelf aside. The elegant golden plate shone back at her. Someone's life had been made miserable to keep the inside of the instrument this spotless.

As her mother had slipped slowly down into bitterness and depression, their piano had suffered at her hands. The always-open top board had caught the spills and refuse of a dozen tantrums; the strings had clogged with fluff and cigarette ends. When they finally fled to Austria, it had become an unrecognizable pile of empty spirit bottles and overflowing ashtrays. Sitting down in front of this fiercely clean instrument was like stepping back in time to when her mother smiled more and snarled less, when the apartment was full of laughter instead of broken glass. The thought was a spear through Sarah's heart.

She lifted the lid, and her hands hovered over the keys.

She thought she could see her mother's face in the music stand, warmer, calmer, and younger than it had been, head rocking gently back and forth, each motion timed to the left-hand chord and imperceptibly circling from side to side to the motion of her right hand.

Sarah found her fingers playing and her foot marking time on the pedals. A gentle and slow waltz was emerging, melancholy and darkly vague, punctuated by almost random drops of high notes, like falling spring rain across the minor bass chords. Raindrops that streak across the windowpane, barely making their presence felt, but ruining the day. The notes sustained into the distance and fell away but reappeared with a slicing suddenness, in the wrong places but at the right time. As the jagged circular melody spiraled round her arms, Sarah felt the box deep inside her split open, and the fear, the sadness, and the loneliness seeped over the edges. She caught her breath and wanted to stop, but couldn't. The notes unpicked her stitches as her fingers traveled right and left. In her mind's eye her mother's head was still rocking to the slow offbeat tempo, but above her hairline her deep red locks were now a mess of blood and glass.

A hand slammed down onto the music rack with such force that Sarah jumped back with a yelp.

The thin uniformed officer was standing over her, a look of disgust on his face. Sarah tried to calm her quaking shoulders as the last discordant notes resonated in the silence.

"Satie was a French degenerate. His experiments in Modernism and Dada were a sickness, the fumblings of a Bolshevist. Where did you learn such filth?" the officer barked.

Inside Sarah was rapidly stuffing, closing, locking, and hiding the box, desperately putting her fears away, conscious of a much more immediate threat. She could not admit to any more weakness. *Attack is the secret of defense; defense is the planning of an attack.*

"My father always said that. This is my mother's favorite piece, but she was a very sick woman," she said quietly and waited, unblinking. Captain Floyd's voice could be heard on the other side of the room.

"Ursula's mother was a long time away from the Fatherland. You see now why I'm so insistent that she gets an appropriate National Socialist education."

The uniformed officer looked back at the headmaster and spoke. "You will ensure that this girl learns only German music. Music appropriate to her talents."

Herr Bauer shrugged and looked away. "If you insist, Klaus."

"I do." The officer turned back to Sarah, who didn't know if she had been dismissed. After a moment, he held out a handkerchief. She regarded the fold of white cotton but found she couldn't move, unable to square this action with the distaste in his expression. Eventually, he tutted and reached for her face. She screamed on the inside as he clasped her chin firmly between his thumb and forefinger, and he deftly wiped her one errant tear away.

He stepped aside and strode from the room. Sarah realized he smelled of oranges.

The headmaster sighed and stared at his desk. "Taking a new girl so far into the term, most inconvenient . . . unprepared for expenses, extra bed and board . . ."

"If money were an object, Herr Bauer, I would leave Ursula in the local *Realschule*," declared the Captain, standing. "Make the arrangements."

"Klaus will be delighted to have another pianist attending," the headmaster mumbled wearily.

Outside, the early evening sun was especially bright, the breeze especially wholesome, as if it were made for the cream of German womanhood. The Captain turned away from the car, where a wizened old man was struggling with Sarah's suitcase.

"Ursula, a little walk, I think."

"Certainly, Onkel."

They ambled with an intense casualness along the front of the school. It was bereft of flower beds, bushes, or anything colorful. Even the grass seemed muted.

"You play very well. I didn't know that about you," the Captain said, something approaching admiration in his voice.

"There's lots you don't know. I think it might be comforting to know you have limits. Anyway, a lady must have some secrets."

"I just wish you'd played something else. Wagner or something?"

"Oh yes, Wagner is very big in Jewish show business families."

"You were lucky that our new friend is a patron of the arts."

Sarah shivered. "Who is he?"

"I don't know," he replied with unusual candor. "I haven't come across him before."

"More ignorance. Mmm . . . this isn't so comforting after all." She spoke with more humor than she felt.

"I'll find out." He placed a hand on her shoulder. "In the meantime, keep him sweet. Learn your Wagner."

They turned the corner of the building. "You're leaving me here, then," she said softly.

"That was the plan."

She felt she was being lowered into a pit of snakes. She needed reassurance from the person holding the rope.

"That man—he's one of your unnecessary uniforms."

"Yes, he is."

"And that's why I'm here?"

"In a way."

They followed the path as it angled away from the school toward a chapel. The courtyard was deserted, but Sarah still felt the need to look over her shoulder.

"What I'm doing here . . . if I stay in *this place* . . . I'm freeing Germany?"

The Captain was about to be flippant, she could see it in his eyes, but something in her face gave him pause.

"You want to leave?" he asked gently.

Sarah took a deep breath and pushed her hands deep into her coat pockets, eyes on the ground. "I didn't say that. I just—" She looked up and tried to make sense of his glazed eyes. "I just want to be sure that it's important."

"How important do you want to be?" The flippancy leaked out.

Sarah stamped a foot and hissed, "I don't want to be some skeleton's piano monkey unless you really need me to be. Does Germany really need me to be? Getting in this man's house— it's that important?"

He held his palms out. "There's nothing in Hans Schäfer's office. He's moved everything to his estate. It's locked down tight. Guarded day and night."

"And he's making the Grapefruit Bomb?" she insisted.

"Maybe. Whatever he's doing, it scared Professor Meitner. Nothing scares Lise Meitner. That . . . disturbs me," he finished softly.

"And you *really* think I can walk up to this Elsa Schäfer and get you an invitation to her father's house?"

"Maybe," he conceded.

She rubbed at her forehead with the tips of her fingers. "That's a lot of maybes."

"There always are."

A cloud passed over the sun. Sarah bit her lip. "What if I mess up?"

"Then I take you home."

"Home?" Sarah laughed. A box room and a fake name. Not enough. "No, I mean what if they discover who I am?"

"We'll cross that bridge when we come to it."

"*More* maybes?"

"Yes."

So many uncertainties. Sarah pulled a shoe through the gravel into a long line. "Have you ever used the floating edge?"

"I have no idea what you mean."

"What is it in English? The . . . *balance beam.*"

He shook his head. She stepped onto the mark she had made and moved her arms behind her, palms up. Slowly, she raised one leg to head level so she was balancing on the other, her foot motionless on the line.

"Just eight centimeters wide, the width of your foot if you're lucky . . ." she explained.

Raising her arms above her head, she swept the leg down and behind her, until it stood straight at right angles to her body.

"It moves as you do, so you have to predict it. Ride it." Her voice sounded strained, tense even to her own ears. "You've walked it endlessly, eyes closed, fallen off over and over, until you can move through the program seamlessly . . . readjusting your balance with your muscles, your toes, never your feet . . ."

She arched her back and bent her outstretched leg. Reaching over her head, she closed her hands over her foot.

"All the while you're being watched, judged, dismissed," she continued. "It's tempting to rush it, but you can't, and you have to commit to the move. If you panic, you're gone.

"Normally, you're a meter from the floor, high enough to break or snap something if you don't fall well. But I used to practice on the banisters at home once they threw me out of class. I had to finish, had to be perfect, because the fall was three meters on one side."

She released her foot and tipped forward, until she was leaning over, balanced by her outstretched leg, before straightening up.

"That's where I am now, aren't I? Except the banister is wet. And the floor is on fire."

"Very poetic." He didn't seem to know what else to say.

"'Art is a lie that makes us realize the truth,' Captain Floyd."

He threw his head back and laughed, a big bright thing that echoed off the school building. It made Sarah smile for its unexpectedness.

"Sarah of Elsengrund, play your part with more care. Good National Socialist girls don't quote Picasso, or play Satie. You've got to be a good dumb little monster now."

"Yes, sir." She clicked her heels together. Playing a part. Doing it well. This was familiar ground.

The sun re-emerged from behind the chapel. Sarah noticed

something and walked toward it. Attached to the front of a dark glass window in the transept was a stone carving of three hares. They were running in a circle, each chasing the tail of the next, somersaulting up and over one another so that their ears were connected at the center.

"Oh," she chirped. "The three hares. It's on . . . it *was* on the synagogue in Karlshorst."

"I thought you didn't go to the synagogue."

"I didn't go *to* synagogue, doesn't mean I never went to *a* synagogue. Why is it here?"

"For Christians it stands for the Trinity—Father, Son, and Holy Ghost. In the Kabbalah, the three levels of the soul. You can find them on churches and shrines from the Silk Road to Great Britain."

Sarah sang quietly.

"Der Hasen und der Löffel drei,
Und doch hat jeder Hase zwei."

"Three hares sharing three ears, yet every one of them has two . . ." She shivered again and cocked her head to one side before continuing. "You know, the Jews are supposed to be the hares. I guess the National Socialists are the dogs. The Jews are persecuted, hunted, hated, but they can run and dodge and you can't wipe them out."

"I suspect they're going to try."

NINE

————

"TWO PERSONAL OBJECTS only on the night table. The suitcase will be removed. This is an example of how your cot will be made." The *Schlafsaalführerin* Liebrich waved her hand across the bed. The sheets were murderously clean and folded into sharp corners. The bedding looked thin. Something must have revealed itself on Sarah's face, because the dormitory leader screwed up her nose in disdain. "You will find it quite adequate. The room is warm enough, even in the winter. We are not permitted to become soft. Luxury is a weakness. We must be hardy, pious—"

"*Fröhlich, frei,*" Sarah chimed in.

The girl carried on as if she hadn't heard. "We wake at six.

Wash and report for exercise before breakfast. You will follow the others."

"Cold showers, I assume?" Sarah spoke almost under her breath. She looked away to the duplicate cots and white cabinets. Bare floorboards, immaculate washstands, and the omnipresent portrait of the Führer, rendered in cheap oils—it had all the charm of a hospital ward.

"Of course. You aren't going to cause us any problems, Haller?" A question, but not a question.

Sarah fixed her eyes on Liebrich's. "Not at all." *Give ground. Nod, something.*

"What happened to your nose? Are you a troublemaker?" Liebrich sneered. Sarah resisted the temptation to touch it. The faded bruising must still be visible. She had grown used to it.

"Only if someone gets in my way."

Dumme Schlampe. This was going all wrong. The girl was taller, bigger, even though she was two years younger. She would make a difficult enemy, and besides, Sarah was on her ground. *Whoever occupies the battleground first and awaits the enemy will be at ease.*

Concede, withdraw.

"I'd be very careful, Haller," Liebrich threatened.

"Just fair warning." Sarah extended a hand. "Ursula."

"Heil." Liebrich jerked her arm into a salute. Sarah felt her skin warm like she'd been slapped, but she slowly, deliberately raised her arm and extended it, letting each muscle tighten until it, too, made a salute.

"Heil," she said, very clearly and with as neutral a tone as she could muster. "I'm still Ursula. Ursula Haller."

Liebrich ignored her. "The vigil is at seven. Someone will collect you. Do everything they say and do not embarrass us, Ursula Haller." She turned on her heel and marched away. Sarah waited for the door to slam, but the handle was oiled and it closed noiselessly. *No slamming of doors here . . . and no noises of approach.* She looked at the floorboards. Thick, old, but there would be creaks. They would have to be learned.

Sarah sat on the bed, the heat of her exchange fading away like the daylight in the windows. A show of strength? Maybe. A new enemy? Maybe that, too. Not even a first name. The cot was hard and cold. It might as well have been a stone slab. She had a stomach-cramping longing for the camp bed in the Captain's airless little box room, with its musty blankets. It was the realization that she had, for a short time, been *safe*. Virtually untouchable.

Sarah seized on this longing and strangled it, squeezing its pitiful and pathetic neck. She was not *safe*. She had not been *safe* for as long as she could remember. Safety was an illusion. Forward motion was everything; to hesitate meant losing balance. Commit. *You have a job. A role to play. The audience is arriving and you are hidden away, already in costume. The overture has started. This is the waiting time before the curtain. Who are you going to be?*

I am Ursula Bettina Haller, she answered. *Good little dumb National Socialist monster. Nobody's enemy. Everybody's friend.*

Alles auf Anfang. Places, please, the voice replied.

"Are you Haller?" asked another, tiny voice. It took Sarah a moment to realize that someone had spoken out loud. At the door was a small and fragile-looking girl. She had untidy braids and absurdly large and frightened eyes. "I'm Mauser, but everyone calls me *die Maus*."

"I wonder why?" Sarah smiled.

"Me, too," the Mouse replied. The girl was so insubstantial that had the doorway been empty, it would have left a greater impression. If there was a less persuasive argument for *die Herrenrasse*, the master race, Sarah had yet to see it. She wondered how someone so weak had gained entry to the school. Maybe she, too, played the piano.

The Mouse squirmed and continued. "Are you ready to join the others?"

"I hope so."

Sarah had seen vigils before. Catholics in May, with torches, banners, and candles, processing the streets in the twilight, singing hymns to Christ's mother. This was just the same, but with a new messiah.

The girls marched down the corridors in well-drilled rows, illuminated only by candlelight, singing softly of the glory of the Fatherland, the virtue of its women, and their love for their leader. They entered the Grand Hall from different directions and merged seamlessly, their fringed banners and flags sliding into place at the head of the formation. They paraded up the grand staircase to meet the older girls descending it, and, turning, they formed a massed choir in front of the rank of teachers by the entrance door. Then, after a silence, one soprano voice soared into life and sang an aria to a hardy Alpine flower and how much the Führer loved it.

Sarah had been escorted to the back of the lines of girls on the ground floor and kept out of the way. She recognized again just how easy it must be to open your heart to all of this. It was unquestionably moving. Every tiny element seemed designed to call out, *Join us*. National Socialist events were always filled with crowds, with torches, with fire, with thick embroidered banners. In the darkest corners, hidden from the firelight, one more convert could slip unnoticed into the throng. If you pushed to the front, there were always willing hands to clap you on as you burned books, kicked bakers, and smashed shop windows.

She had sometimes stolen into a cinema many, many kilometers from home. The walk hurt her feet, but although cinemas weren't officially forbidden to Jews until later, it was safer to be somewhere where she wouldn't be recognized. Besides, she had no money. There she was always rewarded with anonymity and a broken back door. She could sneak in and wedge herself against the threadbare velvet seats in the corner, well out of the sight of curious usherettes. When she was eleven she had inadvertently crept into a film of a really big Nazi rally, *The Triumphant Will* or something, and had sat in rapt amazement at everything she saw. It was beautiful, like an extended dance routine, better choreographed than any American musical she had ever seen. It had seemed to glow from within, a golden sunrise from a forgotten, better childhood, with a god descending from the clouds, bringing joy and inspiration. More than that, it seemed an entire argument for National Socialism. The order, the grace, the majesty. Who wouldn't want to belong to that?

"Where are you from, my friend?" called the fresh-faced youths in uniform before others replied one by one, a roll call of German cities and towns. *Everybody* was there. So swept up in it was she that for those two hours she forgot these were the exact same people throwing stones at her windows and beating her in the street. Making a link between this beautiful dance of pride and celebration and the hate, pain, and humiliation they were dishing out seemed impossible. She must have gotten it wrong somehow. It took most of the walk home to break the spell. Her blisters and thirst reminded her why she had been made to walk fifteen kilometers to find a picture house that she could sneak into.

The singing had stopped, and one of the teachers had stepped forward to speak. His voice was monotonous, so Sarah quickly lost interest. "A bright future . . . a glorious inheritance . . . Polish aggression . . . enemies of the Reich from the outside and from within . . . taking your place . . . the annual River Run, an example of your strength and commitment . . ."

She scanned the crowd for Elsa Schäfer. Among the rows of seemingly identical pupils, immaculate in their *Jungmädel* and

BDM uniforms, it seemed an almost hopeless task, until her eyes were drawn to one tall Final Year girl near the top of the staircase.

She had wavy golden hair tamed in braids, and her face was clear, fresh, and welcoming, pale like alabaster with striking gray eyes. Her arms were muscular and her hips broad. She was a poster for the Third Reich come to life. Around her gathered a group of young women straight from the pages of *Das deutsche Mädel*. Each had strong features, athletic builds, and high-ranking BDM uniforms, yet it was clear who was their leader.

Behind this girl was Elsa. She was fifteen like Sarah, but she was about ten centimeters taller—the kind of growth and maturity that came with a good diet, or enough food of any kind. Her hair was thick and glossy in a way that Sarah's could be when she had time to care for it. Her eyes were wide and friendly, with a touch of vinegar hiding in their vitality.

Then Sarah sensed that she was being watched. Their leader was staring at her intensely. Sarah tried to break eye contact but found that she could not. After an uncomfortable and drawn-out moment, the girl looked away, but only to nudge one of the others and point Sarah out.

Sarah knew, instinctively, that this was a bad thing. She could spot a gang forming with mischief in mind and knew there would be no avoiding it. This leader would be the gate-keeper to the group, and there could be no approach to Elsa without her say-so.

Sarah willed herself to look elsewhere.

The teachers were an unremarkable and miserable-looking collection of aging suits and hair pulled into buns so severe the wearers must have had constant headaches. Herr Bauer was wedged into an oversized seat at the back. Hovering to one side was the skeleton Klaus, his brown uniform letting him blend into the shadows.

Sarah leaned over to her escort.

"Mouse, who is that in the uniform? Is he a teacher?"

The Mouse glanced quickly left and right. "That's Sturmbannführer Klaus Foch. He's not a teacher, he's just sort of *there*. He's in charge of the political purity of our—you know—thoughts. He doesn't do much . . ."

"Not a music teacher, then?"

The Mouse raised her eyebrows. "Oh, oh . . . yes, he likes the piano. He likes music. Or rather, he likes the girls who play music."

"Silence," whispered one of the older girls farther down the line. The Mouse went quiet and bowed her head, but she bounced a little on her toes and kept sneaking a peek at Sarah. After a moment she leaned over again.

"Apparently, he was very high up in the *Sturmabteilung*, you know, the SA, a friend of Röhm's and everything. Somehow Foch survived the Blood Purge when the Führer executed everyone else in the SA, but they say the old skeleton has never been the same since. He's a little, you know, *funny* . . ."

This time the older girl reached over, grabbed the Mouse's

braid, and pulled it. "I said shush," she said, giving the hair one more slow tug before releasing her. Sarah kept looking straight ahead and watched this out of the corner of her eye. She counted thirty seconds before glancing over to the Mouse again. A single tear had drawn a line down her cheek. A bubbling fury threaded its way around Sarah's temples, so she slammed her eyes shut.

There was no film of bullied little girls in that movie of the rally, but Sarah knew that around the edges and out of view, hair was being pulled, just as windows were smashed and innocents dragged off to some camp for re-education.

Choose your battles, Sarah. This is survival of the fittest.

As if she'd opened the door to the street on a winter's evening, Sarah went cold. She realized her transformation to little monster had already begun.

The teacher finished railing against the plans of the Poles and Slavs to oppress the German-speaking people of Europe and was now promising, with regret, a swift and decisive response. His voice rose in volume but lost none of its dullness.

"You must believe in Germany as firmly, clearly, and truly as you believe in the sun, the moon, and the starlight. You must believe in Germany as if Germany were yourself. As you believe your soul strives toward eternity. You must believe in Germany—as your life is but death. And you must fight for Germany until the new dawn comes."

To this climax, the girls saluted and shouted the Führer's

name over and over. It began as a unified chant, but the words and patterns dissolved into a hysterical, excited howling. Grins fixed, eyes wide, faces flushed.

Each time Sarah joined in, it was like a piece of her died away. *Dumb monster, dumb monster,* she repeated to herself. She felt increasingly grubby and unwashed.

Finally, the ceremony was over, and the lines of girls broke into babbling groups. Electric lights flickered into life all over the hall, making everything seem smaller and more childish.

Sarah looked for Elsa Schäfer, but in the disorder she seemed to have vanished. There would be no quick win this first night. Seeing it this way, the scale of the challenge dwarfed her, as did the danger. How long before someone turned and pointed at the dirty Jew among them? Sarah was about to ask the Mouse what they were meant to do next when a voice yelled over the hubbub.

"You, new girl! You don't know the songs."

The girl's voice had command: a Berlin accent that spoke of expensive housing and servants. Sarah felt the Mouse dissolve away before the tall girl, the leader, who strode toward her.

She was flanked by her entourage of high-ranking BDM uniforms, and almost imperceptibly, they encircled Sarah. She had received enough harassment on the streets of Berlin and Vienna to know where this was going, but she quelled the need to flee.

Enter Little Monster, stage left. She pauses. She has no need to fear.

"I'm sorry?" she said, tilting her head to one side and saucering her eyes. Her heart fluttered in her chest, so she breathed out slowly and silently through her nose.

"How did you get this uniform if you don't know our songs?" The girl smiled.

"Oh, well, that's a little embarrassing. I was traveling with my parents a lot, and my time with the *Jungmädel* was very patchy. My uncle is hoping my education will improve here." She was about to add, "I'm sure it will!" brightly, but stopped herself.

"Where were you?" said the girl curiously.

"Spain, mostly. My father was in the Condor Legion."

"Oh, good. Bombing the Republicans into mulch, I hope." More smiles. "What is your name?"

"Haller, Ursula Haller." *This is going too well,* she thought. Something more was on its way.

"Well, Haller." Smile. "You will come to see me tomorrow night and sing each song we sang tonight. For every mistake, for every word you get wrong, Rahn here will pull out one strand of your hair." Smile. "That *will* improve your education, won't it?" Wide-eyed innocence, agreement, satisfaction.

Sarah looked at Rahn, a mountain of a girl whose arms threatened to burst from her shirt. The leader was still smiling, with no trace of anger or hate, while the others smirked. She nodded at Sarah and walked away, calling out, "Shall we say sunset? Yes, let's."

Now everyone was looking at Sarah. Her lips felt dry. Was she blushing? Her neck was warm. The totality of her defeat was shattering, as was its speed. *Close your mouth, dumme Schlampe, you look like a fish.*

"Von Scharnhorst. She's the *Schulsprecherin*, the Head Girl." The Mouse had reappeared and moved from foot to foot. "We only sang four songs tonight . . . or was it five? Not sure. The Ice Queen is going easy on you."

"That's still a lot of hair," croaked Sarah.

TEN

———

"I KNEW IT. I knew you would make trouble." Liebrich paced up and down at the end of Sarah's cot, practically growling. "The last thing we need is Von Scharnhorst making this dorm her latest pet project. Damn you, Haller."

Sarah was sitting cross-legged on the bed, hastily written pages spread out in front of her. She scanned the lines over and over. Some songs, like "The Banner," were easy—she was familiar with the tune—but two of them she'd never heard before. With no melody to hang the words on, they just drifted away, autumn leaves blowing off their branches.

"You aren't making this any easier," Sarah murmured.

"I mean, what *rock* have you been under that you don't know these songs?"

"Yes, that was it, I was under a rock. Not in Spain, under a rock. My best friend was a worm," Sarah said icily.

"Don't get smart, Haller."

"Well, we can't all be like you, can we?"

Liebrich thought about that for a moment. Two of the other girls getting ready for bed behind her stifled a laugh. Liebrich clenched her fists by her side. "If you don't make *die Eiskönigin* happy tomorrow, you'll have another hair-pulling session here right afterward."

"I'll look forward to it. Bring a hat." Sarah didn't look up. She didn't care about Liebrich anymore. There were bigger sausages to fry.

"Lights out," called a voice, and the girls hurried to their cots. Sarah shuffled into the bed and tried to wrap herself in the sheet. Liebrich had lied. It was nowhere near warm enough.

Sarah was running headlong down the alley. She had scratched her cheek and could feel blood running down her chin.

"*JUDE!*" screamed a voice behind her.

"*JU-DE,*" other voices chanted, more distantly.

She glanced back to see how far they were behind her and totally failed to see the three boys from the *Hitlerjugend,* the Hitler Youth, until she was right on top of them. The tallest, a boy of about fifteen, seized her wrists and dragged her to a halt.

"Look, it's the little golden Jewess." He flung her against a wall and wiped his palms on his uniform trousers. The rough brick tore at her back through the thin cotton.

"You've got your hands dirty now, Bernt," said one of the others, slouching against the wall. They were almost twice her size, too big to fight but young enough to keep up with her if she got away. She tried not to breathe heavily, but the moment was too much for her and she ended up panting like a dog.

"They shouldn't be out soiling up the place," muttered the other, blocking Sarah's escape on the other side and making a wet snorting sound.

"Yeah, we should make them wash. Don't you think, Martin?"

Martin stooped and spat in Sarah's face. The phlegm was hot as it slapped into her cheek, splashing into her eye before coming to rest across her ear. She waited for it to slough away, staring at the ground, both eyes wide. She knew better than to look them in the eye at this point. Her only defense was their boredom. *I am nothing, I am not worth bothering with. Walk away.*

"What's a Jew doing with that hair, anyway? Eh?" The leader seized one of her curls and pulled slowly. This was new, and she wasn't sure how to play it. Seeing her confusion, he tugged quickly and tore the hair from her scalp. She cried out despite herself, and she could feel the tears coming.

Don't you dare cry, dumme Schlampe. Better they take every hair on your head than be that weak.

My lovely, lovely hair.

You vain little Hure. *You shouldn't even have hair that color.*

The boys laughed and reached for her head.

"Is this what the master race is doing these days? Bullying a little girl?" The voice made them stagger and turn. "That making you feel big and important?"

The butcher was huge. Tall and broad shouldered, he had arms that were rounded and merged seamlessly into his bald head without stopping for a neck. The front of his white coat was soaked red, with gleaming patches where it was still wet. In his hand was a *chalef*, a long cleaver, with a glittering edge.

In the silence a sphere of blood formed at the end of the blade and dripped onto the cobbles.

"Move on, old man. This is Reich business," Bernt stated, but his voice quavered.

"The business of the Reich? Children menacing children?" He swapped the cleaver into his right hand. The blood left a trail across the ground. "You've got until I count to five to get lost. One." The boys looked at one another.

Bernt stepped forward. "We don't take orders from a Jew."

"Two."

"You take orders from us." Behind him, Martin took a step to the right.

"Three."

The third boy looked at Martin. Martin shrugged.

"Bernt . . ." Martin whispered.

"Shut up," Bernt hissed, but Martin shuffled farther away.

"Four." The butcher took a step forward, and the third boy ran. Bernt took an involuntary step backward and Martin was gone.

"This isn't over, Israel . . ."

"Five."

Bernt ran. He stopped ten meters away and cried out, "Not for you. Not for your little *Hure.*"

The butcher turned slowly toward him, but the boy was gone.

He breathed out slowly and shook his head. He crouched down and shook off his coat. He laid the cleaver down gently on its folds and covered it with a sleeve. Sarah was shaking. He reached out to her, but she pulled away.

"Hey, hey, it's all right, it's all right," he shushed, pulling a bloody handkerchief from a pocket. He reached over and moved the wet hair from her face. "Don't worry. I wouldn't have risked the blade on those lowlifes. Too precious." He gently cleaned the spittle from her face with the cloth that smelled of meat. "When I do this for my son, I usually spit on it, you know?" He laughed gently.

"Those boys . . ." Sarah whispered.

"They're gone; it's over," shushed the butcher.

"It's not over," she rasped. "They'll come back and there'll be more of them, and the SA and . . . aren't you scared?" The butcher's eyes were small brown walnuts in a giant suet pudding. He wasn't.

"Rapunzel, there were pogroms before, there'll be little *Arschlöcher* like that throwing stones through my son's windows in the years to come. Nothing changes. Yet we remain. I can't be scared that there's a storm. It rains. It stops. It'll rain again. Are you scared of the rain?" he asked with mock seriousness.

"No."

"The thunder or the lightning?" He smiled.

"No." Sarah giggled, unexpectedly like a hiccup. It was like a ray of sunshine through the cloud.

"See? Now, you'd better get home."

The sky darkened and the air grew cold. Sarah looked up at the butcher. His smile faded and the light in his eyes grew dull. His right cheek swelled, the skin bruising and blistering, finally cracking with dark blood. The growth spread across the white of his eyeball and it turned a dark red black. His nose grew and snapped to the right, his lips thickening even as broken teeth pushed through them. The sky was night, and the world was lit by fire and screaming. As the butcher sank to his knees, Sarah could see that the floor was littered with broken glass that twinkled like a million stars, as the boots crashed past. About his neck was hanging a board hacked into a crude Star of David, and the rope was tight around his throat. He opened his mouth and leaned toward her. Blood and vomit spilled down the yellow paint.

The blood was running down her face, the vomit in her hair.

She wanted to scream but couldn't; her pulse was hammering in her ears like her head was about to explode. She needed to scream, she needed to force all this away by the power of her voice, but nothing came out. She took a long breath, opened her mouth. But still nothing came out.

"Haller." Small hands reached out to her. Sarah knocked them aside and tried to squirm away.

"Haller! Shhhh . . ."

Sarah looked into the Mouse's face, unmistakable in the moonlight.

"You're having a nightmare."

Sarah stopped fighting. She was slick with sweat and the sheets were damp. The big eyes of the Mouse blinked inquiringly.

"No dogs." Sarah snickered mirthlessly, rubbing her eyes.

"You like dogs? I like dogs. They're nice. Maybe a bit smelly," the Mouse burbled. "What were you dreaming about?"

"I was dreaming about *Kristall*—" Her skin went cold.

She struggled to think straight, pulling the leaves of sleep from her mind. What would she know about that night, as one of them? What would she call it? Not the *Novemberpogrome* . . . no, she was right. *Kristallnacht.* It was a beautiful name they gave to something so horrific. She shook her head and muttered something incoherent.

"It was a bit scary, wasn't it? With all that screaming." The Mouse paused. "Wouldn't you have been in Spain?"

Dumme Schlampe.

"I wasn't there . . . I was just dreaming . . . the Jews were all getting away. No one was listening to me. It's silly . . ."

"No, that would have been horrible." The Mouse nodded as she spoke and seemed content. Sarah tried to marshal her thoughts. The lie, the consequences, the meaning . . . what would Ursula Haller's next question be?

"What was it like? *Kristallnacht*, I mean?"

"Oh, it was very exciting, I suppose. You know, the Jews getting punished and the will of the people and everything. But the glass was everywhere, in all the streets, even where there were no Jewish shops, and it took ages to get cleaned up and I had it in my hair and my shoes were ruined and . . ."

"Mouse." A voice spoke out of the darkness. "Shut up."

The Mouse pulled a face. "You should sleep so you're ready for tomorrow evening," she whispered in a conspiratorial tone. "How are you getting on?"

"I don't know the tunes of half of them. It makes it harder to remember."

"Oh, that's easy, I'll sing them for you. You lie down and sleep and I'll sing them, then you'll remember. Go on."

Sarah couldn't think of what to say. She lay back on the sheet and rolled over, feeling the Mouse lie down behind her.

Sarah didn't want to be touched. It had been a very long time since someone had held her, deliberately, voluntarily, without seeking to deceive someone or hurt her. But the Mouse did not touch her. She just lay ten centimeters away, too close for comfort, too far away to truly matter. Her little willowy voice croaked into life, half-whispering, half-singing, like a faulty gramophone.

> *"We stay in solidarity under our shining flag, all together.*
> *There we find ourselves as one people. No one walks alone now,*
> *No one walks alone now.*
> *All together, we stay dutiful to God, the Führer, and the*
>   *blood . . ."*

Sarah began to slip away, into a misty evening harbor road and the distant sound of dogs.

> *"We want to be as one, all together: Germany, you shall stay*
>   *alight.*
> *We will see your honor in your bright light."*

"Mouse," snarled the voice in the darkness. "Shut. Your. Mouth."

ELEVEN

THE FOOD AT Rothenstadt was cold and disgusting. It had once been fried, but that had been a long time ago. Like most things in the Third Reich, the school's veneer of excellence was a sham, but even knowing this, the quality shocked Sarah. The weeks of eating the Captain's rich and expensive leftovers had made Sarah soft. She gathered the hollow longing for apple cake and hid it deep inside her box. She had, she reminded herself, eaten far worse, and at least this came on a dirty plate, rather than from a dustbin.

Classes were easy. Sarah had been worried about being behind the other girls in arithmetic and algebra, subjects that never came easily to her even before she lost her tutor. But there were no proper sums, or science, or much of anything that she would have recognized as a normal school day. The watchwords appeared to be *Kinder, Küche, Kirche*—children, kitchen, church—the religious component being National Socialism. There were classes in housekeeping, childcare, and ironically, cooking. Sarah was up to most domestic tasks. She'd pretty much run her household for the last few years on increasingly meager rations and supplies.

The rest seemed like a parody of an education. There were exercises that sounded like math questions but were all about how much the Jews stole from the Fatherland. Geography talked about the Germans being harassed in Poland. History was all about the *Volk*—the people—and their achievements. The answers were unimportant; the message was everything.

Any failure, any dubious reply, any work that didn't measure up to the school's frustratingly vague standards resulted in being struck across the palm of the hand with a ruler. Some teachers administered this punishment with only cursory attention. Sarah saw girls who didn't even wince as the wood bounced across their skin. Other teachers took their responsibility far more seriously. One such woman was Fräulein Langefeld.

Fräulein Langefeld carried, or rather wielded, a thick meter-long stick, which she tapped impatiently against the dais at the end of the classroom. Her voice followed its staccato rhythm, each word a weapon, her face pulled into an everlasting frown of sharp distaste. Her stick was used too hard, too often, her tongue clenched between her teeth.

The prime target of her simmering discontent appeared to be the Mouse. The harder Langefeld hit, the more the Mouse stuttered; the higher the upswing of the wood, the deeper the fear in her round eyes. Sarah found herself turning away rather than having to see it.

Dumb. Monster.

Sarah preferred to move in the shadows. It paid to go unnoticed, to watch and not be watched. But over the course of that first day, Sarah realized this was impossible. Word had spread. Von Scharnhorst had set Sarah an impossible task, and her pet maniac Rahn was going to tear Sarah's scalp off. Sarah saw the glances, nudges, and whispers. *Die Eiskönigin*, the Ice Queen, had a new target. The girls pitied her but were relieved. While Haller sat at the bottom of the pile, they weren't there. *Dumb. Monsters.*

Sarah pushed open the heavy double doors to the music room as carefully as she could. The small hall was empty and smelled of mildew. Against the far wall, a pile of songbooks formed an irregular tower. Every copy of *We Girls Sing!* was yellowed and tatty, held together with sticky tape, but to her intense relief, the Mouse was right. The book had all the words and music she needed to learn.

The piano was cheap and dusty. Clearly Herr Bauer's fastidiousness didn't extend beyond his office. In fact everything Sarah had seen so far suggested the school was a rotten apple, shiny and whole on the surface but writhing with decay inside.

Sarah tapped a key. The ivory plating on the bottom C was even held down by the same sticky tape, making it tacky to touch. She sat on the stool and played scales across the octaves. The rollers thudded noisily under the lid, and the strings revealed themselves to be minutely out of tune. Sarah grunted and began working through the songbook.

The tunes were triumphant, even jolly. Some were old German folk songs that Sarah could easily recognize, romantic visions of common purpose. Some she had heard from the passing Hitler Youth—these were more boisterous, more martial, full of darkness and blood. The women were giving, yielding, suffering, yet somehow they were also to be strong, united, and proud. Go east, avenge the wrongs, free the German folk . . . our people to arms!

It was enticing, almost hypnotic, following the notes tripping across the stave. Her voice began quietly but grew in volume. It rose and fell, taking in the words, putting them in the right place for later: "Germany awake and end the . . ."

Sarah stopped. That was wrong. She knew this one. She heard it chanted endlessly by boys with stones and spittle. "Germany awake and death to the Jew," that's how it went. Yet here it said "and end the suffering." Whose suffering? The Jews'? Not the goyim's? How had they suffered? Sarah was annoyed. Why was it changed? Were the girls supposed to ignore the pogrom? Did they not know? *Of course they knew.* It wasn't possible not to know.

Wasn't it?

"'End the suffering.' That's the next bit."

Sarah froze as the scent of oranges filled her nostrils. She read the lie on the page, and against her will, her irritation oozed out.

"It's 'death to the Jew.' Why is it different here?" Sarah snapped. "Are you—are we ashamed of it?" *Shut up, shut up, shut up, dumme Schlampe.*

Behind her, Sarah heard Sturmbannführer Foch take two more steps into the room. Sarah felt a creeping chill, like she'd walked out of the house with wet hair in December. She began to play "Volk, ans Gewehr!" again. In the smeary surface of the open lid, she saw the officer come closer.

"It isn't necessary for women to be part of that action. Theirs is to raise the family and leave the removal of the Jews from public life to us. No one is dying," he said soothingly.

"Death . . ." Sarah murmured, looking down.

"The excitement of youth," he assured her.

A hand rested on her shoulder. Sarah tried to keep playing. The piece was simple, too simple for her to concentrate on. She wanted to pull away, push the hand off, and back into a corner.

The *Sturmbannführer* spoke again. "Do you know any Beethoven, Haller?"

Nothing. There were no notes in her head. *Think of some-*

thing. Say anything. She was being pathetic. *Pathétique.* Sarah nearly laughed. Beethoven's Piano Sonata No. 8. The *Pathétique.* The notes filled her head.

She smacked the keys with venom; she reined it in, then struck again. The gentleness that followed belied the tension, the suggestion of anger and pain. Noise, peace, darkness, light.

The start of this piece had always been fun. It had felt like summoning demons and monsters and lightning before controlling them with the pedals and fingertips. Not this time.

Sarah let her hands run across the keyboard with an unfelt joy and settled into a rocking lullaby, a lullaby of approaching storm clouds, lightning, and destruction. This time her hands weren't free to run. They tugged back just as freedom beckoned. Then the notes flowed in a torrent of trills and runs, the emotion lost in the technical effort. Just numbers and fingertips, mathematics and memory.

The hand tightened on her shoulder. She lost her place, rippling into discord and error. She stopped, the last mistake resonating dully under the lid.

"It's been a while, *Sturmbannführer.*"

"That's fine, Gretel. Next time you'll play it right."

"Ursula, sir." *He's funny,* the Mouse had said. Is this what she meant?

The hand vanished from her shoulder. "Of course. Carry on."

She watched his dark shape shrink and vanish in the piano's reflection. Somewhere an unseen clock ticked. *Count the seconds, wait, take control.*

The room was nearly dark. The light in the window was fading and reddening.

Sunset.

Sarah gathered *We Girls Sing!* to her chest and made for the door.

The room was hot, stiflingly so. A fire was playing in the hearth and the pointed flag tacked crudely to the wall above it moved slowly in the rising air. The steamy window trickled in its struggle to keep out the cold or withstand the heat inside. But that wasn't what made the atmosphere so oppressive. The room dripped with a leery, vicious condescension that coated the peeling walls like mold.

Sarah stood to attention in the center of the room. A trickle of sweat slid down her back, escaping her gathered waistband and continuing downward. It gave her the uncomfortable feeling that she had wet herself. *Get your act together, dumme Schlampe. No rehearsal, this: the press and honored guests await, the electric lights are on, the curtains open.*

The Ice Queen occupied the ancient leather armchair like a throne, one leg lazily draped over the other, and her hands extended along the arms, long fingernails scratching the edges absentmindedly. Her hair was escaping the braid that ran around her head, and a fringe now hung over one of her lamp-like blue eyes. There were smirks and whispers from the older girls in the shadows. Sarah knew Elsa would be there, near enough to touch.

The words she needed squirmed and writhed in the front of Sarah's mind, but she pushed them aside. They would come when called, or they would not. There was nothing to be gained from grabbing frantically at them now.

"Head up, eyes front, new girl. Your posture is appalling."

Sarah stared at the BDM pennant. It was cheap and had loose threads. The eagle was roughly sewn and almost comical, like an injured chicken. "Shall I start?" Sarah asked carefully.

"When I say."

From the corner of her eye, Sarah watched Rahn unfold herself from her slouching position next to the Ice Queen's chair, like a house spider Sarah had once seen after a fly had crashed, buzzing, into its web.

Rahn stalked past Sarah, uncomfortably close. She listened to the taller girl pace back and forth slowly over the carpet behind her.

"You see," the Ice Queen began softly, "you're here for two reasons. Firstly, our people are destined for great things, but the future will be hard won. Only those who can function under stress are worthy of raising the next generation." Her voice was reasonable, even friendly, but not to be crossed. "It's survival of the fittest . . . and we *will* be the fittest. All others will be cast aside."

Rahn coiled a muscular arm around Sarah's neck and began to tighten it slowly. Stale sweat and cheap soap filled her nostrils. Rough fingertips ran across her scalp and through her hair.

"The other reason is you have some catching up to do, and I've found that pain is a terrific motivator. Really focuses the mind."

As the arm squeezed, Sarah had to stand on tiptoe to breathe. The hand closed around a fistful of hair and pulled slowly until it was taut on her scalp. The first few hairs tore away; a squall of lightning pinpricks peppered her head.

"Not that much, Rahn," chided Von Scharnhorst gently. "She's got a long way to go yet. Don't want her looking like a Polack laborer, do we?"

The hand released the clump of hair so it fell over her brow, but neatly wrapped a smaller lock around a finger and heaved. Sarah sucked at her teeth as three strands snapped away with tiny popping noises. The finger froze as her scalp howled.

"So you may begin."

Your cue. Sarah licked her dry lips and began to sing.

> *"In the east, the flags are raised,*
> *By the easterly wind they are praised . . .*
> *Then they sound the signal to depart,*
> *And our blood responds in our hearts . . ."*

The words arrived on cue, joined hands with the melody, and fell from her mouth to a military beat.

> *"The answer comes from that place,*
> *And it has a German face.*

For that, many have bled . . .
This is what that earth has said."

Her voice grew more powerful as she got into her stride, letting defiance creep into her tone.

"In the easterly wind, the flags will wave,
To a journey made for the brave.
Protect yourself and be strong!
If you journey east, you may suffer long."

What are you singing, dumb monster? Going east? When Germany goes east, what will it do? What about the people who are already there?
Concentrate—

Sarah stuttered at the start of the fourth verse, and with a grunt of satisfaction Rahn tore the lock of hair out. The pain came like an explosion of light. Sarah suppressed the shriek, but a whimper escaped as Rahn tightened her grip and wrapped a new curl round her index finger.

Now *look, princess. See what you did.*

My lovely hair!

You vain little Hure. *Concentrate.*

Mutti . . .

No. Sing your songs.

Sarah closed her eyes. She finished "In the East, the Flags Are Raised" and went straight into "All Stand in Solidarity"—flag, Führer, blood . . . more passion, more volume as the words streamed out, faultlessly, perfectly, like the threads of a story she'd told all her life.

As she moved on to "One Flame," Rahn growled and began to pull her forearm into Sarah's windpipe. Sarah's voice became rough, then hoarse. It was almost painless, like a sore throat, but as she continued it became harder to breathe. Each breath gave her less and less air.

"Close the ranks"—heart beating faster and louder in her chest—"let the embers flame"—gasping—"none shall taint or chide it"—her song was now a wordless whisper, the pain—"what lies"—too much—"in our hearts . . ."

Sarah inhaled loudly through her mouth, and Rahn ripped a handful of hair from the roots.

"Rahn . . ." A warning. Who?

Sarah gasped silently, opening her mouth to go on, but nothing came out. The words became dim. The flag was growing dark.

"Rahn . . ."

Rahn dragged a long blonde tress clear of her head, ripping it noisily free.

"Rahn! Enough," the Ice Queen commanded.

Rahn swore and relaxed her arm around Sarah's throat. Sarah crumpled and was given a shove forward. She managed to stop herself in front of Von Scharnhorst's armchair.

The Ice Queen watched Sarah's shoulders rising and falling. She nodded once, her eyes and lips narrowing.

"Nothing wrong with your brain, then," Von Scharnhorst

said, lighting a cigarette. She exhaled noisily, and the cloud of cigarette smoke billowed round Sarah's face. "How old are you, Haller?"

"Thirteen," she rasped. *Liar, liar, liar.*

"Bit small for thirteen, aren't you?" She sounded disappointed.

"I suppose."

"Like I said, you've got some catching up to do. However, you interest me. I've not had a clean slate, a tabula rasa, to work with before. I wonder what we can make of you. Next time, we'll see what your body is capable of, eh?"

Rahn pushed Sarah toward the door as giggles broke out from the shadows behind her. She looked back and for the first time spotted Elsa, her expression one of amused fascination in the firelight. Her eyes followed Sarah's exit. Whom was she standing with? Who were her special friends? What did—

Rahn slapped her in the face with a crack. Stumbling into the wall, Sarah found herself cowering and holding her hands over her face. *Make yourself small and minimize the damage.*

"Rahn! No more," the Ice Queen ordered.

Rahn stood over Sarah and wiped some spittle from the corner of her mouth. "You'll fail, you dumb little girl. Then I'll break you."

The dormitory was trying to look busy, but everyone was evidently waiting for Sarah to return. As she pushed the door open,

Liebrich was blocking the way from the door to her bed.

"You still have some hair. Excellent." The sarcasm was thick in her voice. Sarah just kept walking until they were face-to-face. When she looked up, Liebrich started abruptly, eyes wide, mouth open. Sarah took another step, pushing home this advantage.

"You stay away from me, Liebrich," Sarah croaked, barely audible. "You understand?"

Liebrich nodded, composure gone.

Sarah pushed past her and sat on her bed, facing the wall. She was tired, too tired to undress.

"Haller?" inquired a little voice.

"Hello, Mouse," whispered Sarah.

"Oh, you've lost hardly any hair, that's good, when we've brushed it and cleaned, you know, the blood away a bit, we'll braid it and—" The Mouse stopped as Sarah raised her head.

"What?"

"Your eyes, Haller, oh, your eyes . . ." gasped the Mouse.

"Do you have a mirror, Mouse?"

The small figure darted away and returned a few seconds later clutching an old tortoiseshell compact. Sarah opened the lid.

The whites of her eyes were no longer white. They were a deep, dark red.

How did that BDM song go? *The blood hears the call.*

The whole room was staring at her, wonder, sympathy, and fear on their faces.

TWELVE

THEY PUT HER in the infirmary, supposedly to check that she was all right, but mostly because she was unnerving the other students. The teachers and staff had clearly decided to ignore whatever it was that had happened. Maybe it was easier than trying to deal with it, to admit that something unpleasant had occurred. Maybe they knew and didn't care. It didn't seem to matter.

Even to Sarah, who hadn't gone to school, priorities seemed askew here. The discipline was violent, but the education seemed unimportant. The older girls seemed to be left to run things as they pleased. The Captain had once said that the whole

Third Reich was like this, with no real structure or organization, just fear and jealousy and control and incompetence. If that was true, maybe there was a way to defeat it. Yet the school functioned, endured.

But this bed was warm and the sheets were clean, so Sarah slept. For the most part, the dogs stayed away.

A compact, middle-aged nurse brought her meals, or rather dropped a tray in front of her with a tutting noise. She took Sarah's temperature with a thermometer thrust so vehemently that it made her tongue hurt, but the nurse said nothing. In fact the woman didn't even look her in the face, except once. The glance beneath the severe fringe was filled with such abhorrence that Sarah couldn't meet her gaze. There was no clue what she had done to warrant so pitiless a response.

She had two other visitors.

The Mouse came and talked. The food. The lessons. The running. Dogs and kittens. *Don't visit me. Don't talk to me,* howled Sarah silently. *Do not identify yourself with me. Leave. Me. Alone.*

But instead Sarah sat and nodded, whispered and shrugged . . . She could see light in the Mouse's eyes like a chink of sunshine through a shuttered window. She had trouble remembering a time when she had been the cause of brightness in another human being. Had she *ever* been? While it was strange and claustrophobic after all this time alone, it was warming, too, like cocoa on an icy day. Sarah wanted more of it.

As the Mouse wound a braid across Sarah's head, she wittered away. "You know what everyone is saying? That Haller was sent to the Ice Queen but you passed every test but Rahn hurt you anyway, so you made your eyes bleed on purpose, and she got scared and stopped! Imagine! What a tale. But I think they want to believe it."

"Sent to the Ice Queen?" Sarah felt like she was part of a longer story that she hadn't been told yet. "You talk like this has happened before."

"Oh yes, I mean, there's usually a girl picked to . . . be tested."

"What happens to them?" Sarah felt a growing unease. "What happened to the last one?"

The light went out in the Mouse's face, and she looked down. "Some of them join Von Scharnhorst as a Youth Leader. They get all the best food and they pretty much stop going to classes. There was Kohlmeyer and—"

"What happened to the *last* test subject?" Sarah interrupted, touching her arm. It was cold.

"She . . . They're not . . . considered . . . strong enough. Sometimes there's an accident . . . Sometimes . . ." the Mouse trailed off.

Nothing was going to plan.

What plan? Keeping your head down? Staying quiet? Hiding in the shadows?

No, this is how you finish, by going through the program. You know where the edge is. You know what it is, therefore it cannot hurt you.

Finish the move. Follow through. Don't stop.

The second visitor left a sheet of Beethoven piano music on her lap as she slept.

Sarah did not sleep in the sanatorium again.

The window was ajar, just as it had been earlier. From inside came the smell of blood. Sarah crouched underneath it and glanced down the street. Clear.

She reached up and grasped the windowsill. It was wet with blood. Fighting the feeling of disgust, she gripped the wood firmly and pulled herself up. When her eyes were level with the opening, she stopped, holding herself a few centimeters from the floor. There was no one in the room, but the room was not empty. Perfect.

She elbowed the window open. The hinges squeaked and Sarah froze. Nothing. A shout, a cart, a motorcar, just distant noises of the city. She heaved herself up, swinging her legs between her arms, as she had a thousand times on the bars, careful not to touch the frame. She hopped down onto the floor, which was slick, and slid into the table. She only just kept her balance and had to stop again to listen. No sound, no movement in the doorway.

She looked down at the table and felt her stomach turn. *Oh, grow up, dumme Schlampe.* Her hands, tugging the sack from her coat, were already dripping red. She ignored the saliva gathering in her throat and began shoveling the greasy white, brown, and red entrails into the makeshift bag.

"I can't let you take that, Rapunzel."

Sarah stopped for a second and then continued to quickly drag the meat toward her. "We're hungry. I'm hungry."

"You can't take it."

Sarah stopped and stared at the butcher. She pushed a strand of hair out of her face and left a bloody trail across her cheek. Her chin started to quiver. *Damn it.*

"We. Have. No. Food. No money. We are starving." Blood splashed across her grubby socks and worn-out shoes.

"Well, you could take it, but I won't let you eat it." The butcher folded his arms, the blade resting on the vast chest and shoulder.

"What?" stammered Sarah, confusion overcoming her hunger.

"It's *tref.* Sciatic nerve, veins, sinews, unporged hindquarters—I can't let you eat it."

"It's not kosher?" Sarah laughed in disbelief. "Really? You think I give a damn that it's unclean?"

The butcher looked at the floor and sighed. "No. But I do."

"So you just throw it away?" Sarah slammed the sack onto the table.

"Well, we used to sell it to the goyim. We're not allowed to do that anymore. I haven't the skill to porge the hindquarters properly, so . . ."

"So you throw it away," Sarah said ruefully. "While people are going hungry."

"It's not the end of the world, Rapunzel. Not yet, anyway." He gently lifted the dripping sack from the table. "Come. Come and eat with me."

He sat Sarah on a stool among the hanging carcasses in the next room and reappeared a minute later with sausages.

Sarah attacked the kishke like a wolf.

The sausage was thick, fatty, and still juicy even cold. Her sense of defeat evaporated as her teeth closed around it, tearing at the sweet, rubbery casing and letting the contents pop into her mouth. For a moment she forgot about her life, instead delighting in the dribble of grease that trickled onto her chin.

The butcher watched Sarah attacking the food. "Does your mother not feed you?"

Sarah swiveled her eyes toward him. Mutti. Waiting. Crying. Sleeping.

"Your mother feeds you too much," she snarled, and went on eating. Her ingratitude stung her like a nettle. Between mouthfuls, she tried again. "She's not well. But they won't let her work anyway. There's no money."

"Your father?"

"Pure Aryan stock, so as long as no one knows he's a

race-defiler, he'll be *fine*. Wherever he is. What about you?"

"Everyone needs the shohet because someone has to cut the meat properly. While there's food for anyone, there's food for me." He paused, then shrugged. "I'm lucky."

"How is anyone paying you?"

"What they can." He reached out and offered the remains of his kishke to her. Sarah tried not to snatch it out of his hands, but she was holding it before the thought had fully formed. She hummed her thanks as she attacked it.

Sarah thought of nothing but food these days. At first her stomach seemed to close up, as if she didn't need to eat. Then, slowly, the life had seemed to drain out of her. Her limbs felt heavy and useless. She felt tired, an all-embracing fatigue that never went away. She got cross easily and found it hard to think, every idea lost to the buzzing of emptiness in the back of her head. It was easy to imagine her fragile body being drawn into the void inside, like bathwater through the drain. Every morsel she found only seemed to make her hungrier, as though these repayments were only making the bank aware of how much she owed them. She dreamed of cakes, stews, soup, and fruit, but the reality was so disappointing it was too much to bear. This sausage—so fatty, so beautiful—was a reminder of its own absence. Joy and misery cooked in the same pot, tasting of both and neither.

"Hey, slow down, Rapunzel. You'll make yourself sick." The butcher smiled as he stood up and walked out of the room.

Sarah reveled in the sensation of the oily meat sliding into her stomach. She rested her back against the wall. There weren't very many carcasses hanging up given the size of room. How many men were supposed to be working here? With a pang, Sarah realized that the butcher's apparent wealth was wafer-thin. The boycotts, the Jewish laws putting them out of work . . . How much meat could he sell to people who increasingly owned nothing?

Through the other doorway, Sarah spotted her sack by the window where she'd come in. It was clearly still full, the bottom now soaked in gore.

She looked at the window. She looked at the sack. She looked at the other door.

She hit the cobbles hard, the weight of the sack nearly pulling her over, but she accelerated and stayed on her feet. She tore down the road like the devil himself was on her trail.

She tired easily, and once she was around the corner, she slowed to a lope. The sack was certainly heavy—how much had she loaded into it? She began to walk and slid the sack off her shoulder, feeling the gritty dampness through her dress. She stopped and opened it.

Inside was a perfect side of beef, already kashered in salt the traditional way.

She wasn't sad, but the tears came anyway and washed the blood from her face.

THIRTEEN

SARAH HAD SPENT years skulking. Hiding. Creeping. When that failed, she had run—faster, longer, and, if necessary, smarter than her pursuers. Now suddenly she was famous. Watched. Whispered about behind small hands. Glances of jealousy, admiration, and pity shot from one side of the school to the other. To Liebrich, she was competition. To the Mouse, she was a god. To the Ice Queen, she was a new test subject. For everyone else? Sarah couldn't make sense of it. After the isolation of the last few years, the attention was overpowering. The school seemed very small and overwhelmingly full of girls. The corridors and classrooms, the halls and dorm rooms—wherever she went to be alone, someone was watching, with the Mouse trailing after her at a reverent distance. It was smothering, like a wet blanket.

She avoided the music rooms.

Only outdoors did she feel free. In this school, exercise was considered almost as important as propaganda. Every afternoon, they were chased into the grounds, whatever the weather, to march and dance, perform and stretch, in symmetrical rows. It was a gymnastic version of the flag ceremonies, chants, and songs. As a tiny cog in this National Socialist machine, Sarah regained a certain anonymity. Dumb Monster with a hoop. Dumb Monster touching her toes. Dumb Monster smiles, moving gracefully. Hardy, pious, cheerful, free. When the possibility of standing out presented itself, Sarah intended to fail. She tried to spring clumsily, tumble awkwardly, and jump inelegantly.

But the more she exercised, the more she stretched out her withered muscles, the more food she ate, the stronger she became. She found herself finishing, succeeding, winning. Excelling became a habit, and leaving the daughters of the master race in her wake was a deep-lying thrill that gave her power. She watched the weaker girls and found her first instinct was to sneer, snicker, and scoff. It was easier not to fight it.

The cross-country run was a chance to both shake off her audience and belittle them. It was just too tempting. Sarah easily outran the others as the trail wound into the forest. The soil was hard underfoot, the path beaten clean of rocks and branches. The trees whipped by, and each breath felt sharp in her chest, each exhalation billowing past her in the wind. She was running too fast, but Sarah felt calm. For a few moments she was in total control of everything. She counted the seconds, one, two . . . holding even time in the palm of her hand. Three, four . . . five.

She slowed, feeling the sting of the ground through her feet, the scratching in her chest and throat, the stitch developing in her side. She bathed in the sudden discomfort that she had held at arm's length until she was ready. Already her muscles seemed to be recovering, readying themselves for the next challenge.

She rounded the bend.

Von Scharnhorst, Elsa, and three Final Year girls were blocking the path.

Sarah slid to a stop and saw Rahn coming out of the woods behind her. There was no strength left in her thighs to escape, even if she could get past them. *Dumme Schlampe.*

"Good afternoon, Haller. I'm glad to see you back on your feet." The Ice Queen smiled and beckoned to Sarah. "Come, walk with me."

Sarah glanced back at Rahn, ten meters away, playing with some fallen leaves with her foot. The Ice Queen beckoned again, an expression of wide-eyed encouragement lighting up her face, like she was calling a dog. Just as a hound will follow its owner, however bad-tempered they may be, Sarah followed.

"Come on, that's right . . ."

Sarah glanced at Elsa. These moments were still her best chance to impress the professor's daughter, but the sensation that she was a moth dancing around a lit candle was unshakable.

Elsa watched her the way a small child watches an ice cream

scoop begin its work. Sarah had to look away. The other girls feigned indifference as Sarah passed.

For a few moments the Ice Queen locked step with Sarah. "Your injuries were regrettable. I really should learn to use Rahn with more care." *Eyes front.* "You see, she doesn't think things through, and I suspect she enjoys her work a little too much."

"And you don't?" *Shut up.*

"No," she replied, with a hint of admonishment. "This is all for the Fatherland. The end result is everything. The means are of no interest to me whatsoever. Even the Führer saw fit to make an alliance with the Bolsheviks in the east because it served his purposes."

Sarah swung around. "What's the point of this? Aren't we supposed to be just mothers and *Hausfrauen*?"

"There's no just about it. Raising the next generation— nothing is more sacred or important. We must be fearless and bright as she-wolves." Her eyes were fierce. "You think that fat mass of blubber Bauer and his staff of twisted rodents are the future of this country?" The Ice Queen pointed up the path. The sun broke through the low clouds behind her. "You think there's anything to learn from them? With their rulers and their sticks and their wrath focused on the weak and pointless, like your friend the Mouse? That traitor Foch is the closest thing to a real National Socialist, and he's a jibbering wreck who should have had a bullet in his brain in nineteen thirty-four." She stopped and softened. "No, what *we* do is the real lesson here. We find the strongest and purest. We don't waste time on the chaff."

The sun disappeared behind a cloud, and the warmth vanished from the air.

But, thought Sarah.

"But we have a problem," the older girl went on. "For some reason, the school has formed the idea that you've defied me somehow. It's all my fault, of course, allowing Rahn to get carried away, but this is not in anyone's interests. An experiment that failed. You understand that, don't you?"

"No." This was the logic of the madhouse. "I'm not sure I do."

"It's unfortunate, as you had potential, but I need to reestablish the hierarchy. The physical challenge, the River Race, would have suited you, but I'm afraid you will have to fail. You'll have an accident, all very unfortunate, but you'll live. You'll probably be back next year while I'm walking through the ruins of Paris."

Sarah stopped. *Just let it go, let it happen, ask for forgiveness, beg for mercy.* Instead the mounting bitterness and wailing hysteria deep within escaped the box, even as she pressed the lid down. She felt the heat in her teeth and ears and tried to keep her voice low.

"I won't fail. Then what will you do?"

The Ice Queen smiled and raised her eyebrows. "Oh, *interesting* . . . but, no."

The laughter of their approaching classmates began to fill the air. The Ice Queen cocked her head toward the school.

"Time to start running, Haller."

They got chocolate cake for dessert. As a treat. It was foul.

Elsa, the Ice Queen, and the others weren't eating it. As the Mouse had suggested, they ate and exercised alone. However, the elite of Rothenstadt were sitting on a table at the head of the hall, too remote, too beautiful, and laughing too loud. Elsa was younger than the others but made up for that with volume, though her words were lost in the din of the hall.

Sarah looked at the rest of the school, at the merely average cream of German youth trying to enjoy dessert, and wondered if she should be feeling grateful that the Ice Queen had chosen her as a test subject. Certainly there didn't seem to be any way of approaching Elsa Schäfer otherwise. The act of walking up and starting a conversation would have been beyond her, although Sarah was no longer sure if the mission was befriending Elsa or just surviving. Being Jewish in a Nazi school seemed almost beside the point.

The Mouse was talking. The Mouse was always talking. It should have been overwhelming and irritating, but Sarah found it oddly calming. Sitting with her was better than being alone. The Mouse didn't ask many questions, but Sarah sensed that wasn't because she wasn't interested. She was giving Sarah space, in the only way she could.

Sarah interrupted her. "What is the River Race, Mouse?"

"It's the last race of the term. There's a trophy and every-thing, three kilometers to the bridge and three kilometers back on the other side. It's for the big girls, really, but we're all supposed to cheer them on. The Final Year girls organize it." The Mouse prattled on. "They choose one girl from each class. Liebrich wants it to be her, as she's the *Schlafsaalführerin,* but everyone thinks she's too slow." She giggled. "Not that it matters. The older girls will win . . ." The Mouse stopped, as an unpleasant idea occurred. "Oh . . . is the River Race your challenge?"

"It appears so." Sarah pushed a sour cherry around her plate.

"I'm sorry, Haller."

"I might win," she said, with the confidence of a fox cornered by hounds.

"No. No, I don't think so." The Mouse fell silent and concentrated on trying not to make her fork shriek against the plate.

"What's *wrong* with Sturmbannführer Foch?" Sarah changed the subject.

"I don't know. He cries a lot. I think he wishes they'd shot him along with the others," the Mouse mused. "I hear he did something to survive, something horrible."

What could be worse than being an officer in the SA? Sarah nearly said out loud. She didn't trust herself to talk further.

The Ice Queen's retinue left the room with great ceremony. Some First Year girls even stood up as they went past.

"What do you know about her?" Sarah asked, waving a fork at Elsa as she left the room.

The Mouse made a face like they might be overheard and replied hurriedly, "I don't know anything about her . . . Why?"

"No reason. She's younger than the others . . ."

"It's not about age." The Mouse scraped her fork and drew reproving catcalls from the next table. "Really not very interesting," she added. "How is your cake?"

Sarah made a face and sighed. "Why *is* the food so bad?" she mumbled to the gritty brown mess on her plate.

The Mouse brightened and leaned in toward her. "Apparently, Herr Bauer is taking all the money—well, most of it, the money that comes from the Reich Ministry of Education. You see, the *Napola* schools were created in such a hurry they didn't check anyone out properly, so Bauer managed to talk his way in, but he's on thin ice now, so it's only a matter of time before—" The Mouse stopped, panic in her eyes. She dropped her head.

"Mouse, how do you know all this?" The small girl was absurdly well-informed. A girl who liked secrets almost for secrets' sake. A girl after Sarah's own heart.

"Well, my father is . . . important . . . to do with schools and things like that . . ." the Mouse stammered.

Sarah looked around, but the conversation didn't seem to have been overheard. She realized why the Mouse, so small, so limited, was at a school for the strongest, fastest, most intelligent. She closed in. "Mouse, are you here as a . . . spy?"

The Mouse was shaking gently behind her hair. "Just to notice things . . ."

Sarah laughed—a big, hearty chuckle—and couldn't stop for a minute. "Hey, come on, it's all right. I won't tell anyone," she whispered.

"Promise?" demanded the Mouse in a tiny voice.

"Promise. Would you like some of my cake?" Sarah proffered a dirty spoon.

"Really?" The Mouse brightened.

"Really."

The two spies sat side by side and tried to enjoy the bitter, gritty brown lump and spoiled fruit, surrounded by oblivious monsters.

Jungmädel Ursula Haller is to report to Sturmbannführer Foch in Herr Bauer's office at 1400 hours.

Sarah waited outside the door, feeling the need to catch her breath, as if she was about to dive into the Müggelsee on a cool day. But the air seemed false, inadequate. Sarah found Foch's interest in her discomfiting. He was a storm trooper, wearing the uniform of beatings, broken windows, and fire, but that wasn't quite it. He was also emaciated, coarse, and *ugly*. In any normal circumstance Sarah would have laughed at this. The evil that she had seen, and the wanton hatred she'd experienced, were often immaculately dressed and superficially attractive. But he *felt* wrong, broken, unpredictable, and there was something else she couldn't quite fathom that made his proximity unbearable.

She raised a hand to knock, but before she could make a noise, a voice ordered:

"Enter."

She took one last gulp and turned the cold doorknob.

Sturmbannführer Foch was standing at the window, hands clasped behind his back. Sarah closed the door and stepped to the piano, holding her music to her chest like a shield.

It's a recital, just a recital.

When did I play a recital?

You've seen recitals. The audience applauds and wonders how the soloist can dare stand up in front of everyone. They feel embarrassed in the opening silence. They are frightened. Feed on their fear.

The lid was open, the music stand was clear. Everything was waiting. Her audience stood in silhouette at the window.

Don't look at the audience, dumme Schlampe.

She sat on the stool, dwarfed by the instrument. She needed to adjust the height of the seat but wanted to get started. *Sit, play, leave.* Placing the sheet on the stand, she studied the staves, the notes, the accents. She let her brain slide through the melodies she knew so well, looking for the minute changes where her memory had blurred or erased the detail. She allowed herself to become irritated. She loathed notation. It was a corset that made music wheeze. Like someone explaining a joke.

She hammered the keys with mock melodrama, but there was no light and dark, just noise. She kept time with a vehement precision but couldn't reach the pedals properly, so all the subtlety was lost. *Here's your damn music, Sturmbannführer.*

"Lovely, Gretel. Slow down."

His words, so close behind her, were like being doused with

cold water. He had moved with a catlike silence once again, and now his breath was audible between the notes. She slowed at his command, the scent of oranges filling the air.

Who is Gretel?

Ignore the audience.

"Ursula, sir."

Had Gretel sat on this seat, played this piano?

She stared at the approaching forest of notes and ran for their cover. *Lauf.*

Had he stood this close to her?

"Slowly, Gretel," he whispered.

She broke into the fast section and attacked the keyboard.

Make it stop.

Shush, *dumme Schlampe. Shut up and play.*

Something touched the top of her head, and a chill ran down her scalp like a falling insect. Her shoulders tensed and rose to touch her ears. Her fingers kept moving, but her elbows retreated to her sides, shaking her rhythm.

His fingers ran softly down the outside of her hair, taking in the curves and bumps of her braids, brushing her loose strands flat, and sliding his hands toward her neck. The sensation was like hearing a steel knife across a plate.

Stop touching me.

She tried to move forward, to shrink from his touch, but couldn't seem to escape, as if she was being held. She began to lean over the keys.

Stop playing and run. Lauf!

Her neck grew warm as his hands reached its nape and began again at the top. She was still playing, now merely repeating the same phrases over and over. Her chin started to quiver, so she bit her tongue until it stopped, but to her mortification a slow gurgling whimper began to escape from her throat. She shut her eyes before any tears could appear.

Stop. Touching. Me.

She didn't trust herself to speak without crying out.

Please. Stop.

Her hands were now shaking so much she couldn't press the keys.

"Don't stop, Gretel," Klaus Foch whispered, his voice shaking.

Who is Gretel? What happened to Gretel? What is happening to me?

Sarah stopped her whimper. As she did, she heard the man behind her crying. She pulled her head away from his hands and retreated to the edge of the stool.

"Gretel . . ." he sobbed.

She slammed the lid of the piano closed with a smack. The strings protested with a cacophonous howl as she fled for the door. Papers were carried off the desk as she passed. The rug tried to slide away from her feet, but then she was at the door and pulling at the handle with sweaty fingers.

She was out of the room and down the corridor before the sound from the piano had faded.

FOURTEEN

———

THE ROOM WAS silent except for the noise of pen nibs on rough paper and Fräulein Langefeld's sensible shoes clopping slowly across the floorboards as she prowled among the desks.

Sarah looked at her still-blank sheet. A letter home. She tried to imagine what her ink-stained hands might possibly write.

> Dear Captain Floyd,
>   I thank you for enrolling me in an asylum for the insane. In my short time here, I have become the plaything of one of the Furies of antiquity and been strangled by her attack dog

until my eyes bled. The food is poisonous, the
teachers are psychopathic, and as for the music
staff,

Nausea threatened to overcome her.

*Take me away. Get me out of here. Take me to a clean kitchen
with warm bread and cold sausage, fresh sheets and a safe room with no
windows . . .*

Sarah bit her tongue and drove the weakness away.

*The next time I go running, I could disappear into the woods and
never be found.*

If I had somewhere to go, yes.

Anywhere but here.

*I have a job to do. There's no home, no safety, nothing to run away
to, until it's done.*

*The job? And what's the plan? Defeat the Ice Queen? Save the
Mouse? Lead the chosen people out of Egypt?*

*Go to class. Blend in. Make friends. Wait for an opportunity. Sur-
vive.*

Make enemies, more like.

Maybe. Just commit to the move.

And if I fall?

Then you break and you burn.

The Mouse was scribbling furiously. What was she saying?
Was she detailing the wickedness? How could her father leave
her in this place? If she was spying for him, why had nothing
changed?

"Haller! What are you doing?" Langefeld's voice cut the air in two.

"Nothing," Sarah called, and concentrated on her blank sheet. Langefeld slapped her stick across the desk. It missed Sarah's hands, but the impact sloshed the contents of her inkwell onto the desk.

"That much I can see. What is so interesting about Mauser?"

"I'm sorry, I'll concentrate." *Make it better, make it go away.*

"No, there must be something. Why would you be so transfixed?" Langefeld strode toward the Mouse, who shrank away from her. Sarah quailed as the teacher tore the letter from her desk. "Mauser! This is illegible. What is it supposed to say?"

"It's—just a few—" the Mouse stammered.

"You're hopeless. A waste of skin. What are you?" Langefeld leaned into the Mouse's face.

"A waste . . ." the Mouse said softly.

"Speak up, I can't hear you," Langefeld snarled, little flecks of spittle flying from her mouth.

"I'm a waste of skin!" shrieked the Mouse.

"Stand up."

"Oh no, please, don't, I'm sorry." Tears were already running down the Mouse's face.

"Hands out."

Sarah watched the woman tensing up and raising her stick, her eyes alight with cruelty.

"No . . ."

Sarah began to write. She added each word deliberately and slowly, as the slaps and the stifled cries began.

> Dear Uncle,
>
> Thank you for sending me to this excellent institution. The very cream of our shared and golden future is being prepared for what awaits us all.

"Sarahchen . . . Sarahchen. Where are you?"

Sarah crawled out from under the table, noting that the stove had gone out again. "Mutti, I'm coming."

"Sarah . . ." Her mother's voice was weak and rasping but had lost none of its needle-like effect on Sarah. To resist it would have cut her in two. She stretched as she ran to the bedroom.

Her mother had walked into this room when they moved to the top-floor flat and had never left it. It wasn't the SA driving them from their apartment in Giselhergasse that had pushed her over the edge. It had been selling the piano to a predatory neighbor for a knock-down rate. The instrument that had propped her in a seated position for three years, physically and emotionally, had gone. She and Sarah had shared the bed at first, but the scent of alcohol had grown overpowering. When her mother wet the bed the first time, Sarah slept in the kitchen, beginning an ongoing campaign against Vienna's most insistent cockroaches.

They had been lucky to escape to Austria, but then Germany had followed them, swallowing its neighboring country in the Anschluss, the Joining. And it had all started again, only worse.

Sarah pushed the bedroom door open, hit once again by the smell of whisky and urine. Her mother was bolt upright in bed, hair escaping its clips, eyes red and glistening in the muted, curtained light.

"Mutti, what's wrong?"

"Sarahchen, my medicine has gone."

There was an empty bottle and a cracked tumbler on the nightstand.

"Mutti, that was full yesterday. Surely it hasn't all been drunk?" Sarah wailed. That bottle had cost a teapot and, most painfully of all, half a loaf of bread. "Mother, the last of the piano money has gone. We don't have anything left."

"You're a clever girl, you'll think of something. All this time you've run the house while Mutti's been sick."

"What about the car, Mutti? It's worth—"

"Don't be ridiculous. We'll need the car when we leave." Her mother's voice was dismissive.

Sarah pushed her nails into her palms. She tried again—had to try again—but knew inside where the trail would lead.

"Mutti, when are we leaving? They check papers now crossing the bridges, going to the shops. Soon they won't let us leave at all."

"We wait for your father; he'll come, he'll help us . . ." Her mother's attention was seeping away.

"When? We haven't seen him for *eight years*." Sarah's frustration at the hopeless fairy tale spilled over. "Mutti, he's never coming back . . ."

"*Schnauze, dumme Schlampe!*" her mother screamed at her. "You know nothing, nothing, nothing—"

Sarah raised her head to see the resentment and loathing in her mother's bloodshot green eyes. She waited for it to melt, for the words and spite to ebb away. For all the hate to gurgle away like dishwater. Waiting . . .

In her nightmares, she waited forever.

Her mother's chin began to tremble and the top lip joined it. Her eyebrows rose and the face emptied of viciousness, to be replaced by sadness and regret. Arms reached out for absolution—Sarah could provide that. Would always provide that.

She just had to wait.

Sarah knew her mother loved her.

Sarah knew her mother needed her.

"We just have to wait a little longer, that's all. We can move to a bigger place and get a new piano and . . ."

Sarah stopped listening and just nodded.

Once her mother had smelled of musky perfumes and expensive soaps. It was the smell of safety and love. Now her pores released nothing but sweat and liquor, so Sarah remembered instead. She closed her eyes and imagined the house in Elsengrund and the apartment in Berlin, the thick warmth and full belly, velvet and shiny surfaces, tuned pianos and clean windows.

Her mother had said something.

"Sorry, Mutti, what was that?"

"You'll find me some medicine?" she asked again in Czech.

"Yes, *Máma*. Of course I will," Sarah replied with a perfect Prague accent.

"That's my girl. My clever, clever girl."

It was bitterly cold to be out in athletic gear. Each time the wind blew, it stole tears from Sarah's eyes and brought an audible cry from the waiting girls, quickly lost in the roar of the river. Sarah's hands were so chilled that she found she couldn't touch her thumb to her little finger, a sure sign back in Vienna that she needed to steal more firewood.

The clearing in the woods was a trap that Sarah felt closing around her. Each class stood, awaiting selection by the Final Year girls. The staff stood behind, prison guards unaware of their role.

Dumme Schlampe. You still don't have a plan, do you?

Shut up and let me think.

"Where are we, Mouse?" This day had arrived too quickly.

The information she had gathered was too vague. She needed to know what the enemy knew and more. She needed secrets. She needed more time.

Too late now.

Shush.

"About two kilometers from the school, I think. The bridge we came over just now is the only way over the river for three kilometers in either direction. It's deep and wide and fast-moving this time of year, so no shortcuts, no cheating."

"You *do* notice things, don't you?" Sarah smiled at the Mouse, who lit up.

"Shut your mouths, you two," ordered Liebrich.

"Shut up yourself," answered Sarah with vehemence.

Sarah watched the Ice Queen and her retinue drift from class to class, selecting runners. Fast? Slow? It didn't matter. The exercise in power was everything. The staff didn't need to terrorize the students, not if they could leave it up to the *Schulsprecherin* and her friends.

"*O, it is excellent to have a giant's strength,*" thought Sarah in English, "*but it is tyrannous to use it like a giant.*"

Clear your head, dumme Schlampe. You need to think.

Elsa Schäfer was at the back of the group. She did look small compared to the others, but that was illusory. The Ice Queen's courtiers were giants and the rest of the girls were peons, miniature people. To talk to her, to befriend her was ridiculous. Sarah might as well have been on the moon.

The Ice Queen looked like she might pass the Third Year

class altogether, causing a quiver of hope in Sarah's stomach. That was, of course, her intention.

"*Schlafsaalführerin*," the Ice Queen shouted.

Liebrich stepped forward. "*Meine Schulsprecherin*," the girl barked enthusiastically in response.

"Who is the quickest in this class?"

"I am, *meine Schulsprecherin*."

"A fat little thing like you? No, surely the Reich doesn't have to rely on your swift heels?" The Ice Queen smiled at her retinue. They dutifully laughed, and some thoughtless Third Year girls giggled, too. "No. Not you, but then who?" She made an act of looking around and over the heads of the smaller girls.

Sarah stared ahead and didn't move. *Oh, get on with it.*

"Haller! Come here."

Sarah waited an insubordinate length of time before stepping forward.

The Ice Queen came very close and spoke quietly. "So, here we are. Now is the moment. Remember, this is for the betterment of the Reich. I'll ensure that you can continue to contribute. You do have a keen brain." She paused. Despite the jaunty tone, Von Scharnhorst's blue eyes were infinitely cold and oppressively perfect. "But you don't need your legs for that," she whispered before wheeling away and addressing the whole school.

"Girls! Not only has Haller volunteered for the River Run, but she thinks she might win it!" The Ice Queen waved her hands in the air theatrically. There was a smattering of laughter. "The Führer loves confidence, but when does that become hubris— pride and a fall? This race is dangerous, Haller. Anything could happen. Anything at all . . ."

Sarah listened to the river.

"If I cross the finish line first, then this is over," Sarah called softly, so only the Ice Queen could hear. "No more tests, no more trials."

The older girl turned on her heel. Her mask dropped.

"You will not win," she growled.

"I will cross the line first," Sarah shouted, so everyone could hear. "I do this for the good of the Reich and for the Führer!"

There was a flash of recognition on the Ice Queen's face.

"Well played, Haller, well played," she said, close to Sarah's face. "Again, I wonder why we've been forced into this position, when you have so much potential. But there is no winning. Not for either of us. Shame." She threw her head back and cried, "Haller is dedicating her run to the Führer; win . . . or *lose*, this is noble. Heil Hitler."

The girls cheered. They broke ranks and crowded around the runners. Sarah couldn't hear the questions or feel the back pats over her own desperation.

Whatever the Ice Queen had planned, it didn't sound like Sarah would still be at the school afterward, and that would end the mission. Meeting Elsa on a level footing meant penetrating that inner circle, and that meant proving herself somehow. She didn't really know what the Ice Queen would do if Sarah did win, but survival and any chance of completing the mission? They were now the same thing. To lose meant losing twice over. Being *broken*.

So what's your plan, dumme Schlampe?

I'm going to cross the line first, that's what.

Always with the great plans.

The girls in the crowd were herded toward the starting line and began to gather on either side of the cinder path that marked the start of the course. Here Sarah got a look at the competition.

There were six other runners, all bigger than Sarah, but three were too insubstantial to present a problem. One was possessed of a large bosom and had probably been chosen to supply comic relief. Of the other two, the Final Year girl, Kohlmeyer, who was one of the Ice Queen's train, was clearly the born athlete. Sarah watched her stretch and flex her muscles, saw the strength in the shoulders beneath her shirt, and knew the impossibility of the task. Kohlmeyer was *die Eiskönigin*'s insurance against anything Sarah could muster.

"Good luck, Haller," exclaimed the Mouse, her reedy voice almost lost in the clamor. One of her classmates repeated the phrase, and then, to Sarah's horror, several others began to chant her name.

"HAL-LER!"

Stop it, for the love of God, stop.

"HAL-LER!"

The Ice Queen is right. I am a threat.

Sarah wondered momentarily whether she could lose, be injured, fail, and disappear into the background. It was so tempting to just surrender, to let go, to drown in the circumstance. Forget the mission, run away.

Then she saw the Ice Queen across the clearing, her piercing blue eyes so alive with intelligence and disapproval. Sarah did not want to lose.

Sarah remembered a story from the Brothers Grimm collection, *Kinder- und Hausmärchen.*

Tired of his arrogance and bullying, the hedgehog raced the hare. The slower beast with little crooked legs used his failings—his small size and the fact that all hedgehogs look alike—and turned them to his advantage.

He placed his wife at the finish line at the end of a plow furrow, so no matter how many times the hare ran the course, the hedgehog was always waiting for him.

Finally, a blood vessel in the hare's neck ruptured, and he bled out into the soil without ever knowing the hedgehog's secret.

Sarah would use her size and turn it to her advantage. Sarah would cheat. The Ice Queen was going to bleed and bleed and bleed.

"HAL-LER!

"HAL-LER!

"HAL-LER!"

FIFTEEN

THE SEVEN COMPETITORS were shoulder to shoulder on the line. There wouldn't be room for everyone on the path as it entered the trees. Beyond, roots sprung from the ground to trip the unwary, the track barely visible where bushes had encroached on last year's footsteps. A fast start on the flat ground was a must, especially for a city girl.

Sarah closed her eyes. She pictured a long, smooth running track in an empty stadium. She let the cheering and clapping fade away.

"*Achtung . . .*"

Sarah crouched.

"*Fertig . . .*"

She felt her feet compressing the cinders as she tensed.

"*Los!*"

Eyes snapping open, she exploded out of herself, legs like pistons, hard but light. She kept her body as low as possible, and as the taller girls on either side began to close in, Sarah drifted between and under them, into the clear air.

Three meters from the trees, Kohlmeyer outpaced Sarah, moving in front from the flanks, and was first though the gap.

Sarah followed, the noise of the other girls loud in her ears. The first leg was uphill, pitching her forward, and as her feet slid sideways in the damp earth, she heard two girls collide with a scream behind her. She received the merest shove, which carried her over the mound, allowing her to speed on between the branches.

She looked up to see Kohlmeyer release a branch she'd held out of the way. It swung back across the path, and even though Sarah had time to turn her head, it caught her across her cheek with a slap.

Sarah stumbled into a bush, but her momentum pushed her through. She kept her legs going and bundled down the bank to the river's edge. She slowed herself on the crumbling verge, and as she did so, she saw it: there, right on the bank, was a narrow second track, trodden flat by the summer's fishermen. It wound off into the distance and around the next bend in the river. Not a shortcut but a clear path, slippery with frost but firm underfoot. She hit the track, skidded, regained her balance, and sped away, feeling rather than hearing her footsteps and breathing over the roar of the river.

She upped her pace, going as fast as she could over the good ground. She needed to break away from the pack for what she had in mind—even if she found what she was looking for.

The river was wide, deep, and fast, littered with sharp rocks. She grabbed a twig as she ran and tossed it into the torrent. It vanished in the spray and didn't reappear. To try and swim across was probably suicide.

After *Kristallnacht,* when the Nazis had run riot through the Jewish communities throughout Germany, arresting, killing, and destroying, it was impossible to walk the streets of Vienna. Sarah's blonde hair was too noticeable around the neighborhood, and the prowling gangs of thugs simply couldn't resist harassing her. Anyway, she couldn't stand to see the shopkeepers forced to vandalize their own shop fronts, or to watch the old men being made to scrub the pavements, hands bleeding and backs red from horsewhips. The last few had been given buckets of acid to use instead of water, at least that was what people said. Those men had been taken away afterward, so no one got to ask them for sure.

However, their tiny, stinking, top-floor apartment turned out to have one positive feature: the kitchen window opened onto the roof. Sarah had started off clambering out just to escape the smell. Then she began scrambling up onto the ridge to watch the sunsets over the city, the pinkish-red tiled roofs glowing in the vanishing light. She soon realized that she could move from building to building across the ridges and valleys of the old town's crowded roofs. Leaping the small gaps and riding the fragile dormers was treacherous, but for someone with Sarah's training, quick feet, good balance, and strong fingertips, it was almost safer than running the gauntlet of the storm troopers in the streets. Compared to the floating edge or the horse, this red-tiled landscape was a playground, a playground that became a secret passage and, finally, an escape route.

There was just a three-meter gap that could take Sarah out of the poor Leopoldstadt quarter and into a district of apartment blocks with unguarded windows, wealthy owners, and easily sold valuables. When Sarah stood on the ridge of the roof, planning her raids and choosing her route, she had felt truly free. Untied, unfettered, unencumbered. The dirty Jew, the grubby child, the hungry daughter of a bedridden mother—all this was gone. She charged helter-skelter over the dormers, swinging on the pipework and striding over the guttering, for all the world like a child running circles through a sunlit park, trailing her tiny hands and dress ribbons behind her.

Accelerating across the tiles on the final roof, she reveled in the control. Knowing how dangerous it all was, how far she had to fall, even how forbidden her presence was, only demonstrated the hold she had over her own destiny. All those years of gymnastics, practiced at home when banned from her classes, gave her a perfection in her footwork, in her judgment, and in her power. All this was hers, uncontrollable and untouchable under an open sky . . . and to fly, to truly leave the Earth behind and sail across the final space, with the tiny oppressed animals and their demonic drivers so distant below and blurred by her speed? That was freedom. It was a fire that lit in her stomach and spread to her limbs and brain with a crackle and joyful hooting.

The landing was difficult, painful on every occasion, but she didn't care one bit. The hurt was hers and no one else's. She could fly. The sky belonged to her. She was a bird.

She was a bird and she would fly across the river.

Sarah slowly rose to a standing position on the wide branch, panting. Back toward the river, a lattice of leafless branches was spread before her, a weave of possibilities and dangers.

She had been nearly halfway to the bridge when she had found what she was looking for: a spot where the trees on either bank reached out to each other and almost touched in the center. It hadn't been perfect, but she might not find a better option, and the clock was ticking.

It had also taken an age to find a suitable tree to climb. The trunks that lined the river were tall and smooth, their lowest branches hanging tantalizingly out of reach. She had headed inland through the useless beeches, wishing for a rippled elm or old oak tree, all the while panicking that she had gone too far, wasted too much time, that no shortcut would be short enough to beat the muscled and well-fed competition. The wide tree with deep furrowed bark and clefts for small feet was a gift, but it was too long in coming.

How long? Since she'd left the river? Four minutes? If so, Kohlmeyer and the others would be approaching the bridge and the halfway mark. She had to move.

Look how high you are!

No.

Sarah closed her eyes and waited for the moment to pass.

Trust yourself, dumme Schlampe. You've done this a thousand times. Think wood beam. Think tiles and bricks, gutters and chimney stacks. Better still, don't think at all.

Commit to the move.

Sarah loped along the branch to its end and, as it began to bend, leapt into the next tree, landing cleanly on a wide upward-traveling branch, feeling the heavy permanence under her feet. The floating edge, the vault, Viennese roof ridges, or tree branches: they were the same, she told herself over and over. She went on and jumped again. The limb of the third tree gave a little but held, so Sarah sped up and skipped onto the next. Tiles and bricks. Gutters and chimney stacks. Powdered canvas. She could hear the river grow louder as she ran, but she ignored it. The water was just a street polished bloody by old Jewish men. Nothing to do with her.

She stepped lightly. Quickly. The branches were moist where the night's frost had thawed, but they weren't slippery like wet tile. Sarah noticed the limbs growing thinner as she approached the river, so she chose the biggest for her final three pathways to the other side.

Three.

Sarah passed the bank far below, arms outstretched to counter the slight twist in the branch. She skipped. *Commit to the move.*

Two.

She landed awkwardly as the penultimate limb sagged under her weight. She readjusted her balance by sweeping both arms to the left. She was over the water, the rush of the spray filling her ears. The third branch was just above hers, so she needed to leap and bring both feet up together to keep her momentum. *Commit.*

One.

She faltered as she landed but pushed herself upright with her hands before the branch grew too narrow. She looked up to see it dwindle to nothing ahead, but there, maybe just two meters away, was the beginnings of a new tree. Its slender twigs were the keystone of the bridge, behind them branches that could take her weight. How far behind them Sarah couldn't tell, but she was committed now.

Imagine you've an armful of bratwurst and an empty stomach. Imagine there are angry Viennese Hausfrauen *in pursuit.*

She sprinted the last two meters, and with the limb bending precariously beneath her, she exploded off the end, arms stretching out in front of her.

Flying.

Falling.

Sarah crashed into the spindly parallel branches that snapped instantly under her and tore at her shirt. Her arms wrapped around the largest survivor, her shoulders screaming at her. One hand slipped from the other and was dragged away by her weight. The other tore at the bark . . . and held.

She swayed forward and then back, suspended by her fingertips and a shoulder on fire. Sarah looked down and watched the torrent of water spitting and broiling among the rocks. Her feet grew wet with the spray, but the river couldn't touch her. Sarah grinned in mirthless triumph.

Though now she found her other arm was numb and slow, so she had to heave at the good arm until the weaker limb could wrap itself around the branch. The effort made her cry out loud, a high piercing noise that scared her. Sarah realized that she didn't have much energy left to finish her crossing.

Last lap, dumme Schlampe.

She swung herself back and forth to get her legs up and curled them around the limb. Then, after an agonizing scramble of arms and feet, she climbed onto it. Her fingernails were torn and bloody, her arms wet with tiny scratches.

But she was okay. She'd made it. The way through to the other bank was easier, with thicker limbs and fewer jumps. She slowly climbed to her feet, taking the extra seconds to stretch out her muscles for the last effort. She was safely back on her apartment roof, with a dinner of bratwurst to come. Better than that, she was Trudi Meyer smiling with her gold medal.

She trotted along the branch and skipped over to a wider limb just a meter away. She landed with a hollow clunk—

She hadn't managed to move before the rotten wood split in two and tumbled down into the river, taking Sarah with it.

SIXTEEN

THE PAIN OF the impact was lost instantly in the icy flash of deep, all-over cold. Water filled Sarah's mouth, and her ears howled with the change in pressure. She thrashed her arms and legs, but she couldn't coordinate her movements as she tumbled in the current.

Darkness.

Light.

Darkness.

She grew slow. The deep chill pushed its talons through Sarah's muscles, all the while whispering and hushing and reassuring. It numbed her brain and body, taking control.

Darkness.

Light.

There was something she was doing. Trying to do.

Light.

So cold.

Stab of pain. Something had smacked into her head and neck. It tore at her back with rough fingers. Light . . .

Her face emerged from the water momentarily as she was dragged across the rock.

Breathe.

Then beneath, in the darkness. Not cold anymore. Strangely warm. Had she been cold? She was spinning, like turning cartwheels in the park.

She could hear her mother singing nearby, but she couldn't see her. It was the pirate song from that musical. The girl was cleaning, sweeping the floors . . .

Sarah looked into the light, the darkness, the light, and wondered why she couldn't see her mother when her voice was so close.

The girl, Jenny, was *sweeping the floor.*

The floor.

Sarah reached out. Her fingers sunk into wet sand and gravel and were pulled free. Light. Then, a moment later, the gravel brushed her knuckles. Darkness. Light. She stretched again and her fingers pushed into the sand. Darkness. Longer this time. She extended her limp, cold limbs once more, and this time her fingers slid deep into the silt, catching on larger rocks and slowing her spin. Her shoes caught on something, so she dug the toes down. This seemed important.

She was facedown, digging deeper into the silt as she moved. Her mother stopped singing.

"You see, Sarahchen, right now you're sweeping the floors, but one day . . . they'll be sorry. Really sorry."

Sweeping . . .

Sweep . . .

Ss . . .

. . .

There was a thud and the dull sensation of an impact.

Light.

Dark.

Light.

Air.

Sarah exhaled with a gasp, the stale air bubbling into the shallow water. She raised her head and took a violent inhalation that was like swallowing glass.

She stopped sliding forward and settled on the sandbank, face above the water. She shivered, but her chest was on fire. Laying her forehead against the sand as the water lapped around her, she concentrated on breathing in and out until she didn't have to make herself do so.

She waited for the ache in her head and chest to ebb away, reconstructing the fragments of memory.

Get up.

With difficulty, Sarah rolled over and looked back into the

river. A big rock and a fallen log had created a pool of calmer, shallow water by the bank. She'd hit the rock and been swept into the shallows by the current.

Get up, dumme Schlampe!

Why had she fallen in the water? Shaking uncontrollably, she pushed herself into a sitting position. She had to get out of the water. *Why?*

Ticktock!

A race. The race. Sarah rolled over again and climbed on all fours up the bank. Her numb fingers were bundled into claws, but her feet responded to her as she stood. She looked around, still confused. Which bank was she on? Which direction should she be running? Her teeth chattered, so she clamped her mouth shut.

Think.

Which way, Mutti? Help me.

High bank, upriver. She had been running upriver. She'd climbed the trees on the high bank. She was on the other side.

Ticktock!

Two banks, one bridge, a U-shaped course. A dangerous boast. She staggered into the trees, looking for the path. How long? Had the other runners passed her already? She found the track and then began to limp downstream. There were no fresh tracks . . . maybe she was still ahead.

But she was traveling too slowly. Her body wasn't responding properly, her movements awkward and jerky. The path was uneven and covered in roots masquerading as twigs, with leaf litter concealing potholes. The sense that the others were on her heels was inescapable, like the dream dogs howling behind her. In her head Kohlmeyer loomed, a snout full of teeth and the smell of blood.

Sarah let the panic warm her, feeling her increasing heart rate push life into arms and legs.

Think of the dogs . . .

Sarah let her mind conjure the barking, snarling, and panting, until she could hear them. The trees began to whip past her as she went faster. The ache in her thighs, the tearing skin under the wet clothes, and the pain in her chest and head, it all fed into the flight. She let the fear conquer everything until there was nothing else.

Feet pounding. Arms swinging. The wind whistling in her ears. Her breathing wheezing a rhythm for her stride. She was on her way, and her body was responding. How far was there to go? Could she make it? Surely she couldn't be caught now. Even Kohlmeyer was human.

She began to grunt as she breathed in and out to a tune that had appeared in her head.

Sarah smiled.

Won't they be surprised, she thought, *when I cross the line first?* She couldn't wait to see the Ice Queen's face.

Rahn's shoulder crashed into the side of Sarah's knees as the huge arms wrapped around her legs. With a shriek, they tumbled into the brush, Sarah landing facedown in the mulch and Rahn collapsing onto her feet.

"No, no, no, no . . ." Sarah stammered as she tried to crawl away, tears pricking her eyes. Rahn let Sarah free her feet, then grabbed an ankle and effortlessly dragged Sarah back underneath her. The tears came, and Sarah couldn't stop them. The Final Year girl dropped onto Sarah's back, a giant knee on each arm pinning her to the ground. The smell of sweat was thick like a blanket. Sarah kicked her legs but couldn't move. She could dig her heels into Rahn's back, but there was no power in her kicks.

"Yes, yes, yes," crowed Rahn, pulling Sarah's head back by her hair. "Stop sniveling."

Sarah sagged and sobbed into the leaves, giving herself over to failure. She was beaten. She'd nearly done it, and maybe if she'd not been so pleased with herself, she'd have seen Rahn in the trees.

Think. The Captain will have to come and get you, and you'll be safe. He can't leave you here . . . but then what? What use are you to him? What use will you be to anyone? What is Rahn actually going to do?

"Just get on with it," hissed Sarah.

"Shut your mouth," Rahn grunted, turning around to grab Sarah's ankle. "Give me your foot." Sarah pushed her legs flat to the ground, unwilling to help in her own destruction. Rahn had to rebalance herself and stretch out. "Give it here, you *kleine, dumme Schlampe . . .*"

The locked box where Sarah trapped all the horrors sprang open.

The older girl had taken only the tiniest weight off Sarah's right shoulder, but this placed her knee centimeters from Sarah's cheek. Just as Rahn caught her foot and pulled it upward, Sarah wrenched her face around and sank her teeth into the top of Rahn's calf. She bit down with every strand of rage and fury that was spilling out of her.

Rahn screamed as Sarah's teeth broke through the skin. She dropped the foot and swung away, arms aloft. The movement unbalanced Rahn, and Sarah heaved her off with her left shoulder. The older girl rolled away, her calf still in Sarah's mouth, arms thrashing as she fell.

"Let go!" she screamed, hitting at Sarah's face with her hands, but panicking and not making good contact.

Sarah pushed her hands against the older girl's leg, pulling upward and away with her head. She felt something give, and the leg was free. In the moment that Rahn cried out and grabbed at her leg, Sarah found what she was looking for.

She swung the rock at Rahn's head. She didn't get much speed, but the stone was heavy and sharp. It made a satisfying cracking noise where it hit. Rahn went limp.

Sarah backed away frantically on her hands and knees, clutching the rock. Panting and hot-faced, she spat at the motionless body and waited for Rahn to move. A second passed, her advantage seeping away, but nothing happened. Climbing to her feet, she turned back to the path and, with a last look over her shoulder, limped and staggered away.

What did you do?

Ticktock.

Did you just kill that girl?

Sarah glanced back, but she wasn't being pursued.

You don't even know. Did you kill that girl?

She shook her head, as if she could shrug off the thought. She loped into a jog, stretching out her muscles.

A blood vessel in the hare's neck ruptured, and he bled out into the soil.

She looked back down the path once more. In the distance something moved. Sarah slid to a stop. Just visible through the trees something small and white was traveling at speed toward her. Kohlmeyer.

Sarah started to run. She ignored the pain in her knee, the ache in her chest, the throbbing in her head, and the guilt that sat on her shoulders like baskets of laundry. She imagined the dream dogs, the pursuing Viennese children and boys of the *Hitlerjugend*. She pictured the SA storm troopers with their buckets of acid and Fräulein Langefeld with her stick. She thought of Sturmbannführer Foch with his wrinkled fingers and smell of oranges, letting the sensation run down her scalp and along her spine. She saw the ghost of Rahn rise from the mud with eyes of blood and a mouth of fangs . . .

There was no calculation, no shortcut, and no furrow to

hide in, just a straight run against the hare. But Sarah knew she was no hedgehog. She could be her own hare, albeit a small one. One with a head start.

She sped down the path, panting to a faster beat.

Just keep going. Don't look around.

She turned her head. Kohlmeyer was only a hundred meters away, face contorted with outrage and effort.

Don't look around!

Sarah pushed herself into a full sprint.

Just keep going. Don't look around.

The path narrowed, twisted, and bucked, throwing Sarah off her rhythm, and the track was crowded with bushes and leaves. She pushed through the overhanging branches with her forearms and nearly ran into a girl standing just to one side. The girl started and then, as Sarah passed, cupped her hands around her mouth and yelled, "It's Haller! Haller is leading!"

In the distance Sarah heard shouts.

"It's Haller!"

"Haller . . ."

Sarah rounded a bend in the path and saw the finish line, a clearing at the end of a wide avenue lined with suddenly screaming girls. To her horror, it was still two hundred meters away. The uphill slope was now noticeable, and the ache in her legs had become a stabbing pain that speared her with every step. How much longer could she do this?

She nearly slipped as she leapt onto the cleared ground that had long since been trodden into puddles by hikers. Each had frozen solid, making the home straight desperately icy. She kept her balance and pushed on, fixing her eyes on the clearing and ignoring the bouncing, waving, howling monsters.

Don't look around!

Kohlmeyer hadn't reached the avenue. The lookout was still hopping about, waiting to see who was in second. Sarah looked back at the clearing. Visible now, in front of the dark-clad teachers, was the Ice Queen with her court, tall and impossibly white, improbably golden. Already she must know that her plans were unraveling.

And what will this change? The Ice Queen won't keep her word. You're just kicking the hornet's nest.

"Kohlmeyer!" screamed the lookout behind her.

If Sarah was now the hare, then the Final Year girl was the wolf—faster, stronger, and inevitably victorious.

The crowd was screaming now, chanting her name.

"HAL-LER! HAL-LER!"

Another slip broke her rhythm, and this time she nearly fell. She kept upright by swinging her arms around, but this slowed her down.

The crowd gasped and then cheered more as she quickened her pace, but now they looked behind her, as the wolf bore down.

"HAL-LER! HAL-LER!"

She was just fifty meters from the finish now. The girls moved clear of the tape, a piece of string held across the path by two bored teachers, as the frontrunners closed in. Through the noise Sarah could hear Kohlmeyer's pounding feet. They were so close and so fast, the feet of a wolf on the verge of the kill.

"HAL-LER! HAL-LER!"

As she approached the line, Sarah saw the Ice Queen break into a smile, quickly concealed. The waiting girls squealed. There were hands in front of mouths and defeated faces. Out of the corner of Sarah's eye Kohlmeyer appeared, drawing level effortlessly. Sarah's body had given everything it had to give. They ran shoulder to shoulder for a few more paces, and then Kohlmeyer was in front. She turned her head and sneered as she drifted past, just a few meters from the line. Sarah made a defeated little cry and began to slow, a stinging fatigue engulfing her limbs.

Kohlmeyer was still looking behind her when she trod on the patch of ice. Her left foot slipped into the path of her right leg and she fell, crashing into the earth a meter short of the line. Sarah staggered over her and hit the tape, the string dropping to her feet. The crowd of girls on both sides exploded in a ragged, dancing, cheering mass, invading the track and swallowing Kohlmeyer.

Sarah limped the last few meters to stand defiantly in front of the Ice Queen. A moment later, the other girls surrounded her, lifted her off the ground, and carried her onto their shoulders, up and away.

SEVENTEEN

"AND THE WINNER of the annual River Run is . . ." There was a pause while the teacher checked the name. "Ursula Haller."

The girls, crowded into two lines, went wild as Sarah walked between them to where the Ice Queen waited at the head of the parade. She was clutching a tarnished trophy and staring at Sarah like a butcher appraising a side of beef.

"Heil Hitler, *meine Schulsprecherin*." Sarah saluted with all the verve she could muster. Her armpits and nipples were rubbed raw, and the action was agonizing. The Ice Queen waited a beat before replying, the crowd still burbling and clapping happily.

"So, once more it appears I have underestimated you," she said quietly. "You're wet. You swam?"

"I flew," Sarah said insolently.

"I should have you disqualified."

"It's immaterial. I said I'd cross the finish line first. I did. So we're done."

"And how am I supposed to maintain order, with you running roughshod over the hierarchy?"

"I'm not. I'm one of you, strong, fast, and superior. I'm your ally and, of course, your loyal servant."

You will never be this strong again. Let's hope this works.

Sarah sank to one knee.

"What are you doing?" The Ice Queen cocked her head, puzzled.

"Place your hand on my head, then offer me your hand. That's it." Sarah took the proffered hand and kissed the back of it. She had read this in a book. "Now help me up and tell them I don't want the trophy; it belongs to the Fatherland."

The Ice Queen frowned, then smiled.

"No, stay there a moment." She threw her head back. "Haller rejects these petty spoils. She won the race for the Führer, and she offers him the trophy!" The crowd cheered and a few girls began to chant Sarah's name. "No, my sisters. Don't celebrate Haller— she does not wish it. The glory belongs to the Reich! Heil Hitler!"

The girls saluted and chanted and saluted some more while Sarah knelt in the mud. A teacher began a speech about the war, but the girls' raw enthusiasm drowned him out. The Ice Queen reached down and lifted Sarah to her feet. She came close so she couldn't be overheard.

"Now, Haller. If you are indeed to run with this esteemed company"—she gestured to her lieutenants—"you will be your year's *Schlafsaalführerin* now. You must make that happen, no matter how it is done. You will lead. You will follow no one."

"Very well," replied Sarah. *It's all coming together. I can do this*, she thought.

Elsa Schäfer was standing behind the Ice Queen with the others, watching intently with the same expression of amused fascination. *Be fascinated. Be amused. Be my friend.* Victory was so close that Sarah could taste it.

"And you must stop fraternizing with the weak and point-less, like your friend Mauser."

Little Mouse. Unloved and unwanted. *Weak and pointless.* The only girl who gave a damn about Ursula Haller. Haller's friend . . . *Sarah's* friend. Sarah had a *friend*. She wanted to scream and swing a punch at the Ice Queen.

"No."

"No?" The Ice Queen's eyes betrayed real surprise.

It happened before Sarah could stop it. She was so full of anger and power that she spoke without thinking.

"You're right," Sarah snarled. "I *will* lead, and I will not fol-low anyone. So take your crowd of lickspittles and *verpiss dich*."

The Ice Queen was incredulous. "You don't get to walk away, Haller."

Commit to the move.

"That's exactly what I'm doing. *And* I'm bringing my weak

and pointless friend with me." Sarah pointed at the Ice Queen. "You'll want to be a woman of your word. We're done, and you're done with my class. You stay away," Sarah finished through clenched teeth.

Sarah could feel the opportunity, her way out, the job, sliding away like the sea from the shore . . . but her passion had been bigger, stronger, and in total control. The move was complete.

The older girl's mouth opened, and she seemed on the verge of slapping Sarah. Then her expression changed to a curious mix of animosity and irritation that didn't sit well on her normally blank slate. Around them, the teachers began reorganizing the classes for the walk back to school.

"And where is Rahn?" the Ice Queen asked as Sarah turned.

"I have no idea," Sarah lied with the straightest of faces. "Where did you put her?"

The Ice Queen strode away, calling to her retinue. Elsa glanced at Sarah—a moment's confusion—and they were gone. Sarah breathed out, like she had broken the surface of the water again. She began to shiver, doused in exhaustion. It took the Mouse and two other girls to help her back to school.

The River Run proved very controversial that year. One girl, Rahn, appeared to have been attacked by a wild animal of some kind. Her injuries were serious enough that she'd been sent home to recover. It seemed that the forest was no longer safe, and the teachers were bickering, trying to apportion blame. Some felt that the whole race was dangerous and the Final Year girls had too much power over it. In the end, boredom and indifference reigned. It was too much trouble to do anything about it.

Sarah's victory was endlessly argued about. The impossibility of swimming the river seemed the only certainty, and some would rather believe she had flown across. There was disappointment that the win didn't bring about a sudden end to the Ice Queen's tyranny. Others saw the apparent truce as a betrayal, and many girls began to look over their shoulder, wondering who was the next on the *Schulsprecherin*'s hit list.

Sarah ran a fever for the rest of the week. Confined to the sanatorium and between vivid nightmares, she lay and considered her mission's complete failure. Her failure. She had been welcomed into the inner circle, to rule the school alongside Elsa Schäfer. She hadn't just refused, she had doused that bridge in gasoline and lit the match.

As she berated herself silently, the visiting Mouse gave her a running commentary on life in Rothenstadt, an endless narrative of gossip, politics, and supposition.

"How *did* you get ahead, Haller?" the Mouse jabbered happily.

"I flew, didn't you hear?"

"No. Really?"

"Really," Sarah said.

She had tried to piece together the events over the river,

but even she wasn't quite sure. The whole fragmented experience was laced with pursuing horrors, cabaret songs, and dream dogs. It seemed scarcely believable, even to herself.

Sarah had immediately regretted her willful sabotage of the mission but simultaneously clung to what it had represented. She was no monster, no monster, no monster . . . but her fractured memories of the run told another story. One moment stood out, in crystal-clear fidelity that Sarah relived over and over again: The rock hitting Rahn in the face. The cracking sound. The movement. The intention suddenly exploding out of circumstance. She could have killed her. She *would* have killed her, if the rock had been heavier. She had been willing to do anything to fight her off. Not even to survive, just to avoid pain—to avoid *losing*. It was a deep pitcher of shame and self-loathing that part of her wanted to drink from, just to prove she was still a human being. But the jug was huge. There was enough to drown in.

Once she was well, any sense of triumph deserted her, along with her ethical qualms. She wanted an *erneuter Versuch*, a second go. The mission still stood and now seemed more impossible than ever. She couldn't bring herself to beg the Ice Queen for forgiveness, so without anything better to do, Sarah found herself trailing silently after the Ice Queen's entourage. There was no plan, no idea. She hung about in the shadows, watching them, their habits, and their routines. Hoping for a piece of information she could use, waiting for an opportunity that she knew wouldn't come.

Elsa was loud. It was the boisterousness of someone with something to prove. As the youngest, she must have felt that she had to be rougher, nastier, and noisier than everyone else. When the Ice Queen was absent, their conversation was prosaic. Horses. Boys. Marika Rökk's new song. It was as if the war, the Reich, and *die Judenfrage*—the Jewish Question—didn't exist.

Just once Sarah heard something valuable. She was eavesdropping on the queenless court, who were smoking on a fire escape. She was crouched, back to the wall beneath them, listening to the voices she had come to know so well.

"So who is he preying on now?"

"That new girl Haller."

"Oh, the all-conquering hero—"

"Shut your mouth, Eckel."

"That's what she did on Rahn's leg," Eckel joked.

"Shush. You *really* don't want the Ice Queen to hear you."

"So what's Foch's story, anyway?"

"No clue, but Schäfer knows, don't you?"

"Look at her face! She knows something."

"This is what I heard. I got it from someone whose father knows the staff—" Elsa crowed.

"One of your pets?"

Elsa ignored the interruption. "Foch was a loyal part of

the *Sturmabteilung* from the very start. They put the Führer in power, but Röhm, the head of the SA, he was a *Revolutionär*. And there is no place for those when the revolution is over. He thought he was more important than he was. He loathed Himmler and Heydrich and thought they couldn't touch him."

"Ha! Yeah, that worked out well."

"The SS put an end to the Röhm Putsch and wiped out the SA in just one night," Elsa continued. "A Blood Purge, a night of the long knives. Bang. Bang. Bang." She began to laugh.

"That's not news, Schäfer . . ."

"But Foch wasn't shot with the others, so what happened?"

"Ah, well. When they came for him, he pleaded to be let off. So they made him do something to prove his loyalty. Something *disgusting*."

"What?"

"What's the worst thing you can think of?"

Gretel, thought Sarah.

A distant bell rang. Lit cigarettes dropped one by one at the wet ground beyond Sarah's feet.

Sarah decided that even if she had to break her own fingers, she wasn't going to play the piano for Foch anymore.

EIGHTEEN

November 9, 1939

ROTHENSTADT'S DRIVEWAY WAS filled with expensive cars and elaborate uniforms. There were subservient drivers and mothers who wore silk and fur. The fathers had surreptitious bodyguards and supercilious expressions. Girls ran in search of parents, thoughts full of ice cream and precious attention.

Sarah stood on tiptoe to peck the Captain on the cheek.

"Onkel," she said formally.

"Ursula, I hope you are making me proud," her *Onkel* replied.

"Oh, yes, I am dedicated to my studies." Sarah waited a moment for a boisterous Fourth Year girl to bounce past. When she had gone, Sarah went on in a singsong voice. "A solid month of marching in circles, swallowing lies, tormenting the weak—I excel at them all. I'm the perfect little monster already."

The Captain opened the car door. Sarah always felt that somehow she was cluttering the pristine, minimalist interior, but climbing into a safe space after the weeks of tension and miserable failure was like climbing into a pair of strong arms.

"So where is she?" The Captain climbed in and pretended to adjust his mirror to cover his visual sweep.

"She isn't coming out. Professor Schäfer isn't visiting today. It's the Ninth of the Eleventh, remember? He'll be in Munich for the Speeches from the Führer, flags, marching, etcetera. The usual Nazi *Quatsch*."

"Language," he chided, starting the engine.

The car squeezed through the throng toward the gate, along the tree-lined avenue and past long, chauffeured vehicles.

"Why don't you have a driver? It makes you stand out."

"I'm quite capable of driving a car, thank you. Besides"—he pulled out of the gate and accelerated down the road—"we are short of friends right now."

"We had friends?" Sarah thought she should have asked more questions before, but he had been so evasive that it had grown wearying. The car wound through country lanes as Sarah waited for a response. She pushed. "Close acquaintances?"

The Captain snorted. "There were other agents, but fortunately we were not close."

"*Were?*"

"The Gestapo is cleaning house."

For an instant, the mask slipped and Sarah saw an emotion on the Captain's face. It wasn't fear as such, more a sliver of discomfort. She remembered the nights she had left the Captain in an armchair and found him sitting in it again the next morning. It hadn't occurred to her before that he had sat there all night, but now she thought about it, it had faced the front door.

"You have me," she began to say, but let the sentence tail away to inaudibility.

They passed into the outskirts of Rothenstadt, a lackluster town that showed few signs of the Führer's economic miracle. The paint was peeling, the stone crumbling, and its inhabitants looked surly and underfed.

Did he need *her*? Or just an agent at the school? He *sounded* isolated. Did he need her the way she needed the Mouse—

The thought was like walking into an unseen door. Did she *need* the Mouse?

Did the Captain resent her the way she could not help resenting the Mouse—for being a sign of her weakness and a distraction? Was Sarah a responsibility he didn't need? Like the Mouse, was she a vulnerability that led to impulsive action and failure?

There were too many threads in this tapestry, and Sarah decided that she didn't want to start pulling any of them.

The car purred down out of the town, refusing to fill the awkward silence with enough noise.

"So tell me about Elsa Schäfer," the Captain asked.

The *Schulsprecherin* had been as good as her word, leaving Ursula Haller and her class alone. The court of the Ice Queen was often elsewhere and always unavailable when present. Elsa Schäfer was never alone and virtually untouchable.

She didn't want to tell him anything. She didn't want to admit what she had done.

She didn't want to take responsibility for her failure because she could barely understand it herself. She didn't want to cry and ask to be taken *home*. And she was scared that if she started to speak, she wouldn't be able to stop herself.

"I had a chance to get near her, to be her friend, but I threw it away because I felt sorry for someone. I failed the mission."

It leaked out of her, like she had wet herself. She felt humiliated. *Take me home.*

She hadn't had someone to confide in before, but, like letting the Mouse in and allowing the girl to mean something to her, it could only end badly.

The Captain was quiet. Then he reached over and put his hand on hers.

"All right," he soothed. "But let me show you something. It's a few kilometers ahead."

Sarah felt a pricking at the edges of her eyes. Her guilt was swiftly soaked in bitter anger, and she directed it at him.

"We're wasting our time anyway. Say I get invited to her house, what then? What can I possibly achieve?"

Sarah sat in sullen and defensive muteness, arms folded. The

Bavarian countryside failed to lighten her mood in the cold November light, neither crisp silver winter nor golden autumn. Then she became aware of something alien creeping into view, something that should not be there. An imposing stone wall loomed, a thick scar across the natural landscape, swallowing more and more of the sky until it filled the car windows.

The Captain turned the car onto the road that ran in its shadow. The barrier stretched and curved away to the horizon on either side.

"This is the wall of the Schäfer Estate."

Now that she was closer, Sarah could see that the older stone was repaired and smoothed off, topped by barbed wire. The Captain drove on, and the unchanging fortification rolled past. There were no overhanging trees or indeed life of any kind within touching distance of the barrier. Sarah began to understand why the Captain regarded the estate as inaccessible.

"If I managed to scale that wall—and that's a big 'if'—I'm still a mile or more from the house." The Captain pointed a gloved hand for emphasis. "The grounds are patrolled by guards. Not some local idiots, but by the *Schutzstaffel*. I only have the vaguest notion of what the house looks like, let alone the layout." The wall slid by. "Want to see the way in?"

Up ahead there was some kind of military convoy. Trucks lined the road, and soldiers were milling around them. As they got closer, Sarah realized that this was the gate. Any visiting car had to drive a zigzag path of short stone walls to reach the gate itself, where guards would check the driver's identity again before opening a striped barrier. The soldiers were smart, alert, awake. They eyed the car with suspicion as it drove past. Sarah wanted to shrink from the window, to hide herself from view.

"This place is a fortress. Unless we are invited, we are not getting in."

The wall resumed and filled the passenger door window.

"She hangs out with the Final Year girls. They're in charge." Sarah was defensive.

"Then join them. Make yourself interesting to them."

"They're *monsters*," she complained.

"German High Command is full of monsters," he pressed. "Do you want monsters dropping the Grapefruit Bomb on—"

"Fine, I *get* it. They've only just stopped harassing me. Do you know what that school is? It's a lunatic asylum run by psychopaths, in the name of . . . *bastards*," spat Sarah.

The car sighed across the tarmac. The Captain shook his head slowly, then straightened.

"How did you know that Schäfer is in Munich today?"

"Elsa has a loud voice, and I'm always around trying to *make myself interesting*," Sarah sneered. "Anyway, it's Memorial Day for the Martyrs of the Movement, so—"

"Shush," he interrupted. "Did she—"

"Shush? *Shush?*" Sarah was really annoyed now.

The Captain raised a hand and made a conciliatory move of his head. "Did Elsa say anything else?" he asked with the suggestion of excitement. "Anything at all?"

"She doesn't stop talking." Sarah thought about the endless, meaningless discussions she'd listened to from a distance.

"About the house? About her father?"

"She talked about being left at school on Memorial Day. She talks about horses." Sarah grew bored. "About Anne-something, about how the man who looks after the horses is a drunk and needs to be fired . . ."

The Captain started to laugh.

"Do you want to share the joke?"

"You are an excellent, excellent spy," he said quietly.

Sarah didn't know if he was talking to himself or to her.

The parked car grew cold as the winter sun vanished into the trees, the red ball strangled by thorns and swallowed.

"How do you know the stable master is going to come this way?" Sarah asked, snuggling down into her coat.

The Captain shrugged.

"I don't."

"But you think . . . he's going to go drinking in the town?"

"Possibly."

Sarah thought all this was rather vague. "Not alone? In his bed?"

"Possibly."

This reminded Sarah of the train carriage ten weeks ago and was even more irritating. "But you have a *hunch*," she said.

"Yes."

"And *if* he does?"

"Then he'll probably do it tomorrow and the next night. Drunks are creatures of habit."

Sarah snorted. "And they're lazy and unreliable and unpredictable," she muttered.

"True, but he'd already have lost his job at that point. He drinks enough that a fifteen-year-old girl has noticed, but he's still employed. So my guess, my *hunch*, is it's every night, in the beer hall. *Social* drinking."

"Then what?"

"He has an accident walking home and I take his place."

"Then what?"

"Then I'm in and I can work."

"Tonight?" Sarah was taken aback.

"No, I'm not dressed for it." He smiled. "You know this . . . this profession, is a lot of educated guesswork and waiting around and being disappointed. You need to get used to it."

This was the first time that the Captain had specifically referred to any kind of future. But before Sarah could mention it, there was movement ahead.

"Hello . . ." The Captain stirred and smiled. "There's our stable master."

A scruffy, red-faced man, approaching middle age, walked purposefully around the corner and toward the town.

"He's half your height." She laughed, incredulous.

"I'll slouch."

The car slowed to a stop in the crush of vehicles trying to drop off girls in the twilit driveway, headlights jostling for position.

"The town, the estate, they're only a few kilometers as the crow flies. I want to come," said Sarah, mind made up.

"Tomorrow? No. Ridiculous." The Captain shook his head.

Sarah needed some control, some success, some *say* in the unfolding events. If she was not an "excellent spy," then what use was she? She needed absolution.

"I'm a spy. I want to do spy . . . *things*."

"You're doing *spy things*."

"I can't *stand it* here," she complained. "It's like watching the old men scrubbing the streets of Vienna, but *every single day*. If I can hold your coat and it gets me out of here thirty seconds quicker, then I am going to hold your *gottverdammten* coat."

He watched her glower at him, face on the verge of fury. He rolled his eyes. "Fine. You can get out of here tomorrow night?"

"In a heartbeat." She smiled. "And if it means I don't have to come back, then even quicker than that."

Sarah almost jumped from the car, but as she closed the door she saw something that made her freeze. She began tapping on the car window with a knuckle. When nothing happened, she rapped more frenetically, all the while glancing covertly at the school entrance. The window lowered.

"What?" the Captain asked impatiently.

"Look," rasped Sarah, jerking her head toward Rothen-stadt.

On the steps of the school were Elsa and a man in traditional hunting clothes. Sarah knew, even at this distance, that it was Hans Schäfer.

"Well, look at that. The Führer wasn't the big draw that we thought," the Captain said. "Can you stop trying *not* to look at them?"

"She's staring at me," replied Sarah in a stage whisper.

"She isn't, she's just looking in this direction. Just . . . go back to school."

Everything, everyone, was here in one place. It felt impossible that it couldn't be finished right now.

"Can't you just shoot him here or something?"

The Captain tutted and wound the window up, leaving Sarah feeling exposed.

This is stupid.

She plastered a big smile on her face and walked purposefully toward the school, pausing only to turn and wave at the car, the Captain already invisible behind the glass. As she turned back, Elsa was pointing at her.

Sarah drove herself on, trying not to stare back.

She wasn't pointing at me. She was pointing at someone nearby.

But there was no other Year Four girl there, and none of the Ice Queen's attendants. Now Elsa was talking to her father.

Does she know?

How could she know? There's nothing to know. Not yet, anyway.

As Sarah reached the entrance, Elsa's father kissed his daughter on the cheek. Sarah concentrated on the steps. By the time she reached the top, Hans Schäfer was alone in front of the doors.

"Excuse me, *mein Herr*," said Sarah, her voice squeaking.

"Certainly, *Fräulein*." He stepped out of the way.

As Sarah entered the school, it felt like being passed by a fast-moving vehicle. The sense of power, the movement, the slight tug of the wind, and the billowing aftermath. Once inside, she rested against the doorframe.

One more day here. Maybe just one more day.

NINETEEN

THE DORMITORY SLEPT as Sarah, fully dressed, slipped out from under the covers. She dropped soundlessly into her waiting shoes, but the rain beat on the windows with a ferocity that masked any noise she could make. She wondered if she should plan on returning in wet clothes—find a place to dry them, or leave clean clothes for the next day somewhere—but she just couldn't focus. She was getting out, she was sure of it.

She looked at her nightstand. Should she be taking the contents? Would she need Ursula Haller again? Would that girl vanish and leave her personal effects behind?

"Haller? What are you doing?" the Mouse's voice croaked out of the dark.

God . . .

"I'm going for a pee, shush."

"In your coat?"

"Mouse! Shut up, you're going to wake Liebrich," she pleaded.

"Sorry."

"I'll be back in a minute. Go to sleep."

She slipped soundlessly across the floorboards and was lost in the shadows, hoping that the Mouse would stay where she was.

Sarah knew her escape route well. The landing window was still broken, just as she had left it weeks earlier. *Always have another way out.* The swing to the drainpipe was no kind of challenge. The bushes were evergreen and gave good cover all the way to the crumbling walls. But in the moonless midnight hour, in a rainstorm, each of these things acquired a new peril. The windowsill was slick. The rainwater poured from the blocked guttering and down the outside of the drainpipe. Sarah waited for her eyes to adjust, but the grounds were invisible in the gloom.

She climbed out of the window and felt the water beat against her face. Since the race, she'd started to dislike getting her head wet: she couldn't shake the feeling that the water was going to swallow her up. She'd avoided the showers, and washing her hair had actually been frightening for her. Now the water soaked into her hair and ran down her face. It dripped into her nose and filled her ears. She resisted the emerging chaos inside her, the animal that had to run, to flee, to escape.

When she was calm enough, she swung to the pipe and slid

down the two floors to the ground. She looked up into the deluge and wondered whether she'd be able to climb back up later if it was still so wet—another reason to hope this was it.

She sped through the grounds away from the school, from tree to bush, skipping over the growing puddles until she had no choice but to splash through them. As she reached the wall and leapt onto it, a bright white flash illuminated her. She was relieved to realize it was just lightning. She began counting.

One.

She threw a leg over the top of the wall.

Two.

She rolled over the top and landed smoothly on the other side.

Three.

She took a moment to remember which direction she should be heading, and then cautiously trotted into the darkness.

Four, five, six . . .

The thunder was so loud that Sarah, who was waiting for it, jumped and let out a squeak.

You're pathetic. The storm is two kilometers away . . . but coming or going?

She pushed on into the dark in search of the road, beginning to doubt the wisdom of leaving the school at all. But she didn't want her fate decided without her being there . . . she didn't want to *miss out.*

When she reached the road, the rough tarmac was awash. It looked like a river, although in Sarah's opinion, a very poor sort of river, but it was galling that she had to trample through the undergrowth to stop the rain soaking through her shoes. Her clothes weighed heavy on her, and everything had begun to chafe. Her discomfort preoccupied her as she trudged.

"Your spy-craft needs some work," said a voice in the bushes next to her.

Sarah covered her surprise by pretending to shiver. She put her hands on her hips and stared up the road.

She shrugged. "I'm here, am I not?"

"And moving along the verge like a buffalo," he mocked. "I could hear you coming for the last five minutes . . . and see you."

She pursed her lips. "He's not coming in this weather."

"I think you underestimate the drunk."

The world turned white. "Yes, you understand drunks better than me." Her reply was scornful.

Thunder broke in a series of deep, tearing snaps, a ball bouncing on a drum of broken glass. As it did so, a figure rounded the bend, draped in a waterproof cape and hat. His progress was slow, a protracted stagger that meandered irregularly into and off the road. The Captain gently took Sarah's arm and guided her deeper into the trees.

They waited in silence as the man approached. He was singing.

"*Ein Prosit, ein Prosit . . .*" His gravelly voice trailed off as he scrabbled about for the next line. He gave up and started from the beginning. "*Ein Prosit, ein Prosit . . .* a toast . . . a toast . . . a toast . . ."

"Here." The Captain pushed something toward her.

"What is that?"

"My coat."

Sarah waited an insolent few seconds and took the damp, voluminous overcoat and bag. She bundled them up in her arms. "Great. *Now* I'm helping," she said sarcastically.

"A toast . . . a toast . . ." the man mumbled as he passed.

Sarah felt the Captain tensing up, a coiling snake.

"*Ein Prosit, ein Prosit . . .*"

The Captain emerged from the bushes.

". . . *der Gemütlichkeit! . . .* to good times!" the man sang into the darkness.

The Captain loped after the retreating figure, easily catching him up.

"One, two, three! Drink up!"

With one swift motion of the Captain's arm, the man in the raincoat dropped like a stone onto the tarmac. It was like the Captain had squashed a spider on the way to the kitchen, and his matter-of-factness frightened Sarah.

The Captain dragged the body into the bushes. He pulled the raincoat away from the stable master's limp arms and unbuttoned the man's shirt.

"Open the bag," the Captain ordered.

"Have you killed him?" Sarah was still shocked.

"No, probably not," the Captain said, like he was discussing a forthcoming soccer match. "Still, it's a cold night. He wouldn't be the first drunkard to die of exposure in a ditch."

He seized the man's trousers and began to pull at them. Sarah flushed and turned away. She had never seen an adult man with no clothes on, and she found that the idea made her feel a bit sick.

"Bag," the Captain reiterated. She held out the shoulder bag behind her, and he laughed. "He's not going to bite."

Nevertheless, she wasn't going to look. Something about this *felt* wrong.

She took a step backward and shook the bag. The Captain stuffed something into it. She had an uneasy feeling in the nape of her neck as she realized these were his clothes.

"Take my coat and bag and wait for me in the barn."

"Goodness, spying is glamorous," Sarah gasped theatrically. She was relieved to see the Captain dressed and pouring a bottle of liquor over his head.

"You're saving me a walk back to the car, and it's valuable extra time. Sleeping Beauty here could wake up any minute."

"Then tie him up . . . or . . ."

The Captain froze and rounded on Sarah. "What? Kill him? *You* kill him, then."

Lightning lit up the white, pudgy flesh of the stable master between them, then he was covered in darkness. The Captain waited while Sarah confronted the horror of what she'd almost found herself saying. *Dumb monster.* The thunder crackled and rumbled.

"Storm's getting closer. Time to move," the Captain declared, pulling on the raincoat and hat.

"Good luck," ventured Sarah, unconvinced by his disguise.

"No such thing," sneered the Captain.

"Then break a leg."

Sarah wanted to follow him, to watch him work. To see if feigned drunkenness, a raincoat, and hair washed in cheap spirits would be enough to fool the guards. There was that drive again, a tickling sensation building in her belly. She realized it was hope. Hope that this would all be over soon, that . . . something else would follow, something warmer, dryer, safer. It warmed her as she headed for the rendezvous point.

She picked out the hedges she needed to follow to reach the barn near the school. She'd seen it in the distance on runs. It was dilapidated and probably abandoned. It made a perfect place to wait. There was another flash, lighting up the side of the building ahead, just about visible through sheets of water. Sarah counted as she approached, curving her run away from the door to arrive behind the building. The thunder followed, louder and nearer, meaning the worst was still to come—although Sarah could hardly believe that it could rain any harder.

The slats that formed the walls of the barn had shrunk with age, and the paint had split and peeled away. The darkness within could be seen between the boards, and it made Sarah feel exposed. Anyone inside could probably see her, while they remained invisible. Again, a perfect meeting place. She reached the double doors and listened but couldn't hear anything over the sound of rain beating down on the thatched roof and walls. She gently pulled at the nearest door, and it creaked open.

Inside it was pitch-black and smelled of old hay and animal dung. She took a step in and waited until the lightning broke across the sky again, revealing nothing but a stall and a pile of straw. She felt for the back wall and finally settled onto the straw to wait.

She peeled off her coat and shook it. It was hopelessly soaked. She wrung out her hair and tried to braid it back into place, wondering how long she would be waiting. The barn was dry inside—its roof was a tribute to the thatcher's art. Here, out of the wind, it was almost snug. Sarah could picture a candle, a horse blanket, and a good book. She covered her legs with her coat instead and rested her head against a pillar. She yawned, realizing how her excitement had masked her tiredness. Each yawn made her eyes water. She had always hated that. She never wanted anyone to think she was crying. She closed her eyes so she could wipe them with her sleeve.

"What's all the noise?" Her mother met her by the door, wrapped in her frayed silk kimono.

"There are mobs in the street. They're smashing up

the windows of the Jewish shops, and the SA are beating up anyone they can find. They threw bombs into the Leopoldstädter Temple—everything's burning."

"Well, we're safe up here. You come in, Sarahchen."

Sarah hovered on the threshold. "But there are so many people in danger, who need help . . ." she trailed off.

"But what can we do?" her mother whined. "We need to stay out of it."

"How can we stay out of it? We're *in* it."

As if to illustrate her point, there was hammering and shouting down below, followed by the noise of tearing, smashing wood. Sarah ran to the top of the stairwell and looked down. The curving spiral was dancing with panicked shadows and vanishing lights.

"Sarahchen . . ."

There was a final crash, and the checkerboard floor at the bottom of the well was painted with a rectangle of dancing firelight.

"Come away . . ." her mother tried again.

Dark figures swarmed across it, and the first scream was heard.

"*Dumme Schlampe*, inside now," howled the voice behind her.

The shadows cast by the encroaching gang coiled around the heart of the building. Doors were being set upon. Shouts and the crunch of forced locks traveled up the stairs.

"Now—"

The door of the first-floor apartment had been flung open, and a stream of candlesticks, papers, and bits of furniture were being thrown out of it.

Sarah turned and pushed her mother through the door. "Go through the window in the kitchen onto the roof and close it behind you."

Her mother stopped, surprised. "Sarahchen . . ." she pleaded.

"Go now and stay there until I bang the glass for you." There was command in Sarah's eyes, and her mother took a step back. Sarah softened. "Go on, Mutti, I'll join you soon. I need to block the door, that's all."

Her mother retreated into the kitchen, and Sarah licked her lips in concentration.

Just a coat in a closet, just a coat.

She ran down the corridor, pulling the few pictures off the wall and letting the glass smash on the floor. She crashed into the kitchen and overturned the table, pushing the few pots and pans from the sideboards. She flung the blankets into the hall, and, grabbing an empty bag, her book, and some matches, she entered the small bathroom. She lit the paper and laid it carefully in the sink, taking one apologetic look at the ceiling as it caught. She ran to the bedroom, but her mother had already wrecked that room by living in it. She extinguished the candles, and she pulled off her shoe. In the hall, jumping, she smashed the light bulb, raining slivers of glass into her hair. She ran through the darkness, kicking the blankets out of the door of the apartment onto the landing.

The intruders were just a floor away. She could even see the brown-shirted SA trooper directing the other men. She glanced back to her door and swore loudly. Attached to their doorframe, unnoticed until now, was an old mezuzah case left by a former, more religious resident.

She grabbed hold of it and tugged, but it was screwed tight to the frame, and the edges had been painted over. Sarah gritted her teeth and pulled again.

"Oh, so religious that you've a *gottverdammte* me . . . zu . . . zah . . . too . . . *gottverdammt* . . . lazy . . . to take . . . it . . . *with* you . . ." she complained through her teeth. Finally, the pewter split and the front tore away in her hands. The prayers inside fluttered to the floor, and she stomped on them.

She could hear footsteps on the last flight of stairs.

She dropped to the floor and curled up with her back to the wall. She covered her face in her arms and snorted violently, before summoning a loud wail.

Cry, dumme Schlampe, cry!

She let her empty belly desire sweet, juicy meats and tangy fruits. She allowed the ripples of sadness to travel up from her stomach to clutch her heart and bring a sting to her eyes. The commanded tears rolled down her warm cheeks onto her forearms. She raised her head and looked into the eyes of the beasts as they stepped onto the landing.

"Not again, there's nothing left," she sobbed, feeling the snot gathering behind her eyes and running down through her nose. *Let it drip.*

The men, some wheezing from their exertions, looked at the smashed case and torn parchment, the tumbled blankets, broken glass, and dark corridor. One even stepped inside to see the firelight licking around an open door, the wreckage in the kitchen, and the trailing smoke. They turned and shambled down the stairs, disappointed.

"Disgusting," one of them said to another. "They actually live like this."

Sarah counted slowly to quell a flash of seething rage and waited until the last one disappeared down the stairs.

She doused the fire in the bathroom but left everything else where it was. She tapped on the kitchen skylight, pulled it open, and climbed out.

Everything was red, like the dawn. Screaming and sounds of smashing glass echoed up from the streets below. Her mother was sitting on the roof, her arms around her knees, rocking back and forth and weeping. "What's happening, Sarahchen?"

Sarah sat down and, closing her eyes, wrapped herself around her mother.

Sarah jerked awake, crying ringing in her ears. She had wiped the tears out of her eyes and cursed her carelessness before she realized the moaning was coming from outside the barn. The doors flung open, and a figure hunched in the doorway, a weak flashlight dangling from one hand. Sarah froze, hoping the darkness would conceal her.

At that moment lightning licked the sky above his shoulders, and Sarah saw the barn and the man in front of her. The thunder followed with a noise that set her ears ringing.

It was Captain Floyd.

She got to her feet with a happy little cry, just in time to watch him sag and drop like a toppled bowling pin into the earth.

TWENTY

SARAH STOOD FOR a moment in confusion, too recently awoken and surprised to act, before running over and crouching next to the fallen man.

"Captain? Haller? . . . *Jeremy?*" she shouted, pushing at his shoulder. He convulsed. "What . . . ?" She looked at her hands, now covered with something dark and warm.

"Do *not* push me there again," he said in English. Sarah set to work on turning the Captain over. She had moved her mother many times, but he was taller, heavier, and still awake.

"Too . . . much . . . bratwurst . . . Captain Floyd . . ." she grunted. She couldn't accept the implications, so she concentrated on the practicalities.

"I'll pass your . . . comments . . . to . . . my . . ."

"You don't have a chef, *Arschloch*." She allowed herself to get irritated by his humor so she didn't have to think about the rest.

Sarah rolled him over, and he howled as he pressed on his left shoulder. It was an inhuman noise, and she flinched away from it. She reached over for the flashlight. Its bulb was covered in a white filter to dim the brightness, so she had to unscrew the cap to make it usable. The unfiltered light revealed the Captain's deathly pale skin and blood-soaked shirt. Her own hands were bright red.

"What have you done?" she whispered, feeling everything slipping away under her feet.

"*I* haven't done anything." He coughed.

"Well, someone did something. Come on." She reached under his back and hauled him in slow, painful centimeters onto the bed of straw. She had to look away from his face, which registered every movement as agony. When he was finally off the floor, she went to close the doors. She looked out into the night, but there was nothing but falling water.

She turned back to the Captain, who hadn't moved, and began to remove his coat.

Do not fall now, dumme Schlampe. Stay on that beam.

"The SS guards"—he arched his back as Sarah pulled at his arms—"were not as stupid as I thought."

She drew his dripping shirt away from his shoulder. There was a dark red crater the size of a one-pfennig piece where his arm met his body. Blood was seeping from it.

Oh God, oh God . . .

"You let them *shoot* you? Wasn't that extremely careless of you?"

"They hit my . . . shoulder. The lack of care was all theirs." He coughed again.

Sarah felt his back, but there was no exit wound. "Tell me what to do."

"Pressure. Stop the bleeding."

Sarah pulled a handkerchief from her pocket and pressed it against the wound, pushing her weight against it. He arched again and gasped, chest rising and falling. He opened his eyes and looked at the material in her hands.

"That's ruined."

"It's all right, it's one of yours," Sarah muttered. *Keep it light.* The seconds passed. The barn was lit up by lightning and instantly hammered by a prolonged clap of thunder. The walls shook as it rained even harder. She looked at the Captain, whose very life was oozing out from between her fingers. She wasn't going to be taken away now. Maybe there wouldn't be anyone to take her away at all. The void where her mother used to be would grow and grow until it consumed Sarah and she'd be nothing but loss and loneliness and—

She stuffed that line of thought into the box and slammed the lid.

Sarah looked at her hands. They had grown sticky, rather

than wet. She slowly lifted her weight, and the congealed hand-kerchief stayed in place. The rain was drumming on the walls, where the shadow she cast was expanding and diminishing as the flashlight rolled back and forth. Through the noise of the storm she thought she caught a high-pitched yelping. She was tired. The dream dogs were following her. She bowed her head and closed her eyes, abruptly aware of how much they ached. She heard the dream dogs again, closer this time.

Her head jerked up. There were one, maybe two, real bark-ing dogs in the distance.

"Hey. *Hey.*" The Captain had closed his eyes, and she had to shake his arm to get his attention. "Were you followed?"

He hummed like someone woken from a deep sleep. "Short chase. Lost them."

"You didn't lose them," she groaned. "They're here. Come on, you've got to move." She tugged on his arm, but he was dead weight.

"Just. Need. A rest," he murmured and closed his eyes.

"Come on, *Hurensohn*, move it. *Raus.*"

She grabbed a leg and pulled, but he was already uncon-scious. The dogs barked again, closer, louder, and more nu-merous.

Think.

She looked at the flashlight, which was still rocking from side to side like a ship. She watched the shadow of the stall mov-ing, back and forth, back and forth . . .

She dove into the straw pile and began to bury the Captain until he disappeared beneath it. Then she snatched the flashlight from the floor and, shutting it off, made for the door.

The rain outside was like something that Noah had seen. Sarah hesitated under the eaves, then pulled the double doors shut behind her. No going back. She closed her eyes and pictured the landscape—the forest in front of her, Rothenstadt behind her, and the open farmland to either side—before running out into the night.

When she was halfway to the forest, she stopped again and turned in a slow circle, looking for the pursuers. Beyond the patch of grass that she stood on, all she could see was falling water, like the bars of a cage. She began to feel trapped and lost, doubting her sense of direction.

Commit to the move.

The dogs barked again. In the distance Sarah could just make out three lights, bobbing and crossing, their beams catching the rain. She could easily outrun them, but that wasn't the plan. It couldn't be the plan. The dogs would find the Captain, if their handlers let them. Sarah had to make the men follow her instead and take the dogs with them. That meant being spotted. Being bait.

What if he dies? What will you do?

He was going to have to manage without her for now. He was going to have to *not die*, and if she was going to do this, she couldn't waste her attention and energy worrying about him.

She switched on the flashlight and swung it wildly in the air. She waited. Still the lights bobbed unconvincingly on the horizon. She wiped rainwater from her face and tried again, making sure the bulb faced the oncoming soldiers. Lightning created a web across the sky—the four soldiers and two dogs were absurdly close. Surely they'd see her? But as the thunder exploded overhead, the lights kept up their random dance. She had until the next flash to attract their attention, otherwise the light would reveal a girl, a distraction, not the man they were following. She tried again.

This time the distant flashlights swept in her direction. Sarah trotted toward the trees, keeping her beam pointed roughly at them.

Follow my light.

One of her father's books described this. *The Doomed Spy, in the open for the purposes of deception.*

Their flashlights moved as one with new purpose. The dogs started baying.

Follow my light, follow my light, follow my light, follow my light, she repeated to herself as she crashed into the cover of the trees.

It was raining like the oceans were being tipped over the Earth. There didn't seem to be separate drops but one long sluice from a billion hosepipes.

Sarah slid to a halt, tearing a muddy trench in the ground and stumbling over a hidden root. She squinted back into the darkness, dragging strips of sodden hair away from her eyes. *Where are they?* The trees were thick with movement, branches swayed, leaves shook, and every tree was a soldier with a dog.

You've lost them. Dumme Schlampe.

No, no, no, no, no, no, Sarah repeated to herself, *not lost, far enough back for safety, near enough to follow the trail.*

Then where are they?

She switched the flashlight on again and dragged it back and forth in a wide arc. The branches and shadows danced like a cardboard puppet show. She turned off the light and clamped her eyes shut, the pulsing red flashes fading in her vision. She listened. The rain on the leaves, needles, and bare branches—like frying sausages. Water running down the slope—gurgling, gargling. Wind—a distant howling almost lost in the deluge. Rustling?

"*Da drüben,*" called a voice. *Over there.*

Very close. *Too close.*

Sarah spun in the sludge and slipped frantically into motion, every third step a skid in a wrong direction. When she was up to speed, she smacked the flashlight back into life and waggled it along the ground, side to side through the brush.

Follow my light, follow my light, follow my light, follow my light, she repeated to herself as she pushed through the trees. Branches slapped into her face and across her arm.

A high bar fence loomed out of the dark. Sarah got one good foothold in the slime and launched herself up to the top, clasped at the soaking wood, and swung herself over. She flew through the rain with a yelp of triumph, overcoat fluttering like wings, with only the splinters tearing into the palm of her hand to tie her to the Earth. Then she was over the side and falling.

She hit the water with an explosive burst of shocking cold. She sank through the black liquid up to her neck before settling on the bottom, her face briefly submerged by a wave of brackish rainwater. She gasped and spat her mouth clear. *Keep moving.* She dug her fingers into the remains of the grass and pulled herself out of the ditch, dragging her legs out of the water and staggering to her feet.

Stretching out in front of her was a wide field, with undulating grass in all directions, that disappeared into the pale sheets of water. If Sarah followed the fence in search of the trees, the soldiers would be on top of her in no time. If she carried on across the paddock, she'd be visible when they reached the fence. Then they would know.

Unless she was quick. She turned off the flashlight, noticing that the blood on her hands had washed away. She set off, skipping from hillock to hillock, willing her shoes to grip the mud, conscious of the closing pursuit, waiting for the shouts of recognition.

They are going to see you. They are going to see you and they are going to shoot you in the back.

They won't . . . hop . . . *shoot me* . . . skip, hop . . . *I'm just* . . . skip . . . *a little* . . . hop . . . *girl* . . .

She realized what she was doing, the skipping, the hopping, the continual movement of her eyes over the ground just in front. She was playing *Himmel und Hölle*, kicking the stone to the next square and hopping toward it, within the white lines but never touching. From Earth to heaven, skipping over hell, and back. And back again. And again. Sarah would just keep playing. She always played this game alone, even before the other children were told not to go near her. Over and over until the sky grew dark, waiting in vain for her mother to call her in.

Erde, skip, *zwei*, hop, *drei* . . . Her movement was fast and fluid now, skip, *silence!* . . . skip, *no laughing!* . . . each step swift and sure . . . *four, five*, skip, *six*, skip . . . coming up on hell, ready to make that double jump to heaven . . .

The lightning split the sky in two and bathed the water-filled world in white light. A black monster loomed in front of her, its eyes wild and tall ears back, baring its white teeth like the night had torn itself a mouth. The teeth opened and it started to scream. Sarah tried to stop, but her momentum carried her forward. She lost her footing and fell toward the beast.

She screamed. It screamed. The night screamed.

Sarah smacked into the side of the leathery beast and fell down into the water. The slope was liquefying under her hands and elbows. Hooves hammered into the mud around her. She had to turn her back on the monster that reared over her to climb slowly up and out of the trench, all the while waiting for the killing blow.

As she reached the top, she identified the smell. Rather than a vicious monster, she saw a black horse, its back legs stuck in the mud. Its eyes were wild but pleading, desperate, and frightened. Sarah wondered how often her own eyes had looked that way.

Sarah reached out a hand, and the horse moved its head to meet it. She touched its muzzle, warm and rough like suede.

What are you doing, dumme Schlampe? Run . . .

She found it was still wearing a bridle of some kind and closed her hand around the noseband.

Through the rain a gray-clad soldier appeared, stumbling over the mounds and hillocks. He was so close he couldn't help but see her, yet his eyes were planted firmly on his own feet. There was nowhere for Sarah to go, nowhere to hide and nothing to do but stand in plain sight. Sarah held her breath, then breathed out and tugged wildly on the bridle.

"You! Soldier. Help me!" she screamed over the noise of the rain. The soldier marched on. "Hey!"

He saw her and then stood, his mouth open just enough to indicate a failure of thought. He was young, so young he might still have been in school, and what he was seeing was so unexpected he couldn't quite fathom it.

"Well, help me, then!" Sarah howled, jerking her head toward the horse. She turned back to the horse and pulled with everything she had. "Come on, boy . . . you," she said to the animal, realizing she had no idea what it was and spotting a lie that might betray her. The soldier stood beside her.

"What's wrong?" he asked, still confused.

"He's trying to fly away, what do you think?" The boy looked blankly back at her. "The horse—is—stuck—in—the mud. He'll break his legs. We have to get him out."

"What's going on here? Who is this, Stern?" An older, keener-looking soldier appeared over his shoulder, his voice a piercing nasal whine.

"The little girl's horse is stuck, *Scharführer*," he explained. "We have to get him out."

"What are you doing here at this time of night?" the *Scharführer* shouted.

"My brother is fighting in Poland, and there isn't anyone else to check on the livestock." The lie emerged, fully formed, without time to think it through. "Look, if you're not going to help, then just carry on like your mate who just passed here a minute ago."

"Who passed through here?" the *Scharführer* demanded as a third soldier with two dogs loomed out of the gloom.

"Some idiot with a limp and a flashlight, wouldn't stop." She waved a hand vaguely away from the barn. "Help me or go—your dogs are scaring my horse."

"Stern, help this girl. You!" He pointed at the dog handler. "With me." They jogged into the night, dragging the protesting dogs with them.

"Well, that's just brilliant, thank you *so* much," she called, rolling her eyes theatrically. *This is working. How is it working?* "You know anything about horses?"

The boy shook his head. "I'm from Dresden," he admitted, as if that explained it all. *Good,* thought Sarah. *Neither do I.*

"Well, grab this and pull. On three . . ." Stern took hold of the noseband, and they planted their heels into the mud.

"One. Two." They looked at each other. "Three!" They hauled on the bridle.

The horse screamed and thrashed its front legs, throwing up great sluices of muddy water. Their heels slid out of their footholds as it tried to pull away. After a minute they stopped, exhausted, hands white and raw with effort.

"Again," Sarah urged, looking into the horse's eyes and seeing the panic broiling just beneath the surface.

"It's no use—"

"No, again!" Sarah hauled on the bridle, not knowing now if she wanted the horse free as part of the ruse or because she herself needed it to be so.

"Wait!" shouted Stern, and he jumped down into the trench beside the beast.

"What are you doing? He'll kick you!" The last thing Sarah needed was an unconscious SS guard.

"No, wait!"

The soldier busied himself around the horse's hindquarters, digging through the mud as Sarah stood, hopelessly wet and muddied, stroking its muzzle.

"This is crazy, huh?" she whispered to the animal in a tone

she could reasonably argue was comforting. "If you kick him in the head, I could go home, maybe? What do you think?" The horse whinnied and flicked its ears. "Oh, you're right, of course. They'd look for me then, wouldn't they? Fine, don't kill him, I don't care."

"Try now," the boy shouted. Sarah took a breath and pulled on the bridle. The horse lurched to one side, and with a scream it took one step up the slope with its free back leg.

"Yes!" cheered Sarah. "Come on . . ."

She hauled again, and Stern's hands closed around hers. The animal inched itself out of the trench.

"Come on," they both shouted, adjusting their feet, pulling, stabilizing, pulling again, then finding new higher footholds until finally the remaining hoof was dragged out of the mud. The horse broke into a trot and mounted the crest of the hillock, taking Sarah and the boy with it. He let go, but her hand was caught in the nose strap, and she was carried down the slope and up the next on her back, dodging the pounding hooves, until her hand slipped out from under the bridle. The horse effort-lessly leapt over her and was gone.

Sarah lay in the mud and degenerated into helpless, hysterical laughter—big-belly, side-splitting, couldn't-breathe-properly whooping cries of pain and joy.

"Are you all right?" asked Stern. He was covered in mud from hair to boots.

"Yes." Sarah giggled. *That's all it took,* she thought. *A helpful*

Schutzstaffel *trooper to crawl about in the mud for you.*

"Will she be okay?" He tried to help her up, but she slipped back onto the ground through his hands.

"He. He's a he," she declared with certainty. *You have no idea.* "If he can stay out of trouble tonight, he'll be fine." The soldier finally brought her to her feet. He was barely old enough for the uniform, barely old enough for his size, a face of compassion and innocence. Sarah felt disarmed. Transparent.

They were lit up by the lightning arcing in the sky, a spotlight in a windswept dance hall. The rain eased into larger, messy splashes. Sarah realized her mouth was open.

"I should walk you home," he said at last. The thunder boomed dully.

"Erm, no, I'm fine. It's not far. I . . . couldn't show up in the middle of the night with a soldier, could I? My Mutti would be *mad.*" She laughed, that caustic fake laugh she'd heard from her mother's friends when she was little. "Go and do . . . the thing you're doing . . . the thing . . ." Sarah grasped hold of her intellect. *You're going to screw this up, concentrate.* "What *is* it that you're doing?"

"Oh, we're following a criminal who broke into a nearby estate," he said proudly.

"Oh! You know who it is, though? You can just go and wait for him where he lives?" she probed.

"No idea who he is, or where he lives, or what he wanted."

"Oh dear." *Good.*

"But we shot him, so he won't last long."

There was a split second where his eyes were those of a little monster. A little monster with a gun.

"Well, thanks for your help. I have to go, try to sleep before school tomorrow." She headed back the way she came. So close to freedom and success. *Act normal.* One o'clock in the morning. In a rainstorm. With the SS. And a horse. Nothing could be more normal.

Her path was still lit by his flashlight, so he must be watching her. Without the horse or the chase to distract her, fear filled the space.

Let me go.

Then everything went black. She looked back to see his silhouette picking through the paddock, the foggy ring of light bobbing ahead of him.

She started to run.

From the darkness, there was a loud whinny and snort.

You're welcome.

TWENTY-ONE

THE CAPTAIN WAS unconscious when she got back to him. The bleeding seemed to have stopped, as best she could tell in the dark, but she wouldn't have dared move him even if she could have. He was hidden and dry, so the barn was as good a place as any. But he was going to need water, food, clean dressings.

So Sarah went back to Rothenstadt.

It had taken more than an hour to rinse the blood and mud from her clothes, then longer to find somewhere for it all to dry where it wouldn't be found. She had swept her muddy footprints from the corridors as well, but the school was so grubby that it barely mattered. When she finally climbed into her cot, she found her heart was beating too fast to sleep.

She dozed through the next day's lessons, with the winter light and buzzing electric bulbs cruelly bright to her twitching eyes. She was barely capable of evading the Mouse's innocuous but probing questions. *In the bathroom. Going for a walk. Watching the storm. Couldn't sleep. Just stepped out. Yes, and my socks.* At dinner she was dropping a dry roll into her pocket when she realized her constant companion was watching.

"What are you doing with that bread?" asked the Mouse, sounding only faintly curious. *Not again*, thought Sarah.

"Keeping it for later. I sometimes get hungry."

"You could eat it on your walk . . ."

Sarah swung on the Mouse, but she was already busying herself with the salt.

"Mouse," Sarah began after squashing her anger. "Sometimes this place is so . . . horrible, that I can't be here anymore. Do you understand that? I mean, I'm not leaving. I just need to be outside from time to time."

The Mouse pushed an unconvincing vegetable around her plate. "You wouldn't leave me here, would you? Alone, I mean."

Sarah answered immediately, knowing a pause would be damning. "No, of course not." She smiled. *With your eyes.*

"Do you promise?" she pleaded.

Shut up, shut up, shut up.

"Yes." *Liar, liar, liar.*

"Here, take my bread," the Mouse offered. Sarah took it, and the uncomfortable feeling that she was stealing, with a tired smile.

Maybe I'll be here forever after all.

Although the sanatorium had all the dressings and tools she thought she might need, she was faced with the problem of transporting water to the barn. In the end she resorted to using a flower vase that sloshed its precious contents at every opportunity onto her still-wet coat. The moonless night provided a series of trip hazards and mysterious puddles for her tired feet to find. Twice she found herself in the wrong place and had to correct her course, taking an age to reach the barn, all the time worrying that he'd been found.

She tried watching the barn from a distance, but there wasn't enough light for her to tell if anyone was inside, outside, or surrounding it. Finally, she just walked up to the entrance to find it exactly as she'd left it.

"Hello?"

She pushed her way in and tugged the doors closed behind her, pulling a candle and matches from her pocket. With her eyes closed against the flare of sulfur to keep her night vision, she struck the match and waited for the red glow through her eyelids to fade. The barn seemed empty, except for dancing shadows. The candle sputtered and eventually came to life.

"Captain?"

"You know, the nurses haven't been in to see me all day," a voice croaked from the straw. Inside Sarah a little fire ignited, fed by hope and relief.

"I hid you very well."

"Yes, and now I smell of dung. Thank you for that." He sounded pitifully weak, but the words were still his. This pleased her, not just because he was alive and she was not alone.

Sarah knelt next to the pile and brushed the straw from his head and shoulders. He was a sickly white, and his lips were chapped and dry. His eyes opened long enough to look at her and then closed again. She put the vase down and began to unpack her pockets.

"It makes a difference from the whiff of impropriety, doesn't it?"

He tried to laugh, but the sound rattled in his chest. "The girl who ate a dictionary."

"A girl who *knows things*. *So* unusual. How does the world cope?" She wriggled behind him, and with difficulty she slid her knees under his shoulders. "Hup," she ordered. He cried out as she pulled his head into her lap. She reached for the vase and tipped it toward his mouth. "Drink."

It was a messy process, but he gulped down the tepid water. It seemed to have an immediate effect on him. His eyes opened wider, and it was probably Sarah's imagination, but the cool blue seemed to gain a spark of life again.

"You led them away?"

"Oh yes, I told them, no British spies here. You have the wrong address."

"Are they still looking?" He sounded like he didn't care, but he probably couldn't.

"They didn't inform me otherwise. Drink." He swallowed another few mouthfuls.

How will you keep him fed? How will you get him home?

"They didn't know who you were, or why you were there," she explained.

"How do you know that?"

"A very nice SS trooper called . . . Sturm, Stern? He's from Dresden." The Captain made a curious noise. "I *know things*, remember? Let me look at your shoulder."

The coat pulled away, but the shirt underneath was stuck to the wound by a dark brown crust, along with Sarah's handkerchief. A giant scab. Maybe. What was the first thing her mother would have done?

"This needs cleaning. Tell me what to do." Sarah tapped his good shoulder. "Come on."

"I don't know."

"What do you mean, you don't know?" She was flabbergasted. "Were you shot before? Someone you know must have been shot, you're a *gottverdammter* soldier. You were in the last war, weren't you?"

"I'm not a medic, and yes, I was shot before. There were doctors and nurses, with a good bedside manner."

"Fine. They cleaned it?" He nodded. "Then, bandage . . . things? Right."

Sarah did not like *him* not knowing things. He always knew things when she did not.

She poured a little water over his shoulder and used it to dissolve the crust. He hissed as she began to pull the shirt away. The wound wept blood but didn't open.

"There's a bullet in here, isn't there?" Sarah demanded. "Does that need to come out?"

"I don't know," he whined, shaking his head.

"Hey. Stop sniveling," she barked. "Straight yes or no answer."

"I don't have any useful information for you," he said, regaining his composure. He winced again as Sarah bathed the wound. She slowly and clumsily tried to bandage his shoulder. He began sweating with the effort of moving and gritted his teeth.

"Talk to me. Tell me about the Grapefruit Bomb," Sarah said.

"What about it?"

"See, this is the bit where I get you to talk about something to take your mind off what I'm doing. So just . . . *things*, Captain Floyd. Consider it an opportunity to reveal my ignorance. How does it work?"

"It's complicated."

"So make it simple." She was the one that needed to take her mind elsewhere. Her dressing was hopelessly amateur.

"Professor Meitner says, there's . . . an element, uranium. It's unstable."

"Unstable. What does that mean?"

"It doesn't like being together . . . It wants to be smaller, to become something else."

"Don't we all."

She just needed him to talk.

"If it's hit with a spare neutron, a small bit of another atom, it can split to become two new things."

"This sounds very technical. Carry on."

"When that happens, it releases a little burst of energy. Like a breaking stick making a sound. Tiny but . . . *Jesus.*"

The wound started to seep again.

"Keep still. Go on."

"It also spits out three neutrons. Remember the small bit?"

"Indeed." Sarah was mopping up the blood with her skirt. She hoped it wouldn't show.

"These extra bits can hit another big bit and make that spit out some more extra bits. They'll make more and so on in a big chain."

"The bits spit, the spit hits, and then the bits spit some more. It's a tongue-twister," Sarah chimed in with her mother's best party voice.

"Eventually, all the bits that make up the Grapefruit Bomb would be spitting and hitting all at once and—boom."

She pulled the bandage tighter, hoping the pressure would help. "Like gunpowder."

"No. Much, much more powerful. Millions and millions of times. Are you bandaging me or tying me up?" He winced.

"Sorry. Enough talking. Now eat." She unwrapped her meager supplies and tore the bread into small chunks before feeding them to him like a bird. If the wound opened again when she was gone, would the bleeding stop, or would it keep going until there was nothing left? Would she be bringing tomorrow's lunch to a corpse?

Kommt Zeit, kommt Rat—*you'll deal with that in good time.*

"Thif breadf is schtale."

"Day-old bread is cheaper, didn't you know? They'd say you'd have to be Jewish to know that trick, but this?" She held up a piece of dry bread. "This is pure Aryan greed."

"What's that?" He looked at the rectangular bundle that was left.

"It's a book."

"A book?" He started to laugh again, a dry, hacking sound, but he had to stop.

She bristled at his ingratitude. "I thought you might get bored."

An arm reached out of the straw for it and made a hand-clenching gesture. "*Mein Kampf?*" he said on seeing the book. "I've read it; it's *rubbish.*"

"Rothenstadt's library is *very* limited."

_____

Sarah was so tired when she got back to the dorm she could barely get undressed. She almost failed to see the Mouse waiting in the dark but nodded in her direction to acknowledge the moment.

Sarah climbed into her cot. She couldn't worry about the Mouse. Her mind was already full.

How long are you going to be able to do this?

As long as it takes.

Long enough for him to die or for you to get caught?

Exactly that long.

He was not a corpse. In fact he claimed to feel better.

"So what's happening in the war? Why has nothing happened since September?" she asked.

Sarah ladled the soup into the Captain's mouth. The tin container was a real find, but entering the kitchens and seeing how their food was prepared had been the price. Feeling around in the dark for food while the cockroaches played was bad enough, but finding maggots on the ham was nauseating. The soup had been out too long, but it smelled all right. She fully expected it to make a reappearance in the dining hall tomorrow, anyway. One way or another.

"I'd rather hear about Elsa Schäfer," he said, the spoon at his lips.

"You're kidding, right?" she exploded. "When would I have had time, the *energy* to do anything about her?"

"You're spilling the—"

"I believe we're dealing with the results of your little phase of the operation right now. If you want me to stop stealing food for you and smuggling it out, just let me know."

She waited for an answer, but he just watched her. Her fury burned itself out over the seconds—it was too exhausting.

Finally, he spoke. "So shall I eat that food or catch you up on world events?"

"It's hard to be superior with soup dripping down your chin. Swallow, then talk."

He obeyed. "Well, as of three days ago . . . bad weather stopped the invasion of France. No more fighting this winter. The British were in place by October anyway, makes no difference."

"So what will happen in the spring?" Sarah found something unpleasant on the spoon and wiped it off on her sleeve. It seemed strange to be talking about the idea of spring, of the future, when survival meant dealing with one day at a time.

"Optimistically?"

"If you like." She liked the sound of that right now.

"The Allies will give Manstein a bloody nose in Belgium, and it'll all grind to a halt."

"And realistically?"

"Guderian is right, and they'll be too fast and too strong. The British will be lucky to stop them outside Paris while the French are still sitting in their trenches, waiting for the last war to start again."

"You're very well-informed."

"I go to the right parties."

"This would be easier if you fed yourself," Sarah remarked, giving up on the last few trails at the bottom of the can.

"I can't move my arm right now."

She reached out and touched his arm gently. Then she took it between her thumb and forefinger, repositioning it. He blanched and turned his head away.

"Not better, then," she murmured, peeling his coat away from his dressing.

"Give it time," he said.

She touched the skin next to the wound. "This is . . . warm. Is that normal?"

"Means it's getting better."

Despite Sarah's experience, she could not tell when he was lying. He might just be tired, or he might be a professional liar.

"Cookies, then. You can put those in your own mouth. The best weevils the Reich has to offer." She offered a napkin of powdery beige mush. "So, tell me more about the bomb. Is that going to be ready for spring?"

"No, but sooner than I imagined." He picked out a weevil, then another, before giving up. "A few months ago, I thought a bomb like this was . . . going to need several tons of uranium. Too big to use. That's why Schäfer had a Zeppelin refitted to carry it."

"Ah, that's where I came in." She immediately recoiled from the memory of that day and began to pack up the picnic.

"But now Professor Meitner thinks they'll need just a few kilograms. A bomb you could drop from a plane . . . or even carry."

"You'd want to fly away very fast."

"I have a friend at Siemens. He says they're working on planes without pilots. Rockets. You know what a rocket is?"

"Fireworks." She almost laughed.

"Oh, so much bigger than that . . ." He winced. "I need to rest. You should go back."

Sarah didn't think he looked too good. "How is the book?"

"Ideal, thank you. I found a perfect use for the Führer's prose."

"Oh really?"

"Like the revolutionary Soft-Tuff ScotTissue Towel: no lint, no tear, no waste. It set a new standard for softness and absorbency, yet was amazingly stronger in service . . ."

The stick hit the wood with a crack. Sarah's eyes snapped open, and she jerked into a sitting position. She looked dead ahead, aware that a trail of dribble was running under her chin from a crusty deposit on the corner of her mouth.

"Were you *sleeping*?" Fräulein Langefeld growled. "Were you actually so impertinent that you'd *fall asleep* in my lesson?"

The room was beyond silent. Even the clock seemed to have stopped ticking. The floorboards were embarrassed to creak as Langefeld readjusted her weight.

Lie? Silence? Apology?

"Sorry, *Fräulein*."

The stick struck the desk again. "No one said you could speak, *kleine Hure*."

Silence.

To her horror, Sarah began to shake. Her veins seemed to be filling up with fire.

Do not cry.

It might work . . .

Not with her.

"Stand," Langefeld commanded. Sarah stood, her chair shrieking and clunking into the desk behind her. Without the desk Sarah felt defenseless. The teacher disappeared from view, counting time with the rod against the floor.

"Who thinks it's acceptable to doze during my classes? Liebrich?"

"No, *Fräulein*."

"Posipal?"

"No, *Fräulein*."

"Mauser?"

"Erm . . . no," quavered a little voice.

"What?"

Sarah closed her eyes. *No . . .*

"No, *Fräulein*," the Mouse said, her panic audible.

"Do you agree with Haller? You think we should all have a *Schlummer* in my lesson?"

Sarah watched Langefeld towering over the Mouse's desk.

Only the girl's quivering legs were visible.

Sarah looked to the front again and kicked her chair so it made another shriek. She heard Langefeld turn behind her.

"You're a bad influence, Haller. You've got a stinking little Polack like the Mouse all confused. I won't have it."

The pain across the back of her legs was like touching a hot stove. It lapped up and down her thighs like boiling bathwater. A low groan escaped from Sarah's mouth to fill the space left by the cry she smothered.

She'd been doing this for four days? Five?

"You can stand for the rest of the lesson. That should keep you awake." Langefeld came into view as she walked back to the front of the class. In Sarah's head, unbidden, she saw herself swinging a rock at the teacher's head.

TWENTY-TWO

"YOU SMELL BAD."

"Well, this hotel room is missing many modern conveniences."

"Shall I call housekeeping for you?"

"I don't have any change for . . . the tip."

Sarah approached the Captain with the candle. He was sitting up, but he was rimed in sweat. Little wisps of heat seemed to be leeching away from him in the winter air.

"Well, this is our last sea-view room," Sarah burbled with faux jollity.

"You can barely see it at this distance. I'll report you to the Board of Trade . . ."

"That's a very British-sounding organization, Herr Haller. Wherever did you ever hear of such a thing?"

He smiled, but in slow motion. Something was very wrong. The smell wasn't wet straw. It wasn't human or horse dung. Not sweat or urine.

"Just leave the tray on the table, please."

"Some water first, I think."

He was hot to the touch and gulped down the water.

"Let's see your wound," she asked.

"No, let's not." His reply was too quick, and the effort made him cough.

She lifted his coat lapel and pushed the shirt away from his shoulder. The dressing was stained and wet. This was the source of the smell: a stench like meat starting to rot. She began to unwind the bandage, slowly at first but increasingly quickly as something greenish white oozed from under the gauze. The last piece slid away. She swallowed hard, gagging.

"It's infected," she whispered. She could feel something leaking out of the box and coiling round it.

"Now she's a doctor, too."

"We should have taken the bullet out." The panic took ahold, its tail rattling.

"Hindsight is a wonderful thing."

The panic slithered up her neck. "What do we do?"

"Oh, Sarah of Elsengrund, not even you can stop an infection." He said this gently and without malice.

She seized on the loose emotion and squeezed. "We have to do something . . . I can take you to a doctor . . ." She was gabbling, not thinking. She looked down at him, prone and pale. "I could bring one here."

"You don't think the *Sicherheitspolizei* haven't been looking for someone with a hole and an SS round in them?"

"So what if they know? It's better than dying here!"

"Don't be naïve," he snapped. "You've seen what these people do." He sagged and took hold of her hand with his good arm. "What they do to the innocent. What do you think would happen to me, an enemy, a spy? I'd be lucky if they shot me in the face to start with. Besides . . ." He squeezed her hand. "You need a way out, and I have to buy you time."

Sarah felt the world fracture and fall away in pieces around her. She was the little girl waiting for her father to visit as her mother sobbed. She stood next to her mother's Mercedes, the only person she loved in the world inside, with a hole where the back of her head should be. She heard the dogs coming for her across the broken glass . . .

No.

She jumped to her feet, as if doused with a bucket of water.

"No. No, you're not. I'm not going anywhere."

"We played the game. We lost. Call this a tactical withdrawal."

Her head shook slowly from side to side. "No. What do you need? What would a doctor do?" she demanded.

"Sarah . . ."

"What would he *do*?" she screamed.

"He'd clean the wound, maybe take out the bullet, but you'd need prontosil or some other kind of sulfonamide to kill the infection."

"Where will I find sulfonamide?" She seized on this and dug her nails into her palms.

"Jesus, girl, listen to yourself!" he shouted.

"A doctor? An *Apotheke*? In town? If you don't tell me, I'll just look for it . . ."

"You need to get back to Berlin," he began again, more calmly. "Take the money from my coat pocket . . ."

"No!"

"It's just enough, as long as you don't eat . . ." He kept talking.

"No. Are you not hearing me?"

"Have the concierge let you into the apartment . . ."

Sarah covered her ears as she left.

There was enough moon to paint everything with a silver brush. The leaves shimmered, and the grass was like finely woven silk.

Sarah sat on the fence and watched her breath curl away, wondering how something so beautiful could exist while everything else was rotting, fetid as the Captain's gunshot wound. She had places to be, things to look for, sleep to catch up on, but she simply couldn't move. She wasn't even comfortable there. The wood bit into legs still tender from the stick. She let the pain happen, felt its contours and peaks, holding onto it, controlling it.

The way out was right there, in the barn. All she had to do was walk back and take it. Ahead of her, more danger, more pain, a scenic train ride through a warped and twisted amusement park, all fear and no end. To go back to Rothenstadt, to find the town and steal supplies, all with no guarantee of anything but a corpse at the end? She sat on the fence, doing neither, as if she could sit there forever.

A distant whinnying carried through the dark. Sarah couldn't see it, but she knew it was her horse. *You didn't leave me*, it seemed to say.

You were a diversion.

No, you waited when you could have run. They'd lost you.

Sarah wondered. Could she have left it? Any more than she could leave the Captain? Or the Mouse? Could she leave something as lost and vulnerable as herself?

The horse whinnied again.

You're welcome, it said.

The doctor's office was leather-bound, padded, varnished. Old but expensive. The front door was heavy, and the hall smelled of privilege. A well-dressed woman with graying temples shuffled paperwork behind an antique desk under the watchful eye of the Führer on the wall behind her.

"Excuse me, madam. I've been sent by NPEA Rothenstadt

to pick up some medicines and supplies." She was flawlessly polite and formal. She had considered borrowing the Ice Queen's bullying arrogance, but one look at the receptionist dissuaded her.

"That's rather irregular. Why didn't they call?" She was stern, organized, *irritated*.

Yes, why didn't they call, dumme Schlampe?

Sarah had to make her want rid of this *Napola* girl by giving her what she wanted.

"Oh, I think they're in something of a rush. They wanted to make sure they received everything today."

"Is there an emergency?"

The lie spilt out easily but lay on the floor around her feet, ready to be tripped over. "Well, there's a girl who scratched her leg up pretty badly a week or so ago. I think it's gone a bit . . . *schmutzig*." Sarah made a face. "The nurse wanted some . . . prontosil?" The woman looked blankly at her. "Suff . . . sulf . . . sulfano . . ."

"Sulfonamide."

"Oh yes, that's it." Sarah beamed.

"Expensive."

"They said to invoice the school, and they'll pay by return."

"That's what they always say." The woman rolled her eyes. "And Frau Klose sent you?"

Trap.

"The nurse? I don't know her name. She didn't send me personally. Fräulein Langefeld sent me."

"You have a list?"

"No, I memorized it."

The woman seemed to make up her mind. "Come with me . . . What was your name?"

"Liebrich. Marta Liebrich." Sarah hoped to be long gone before they asked her dorm leader any questions, but she could feel the deceptions piling up. Maybe she should have just come in through the window?

The woman led Sarah through a windowless corridor and asked her to wait on a bench in a small wood-paneled room. Sarah had the uneasy sensation of being cornered. Were they calling the school right now? Would they find Liebrich safe and sound in the dormitory? Would they call attendance and discover Haller was the one gone? She could talk her way out of anything, but she couldn't do much in here. She needed to know what was happening on the other side of the door.

Breathe.

They've got me. How will I ever explain this? What am I doing?

There was a deep *click*, and the door swung slowly open. In the doorway stood the school's nurse.

"The girl with bleeding eyes," she said, blocking the door.

"Oh, Frau Klose," stammered Sarah. "I . . ."

Say something. Talk your way out of this then.

"You're not Liebrich. She's the *Schlafsaalführerin* in the Third Year, the one that's getting fat. You're Haller."

Cry. Start crying.

Shut up.

"Yes—that's right—but I came in her place. I didn't want to get her in trouble."

Frau Klose made a dismissive noise with her lips. "*Gówno prawda*—and I asked for sulfa drugs, did I?"

"Fräulein Langefeld told me—"

"That stupid *debil* wouldn't know a medicine if she could beat on it with a stick. Stop lying to me," she snarled.

Cry, cry now.

"I'm not—"

Frau Klose grunted, grabbed Sarah by the wrist, and, with an excruciating tug, dragged her down the corridor.

"No, that hurts . . . stop," Sarah cried, the desired tears welling up.

The nurse flung open another door and manhandled Sarah into an examination room. In the time it took Sarah to regain her balance, the only door was closed and locked. Frau Klose folded her large arms, her whole stance dripping with distaste. "Talk."

Sarah let a tear slide down her cheek.

Frau Klose tutted. "That won't work on me," she jeered. "You people don't have feelings."

She knows. *She knows that you're Jewish. That's why she gave you a hard time.*

So why didn't she report me?

Think, dumme Schlampe.

The tiled floor was too slippery to run past her. The objects on the shelves were too far away. She felt the couch behind her: bolted to the floor.

No, think.

"Well? Shall I just call the school and let them find out what's going on?"

"No—" Sarah spluttered. *Too fast.*

"What are you little *dziwki* up to?" Her loathing turned into an appalled curiosity. "Stealing drugs now? You don't have enough of everything?"

Dziwki . . .

"I need some for a friend," Sarah said desperately.

"You don't have *friends*. You're parasites."

She knows! She thinks you're a Jewish parasite, what else could she mean?

No. *Think.*

"She's . . ."

Dziwki. Debil. Gówno prawda. Klose.

Like sunshine from behind a cloud, she realized where the nurse was from.

"He's hurt," Sarah whispered in broken Polish. "Needs sulfonamide. Or going to die."

After a brief moment of surprise, the nurse recovered, but something in her demeanor altered. "Who?"

"A *friend*," whispered Sarah firmly. *Think now.* "He is a . . ." She switched back into German. "A poacher? *Kłusownik*? He needed food. They shot him."

"Poor place, this. Nobody has a full belly all the time." She was unconvinced. "They don't all steal."

"He's very hungry," she finished weakly.

"He's Jewish?"

Sarah couldn't help reacting and struggled to create the right response. "No," she began.

The nurse raised a hand. "Fine. Have it your way."

She walked over to the shelves and began pulling boxes and objects into a leather bag. Sarah was uncertain what had just happened.

"Is the bullet out?" Klose had a knife in her hand.

"No."

The nurse dropped the scalpel and a bottle of something into the bag.

Sarah couldn't reconcile the nurse's mood with her sudden, unexpected victory. The flickers of hope seemed misplaced, but it did look like she was getting help. Then her curiosity got the better of her. "You're Polish?"

Klose wheeled and for a moment seemed like she would strike Sarah. Then she laughed bitterly. "No, girl, I'm German. Or I was. Now I'm a second-class German, a German that Germany doesn't want anymore, thanks to people like you." She closed the bag. "Are you ready?"

"Ready for what?"

"To take me to your poacher."

Everything looked different in daylight. The barn looked fragile and horribly exposed. Treading the same paths seemed reckless. To bring another person, fatal.

"You were lucky to find this place when you did. In spring this barn would be crawling with lambs and farmhands." Frau Klose didn't sound impressed. She looked around. "Where exactly would he have been poaching?"

"I don't know. I found him here," Sarah evaded, still suspicious.

"And what were you doing here?"

Sarah stopped walking and waited for Frau Klose to turn back, a spark of fire returning to her eyes. "You ask a lot of questions."

"Because when the *Sicherheitspolizei* ask me theirs, I'll have something to tell them."

She doesn't hate Jews. She hates me, thought Sarah. *Or rather she hates Ursula, the little Nazi.*

The enemy of my enemy.

Sarah pushed past her toward the doors.

"Helmut? Helmut? It's Ursula, I'm coming in." She pulled the doors apart and peered into the shadows, all at once frightened what she'd find. "I've brought a friend to help."

Sarah stepped toward the straw pile until she could make out the Captain's form. He looked asleep. Or worse. Kneeling, she held a hand over his mouth and felt for the movement of air from his nostrils.

He's alive. I am still on the beam.

She wanted to clap her hands and laugh.

His eyes rolled open, and he smiled, very slowly. Then he saw the silhouette of the nurse in the doorway. Sarah made a reassuring noise and stroked his brow, which was hot to the touch.

"It's okay, Helmut. This is Frau Klose. She's here to help you. She doesn't care that you're a poacher."

"I don't care that you're Jewish, is what she means," called the nurse, shutting the door.

"He's not Jewish," complained Sarah.

"Is that what you told her, huh, Israel? How can the master race be so gullible?" The nurse shooed Sarah away and plonked herself down in the straw next to the Captain. She briefly examined his shoulder and then busied herself with her bag.

"Messy, messy, messy. Drink this . . ." She poured something into his mouth. "Did you dress this wound, girl?"

"Yes." Sarah was in two minds about surrendering him to her. There was no choice, that was clear, but he was her responsibility. He was all she had.

Sarah batted this thought away.

"It's atrocious. You've nearly cut off the blood in his arm. Did you clean the wound?"

"Yes, of course I did."

"But you left the bullet in?"

"No, I reached in and pulled it out with my fingers," Sarah replied acerbically.

Frau Klose laughed. "Come, sit on the other side and help me. Come on." She handed Sarah a bottle as the girl knelt into the straw. "Pour a little of this on your hands and rub it in. That's right. Now when I say, hand it back to me. See? Now you're a nurse."

"Is he going to live?" Sarah whispered. He was all she had.

"Your bedside manner needs some work. The patient is still awake. Pass the bottle, now." The nurse began to clean her hands. "Here, take this and this. Soak the cloth, then hold it over his nose and mouth." Sarah fumbled with the new bottle. "Go on."

She eventually unscrewed the lid. The smell was over-whelming, sickly, sweet, and sharp, and it hurt her nose. She lowered it onto his face, but he squirmed and moaned.

"Just do it, girl," urged the nurse. "The alternative is much worse, trust me."

Sarah pushed down with the cloth. The Captain writhed for a few seconds but soon stopped struggling.

"It'll dry out, so keep it wet," Frau Klose instructed. "Then put your fingers there just to the side of the windpipe, there . . . Feel the pulse? Don't let that get too slow. If it does, take off the cloth, got it?"

Sarah nodded, the smell beginning to make her nauseous. With the Captain's heartbeat nuzzling her fingertips and her other hand over his mouth and nose, she couldn't shake the sensation that she was doing something treacherous.

Frau Klose was injecting something into his arm. "He's in a bad way. I may not be able to save him. I need to remove the bullet, and there's probably some shirt in there, too. Then I'll clean the wound out. If he survives that, it's up to the sulfonamide."

Sarah nodded, but inside, her initial optimism, the sense of victory was extinguished.

Just stay upright, use your toes to stay balanced.

The seconds passed. Sarah felt his heart drumming like lazy fingers on a kitchen table. She counted each beat and tried to mark time, but the numbers got lost in her head. The drums sped up as the nurse opened up the wound and began swabbing the pus away with cotton wool. Sarah wasn't squeamish—she'd seen worse—but she found she couldn't watch and concentrated on the cloth. He struggled slightly like a dog in sleep, so Sarah trickled on a little more of the liquid. She found his pulse again. It was slower, maybe one beat each second. His fragility in her hands was terrifying—yet thrilling, too. She looked at the intense effort creasing Frau Klose's face, her tongue busily licking her lower lip in concentration.

"Why are you doing this?" Sarah asked.

"Why are *you* doing this?"

Sarah shrugged, unable to comfortably lie. The glass web of deceit and misdirection lay underfoot and breakable all around them. After a minute Frau Klose started talking.

"I was a nurse in the *Weltkrieg*. Just a little girl really, head full of flowers and kittens, suddenly pulling shrapnel out of boys my own age. Boys with missing arms. Missing jaws." She picked up her forceps and slid them into the wound. "I met a doctor, a surgeon. He was good to me; it didn't matter that I was a woman, he recognized my skill, taught me, encouraged me. We saved so many men together."

She pulled the forceps out with a grunt. Glistening between them was a crumpled star of metal, a flattened pinecone of iron. Holding it up, she twisted the forceps to get a clear look at it.

"Military ammunition. Dangerous being a poacher around here, huh?" She dropped the bullet into a tin tray and inserted the forceps again. "We worked together for nearly twenty years. He said I should have become a doctor, but I didn't want to break up the team." She drew a long scrap of wet black cloth from the wound. "Ha, there it is. *Verflixt*, he's bleeding." Her fingers began moving quickly, thread and needle, cotton wool and cloth. She worked through the dark red mess, seeing something that Sarah could not.

"Then four years ago—" She cut a thread with her teeth. "*Your lot* showed up. Threw him out of the hospital. Can't have a dirty Jew saving Aryan lives, can we? I went with him, of course. Working out of somebody's office, then someone's sitting room, without the right equipment or supplies. It was like nineteen eighteen all over again." Sitting back, she ran a bloody forearm across her brow. "Eventually, he told me to leave. It was too dangerous. I was scared by then, by the violence, by the broken windows, by the words painted on my front door. So I left." She looked at Sarah with undisguised hatred. "Last November they came to take him away. No one has seen him since."

"I'm sorry," said Sarah after a moment.

"You're *sorry*?" Frau Klose snapped, her stare poisonous. "Well, that makes it all better, doesn't it? The little Nazi is *sorry*." For a moment Sarah thought the nurse would attack her. "He was just one of many. I've lost count already. Now they're starting on the Poles. You know no hospital will employ me? I have *medals*. Who's next, little Nazi? Who's next?"

Sarah felt the blame. She felt responsible. The irony was not lost on her. The Captain's breath, through the cloth, seemed to be laughing.

Klose worked in silence. Swabbing, cleaning, injecting, sewing.

"Will he live?" Sarah asked. *He's all I have.*

"Time will tell. The drugs will work, or they won't. These aren't exactly sterile conditions. So why *are* you doing this, little Nazi?"

Sarah told the truth. "For Germany."

The nurse regarded her curiously, then nodded. "You need to be very careful. You're a flea on a tiger. You'll kid yourself that you're part of the animal, but if you jump around too much, it'll scratch you off with the rest."

TWENTY-THREE

"NATURE'S LAWS OF heredity are undeniably true. All living creatures, humans included, are subject to these laws." Fräulein Langefeld talked and walked, swinging her stick. "Note that humans are not all equal, but rather they are of differing races. The drives and strengths that create cultures are rooted in a race's genes . . ."

Sarah felt that this lesson, these words had been rolling in a circle, always arriving back in the same place. It was a strip of paper looped and twisted, giving it just one side. Her left eye was twitching, like a wasp trying to escape the drapes and return to the sun. Staying awake was the mission; Elsa would have to wait. *One move at a time.* Sarah leaned one elbow on her desk, propping up her head, and covering the offending eye with a clenched fist. She had noticed at breakfast that there was still dried blood under her fingernails.

"The success and final victory of our great task depends on the law of selection, on the elimination of those with hereditary illness, on the promotion of genetically strong lines, and on maintaining the purity of the blood . . ."

Out of the corner of her working eye, she could see the Mouse staring off into space, her mouth hanging open. Sarah was irritated by the small girl's lack of survival instincts. Maybe the National Socialists had that right, she mused. Maybe some people just weren't supposed to make it.

"In the case of plants and animals cultivated by humans, care is taken to weed out the less valuable. Only the useful and valuable genetic material is preserved. That is also what nature wants through the law of selection. Should we not do the same with people?"

Sarah hated herself, suddenly and deeply, with a strength that made her want to vomit. She might be a flea, but she knew she wasn't part of this animal.

"This fulfills the command for loving one's neighbor, and is consistent with God-given natural laws. The persons affected by the law make a great sacrifice for the whole of the people."

Sacrifice. For the first time since Memorial Day, she thought about the *Sturmbannführer*. She'd heard that he was crying by the piano day and night now. She wondered what he had sacrificed, or rather whom . . .

"In Upper Bavaria, there were twenty-five beds for the mentally ill in nineteen oh one. In nineteen twenty-seven, there were four thousand. If this trend is allowed to continue, how many beds will be needed by nineteen fifty-three?"

Sarah came to attention. She couldn't juggle the numbers. They kept slipping away from her like a handful of sand. A few hands were raised until it was no longer safe not to do so.

Don't ask me. Don't choose me.

"Mauser? Do you not know?" barked Langefeld.

Not again.

"Er . . . seven thousand, nine hundred, and seventy-five," the Mouse announced brightly.

There was a gasp of admiration, followed by a series of sharp inhalations as one by one they realized the error.

"Mauser, you are as feebleminded as the retarded children in those hospital beds. *Think.* What is the correct answer?"

The room was silent except for the tap-tap-tap of the Mouse's leg as it quivered beneath the desk.

"It's an extra three thousand . . . nine hundred . . . and seventy-five . . . plus four thousand . . . is . . ."

"No, you imbecile. Stand up." Langefeld towered over the girl, her feet apart, ready to strike.

The Mouse's chair scraped along the floor. "I don't understand. It's another twenty-six years . . ."

"You don't understand anything, do you, Mauser? You're a moron. What are you?"

"A moron."

"*Schlafsaalführerin*, what is the answer?"

Liebrich jumped to her feet as if she had touched an electric fence, panic in her eyes. "One hundred and sixty times four thousand, which is . . . one hundred and sixty thousand, times four which is . . ."

"Close enough, girl, sit." Liebrich collapsed back into her seat in relief. "See, Mauser? Everyone knows the answer except you. Now the *Schlafsaalführerin* has given it to you, can you tell me what would happen twenty-six years after that?"

"I don't know." The Mouse's voice was so small it was barely audible.

"How is that possible?" Langefeld shrieked. "You've been given all the information you need."

"I don't understand . . ." The Mouse was crying now.

Langefeld grabbed the Mouse's wrist and dragged her to the front of the class, knocking into desks and scattering books and paper on the floor. She hauled the girl onto the dais, her bare shins cracking loudly on the wooden platform. By the time the Mouse was shoved against the blackboard, tears were streaming down her face.

"You're a parasite, Mauser, an imbecile living off the Fatherland. What are you?"

"An imbec . . . a para . . . a . . ."

"Give me the answer in five seconds or I'll take the skin off your palms." Langefeld's own shoulders were rising and falling in excitement.

"I don't—I mean—"

"Five . . ."

"No, please . . ."

"Four . . ."

"Please!"

"Three . . ."

"No—"

"Two . . ."

"I . . . I . . ."

"One . . ."

"ENOUGH."

Everyone froze. The room went silent except for the whimpers of the Mouse. Sarah was standing in the aisle next to her desk, hands at her sides.

"What did you say?" gasped the teacher, her face red.

"Enough. She doesn't know. She isn't *going* to know, so LEAVE. HER. ALONE."

The clock ticked.

"How dare you—"

The wave of righteous madness was ebbing, leaving Sarah with the feeling of being soaking wet in a rising wind.

"Leave her alone," Sarah said again, this time quietly. "No one is learning anything when you pick on her."

"Don't you tell me what to do, you little *Hure,* don't ever tell me—" Langefeld could barely get the words out. As she stepped off the dais toward Sarah, she was so furious that she was shaking, her hands opening and closing on her wooden rod. Sarah saw only spite and hate leaking out of the woman's soul.

The scale of what she had just unleashed hit her, turning her bowels to water.

Ask for forgiveness, beg for mercy.

Don't you dare.

Sarah took a step forward and stuck her hand out, palm up in front of the teacher. She braced herself, feeling her leg muscles tighten.

"You plead for mercy or I swear I'll flay you alive." Langefeld raised the rod above her head. The wall clock ticked.

Sarah closed her eyes. "Just get on with it," she said with a sigh.

The first strike was a thousand nettle stings. It wasn't just her hand. She felt it down her arm, through her elbow, tightening in her neck like a tourniquet. She felt a flurry of panic in her chest that demanded she run, escape, fight back.

You are *fighting back.*

The second blow was worse. It was every burn, tear, and scratch, every rip, twist, and pinch, returning to remind her of what she'd forgotten, in just one instant. Sarah clenched her teeth together until her cheeks hurt.

She began to unpick the stitches over her misery and anger, to pry open the box where she hid the horrors, desperately trying to feed the seething, teeth-grinding fury and its insulating arms.

She gained a moment's clarity.

You can hurt me. But you do not scare me.

She opened her eyes and looked at Langefeld's lipstick, with its creases revealing the roughness of what was underneath. *Smack.* She saw the beginnings of lines around Langefeld's mouth. *Smack.* The faint diamonds of sweat building on her top lip and the few stray black hairs that the tweezers had missed. *Smack.* Her bared teeth, yellowing from coffee and cigarettes. *Smack.* The roots of her hair black where it had grown since the last bleaching. *Smack.*

This hurts. This hurts so much. I could cry and squeal to make it go away. Make it stop.

No, it can only hurt me. I know what that is, so I will not fear it.

Sarah noticed the flecks of brown in Langefeld's green irises. *Smack.* The veins in the whites of her eyes gathering in the corners. *Smack.* The mascara congealing in the eyelashes. *Smack. Smack. Smack.*

Use the fear. Fear is an energy. Break it up and build something new.

The stick caught in her fingers on the upswing. *Don't look at it.* They had begun to curl with the bruising. The hand looked red and torn, but it was numb and Sarah could no longer feel it. She was winning.

She looked up into Langefeld's eyes and saw the merest hint of uncertainty there.

Sarah *smiled.*

The woman dragged Sarah by the hair down onto her desk

with such violence that the other girls scattered to get away. She held Sarah facedown on the wood and slapped the rod across her back. Then did it again. And again.

Sarah closed her eyes. Fending off the squealing, howling little girl inside her, she searched for a memory, somewhere to go, a place where she had never been in pain or frightened or hungry. There was nowhere. If she ever had been happy, she could no longer remember it.

The frantic blows had no rhythm now. Her back was one endless fire, annihilating all her thoughts, stripping away the defenses to her fear and agony.

She just let go of your hair.

Then Sarah realized that she had little to lose, little to hope for, nothing that she wanted or needed, nothing she could imagine that could ever be a reality—except for this to stop. And nothing could carry on forever.

She just let go of your hair.

Sarah twisted like a corkscrew, and as the next blow hit home across her chest, she grabbed the rod with her good hand and twisted it out of Langefeld's grip. She rolled off the desk and staggered to her feet on the other side.

Her feet slid away from her, and the floor seemed to be pitching upward. She tried to look Langefeld in the eye but couldn't focus. The wood in her hand was slick with blood, and Sarah couldn't think why. The stick . . .

She jammed it between the legs of the desk and pulled

violently. It snapped into several pieces, leaving a thirty-centimeter piece in her hand. She waved it in the air and then tossed it across the room. Sarah's chest rose and fell as she faced Langefeld across the desk.

Sarah, the dirty Jewess. Beaten but *not* beaten. A warmth spread across her face. She wanted to smile.

"I'm not scared of you."

Langefeld turned the desk over with a scream and punched Sarah in the face. Sarah saw a burst of bright lights, like New Year's fireworks. Langefeld threw her into the next row of desks, and she crashed to the floor. The other girls began screaming and pushing to get out of the way, knocking furniture over in the stampede.

Langefeld reached down and pulled Sarah to her feet before hitting her again. This time there were no sparks, just a dull grayness with only the vaguest feeling of hitting a chair and landing on the floor.

Sarah saw the ceiling, the peeling plaster, the heaters that were never on, the missing bulbs in the light fittings. There was more screaming, noise of a struggle, and swearing. Langefeld loomed over her and drew back a fist, but her swing missed as Sturmbannführer Foch wrapped his arms around her and carried her away.

Sarah closed her eyes.

She could feel crisp golden crust breaking between her teeth; soft white bread; creamy, cold cheese; and slices of tangy sausage . . . as the dream dissolved to the metallic taste of blood in her mouth, Sarah remembered being happy.

"You're in here far too much, you know that? Mouth." Frau Klose shoved her thermometer under Sarah's tongue and maneuvered her face from side to side. A few days later, her fat lip was already healing, but her eye was still swollen. "You're very clumsy." She yanked the glass out of Sarah's mouth and stood up to examine the mercury under a light. "Let me see your back."

She pulled Sarah's nightdress up to her neck and saw a series of horizontal welts running down from her shoulder blades to her backside. Still visible under the antiseptic cream were the scabs where the rod had broken the skin.

"Even the army doesn't flog their soldiers anymore. That woman is everything that's wrong with this country," said Klose, more sad than angry, reapplying cream where it had rubbed off.

"Thought you didn't like us." Sarah squirmed. Each stroke was exquisitely sore.

"I don't. If someone dropped a bomb on this place with you all inside, the world would be a better place. Still, she's gone now."

"Where did she go?" Sarah was surprised, even pleased.

"Away from here, with her suitcase packed. That SA *Arschloch* insisted. He had to be stopped from putting a bullet in her head. Lunatics running an asylum, in every sense." She began to prepare a syringe. "You should thank your little friend for fetching him."

"Who?"

"What's she called? Mauser. Off like a shot as that *obrzydliwa suka* laid into you. Found the one person here who would give a damn. Clever girl."

Sarah cried out as the nurse pushed the drug into her back. "What about my hand?"

"What about it?"

"I still can't feel one of my fingers."

"Can you move it?"

"Yes."

"Then get over it."

"My wrist is sore," she complained.

"Because she broke it. Rest it. Wipe your *dupa* with your other hand."

Then Sarah thought about the Captain, about Elsa, about bombs and flattened cities.

"When can I get out of here?"

"I've seen to your friend. Not over the hump, but he's alive. Still sleeping. I gave him some more sulfonamide, but I had to keep some back for you, you selfish *księżniczka*." She collected her things. "Stay in bed. If you rub that back on anything, you'll look like a washboard for the rest of your life."

TWENTY-FOUR

Ursula Haller,

    You are commanded to come before der
Werwolf.

    Midnight in the chapel.

    Tell no one.

SARAH FOUND ALL the doors from the dormitory to the chapel unlocked. The way was prepared for her. She had considered not going, but whoever it was would find her eventually. Sarah thought of Julius Caesar marching to Rome to declare himself emperor. He stopped at the river, marking the border, knowing that to march his legions across it was a crime. Once he'd done that, there was no way back. It was all or nothing. Of course, it was too late to turn back by then anyway: trouble was coming regardless.

One way or another, Sarah felt the move had already begun, and she was, like the Roman general, already committed. There was nowhere to hide and nowhere else to go and no fear left. She was also deeply curious. The Ice Queen had to be behind this, and with the Captain still alive, her mission still stood.

She crept along the wooden floors out of habit, but she knew she could have marched through the corridors whistling. The invitation was probably the work of the *Schulsprecherin*, and Sarah was under no illusion as to who really ran the school.

An orange light spilled from the chapel doorway. It might have looked welcoming if it wasn't for the icy air. Sarah hadn't worn her coat, as it hurt her back too much. She let her body shiver and breathed into her cupped hands for a minute before entering.

Don't creep onto the stage. Let everyone see you, no matter how small your part.

Sarah pushed the door wide open, scraping and creaking on the stone floor.

The chapel was filled with hundreds of lit candles. In their light, Sarah could see the pews had been pushed out of the way to make a central space. Eight girls stood in a circle— Elsa, Eckel, Kohlmeyer, and the others—robed in white, like crusading knights from a painting. At their center stood the Ice Queen, her hands on the hilt of a broadsword so tall that its tip sat on the flagstones.

The need to know eclipsed her suspicions, like a badly written book that had to be read to the end.

"Enter, sister."

The chapel was small, and where Sarah had expected the girl's voice to reverberate, it was close and muffled. Sarah stepped into the ring, her heart racing. Try as she might to control it, the breath curling out of her nostrils betrayed her. Sarah looked behind the older girl and could see, in one gloomy corner, the silhouette of the three stone hares on the outside of the transept window.

Endless, circling, always running, but never to be caught.

The Ice Queen began to talk.

"Long ago, the Teutonic Knights traveled these Germanic forests, driving lesser peoples from our land, performing acts of valor and self-sacrifice. Our people are only now remembering who we are and where we come from.

"We stand in this place of worship, a monument to a dying and irrelevant god, as we form a New Order. An Order committed to the one people, the one Reich, the one Germany."

The sword was dull and pitted with rust spots, as if it had hung unused for decades. Whatever the girls had planned for her, it did not involve the blade. She glanced at Elsa, but her eyes were hidden from view.

The Ice Queen raised her voice. "The Führer is human and will one day leave us, but the Reich will last for a thousand years in our care. We are *der Werwolf*, the fastest and most feared hunters of the forest. We will hide among the weak and overlooked, only to rise when called to devastate, to decimate, to dominate.

"Ursula Haller, you have shown yourself once intelligent, twice cunning, and thrice strong. You are a worthy daughter of the Third Reich. And now is your time to join us."

Sarah felt something wake deep inside her. It bubbled up, entering her mouth like a train, and exploding into the air before she could stop it.

She laughed, a surprised and derisive exclamation that subsided into a helpless giggle. Like Caesar, sandals wet and silted, climbing up the bank, there was no going back.

"Sorry, go on," Sarah said as she got herself under control, hand in front of her mouth.

The Ice Queen tilted her head and narrowed her eyes. Then the cloud passed.

"I was very wrong about you, Haller . . . and you go on surprising me. I mistook your size for weakness, your obstinacy for pride. But you are *fearless*." She could not keep the admiration out of her voice. Then she smiled, a true, joyful grin that changed her face completely. "It's a valuable trait. We need women who are fearless. Langefeld liked the means too much, and she didn't really believe in the ends. Removing her was an act of valor and self-sacrifice." The smile vanished. "Take hold of the blade."

Sarah cautiously took the sword in her hands, using her fingertips to cling to it over her bandage and splint.

"Tighter, that's right," the Ice Queen ordered. "Now, repeat after me."

She spoke the lines and Sarah repeated them, lying with the ease of an actress.

> "I swear allegiance to *der Werwolf* and my fellow wolf-sisters
> With the aim to maintain the Reich for a thousand years in thought and deed,
> To wait patiently until called and then rise like vengeance,
> To commit whatever acts are necessary for our continued glory,
> And I swear that if one dark day the enemies of Germany overwhelm us,
> And I am the last true Aryan warrior,
> My last act will be to destroy all that is within my power to destroy,
> Kill all those it is within my power to kill,
> And, finding myself in hell, to make the devil himself fear me."

The Ice Queen pulled the blade up suddenly, and Sarah felt the rough edge break her skin. The other girls crowded about her and wrapped their hands around hers, grabbing and pulling until her blood was smeared on their hands.

This is insane, thought Sarah.

"Your pure German blood, mixed with ours," the Ice Queen whispered reverently, before shouting, "you are now one of us!"

The other girls threw their hands into the air and began to howl like dogs.

Sarah choked down another laughing fit and, letting her head fall back, she joined in.

Take my dirty, filthy, Jewish, lesser people's, substandard, communist, Mischlings, Untermenschen *blood and drink that down, you deluded little monsters. I hope it infects you. I hope you choke on it.*

The others rubbed her gore across their cheeks as they wailed, so Sarah clenched her fist to squeeze out a little more blood and painted her own face. Then she raised her hands and looked into the Ice Queen's eyes.

This I swear . . . Sarah thought.

> I will wait patiently until called, and then I will rise like vengeance
>
> To commit whatever acts are necessary to end your glory,
>
> And I swear that if one dark day you, the enemies of Germany, overwhelm me,
>
> And I am the last true German,
>
> My last act will be to destroy all that is within my power to destroy,
>
> Kill all those it is within my power to kill,
>
> And, finding myself in hell, deliver you to the devil myself.

The girls were removing their robes and putting out the candles when the Ice Queen beckoned Sarah.

"Your place in *der Werwolf* is, like its existence, a secret. Should you wish to continue plowing your lonely furrow surrounded by the feeble and pathetic, then you may." She turned to go, folding her robe. Sarah raised a hand to stop her and shook her head.

"Why am I here if the Mouse is so pointless?" Her voice was incredulous.

"You stood up for someone under your command. That was noble. Such sacrifices may be needed before the final victory. Besides"—her voice dropped—"you have been our shadow these last few weeks. You know your mistake." With that, Sarah's elevation became her acquiescence. "And I have been persuaded of your value by others. I think you know what you must do."

"Yes, *Schulsprecherin*," Sarah said. Submission. Subjugation. She forced a smile, and it felt like grease oozing out of an engine.

"Good. Carry on." The Ice Queen marched toward the chapel door as the last few candles were snuffed out.

"Hello, Haller," said a voice.

"What now?" groaned Sarah. She was tired and had lost interest in this game.

"I thought I should introduce myself properly, now that you're one of us. My name is Elsa Schäfer."

"Wake up. Come on, hup."

The Captain groaned and opened one eye. "What in hell's name did you tell that Polack about me?"

His voice was still weak, but now it seemed like it was carrying toward her from a distant hill, rather than away into the wind.

"That you're a dirty communist Jew and British spy . . . or that you're a poacher, I forget which. Anyway, guess what? As of last night, I'm friends with Schäfer, or at least whatever passes for friendship among the little monsters," Sarah reported joyfully, as she sorted through her pilfered food.

"What happened to your hand?"

"Fun and games."

"How . . . Never mind. What do you think of Fräulein Schäfer?"

Sarah thought about this. "There's something . . . different about her. Something wrong."

The Captain snorted. "There's something wrong with all of them."

"More than that . . ."

I heard what you did to Langefeld. That was . . . very special. It impressed us, impressed me.

Just couldn't . . . she kept . . . she was a bad teacher.

Yes, she was—and you just took it and took it until she couldn't do it anymore?

Something like that.

That's very brave, I think. To deal with that. Just the kind of person I was looking for. I like your hair.

Thank you, yours is . . . really nice, too.

I think we should be friends.

Are we allowed friends?

Oh, yes. Just people at our level. You're one of us now.

There was something about her self-confidence, her arro-gance that was . . . desperate.

"Well . . ." The Captain pulled himself into a sitting posi-tion, his voice growing stronger. "Tell her I'm away this Christ-mas, that you'll be all alone. Ask if you can stay with her. Get yourself in that house. Any way you can."

"You're mistaking me for someone likable again," she said, handing him some food. But Sarah didn't feel that way. Not anymore.

"Fake it. You know you can."

She did. She could do this. But what was *this*? "And then what?"

"Do the little-girl-lost act. Wander around until you find his labs, find out everything you can. Steal his notes. Sabotage stuff. You're an amazing thief and a nosy little madam. Just be *yourself*."

"Oh, you have a *plan*," she declared theatrically. "Here I was thinking we were making this up as we went along. Very reas-suring." She fished a bottle from the bag and knelt next to him. "*Really?* I don't even understand what I'm looking for."

"The plan was for you to let me in so *I* could snoop around. But thanks to your clinical negligence, you'll be lucky if I'm waiting for you outside in the car . . ."

He winced suddenly and went pale. Sarah's stomach heaved at how precarious her triumph was. *Not now. Not this close. He's all I have.* She moved in and wrapped an arm around his head. "Have some water."

"I'm sick of water. I've been in prisons with better service."

"It's the last lap. Not long to go."

Sarah was at the top of the drainpipe and had just put her arm over the sill when the voice spoke.

"Where've you been?"

Startled, she immediately lost her footing on the brickwork and began to fall. The girl above grabbed her and dragged Sarah up and through the window. They collapsed onto the landing, Sarah on top.

"You're a walking accident, Haller." Elsa giggled. "Now you owe me your life."

"Many thanks," said Sarah, rubbing her wrist. She was desperately tired.

"The question stands, though. Why are you wandering around outside? Why are you *always* wandering around in the middle of the night?" Elsa was beyond curious. This was an accusation.

"I'm not *always* wandering." *Think.*

"Tonight, last night . . ."

"The *secret meeting* was last night," Sarah scoffed.

"But where were you all of last week? Where were you *tonight*?"

"Haller? Is that you?" The Mouse was standing in her night-dress at the end of the landing, rubbing her eyes.

"Yes, Mouse. Go back to bed," snapped Sarah.

"Who's that with you?" The Mouse looked quizzical, but also betrayed. Hurt.

"Mouse . . ." Sarah looked at Elsa's face, fox-like, judging. "It's none of your business," finished Sarah with spite. The Mouse's eyes widened.

"B-but," the Mouse stuttered. "What are you doing with her? Haller, you don't—"

"Go to bed and leave me alone. Now." The Mouse looked like she'd been struck. Her bottom lip quivered once, and then she ran. Sarah felt dirty, but she wasn't done. Elsa would demand more. Elsa would want more. "*Gottverdammtes* girl. Always trailing after me."

"Well, some of us are leaders and some of us are followers." Elsa nodded. "She's keeping tabs on you, though. If you've got a secret, she's dangerous . . . So what is your secret, Haller?" She grinned the way a dog grins before it attacks.

"Oh, goodness. Come on, then," Sarah moaned, climbing out of the window.

"Come on, what?"

"Come and see what I've been doing." Sarah swung out and slid down the drainpipe.

"This is it?"

"Yep. What do you think?"

Elsa put her hands on her hips and watched the horse canter toward them in the moonlight. "This is the ugliest, cheapest carthorse I've ever seen."

Sarah shrugged from the top of the paddock fence.

"I don't know anything about horses. I just thought she was beautiful. Or him. I've no idea." The horse trotted the last few meters and stopped, nodding in front of her. *Bless you*, she thought. "I grew up in Berlin. Didn't see a galloping horse until I was in Spain—and then there was too much else going on."

"*He's* a scraggy farm beast. Haller, really. You need to see a proper horse. Have you ridden him yet?"

Sarah stroked his nose and he whinnied. "Hello again. Twice in one night, eh?" *You* are *returning the favor, aren't you?* His skin was almost steaming. "No, I've never ridden anything. You need a saddle, don't you?"

"God no, you go bareback. It's the only way to do it." There was a joy in Elsa's voice that Sarah had never heard. "Woman and beast in perfect harmony and all that. I'll show you."

Elsa jumped up to the top of the fence and, gathering her skirt up, swung onto the horse. He gave a surprised neigh and took a step back, but then decided he was fine with it. She curled her fingers into the mane and slid into position.

"Watch. You're farther forward than usual, between the barrel and the shoulder—"

"What's a barrel?"

"The barrel, you know. God, Haller, you don't know *any-thing*."

"Teach me."

"You sit here, keep your toes up, heels down. Adjust your balance with the mane—you *know* what a mane is?"

"Yes, thank you." Sarah was relieved that her ignorance turned out to be her cover story. She let Elsa talk, instruct, lead.

"Then you just ride him." She laughed, tapping the horse's flanks and coaxing him into a walk. She steered him into the paddock, and up to canter. "God, this field is a nightmare. It's all bloody ditches and lumps," she shouted.

Sarah watched Elsa with a growing envy. She had a sudden hankering to be that graceful, that developed, that in tune with the world around her. Easy, smooth, and fluent. Muscles and silver moonlight.

That's my horse, she thought, then dismissed the idea.

Elsa was explaining the art of riding, but Sarah just nodded and smiled. Now she'd diverted the other girl from the truth, the fear that had driven away her fatigue was evaporating.

"Oi!"

The call echoed across the fields, the small figure of the farmer already marching across the paddock.

"*Scheiße*," hissed Elsa as she galloped back to Sarah. She pulled up with such violence that the horse brayed in panic. She dismounted shambolically, landing on the ground with a bump.

Sarah hauled her to her feet.

"Come on, Haller, move it! Run!"

They sped away into the darkness of the forest, laughing helplessly, with the farmer swearing retribution behind.

"Do you do this all the time?" asked Elsa.

"Nobody gets on any horses, if that's what you mean."

"We need to do this again. You should come to my house and I'll teach you to ride."

There it was. Sarah looked down, feeling her cheeks flushing in the gloom.

How . . .

Come on, dumme Schlampe. Now.

"Well, my uncle is away over Christmas, I was going to be stuck with some ghastly relatives . . ."

"That's settled, then. You're coming to my house."

Sarah wanted to scream and throw her arms into the air. Swamped in emotions, she managed to give Elsa her best *oh good* smile and caught Elsa's expression. Sarah couldn't figure it out. It looked like shame, sympathy, and disgust, all at once. The effect was disconcerting.

"Are you sure?"

The look was replaced with a more familiar one of devilment and a big, toothy smile.

"It'll be wonderful. You'll never, ever forget it."

TWENTY-FIVE

ELSA WANTED TO be there, but Sarah insisted she watch the putsch from a distance. Liebrich was a tired, washed-out version of the girl who'd showed Sarah the dormitory just a few months ago.

"I can take you, Haller. I'm still bigger than you."

Sarah was cold. "But you won't."

Liebrich's chin quivered. "This isn't fair . . ." she gasped. Then she rounded on Sarah. "What does your father do, Haller?"

"My uncle makes wireless sets."

Liebrich laughed callously. "Then you have *no idea*. My father is an *Oberführer* in the SS. Nothing but perfection is enough for him. The weak, the stupid, the incapable—as far as he's concerned, they're going to fry along with the Jews and the communists. If he hears I've been replaced, I don't know what will happen to me."

Sarah wanted to reassure her, to make it better, to leave her alone, but the only way out was through. So she put her compassion in the box along with her fear. "I am the new *Schlafsaalführerin*. You will raise a hand to no one without my leave and you will obey my commands. Are we clear?"

Liebrich stood defiantly. Sarah moved very close to her.

"You know, I hear Rahn will be back next term, and I believe she's now my best friend," Sarah whispered, using the Ice Queen's emotionless delivery. "She's in a very bad mood right now, and she's probably looking for someone to take it out on, especially since she can't touch me."

Liebrich nodded gently, face red.

"Obedience. Your father will understand that, surely?"

"And what about your friend the Mouse? Where does she stand now?"

Sarah didn't want Liebrich to see her face. "I couldn't care less."

"You're late."

He was still pale and tired, but he was sitting up and dressed.

"Extra precautions. You know . . . spy thing." She bustled in and busied herself with the door.

"So how was your day?"

Sarah opened the bag of food and sorted through it. "Embraced the politics of the Reich and condemned an enemy to a beating at the hands of her father. Same old thing. Fun and games." She sat and handed him a tin of beef. "I can't stay long, I'm being missed."

"Who by?"

"My hostess for the Christmas break." She smiled. "Done and dusted. *Alles in Butter.*"

For just a moment his mask slipped, and Sarah saw something close to delight and pride. Then it was gone. It was enough.

"Good, I can get the hell out of this place. See if my car is still there."

"Can you walk?"

"Just. Well enough."

"Well, then."

Sarah felt there was something that needed to be said, but she couldn't quite form the thought. It seemed to her that he was having the same trouble. Then the space for it vanished.

"Right, in town there are rooms over the beer hall, the Gästehaus Rot. I'll be there on Christmas Eve and until you come and find me. This"—he handed her a scrap of paper with a number on it—"this is how you can contact me. They'll be listening, so watch what you say, *niece.* If I have to get you, I can't go to the house. They'll recognize me. You'll have to meet me on the road. Take some money."

Sarah committed the instructions to memory and secreted the banknotes away. The Captain offered a hand.

"Good luck," he said. She was about to take it, but then she smiled.

"Take a bath. You stink," she replied, standing up. "See you after Christmas." She reached the barn door and then stopped. She was frightened to open it, scared to go on. "Why are you so sure I can find out anything?" she asked.

She couldn't read his face in the dark.

"You're a smart little girl. They aren't expecting a smart little girl." It was enough.

Something else occurred to her. "Am I coming back to Rothenstadt? Ever?"

"Probably not."

Amid the relief, there was unfinished business. "Then I have one last thing to do."

"Liebrich said you wanted to see me."

The Mouse stood at the door of the dormitory. She looked especially small against the doorframe, like a doll who had wandered into a real house.

"Come in, Mauser."

It would be easier for Sarah to threaten the Mouse as she had belittled and rejected Liebrich. Tearing the sticking plaster away quickly. But now she looked into the Mouse's wide eyes, she realized that would be impossible. In the end, the Mouse broke the silence.

"You're not allowed to talk to me anymore," the Mouse prompted.

"Yes—but—"

"I guessed when I saw you with . . . that older girl." She stopped and seemed to be staring off into space. Sarah was about to lean forward to nudge her when she continued. "It's all right. No one talked to me before you came . . . much, so I guess it'll be just like that." It was almost as if the Mouse was trying to make her feel better. This wasn't what Sarah wanted either.

"Mouse, you have to leave here," she pleaded. "Don't come back after Christmas. Tell your father all you know, the corruption, the violence—"

"Haller," the Mouse interrupted with a whole new tone that Sarah had never heard before. "You know when Langefeld called me a waste of skin? She was right. I'm useless. Except here. Here I'm useful, I'm doing something. If I tell him, he'll take me away, and then I'm nothing again."

This horrified Sarah, who could see that the Mouse meant every word.

"Oh, Mouse, you're not useless," said Sarah softly.

"Really? Then why would you give me up for the Ice Queen?" There was a real defiance in her voice. "It's fine, Haller. Just don't lie to me and say that I'm worth more."

Sarah had the urge to snap at the Mouse, but her anger would have been misdirected. The price of Elsa's continued friendship, the bill to be paid for taking the next step, was having to live with what she'd just done.

"There's more to life than this school, Mouse."

"I'm doing my job."

So am I, Sarah wanted to cry. She envisioned a way out, a chink of redemption.

"What if I told you I was working, too? That I *have* to make the Ice Queen like me?"

"Then I'd say you're just like all the others," the Mouse said sadly.

Sarah tried again. "I told you I'd never leave you, Mouse. I might be missing for a bit, but I will come back to you."

"Tell yourself what you need to, *meine Schlafsaalführerin*."

Paid in Full. With Thanks.

"Thank you, Mauser; you can go." Sarah closed her heart and slowly pushed the Mouse and this conversation into her box of horrors.

"You should be careful, Haller. You think this is all wonderful and by the time you realize it isn't, it'll be too late."

Sarah ignored this final warning. She was already more alone than she had ever felt.

Her mother had bolted the door from the inside. Sarah couldn't pick a lock that she couldn't touch, and there must be something else behind the door because it didn't move a centimeter when kicked. She had tried to climb down to the window, but the outside of the building on that side was sheer brick. Anyway, the window would have been too small to climb through, even for an emaciated girl.

She had known her mother was still alive, because she

could hear her screaming. It had gone on for four days. At first Sarah pleaded with her mother to open the door and begged to know what was happening, sobbing in frustration. Then, slowly, Sarah began to withdraw, preparing herself for the worst. She slept on the roof to escape the noise.

This morning, however, as Sarah climbed in through the kitchen window, she was hit by the silence. The bedroom was empty. Sarah closed the door against the stench. She checked the bathroom and the hall, panic rising.

She burst through the front door onto the landing to see someone coming up the staircase.

"Mutti! Where—"

Her mother, *her real mother*, reached the top step. Gone were the wide, red-rimmed eyes; the pale pockmarked skin; and yellow teeth. Instead her face was made up to perfection, and she was dressed in a feathered hat and her best fur coat—a coat that Sarah would have sold for food long ago if she'd known her mother still owned it. It wasn't a perfect performance, but it was like sunlight on a cold spring morning. The suggestion of better things to come.

"Sarahchen, it's time to go. Anything you want to bring, put it in the car now."

Sarah stood, openmouthed, before recovering her composure. "We don't have a car anymore, Mutti."

"The Mercedes is outside, waiting." She gave a tiny wriggle of her shoulders.

"How did you manage that?" Sarah did not like being

confused. Then her mother flashed a cunning grin, and Sarah came to a realization. "Mutti, did you *steal* back our car?"

"You know, they never took my car keys. They must have wanted me to use them. Quick now, we have to get to Friedrichshafen and it's a long drive. I've sent a message to your father to meet us in Switzerland."

There was a light in her mother's eyes that had been missing for . . . months? Years? Sarah had begun to suspect that her mother only glittered in her imagination and that she'd always been sour, stinking, and bloodshot. Yet here she was. Sarah knew that her father hadn't answered and he wouldn't be waiting for them, not after all these years of silence. She'd long since given up caring . . . but maybe it didn't really matter what her mother believed now.

"But our papers? Do we have visas? How will we—"

"Shush, shush, don't you worry about all that."

Her mother opened her arms and Sarah fell into them. The scent of whisky and sick had faded, swamped by soap, perfume, and mothballs.

Don't we need a visa? Unstamped papers? Money?

Shush.

A stolen car?

Shush.

But—

Shush.

TWENTY-SIX

December 23, 1939

THE SCHÄFERS' CAR was sumptuous. Its polish glistened in a shaft of winter sunshine that appeared as if to herald its arrival. Climbing into it felt like taking steps up to some kind of temple. It smelled of clean, waxed leather, and the seats were covered in thick, soft blankets, but the car was warm—warm in a way Sarah had forgotten, warm like cocoa, warm like the edge of old firelight.

The driver was in an SS uniform.

Elsa had sweets. Tangy, sour-edged flashes of flavor, a little explosion of sherbet that was too exquisite to experience without grinning.

There was a machine gun on the front passenger seat.

There were books in the back with beautiful covers, telling wild tales of pirates and wizards in adventure after adventure. For weeks Sarah had seen only dull black type and questionable facts, but now rosy-cheeked children and fearsome beasts, islands of brave knights, quests, and princesses all jumped from the illustrations.

Among them was *Der Giftpilz*, a warning to all children of the dangers of the Jews, the poisonous mushrooms of the Aryan forest.

Elsa talked of banquets and satin dresses, horses and parties in one long uninterrupted story of amusing escapades and delightful pleasures. She asked Sarah no questions about herself. This suited Sarah fine, but it began to occur to her that this was not entirely right. Unlike the Mouse, who could deliver a long and meaningless monologue to fill a silence but would stop whenever someone else talked, Elsa's conversation filled the air so full of words that no others could fit. So animated were her phrases and anecdotes that other words seemed pale and pointless in comparison. Sarah felt swamped, held under by the same hand that stopped her being swept away. She wondered if this was how happy, normal children spoke. It was eerily like listening to her mother.

Sarah pushed that thought away and risked a question as Elsa breathed in.

"What does your father do?"

Elsa's face changed. It was like a cloud had passed across the sun. "He is a scientist. He does experiments. It's very dull." Elsa looked out of the car window at the rushing hedgerows.

"What about your mother? What is she like?" Sarah hurried on.

"My mother was taken away from us four years ago."

Dumme Schlampe. "That's a shame. I'm sorry."

"Don't be. She was a weak, cowardly bitch." The words seemed like they would burn through the chassis onto the road.

"My mother is in a lunatic asylum," Sarah volunteered.

Sarah let those words settle and watched the passing countryside. She felt warm fingers coil around hers on the seat. Where the Mouse had calloused, damaged fingers, Elsa's were soft and smooth like a polished banister. She reached out her other hand and touched Sarah's cheek.

"I'm sorry." She ran her finger down one of Sarah's braids. "I'm sorry about everything."

Sarah didn't know what to say. Elsa's face, unreadable, switched to devilment as she sat back and squeezed Sarah's hand. "Do you like boys yet?"

"Oh, I haven't given them any thought." She was relieved by the change in atmosphere but had nothing to contribute on this subject. She was dimly aware that this was a source of frenzied excitement for other, older people, but her mother had never really talked of it, and the books she had read also skirted the details.

"You must. You must think about them all the time! My father's guards, they're so handsome, and strong, and rugged—

they make me feel tickly inside." She snickered and Sarah joined in. Whatever else, her enthusiasm was infectious. Then she leaned forward and prodded the driver. "Not you, Kurt! You're an old, old, wrinkly man." She laughed. Sarah saw the figure in the front straighten his shoulders. She squashed the desire to wince and giggled her mother's best coquettish giggle, like a music box with its key turned too fast.

The road to the estate took a circuitous route. They trailed through the town, the driver sounding his horn to scatter the locals. Sarah looked sideways at the passing buildings, waiting for the beer hall, and then, from the corner of her eye, she saw the guesthouse's grubby sign on a peeling red facade. She imagined the Captain sitting on a threadbare mattress, weakened and waiting. *So far so good,* thought Sarah, although Elsa was doing most of the heavy lifting. Maybe it would all be this easy . . .

She began mapping her escape, backward from that point.

The next delay was the wall of the estate, the enormous stretch of black brickwork, topped by barbed wire and unfriendly crenulations, a monster ready to swallow Sarah whole. She hoped that the other side was less intimidating, and that a wall designed to keep people out would prove unable to keep her in.

They came to the entrance, and Sarah felt a familiar fear. There were crisp black-and-silver uniforms on show, but the soldiers in their drab forest camouflage unnerved her the most. They lacked the pomposity and arrogance of the officers. It seemed inconceivable that one of them wouldn't turn and see the dirty Jew for what she was—a cuckoo in the nest. Sarah imagined them pointing and screaming at her. Willingly walking into this place was like a rodent climbing into the mouth of a snake.

Run. Flee! Get out while you can.

She rubbed her forehead to conceal her face, then stopped. This was no different from Rothenstadt, she thought. These soldiers were no less zealous than the Ice Queen, and she had made Sarah one of them.

Through the first checkpoint, the car drove the winding, zigzag path of concrete blocks toward the gate itself. Elsa wittered on, pointing out the prettiest, the most handsome, the "most innocent-looking," one of the many things that Sarah didn't understand.

Finally, the car emerged into a vast stretch of well-tended countryside. The wall fell away on either side, and the driveway diminished into the distance with no house in sight. The scale of it amazed Sarah. She could see fences, paddocks, animals, but no hiding places, no cover. Patrolling dogs were everywhere.

Sarah watched the barricade close behind her.

You're in it now, dumme Schlampe.

Just as rehearsed. Little Monsters on holiday.

"Look, Haller, my horse," Elsa burst out, smacking Sarah

on the shoulder. She threw open a window. *"Anneliese!* Mutti's home!" she bellowed.

"She looks . . . lovely." Sarah had no idea of the right terminology.

"Oh, she is; just wait until you see her close up. I really thought I'd lost her . . ."

"Why would you have lost her?"

"Oh, you know. I don't get to keep her unless I'm *good.*"

Elsa made the word *good* sounded onerous. Wrong.

Sarah didn't really understand other children, their expressions, their moods. She had been isolated by her mother's will, then by that of the German people. She had once found the companionship of her peers a rare treat, then an increasingly uncomfortable experience until she simply saw no one. So a few weeks with Elsa hadn't been long enough for Sarah to figure her out.

It's not enough to know your own lines, darling. You must listen to the others, feed off what they say, perceive the meaning in what they don't. That's how to perform.

I don't do people. I told you that.

People are simple. They desire. Some hide it, some don't. They hurt. Some hide it, some don't.

"So, have you been good?" Sarah tried to joke, feeling the clumsy intention in her words.

Elsa looked at Sarah. *Shame. Sympathy. Disgust.* "Yes. Yes, I have."

The house rose over the brow of a hill. It was huge, bigger than Rothenstadt, larger than many government buildings in Berlin. Sarah marveled that any single family could live in such opulence. The central house was classical in style, the entrance flanked by columns and a portico, with grand steps up to the double doors. On either side, newer wings had been added in increasingly aggressive and modernist styles, until, at the fringes, utilitarian concerns had swallowed the art entirely, leaving concrete bunkers and iron sheds. Behind it, an ornate greenhouse almost dwarfed the house itself.

As she often had cause to notice, Sarah wondered that there might be *one people, one leader, one nation*, but there was still another, more privileged Germany.

A servant with white gloves opened the car door before Sarah could reach the handle. He offered a hand to help her out even as she scrambled on her coat. The gravel Sarah stepped onto was deep and gave underfoot. *Thick*, she thought. *Expensive.* Another servant was replying in hushed tones to Elsa's chatter, and others busied themselves with the luggage. The house loomed over Sarah, recalling the beast-like visage of the school. Yet this one was spotless, polished, and well cared for. It was a predator of an entirely superior kind.

"Come on, Haller, let me show you the place," shouted Elsa, already skipping up the stairs.

The hall was a palace of white marble. Two enormous staircases rose up, around and over Sarah's head, their black iron banisters an intricate set of spirals and flowers. A life-sized portrait of the Führer dominated the room, and underneath it, lighting a pipe, was Hans Schäfer. His face was alive with humor, lit by recognition. He couldn't have looked less like the evil scientists of the movies. If anything, Sarah felt like the predator, coming to his house with an ulterior motive.

"My dear, welcome home." His voice was soft and friendly.

"Father," Elsa replied quite formally, curtseying in front of him. He bent down and put his arms about her, kissing her cheek.

"And whom do we have here?" He straightened up, hands on his hips, pipe in mouth.

"This is Ursula Haller," Elsa pronounced with pride. "Third Year *Schlafsaalführerin* and winner of the River Run."

"A Third Year? The winner? Goodness me," he enthused.

"Heil Hitler." Sarah saluted.

"Oh, we don't stand on ceremony here, Ursula. The Führer is secure in the knowledge of our support. Besides, it gets really dull: Heil, Heil, Heil, Hitler, Hitler, Hitler, Sieg Heil, Sieg Heil . . ." He saluted over and over with an increasingly comedic voice.

The girls laughed. This was going to be so much easier than Sarah thought.

"So, you have done well," he finished.

"Thank you," said Sarah and Elsa together.

"Well, dinner at eight. Dress up, please—there are surprises for you both in your bedroom, Elsa."

Elsa clapped her hands and then, after quickly curtseying,

ran up the stairs. Schäfer beamed at Sarah and cocked his head after his daughter. *Go on*, he meant. Sarah smiled, a real joyful thing that spilt out of her face and made her cheeks ache. It felt strange. She skipped up the stairs after Elsa.

The carpets were thick. The door handles were golden. The picture frames were dusted and polished. The light shimmered from crystal chandeliers with a million captured rainbows. Sarah chased Elsa down the corridors, up the stairs, around the corners, and finally through a doorway into a room the size of Sarah's first apartment in Vienna. To be here, with permission, to experience such luxury, triggered long-dormant memories of Sarah's past. It was intoxicating.

On the four-poster bed were two large white boxes. "Let's open them together—this is yours. You ready?" Elsa grinned. "Three, two, one, go."

The box seemed to suck the lid back down as Sarah pulled at it, and she had to push her fingernails under the edge to heave it off. Revealing a nest of tissue paper, she peeled the top layer away.

Inside there was what looked like a bolt of dark green silk that gave with a rustle. It was a ball gown, a soft, cool, and lavish creation that whispered luxury and extravagance. There seemed to be enough material for many normal dresses, yet the silk fabric felt light, almost buoyant. It was something an American film star would wear.

Sarah knew nothing of fashion, but what she held in her hands was clearly a work of art. She felt too grubby to be touching it, but it had the power to change her.

"Will it fit?" she gasped.

"Of course it will. It was made for you." Elsa was holding the exact same dress to her chest. "We'll be like twins."

Sarah looked at the taller, more womanly creature next to her. "I'll probably spill something on it. I can't wear it."

"Then spill something on it. Spill everything on it! It doesn't matter. It's yours to ruin."

"I can't accept this." The polite phrase belonged to another lifetime, when things could be refused.

"Shoes, too," Elsa pointed out. "What, there were no balls in Spain? Come on, let me show you around before dinner."

As they approached the stables, Sarah noted that the bunkers and greenhouse hadn't been on the tour.

"So what's in there?" she asked, waving in their general direction.

"Father's stuff." Elsa dismissed the subject. Then she added, "The greenhouses were my mother's obsession. Everything is dead now."

Sarah waited a respectful moment. Clearly this was the part of the house that she needed to see. She might not have another chance to raise the subject.

"Why are there so many guards? What are they protecting?"

"I don't know. Whatever he's got in there, I expect."

Sarah couldn't understand Elsa's lack of inquisitiveness. "Aren't you curious?"

"I don't bloody care, Haller," snarled Elsa.

Sarah walked alongside her in silence. "Sorry," she said eventually.

After a moment, Elsa carried on. "Look, there she is! There's my baby." She broke into a jog and then a run for the stable doors. A jet-black mare was being led inside by a stable hand. The horse turned to the noise of Elsa's feet and then, when she saw her, let out a fulsome whinny, bucking and refusing to follow the boy. "There you are." Elsa buried her face in the mare's neck. The horse nodded and blew her approval. "See, Haller, *this* is a horse." She smiled, and this time her eyes smiled, too.

"Miss, she has to get down for the night," interrupted the boy in a thick country accent.

"Of course. Tomorrow, my love, tomorrow." Elsa released the mare's muzzle and gave her a gentle shove. She moved away as if ordered. Sarah saw the light leaving Elsa's face.

"She is pretty," Sarah said, struggling for the right words.

"She's more than pretty." Elsa turned on Sarah. "I'm *pretty. Pretty* is nothing."

She strode back to the house, leaving Sarah alone in the gathering gloom.

"This dress has no *back*," Sarah moaned, looking over her shoulder in the mirror.

"Are you worried about the whip marks? You can barely see them. Besides, they're like dueling scars. You should be proud."

"No, the dress is *missing* a whole piece."

"Silly, that's the style. You look like Carole Lombard."

"I look half-dressed." Sarah scowled at the mirror. The cinched waist and the extra material in the cowl neck gave her the shape of an older girl. She seemed painted in green light, and each little curve had a tiny halo of silver stars. She felt a pang of realization: that what she was looking at was more than the sum of its parts, that it was somehow appealing. She didn't know what to do with this knowledge, so it sat at the top of her belly and fluttered like a trapped moth.

As she looked at herself, Elsa tousled Sarah's hair, wrapping, twisting, braiding, brushing. It made it luscious, luminous. It also made it identical to Elsa's own. The two stood side by side in matching dresses, like two nested *matryoshka* dolls.

Elsa hummed. "Pretty enough," she said with a sigh.

TWENTY-SEVEN

"MY, DON'T YOU both look beautiful."

Hans Schäfer stood at the far end of the table in a dinner jacket, at the center of an array of silverware and crockery. At first Sarah thought he was polishing everything, as she had often done in the springtime with the maid when she was little. Then she realized they were expected to use it all. There were three chairs, so there were to be no other guests.

The dining room matched the rest of the house. It was almost as big as the hall at Rothenstadt, with a ceiling so lofty that it couldn't be seen without hurting your neck. The walls were filled with portraits of disapproving relatives and their horses.

Footmen guided the girls to their seats.

Sarah felt exposed. Her dress felt too fine, too figure-hugging. Now that she was apart from her double, it didn't feel like there was enough material between her and nakedness. She felt watched. Looked at.

Professor Schäfer pulled out Sarah's chair, then his daughter's.

"You look tremendous, really. It must be a relief to be out of those uniforms, I expect?"

"Oh, yes, Father."

"There's something to be said for all looking the same, though," said Sarah.

Shut up, dumme Schlampe.

"Why would you say that, Ursula?" the professor asked.

"We're *ein Volk*, one people, rich or poor." She felt there was something amiss with the Schäfers' attitude, or with what it should have been.

"You're an excellent National Socialist. I'm pleased. But here, well, this is a place of learning, of science. We make a huge contribution to the Reich. So we may also enjoy the fruits and rewards for our work," he pontificated. "That's fitting, don't you think?"

Sarah thought it was hypocritical, but said nothing.

Elsa changed the subject. "Ursula's father flew in Spain with the Condor Legion."

"Then you yourself are worthy of reward," he enthused. "Did he fly in Poland, too?"

"I'm sorry to say he was killed in Spain," Sarah said quietly. *Take that.*

His face changed immediately, showing guilt and then sympathy. He reached out and took her hand. His was warm, and he smelled of good soap and a touch of musky aftershave.

"I'm so sorry, little one." He sounded bereft. "You're too young for that to have happened."

You have an advantage. Push it home. Cry. Cry now.

"Is it not a worthy sacrifice for the Reich?" She let her voice crack just slightly.

"No one so sweet should have to suffer so." His voice was soft and comforting. "Not for anyone." No adult had been this caring toward Sarah for many years.

Sarah drew a brave smile on her face. He patted her hand and didn't let go of it. She accessed a shaft of her real loneliness and grief, then rode its dark troughs and cold peaks, allowing his unexpected warmth to point to a brighter, less dismal destination in the range of her misery.

She looked over to Elsa. *Shame. Sympathy. Disgust.*

"Well, for sadness, God created wine." Professor Schäfer gestured to the footman. "The Führer himself does not partake, but he has an extensive cellar for his guests, as I myself have discovered," he boasted, before he smiled indulgently at Sarah. "So this bears the stamp of approval of the highest authority, *Fräulein.*"

"I'm too young for wine, surely?" Sarah frowned.

"Nonsense. In Paris children drink wine every day."

"Aren't the French degenerates?"

He slapped the table and chuckled. "Not when it comes to wine." He had the footman fill Sarah's glass to the top.

Elsa took a giant gulp of hers and then gestured to Sarah, who put the glass to her lips. The chilled wine was creating condensation on the rim, and it smelled not the least bit fruit-like—in fact, it reminded Sarah of her mother's breath. She overcame this and finally took a sip.

The sourness caused her to suck in her cheeks. Her teeth ached and her throat protested, but somewhere on her tongue there was the hint of something sweeter and less aggressive.

Elsa laughed. "You get used to it."

The ache in Sarah's cheeks receded but didn't disappear. It became strangely pleasant, along with a warm sensation in her chest.

The meal proceeded under the guise of a banquet, courses rolling into the room with a team of servants. There was horseradish, mustard, breads, and sausage, as Sarah's glass was refilled. The vegetables were crisp to the bite and succulent inside. Meats were juicy and rich. Fried marinated herring followed before the wine changed color to a dark, bloody draft that smelled of a wood fire and spices. There was a thick gamey soup of wild boar, stocky and warm like a hug. Sarah's glass emptied and filled as a venison sauerbraten slid down, with potatoes so creamy they dissolved on the tongue.

Sarah couldn't remember being so sated. Hans Schäfer asked her a constant stream of questions and took an interest in all her answers. While she found constantly divining what Ursula Haller would think and feel tiring, the attention was comforting. Desirable. She wondered if this was how normal children felt, living in a world that was attentive and curious.

Elsa was unusually quiet throughout.

"You've met the Führer?" Sarah asked, fascinated.

"Indeed, many times," Schäfer enthused.

"What is he like? In person, I mean."

"He is a very sweet and thoughtful man, excellent with children. But he is also passionate and loves to talk, even in the middle of movies." He leaned on one elbow, as if confiding a great secret. "I've watched one Gary Cooper movie with him several times, and he always talked all the way through. I still don't know how it ends!"

He laughed and Sarah giggled. His story wasn't that funny, but the mirth seemed inevitable, as if everything he said was hilarious. Everything seemed that extra bit shinier, tasted that extra bit better. Even Elsa's growing frown seemed increasingly amusing.

"So what do you do for the Reich, then?" Sarah assumed a theatrically serious voice. *Big questions to ask.*

"Very important work."

"Boring work," Elsa spat.

"No, really, what *exactly*?" *Secret questions.*

"I'm not sure you'd understand."

"Try me, I'm very, very clever, *a really smart little girl*. No, wait, that's a secret, shhhhh."

Hans Schäfer smiled indulgently. His face had stopped making sense to Sarah. "I study nuclear physics," he said self-importantly.

"Oh, oh, I know what that is . . . it's . . . it's . . ." *Thought gone.* "What is it?"

"Everything is made of tiny atoms, each of these atoms is made of smaller particles. They can be persuaded to change or swap atoms, to great effect."

"My uncle mentioned that once." *Careful.* "He read it in a really dull magazine he gets. One that looks like a book with no cover."

"What does your uncle do?"

Yes, what does he do?

"He makes wireless sets, *everyone* has one of his *radios*. But he says one needs to know about the latest discoveries that we could use to . . . you know, win."

"He's a smart man."

What were you asking? Really *important.*

"So, what *exactly* are those effects? And why should anyone care?"

Shut up now, dumme Schlampe.

Shut up, yourself.

You are not thinking clearly.

"It's going to change the world." He was suddenly serious.

Sarah's thoughts were like cats, darting away from her as she bent to pick them up. "Wow, that sounds exciting. Elss-sa, you said it was *boring*."

"It *is* boring. Night after night with his big machines, making tiny, tiny amounts of something you can't even touch or it'll make you sick," Elsa ranted. "It's *stupid*."

"Alas, I don't think my daughter is destined to be a scientist." He sounded sorrowful.

"All we're taught to do is hate Jews and have babies. I don't think any of us are going to be scientists," Sarah complained.

"Well, that's where the Führer and I differ. I would love Elsa to understand me better . . ." There was a sadness to his voice that cut into Sarah's heart.

"Oh, you want to understand your father, don't you, Els-sa?"

Elsa's frown deepened further. "I'm not sure I ever want to truly understand him."

Sarah looked from the fuming Elsa to her impassive father. Why would she say that? She wanted to fix it, to make her happy.

Stop talking.

She pressed on. "Well, tell me and then maybe I can explain to Elsa what you mean."

"Oh, he'll tell you, don't worry about that. Don't worry one bit."

Venomous. Really, really upset with someone.

Sarah was confused. Everything was very brightly lit but seemed to be on the other side of a piece of curved glass. Her thoughts were foggy, a little like having a fever. Her back was itching, so she began squirming against the embroidered chair.

"Let's not argue. Look, here comes dessert," said Professor Schäfer.

Into the room rolled the largest Black Forest cake that Sarah had ever seen. It filled a vast silver salver, its frosted cream sides like an alpine mountain, the cherries the size of golf balls. *Hungry. Something sweet.*

"Look, Elsa! I bet this one doesn't have rancid cream and rotten cherries."

"You ate that? That's a First Year mistake." Elsa seemed happy again. *Good.*

The cake was every bit as moist as it looked, with fruit that was tart and sweet at once and the thickest cream. When she'd finished her piece, Sarah looked down to see a visible swelling under her silk dress, a dress that—of course—had food spilt down it. She showed Elsa.

"Told you. So, Herr, Professor, Doctor . . . Schäfer, are you going to show me your experiment . . . lab . . . thing?"

"I'm afraid it's all very secret." *No! Serious voice.*

"Not fair! Elsa's seen it. Come on. Want to see." Sarah let a petulant tone slip into her voice. She was enjoying this far too much.

"Not tonight."

"Ah, you mean not at all." She slumped in her seat. Her back was hurting now.

"I think you should take her, Father. *Alone*, of course, as I think it's all really dull."

The professor watched his daughter for a few seconds, then came to a decision. "More wine first, then." He clapped his hands together.

Sarah felt as if the floor were rolling like the deck of a ship. Professor Schäfer tried to guide her.

"Stop jostling me, Professor." Sarah giggled.

This part of the building was gloomy with bright pools of light to guide the way. As Sarah weaved through one of them, he stopped her.

"What happened to your back?" He sounded shocked. He held her shoulders and examined the welts in the lamplight.

"Oh, I wouldn't let one of the teachers at Rothenstadt beat a weaker student. She beat me instead," she said grandly. *I'm a hero. A Werwolf. Shhhhh.*

"That's barbaric." He ran a finger down her back.

"That's the school you send your daughter to. Don't tell me you didn't know."

"I had no idea." His finger reached the small of her back.

Sarah squirmed and faced him, almost losing her balance. "Well, we're all really happy about your ignorance, Professor." Something had made her really angry, and she couldn't turn it off. "You and all the other Nazis, happy to see your children starved, beaten, and generally abused. Many thanks for that."

"You talk about the party as if you aren't part of it," he said in a very different tone.

Suspicion, exposure, capture. *Fix it, dumme Schlampe.*

"Well, you know—*I'm just a little, little girl.* I don't care whether—you know, our misery makes Germany great or not. I know I should, but—"

"Shhh . . . it's all right." He reached out and stroked her hair.

"Careful, you'll mess it up." The danger had passed. "Elsa spent ages on it."

"I know, it looks just like hers. Just a few years ago," he said, so softly that Sarah almost missed it.

"Come on." She bounced crookedly down the corridor. "I want to see all the experiments. Tell me what you do again. Properly, this time."

Careful.

Why? This is working!

Something . . .

Professor Schäfer caught up with her as she reached a thick steel door. A sign on it read *Zutritt verboten.*

Sarah had nearly walked into the guard sitting on a stool next to it, only seeing him as he shuffled to his feet and saluted.

"Good evening, Max, and merry Christmas," Professor Schäfer said, returning the salute.

"Merry Christmas to you, sir." He was deferential and cautious.

Schäfer produced three keys and opened three locks, top, middle, and bottom. "Are you off tomorrow with all the others?"

"Yes, sir. You'll still have the perimeter, obviously."

"Well, give my love to your family."

"Yes, sir."

Sarah grew bored and hopped from leg to leg. She thought she might need the toilet. The professor pushed the massive door handle up, and the door swung open.

"Sir? Are you bringing the girl with you?"

"Yes. I am." He was brusque.

The soldier fidgeted. "Yes, sir."

"You get off back to barracks, now."

"Yes, sir."

Come on, get on with it.

He saluted and marched away down the corridor. Professor Schäfer turned to Sarah. "Well, Fräulein Haller. You wanted to see the science? Step into my office."

It was pitch-black. Sarah thought they had gone outside, but this place was warm like a summer evening. It must have been a vast space, judging from the echoes as they clattered down the steel staircase. A legion of competing buzzing, pumping, rattling machine noises rose to meet them.

"There is an element called uranium," he began. "It is common and can be pulled from any colonial dirt hole. If you hit it with a fast-moving neutron, one of the individual atoms will split apart."

His voice was soft and warm. Sarah let the familiar words wash over her, thinking about the Captain and the *bits, spit, split*. *He'll be so proud*, she thought. She leaned into the professor for support.

"You get two new elements, three new flying neutrons, and a burst of heat and light. A Jewess from the Institute wanted to call it fission, a dull word to describe something so powerful and violent. It's like Odin releasing his ravens to start the end of all things and calling it flap-flap."

Sarah found this increasingly hard to follow. She was getting tired. She hoped she'd be able to recall anything important later.

"Then each of those flying neutrons can hit another atom and start the process all over again. Three times, then nine times, then eighty-one times—the energy just grows and grows . . ."

They stepped off the stairs onto a rough floor, as if they had stepped into the woods. This made no sense to her.

"In fact, all it takes is for you to bring together enough uranium, with enough violence, and this reaction will just spread out like a web and every atom will split simultaneously."

"That sounds like a bomb," Sarah interjected. She felt woozy. Now she was here, she began to doubt she was capable of . . . whatever was needed of her.

"Exactly. Now, everyone thinks the amount of uranium you need is thirty tons, or something equally ridiculous." He let go of Sarah's shoulders and began turning a switch Sarah couldn't see. "Some people, like that fraud Heisenberg, think you need to wrap it in carbon or heavy water. No—all you need is the *right* kind of uranium . . ."

The lights began to flicker on.

"All you need to make that is space . . ."

They were in the enormous greenhouse. The white pillars that supported the glass domes gleamed in the faint, sickly light, wrapped in pipes and wires.

"And power . . ."

The entire structure was filled with gas tanks, pipes, and humming machines, the same huge structure repeating over and over, lining the wide tiled avenues that traveled off into the distance.

"And patience."

But it was not the vast machines that caught Sarah's attention. Between the gray steel machines, across the floors, around the columns, and in the crumbling flower beds, the greenhouse's vegetation had remained, wizened, brown, and rotting.

"Everything's dead—all the plants," Sarah whispered.

Among the chemicals, grease, oil, and ozone, there was the thick funk of death. Sarah began to feel queasy.

"You're missing the point, dear," he went on excitedly. "None of that is important. Let me show you what is."

He guided Sarah along the machines, arm around her waist, waving at different parts of the machine.

"I push the uranium gas into these tanks through a membrane, and all the good stuff separates out. The secret is the cooling. I've used the greenhouse's natural gas heating system to create electricity right here. I do this again and again and finally . . ."

Membrane . . . gas heating . . . Sarah wanted to stop listening.

They came to the end of a long row of devices. He pulled on a pair of rubber gloves that went up to his elbows and picked up a small, dull silver rock. To Sarah, it looked utterly banal.

"This is pure uranium 235." His voice lowered to a whisper. "Or as I call it, *Ragnarök* . . . the end of the world, when even the gods themselves will burn."

She took an involuntary step back, and he laughed.

Sarah felt dizzy, as if she had spun around in the center of the nursery and wandered out into the grown-ups' part of the house.

Why am I here?

To ask questions.

No, yes—but why am I allowed in here?

What does that mean? Ask your questions.

"So you'll build a bomb using this?"

"Better than that," he said excitedly. "Come with me."

He slid a wide metal door slowly to one side and revealed a laboratory, all white tiles and new concrete, shining contraptions, dials, and pipes. At one end there was a furnace and a milling machine, but Sarah didn't see any of this at first, because the room was dominated by something that chilled her through the room's heat.

It was a long black metal tube, maybe three meters long and a meter thick, rounded at the ends, with fins and a tail.

It was clearly a bomb.

It had been opened lengthways to reveal the inside. Sarah walked toward it like she was approaching a tiger at the zoo, without being entirely convinced the cage door was properly closed.

Her head began to throb. This was it, the purpose of everything. She had to tell the Captain . . . no, she had to do something herself. What was she doing here? Questions . . .

"You've built it," she managed. "Is it ready?"

Professor Schäfer sat at a bench and opened a thick and much-repaired notebook. He jotted something down.

"Not quite. If it fired now, it would . . . what would the Jewess call it? *Fizzle*. Probably like a powerful explosive . . . but very soon it will be the greatest weapon the Earth has ever seen. Only a small amount of 235 needed now." He returned to her side. "See? Here, conventional explosives fire a pellet of uranium down this tube—it's an artillery barrel, the whole thing is—until it hits this ring of uranium, here. When the two pieces are together, that much 235 undergoes a chain reaction and . . . Götterdämmerung! The twilight of the gods."

Sarah couldn't remember what he had just said. She wasn't even sure how she had gotten here. Her mouth was filling with saliva. She held on to him for balance. *Questions.*

"What happens when this goes off?"

"Theoretically? The energy trapped inside, the mass of the metal multiplied by the speed of light squared, will appear all at once. There will be a flash so bright and hot that anyone within a kilometer of the explosion will simply disappear." He stood, both hands in the air, *smiling*. "Everything within two kilometers will burst into flames. Everyone within three and a half kilometers will be dead instantly as the blast wave expands across the target . . ."

Sarah began to shake. *Questions.*

"What happens when everyone has these bombs?"

He came over to her and put his arms round her. She realized she didn't want to be touched. "No one does. Not even the Reich knows about this yet," he said soothingly. "We'll use it to destroy our enemies, and it'll never be needed again."

Our enemies. Sarah knew what they looked like. What it felt like being one.

"I bet the first human to pick up a big stick said something similar," she said without thinking.

"You're an unusual girl, Ursula Haller." He pointed at his notebook. "I just added something to my records." His voice sounded like he was singing a song. "Tonight, the twenty-third of December, I found something more brilliant and more beautiful than my Ragnarök."

Sarah closed her eyes and swayed. "What?"

"You. You are so clever—and so, so beautiful."

Sarah twisted out of his arms and retched violently, a thick, red, stinking vomit. She continued to heave long after her stomach was empty and Elsa was carrying her to her room.

TWENTY-EIGHT

THE CEILING WAS an intricate flower whose petals wove up and under one another into concentric shapes, drifting out from its center like a circular tide. It was very white and very bright, except for one dusty strand of cobweb sailing in an unseen breeze.

Sarah stretched, and a piercing ache cut through her head. It was replaced by a throbbing twinge, like her brain was wearing an undersized, rough shirt. Daylight bathed the room, but the window was too intense to look at.

She was somewhere . . . didn't remember how . . .

The door burst open, and Elsa walked in carrying a tray, dressed in riding gear.

"Wakey-wakey! I have breakfast and a remedy to cure many ills."

Sarah opened her mouth, which was dry and crusty. She smelled of vomit.

"I threw up?" she croaked. She coughed, and a bitter taste filled her mouth.

"Never has French couture been so comprehensively ruined," Elsa proclaimed. "You threw up on my father, too. That suit was Italian, so you've offended the fashion houses of our allies as well as our enemies."

"Oh . . . no. I don't think I remember that." Sarah felt shame that was barely distinguishable from her nausea.

"That's why men drink wine, *to forget*. Sit up."

Sarah's body ached like a dose of flu, and queasiness rippled through her as she moved, but her head was the center of her misery; its stabbing pain consumed her. She tried to piece together the flashing fragments of the previous night, but there were lengthy gaps and an incomplete denouement.

Elsa plumped a pillow behind Sarah and placed the tray on her lap. "So, we have, in order—water, fruit juice, and a pill for your headache; milk for your stomach; fried sausages and sugary black coffee for energy; and finally, the finest cognac, now denied to the Reich by French aggression."

"More alcohol?" Sarah suppressed a heave.

"Naturally! That is how the upper classes function. It's a *Katerbier*, or as they say in the British Empire, the hair of the dog that bit you."

"Disgusting thought," complained Sarah as she worked her way along the line of glasses and plates. Elsa patted her head and stood up.

"When you're done, please bathe. You smell of red wine vomit. Then you have riding clothes on the chair. Everybody's left for Christmas, we have the whole place to ourselves, and I have to ride my baby. Brandy now, please."

The dark liquid smelled of burnt sugar. Sarah held her breath and drank it in one gulp. It burned all the way down and it brought tears to her eyes, but it delivered a vaguely pleasant buzzing behind her nose.

"Is your father angry?" Sarah asked, trying to remember.

"He is, but not for the reason you think." Elsa wrinkled her nose and smiled. "It's his fault completely, so don't worry. So"— she cocked her head to one side—"did you enjoy the tour? I get the feeling you didn't *finish it*."

"I'm not sure I remember." *Or understand.*

"Then you didn't. You never forget."

Sarah lay in the warm water and tried to remember. She hadn't been able to take baths at Rothenstadt. There was very little hot water, the baths were too dirty, and besides, it would have left her open to attack. The showers were quick, but the water in her face and mouth made her anxious, and she often found herself panicking. So this was the first soak she'd managed since leaving the Captain's apartment. But it couldn't make her feel clean.

Self-loathing stuck to her like dried vomit. She couldn't wipe it off or shake it away.

She remembered the greenhouse . . . dead plants, thousands of dead plants . . . the machines that made the *right kind of* uranium . . . something about Norse mythology? The bomb. A bomb that could make people disappear. Sarah's imagination filled in the blanks with all kinds of terrible, mission-destroying moments.

What did she do? What did she admit to?

What did she say?

I'm a smart little girl.

Did she say that? What else came out of her mouth? Were the Gestapo already on their way? Had the little girl proved herself to be an older, Jewish, British spy as she wandered drunkenly through a secret laboratory—incapable, foolish, an embarrassment?

The water was beginning to make her feel uneasy, like she shouldn't be in it. She gripped the sides of the bath.

There was something else, something important. Something that didn't make sense at the time. What was it?

The *notebook*. His notebook, the tattered, much-repaired notebook. It had his notes and thoughts.

She wondered about the sabotage part of her mission. Clearly the Captain had no idea of the scale of what she'd find. There had to be a million ways of breaking the apparatus, but realistically there was very little she could do to make it go away. And it had to go away. Sarah felt this very, very strongly, especially now Professor Schäfer had been good enough to show her everything. But the notebook, that was something she could do—

"HALLER! *Raus!*" screamed Elsa outside the door.

There were no guards and no servants anywhere. The corridors and halls were deserted. Even the stables were empty of humans, so the horses were happy to see Elsa and Sarah. They whinnied and snorted their greetings and approval, with Elsa striding between the stalls calling out to them in turn.

"Who needs *food*? Good day to you, Thor—no, you've plenty, I *know*, harsh but fair. Freyr, what a good boy! A bit more for you later. Freya! You're going to carry my friend today, so ride gentle. Hello, Sigyn and little Loki, Christmas dinner for everyone, then . . . hey, little girl, Mutti's home, yes, I've missed you, too."

Sarah found her in the final stall, wrapped around her horse's muzzle. The mare looked at her as if she were an interloper.

"They all have Norse names. Why is she called Anneliese?"

Elsa let the horse go and fetched a bale of hay. "Here, make yourself useful." Elsa dropped the hay into Sarah's arms, nearly flattening her. "Give this to Freyr, the dappled one. Go on."

"Does that mean spotty?" Sarah guessed.

Elsa tutted as she lumped another bale into a stall. While Sarah dragged hers along the floor, she heard Elsa's voice. "I named her. Anneliese was my nanny."

"Oh, that's nice." Sarah was struggling. Her headache had returned, and the smell of dung was making her feel queasy.

"She always protected me, and Father made her go away."

"Uh-huh." Sarah couldn't figure out how the bale fitted the manger, which was almost as tall as she was. She heaved the hay up and toppled it into the cage. It stuck out like an ice-cream wafer.

What was that? About her father?

"Come on, Haller. Let's teach you to ride."

"You really don't have to." Given a choice she would rather have curled up in the straw.

"Yes, I do. I won't have you riding that mangy beast back at school." She pushed open another stall to reveal a friendly looking brown mare waggling her ears at her. "So meet Freya. She's no Arabian like Anneliese, but she's *zuverlässig*, solid and reliable."

Sarah looked at the beast. It was also fed and housed in exchange for work, so she smiled at it. *We need to stick together.*

The horse nickered.

"It's going to kill me!" Sarah screamed.

"*She. She* is going to kill you."

The two horses trotted side by side around the paddock in perfect sync. Elsa held on to Sarah as she slipped around on the horse's back. She hated *not knowing* things but hated being taught more.

"Do not pull on the reins when you're falling. Do *not* pull—*Jesus*, Haller—"

"How do I stop falling off then?" Sarah complained. This was unlike any balancing trick she had ever done.

"The mane, grab her *mane*."

"The hair, right?"

"No, the *mane,* you moron. They have hair all over." Elsa slapped her leg. "Toes up. Up!"

"Why does it matter what my feet are doing?" Sarah wanted a book, not a teacher.

"Because you need your heels to change direction, like this." She slid her right foot back, and Anneliese veered to the right.

"Don't let go," Sarah screamed as she leaned to the right. "Can't I just have a saddle?"

"No. It teaches you bad habits and it's less comfortable."

"Falling off is more comfortable?" Sarah regained her balance but closed her heels on the horse's flanks. It broke into a canter.

"Don't kick your heels together, she'll speed up. Freya! Easy, girl." The horse slowed.

"Just tell her what to do, if you can talk to the *verfluchtes* thing."

"I can, you can't, so learn the cues. Steady." The horses formed up. "Good, now you're level. Toes up, draw your left leg back." Sarah concentrated on keeping her toes up and shifted her foot down the horse's flank. "There!" Elsa whooped.

Sarah peeled left, held the mane to keep her balance with her good hand, and then straightened out. She felt her thigh muscles begin to respond, to adapt their hard-earned memory to this situation. Her inner ear began to make predictions, to provide useful feedback. This was just another piece of apparatus. *Commit to the move.*

She wheeled the horse around to face Elsa. "What do you mean by your nanny protecting—"

"Now you're riding! Look at you!" cried Elsa.

"I still want a *gottverdammten* saddle."

As the girls walked back to the house, a young SS guard emerged from the kitchen door. Sarah instinctively slanted away from him, but Elsa waited for the right moment and shoved her into his path. Sarah shrieked and staggered into the guard. He caught her arms and straightened her up. She looked up at him to apologize.

He was barely old enough for the uniform, barely old enough for his size. Sarah's mouth fell open.

"It's you," he said, amazed.

For a moment, Sarah thought of ignoring him or denying that they'd met. His name appeared in her head. "Hi—Stern, wasn't it?" she asked, polite but friendly.

"Yes, *Fräulein*." He looked confused, but Sarah knew his brain was only slow-moving, not incapable. "Are you a guest of the Schäfers'?"

"Well, obviously, *boy*," sneered Elsa.

"Of course, apologies—but I thought you were—" Stern stammered.

Sarah interrupted him. She had to get rid of Elsa. The less she knew about their history the better, and Sarah needed to be able to lie with impunity now. "Elsa, would you give us a minute? Please?"

Elsa was confused, then she winked before flouncing away. Sarah saw her hover by the kitchen door.

What did he need to know to go away?

Sarah thought of her mother. How did she move at parties? How did she behave around men? What would she say? The memories were dim and painful, but distinct enough.

Alles auf Anfang. Places, please.

"It's good to see you."

Smile, flutter your eyes, twirl your hair.

"I thought you were a farmer's daughter?" He seemed unmoved.

"I am, but I go to the same school as Elsa."

"You go to the *Napola*? Really? That's a boarding school—"

"Oh, I get to go home often because it's so close."

"It's also expensive."

"My uncle pays. He's a bit rich."

"What was your name?" He sounded like an interrogator.

Make light of it, don't accept it. He's just a silly boy.

"Are you going to arrest me?" Sarah laughed. *Now . . . knees together, right leg out, rock head from side to side.*

Then she imitated him with a deep voice. "What is your

name?" She laughed again and put her finger in her mouth.

This is not working.

Stay calm.

He smiled at her, his shoulders relaxing. He sagged out of a military stance.

"I'm sorry, I was just confused . . . These horses are very different from your nag, huh?"

Bull's-eye.

"Oh, yes, I'm not any better riding them, though." *Dumme Schlampe, you're a farmer's daughter!* "I mean, you know, I've never been very good at riding, just setting up carts and things . . ."

"You really don't sound like you come from a farming family."

Joke? Criticism? Interrogation? Sarah couldn't decide.

"That's what they say, too. They think I'm weird."

"I don't think you're weird," he said gently.

It was half a compliment, but she became breathless . . .

Beautiful . . .

She wanted to hit him, to run away. She began to hyperventilate. He was a *threat.*

"Are you all right?" He reached out to her, and she flinched away.

"Just leave me alone," she hissed, and then ran past him toward the kitchen.

He stood, hands on hips, bemused in her wake.

"You little *Metze*," said Elsa in astonishment as Sarah ran past.

"Shut up," Sarah cried.

Sarah spewed into a trough-like sink. The vomit was bitter, full of bile and chewed sausages. Elsa clapped her on the back unhelpfully.

"Jesus, Haller, I feel funny when I see a cute boy, but this is ridiculous."

"It's the alcohol," Sarah breathed, but in truth she wasn't sure. This sudden and dangerous lack of self-control frightened her. Not knowing what she'd said or what she had done, now not understanding what she felt . . . it was all potentially ruinous. All it would take was for her to use her real name or get her cover story mixed up to be exposed as a spy, as a Jew. For the Gestapo to come for the Captain sitting wounded on his threadbare mattress, so weak and alone.

She ran the taps and watched the evidence wash away.

"Come on, let's make some food." Elsa began pulling packets out of the larder. "We have to do our own at Christmas, but we don't have to dress for dinner, which is good."

Sarah pushed herself from the sink and settled into a chair by the huge timber table, watching the ingredients stack up in front of her. It was a mishmash of components that didn't quite amount to a meal. One pot of light-brown, mustard-looking paste caught Sarah's eye. The label was in English, but the words made no sense. She held it up for Elsa to see.

"What is this?"

"Oh, that's brilliant. Father brought it back from America on his last trip. It's called peanut butter. Here, smear it on bread, go on."

Sarah maneuvered some out of the pot with a butter knife and onto a *Brötchen*. It was so sticky and lumpy that half of it stuck to the cutlery and most of the rest landed on the table. The roll became soggy with oil. Sarah looked up, unconvinced.

"I *know*. Just try it," encouraged Elsa.

Sarah bit into the roll. The paste instantly stuck itself to the roof of her mouth, and as she tore the roll with her teeth, she needed to contort her tongue to pry the mouthful away. She sucked in her cheeks and went wide-eyed with the effort. Elsa slapped her thighs in amusement. Then Sarah turned the bread over in her mouth, and the gunk engulfed her tongue. She groaned as the nutty, sweet, strangely salty flavor had the run of her mouth. It went on long after it should have diminished, and even after Sarah had swallowed, there was a glorious aftertaste, with a residue to lick away and peanut fragments to crunch. Sarah had simply not known its like.

"Thath ith . . ." Sarah sucked at one half of her mouth. "Tremendous." Something occurred to her. "What was your father doing in America? I thought everything he did was all hush-hush. Aren't they the enemy?" She crammed the remaining bread into her mouth and went to work on it.

"Oh, he's got more friends there than here. America's chock-full of Nazis. If anything, they're more rabid than they are here, more . . . insidious, because they're all pretending otherwise." Elsa was scathing. "They're all too happy to give my father money for his little experiments."

"They know what he's working on?" Sarah felt cold at the idea that the bomb might not be a secret.

"Maybe. Who cares?"

"Sounds like a secrecy problem for the Reich—"

"Haller, you haven't fallen for all that *Käse*, have you?" Elsa sneered. "It doesn't matter what we do or what we worry about, it's not going to change anything. The Reich doesn't care about us, and it won't look after us either." She was ranting now. "Look at that *gottverdammte* school. No one was bothered about what was going on there. It took one of *us* to stop Langefeld. That's what Von Scharnhorst recognized about you. *Der Werwolf* isn't there to protect the Reich, it's there to protect *us*." She smacked her chest. "It's about getting ready for this whole thing to come down in flames."

Sarah felt overwhelmed by the outburst and was too tired to dig further. So she just kept applying peanut butter to bread.

"I mean, no one looks after you. That's why you're here," Elsa continued.

Sarah was putting bread to her mouth as these words sunk in. "What does that mean?"

Elsa's lips twitched. "Nothing. It means nothing. Ignore me." She pushed a casserole dish holding the remains of the *Sauerbraten* toward Sarah. "As the man says, 'Life is hard for many, but it is hardest if you are unhappy and have no faith.'"

Sarah picked up a dry dumpling before replying with more words from the Führer. "'The time of individual happiness is past.'"

TWENTY-NINE

THE SITTING ROOM was small in comparison to the rest of the house, but it was still palatial. It had a thick carpet and a roaring fire. It conjured a picture of intimacy, yet Sarah noted the lack of *things*. There were no personal items here, as if the Schäfers were, like her, just pretending.

Dominating the room was the biggest Christmas tree Sarah had ever seen. It was grander than the ones they erected outdoors in town squares, festooned with glass baubles, lights, and tinsel. It was inevitably topped by a silvered swastika, as if something so joyful could only exist under their control.

Beneath it were strewn dozens of presents, wrapped and

bowed with precision in red, black, and white. Elsa whispered to Sarah as they entered the room.

"Most of them are fake. He likes how it looks. Christmas was never the same for me once I knew that," she said bitterly. "Like a lot of things."

To Sarah, it looked like something from a picture book, a wonderful spell cast over the room by a benign sorcerer. She had always coveted Christmas and could never see why they shouldn't be able to join in, especially since her mother didn't observe any Jewish holidays, either.

They're so gottverdammte *miserable, Sarahchen, always with the atoning and the woe-ing. You're missing nothing, darling.*

Getting cross about this always seemed easier to Sarah than getting upset about anything that mattered.

"But some of them are for you, right?" Sarah asked, unable to voice the thought that occurred the moment she had seen the tree. Was there something for her?

You stupid little girl.

"Yeah, something pointlessly expensive, as if that's what matters."

Professor Schäfer stood and beamed at them both. "Ladies! Thank you for joining me. Fräulein Haller, you look much better."

Sarah needed absolution, reassurance. "Herr Professor, I must apologize—"

"Not at all, I won't have it. We all feel ill from time to time.

Science has not provided an infallible panacea, so until then we must bear the brunt of nature's occasional displeasure. I'm only sorry that your pretty dress was ruined."

"I'm mortified, I should replace it—" Was this really the extent of her humiliation?

"You can if you wish, but the dress was yours to ruin. A gift. I won't accept any form of restitution."

"That's very generous." Had Sarah got away with it, completely?

Elsa butted in. "I want a drink."

"Naturally, my dear. I'm forgetting my manners." He returned to a side table. He held up a bottle and made a theatrically sad face. "Regrettably, this is the last champagne for some time. Deliveries from France have, for obvious reasons, ceased." He busied himself with the top. "You would think that I would have planned ahead, but alas, no. My dear, shall I open it like a philistine?"

Elsa jumped to her feet and clapped her hands. "Yes, yes, please do." She pushed Sarah backward to the center of the room.

"What?" Sarah cried.

"We have to catch it! It's good luck."

"What's good luck?"

An explosive pop made Sarah jump, and Elsa backed up, her eyes scanning the air. Sarah looked up at something dark arcing across the white ceiling. She took a step back and neatly caught the cork, to delayed applause from Elsa and Professor Schäfer.

"Congratulations, Ursula. And here is your prize." He proffered a champagne flute.

"No, I shouldn't, I was so ill . . ."

"No, please, have some . . ."

Elsa went to take the glass, but he pulled away and moved it closer to Sarah.

"Erm . . ." Sarah couldn't decide if this would be repeating last night's error or if refusing would be an insult.

"Please, I insist."

"Take the bloody drink, Haller," Elsa interrupted.

Just take the drink, dumme Schlampe.

Sarah felt she had no choice. "Thank you, just one."

The professor passed a flute to his daughter and made a toast. "Ladies, to the Führer."

Sarah raised her glass, and then she watched the others drink. He stared at her and nodded as he drank.

Drink. Sarah put the glass to her lips and felt the effervescence tickle her nose. She was in the clear. With some sleep and another day to get back into the greenhouse—she could remember so much more now—she could get that notebook. Could she call the Captain? He'd be impressed with her progress . . . The liquid fizzed on her tongue and immediately disappeared, leaving a faintly sour aftertaste. She felt it in her cheeks and it brought an involuntary smile.

The professor beamed. "Come! Gather next to the tree. We

have dates, oranges, and chocolates, and, of course, presents for all the good children." His voice was soothing, and Sarah was thrilled. A gift! The espionage could wait for tomorrow.

The professor found the first present. "For my firstborn and only, Elsa."

Elsa took the red parcel and slipped off the white ribbon. She tore the paper away from a leather case, opened the lid, and made a half-smile.

"Thank you, Father." Elsa drew the necklace from the velvet and held it up for Sarah to see. It was a silver chain with what could only be a diamond pendant. Its facets winked as it swung in the firelight. Sarah wondered just how many people in Leopoldstadt you could feed and for how long with just half of what it might have cost . . . then buried the thought as Elsa looked at Sarah and rolled her eyes. *Something pointlessly expensive, as if that's what matters.*

"And for our guest," the professor said softly, handing Sarah her own white box with a black ribbon.

She was delighted. It had been so long since she had been gifted anything face-to-face that she had to take another drink to cover her blushes.

She carefully untied the ribbon and slipped a fingernail under the lip of the wrapping to peel the paper away without tearing it. It was too immaculate, too perfect to be destroyed. It revealed another leather box. Surely she wouldn't receive the same thing? She opened it.

Inside was a diamond necklace. Not a pendant, but an elaborate web of stones, almost crammed into the box. Sarah closed the lid. "I can't—I mean . . . it's too much, I can't—"

"Yes, you can. Our good fortune is yours." He laughed.

Sarah looked to Elsa. There was no envy on her face, just that look. Shame, sympathy, and disgust. All at once. The stones must be fake. Had to be.

"Let me help you put it on." The professor took the box.

"Thank you—I don't know how to thank you enough," Sarah said, going to hold her hair out of the way and realizing it was already up. She laughed at herself. She was funny.

He drew the chain around her and touched the back of her neck. She felt queasy and a little dizzy, so she had to take another mouthful of champagne to settle her stomach. *The hair of the dog.* There was that sour aftertaste again. Wasn't champagne supposed to be better than wine? It tasted like a doctor's office.

"There," he said proudly. "What do you think, Elsa?"

"I think she's the new princess," Elsa said deliberately.

Sarah couldn't see the necklace past her chin and made herself laugh trying to move it out of the way. It was very amusing, all of a sudden. Such a big chin she had! She moved it again like it wasn't part of her. She giggled.

Elsa made an angry noise and seized Sarah's champagne glass, throwing the contents into the fire. Sarah made a noise of protest.

I was drinking that! she wanted to say. *Cheeky. I want another one. No, another two.*

She tried to see herself in the polished surface of the dark marble fireplace, but she couldn't quite focus on her reflection, so she turned to see Elsa open another gift, a board game called *Juden Raus!* It was about deporting Jews. Sarah wanted to be angry but knew she shouldn't be. Why shouldn't she be angry?

"If you manage to see off six Jews, you've won a clear victory!" Sarah read from the board. "S'lovely."

Elsa didn't reply. She put the game on the floor.

"And a second present for the guest." The professor handed Sarah a much bigger box.

This time she tore off the paper. There seemed to be so much of it. Underneath was a white box similar to the one from the French couturier the day before. With difficulty she dragged the lid open to reveal a folded piece of red silk and lace. She prodded it before looking up.

"Issa nightdress?" What a strange gift. Sarah had a nightdress, although the professor wouldn't know that . . .

"Oh God," muttered Elsa.

"Yes, a very special one," he answered softly. "Like the champagne, the last for a good while."

"Erm . . . thanks . . ." Sarah felt tired. She was having trouble remembering words and wrestled with her eyes. Sleep, she needed to sleep. "I's sorry, I seem to be a little . . . I think I need to . . . lie down."

"Elsa, would you take Ursula to her room?" An order. "I think she needs to be there now."

Sarah closed her eyes, and then she was in Elsa's arms.

"Don't," said Elsa to someone. "Please don't."

Sarah mumbled an apology, not knowing what she was doing.

"Do as you're told, girl."

"Drink this, quick."

Elsa held up the mug to Sarah's lips and poured the syrupy coffee dregs into her mouth. Sarah coughed.

"Disgusting," she uttered. "Sleepy . . ."

Elsa emptied the rest of the drink into Sarah and then put her head under Sarah's arm. They hobbled out of the kitchen and up the staircase, Elsa crushing a box under her other arm.

Sarah had to get into bed. She was feeling detached. Her thoughts were trailing away, and she was forgetting things. She found herself on the landing with little idea of how she got there. Everything seemed dim and mundane, where it had been amusing and fascinating before.

Where are you and what is happening?

She was leaning against a wall.

Elsa was making her swallow something small and white. Holding her mouth closed. "Take this. It'll counteract it. You'll need it to fight."

"Fight who? Counter what . . . ?"

Elsa was crying.

A corridor.

"I'm sorry."

"For what?"

The bedroom.

The shock of cold water. *In the river, tumbling in the river.* Sarah thrashed about, panicking, and tried to get away, but something was pushing her head under the tap. Then she was free and breathing, water pouring down her neck. Elsa was holding her shoulders. "Haller, look at me."

Sarah looked but didn't see. There was a smack, a dull snapping pain on Sarah's face. Elsa had slapped her. *Why?* Sarah looked at her and saw fear, pain, shame, sympathy, and disgust.

"You have to fight, even if it makes no difference, you understand? It makes it easier afterward."

Sarah's head grew cold. Elsa's words didn't mean anything.

"I'm sorry." It was the softest, warmest, and sweetest that Elsa had sounded, but also the saddest. She touched Sarah's face.

Then Sarah was alone in the darkened room. A spark of life arced within her brain. It babbled of trouble, of danger. She couldn't find anything to connect it to. She couldn't find her luggage. She needed to lie down. She needed to be careful. She needed to fight. Her riding clothes were tight and uncomfortable. The boots hurt. She sat on the bed and struggled to get them off her feet. She needed something to wear. Where were her clothes?

Wake up.

Sleep.

Wake up.

She peeled off her riding gear and looked for her luggage again. Somebody knocked on her door.

"Elsa?" Sarah called out. She realized she was naked and this was wrong. She found the twisted shape of her jodhpurs on the floor confusing, so she pulled the nightdress out of the crumpled box and held it in front of her.

"Ursula." A man's voice. "Can I come in?"

Sarah needed to be dressed. She shuffled the nightdress on over her head. It got damp as she pulled it over her wet hair. She had a moment of clarity.

Why is he here?

She realized that she did not want Professor Schäfer on her side of the door. At all.

"I'm going to sleep," Sarah shouted.

"Please, just for a moment," he implored.

"No." Sarah felt the power of the word. It gave her strength. Her brain was crystallizing. The fragments were coming together. Something was happening, more dangerous than being a Jew at a *Napola* or being a spy in a bomb laboratory. She had to wake. To fight.

The door opened, spilling light into the room. His silhouette filled the space.

"What do you want?" Sarah kept her voice level even as her terror grew.

Show no weakness. Fight, dumme Schlampe.

Schäfer closed the door behind him. "Still awake? That's good. I worried you'd be asleep already."

Sarah felt her consciousness rise slowly from the mire, pulling away the tendrils of fatigue. She saw the pieces of the evening's events and began to assemble them.

Sarah put all of her concentration into her voice, clinging to this one certainty. "Please go away. I want you to go away."

"I don't think you do," he teased.

Sarah took a step back and hit the foot of the bed. She sidled along it until she reached its edge. "Yes, I do."

"Then why are you dressed like that?"

What am I wearing?

"I couldn't find my clothes," she explained.

"You're wearing my gift."

"I forgot. Go away." Sarah tried to pull the necklace off, but the clasp held.

"You are so beautiful, Ursula. Did you know that?"

Sarah wanted to vomit. The coming fury was like a shrieking in her ears, but it was swamped in fear. Her mind was clearing and the danger was unmasked. She could see the door, but she wouldn't make it over the bed before he caught her. She took another step back. "You said that last night. I remember now."

"How did that make you feel?"

"Sick. Frightened. I don't care."

"Oh, Ursula, that's not true." His tone was patronizing. "Every girl wants to know that she's beautiful. Desirable."

"Go—away." She wanted to scream, but would not show weakness.

Another step. Another step back.

"Elsa wanted to know she was desirable. It made her very happy."

"I don't believe that." Sarah became aware of a swollen, growing boil of revulsion, of terrible reality and understanding.

"It's true. She's sad that she's no longer beautiful to me. I'm sad."

The horror split open and doused Sarah in a disgusting knowledge of things as they were. She was soaked in appalling empathy. Sarah thought she might be sick, but every moment was precious and she needed every instant. She felt what must be Elsa's last gift passing into her blood, waking her—she couldn't lose it.

Sarah took another step and clattered into her breakfast tray. She dropped to the floor and ran her hand over the tray, looking for the plate. She moved awkwardly, but her hand closed around something sharp. She rose and held the knife out in front of her.

"Oh, Ursula, what have you got there?" he mocked.

"Get back, or I'll cut . . . stab you."

"You don't even know what to call it." He was scornful.

"I will hurt you."

"I don't think you can."

Sarah pictured herself drawing blood. She envisioned the movement—a quick stab, a rapid slash. But all she could see was Rahn's eye socket cracking, her teeth tearing through Rahn's skin, and the nightmares that followed.

"Back," she ordered.

He took another step forward into the light, revealing a face of total confidence. She gave ground again, and he kicked the tray under the bed with a clatter of crockery.

She drew back her arm and commanded it to follow through. *Now.* Now. *Now . . .*

But he was right. She couldn't. She was defeated.

He pulled the knife by the blade, and it slipped through her fingers. She couldn't hold on to it. She stepped back into the bedside table. She was trapped. Holding it up, he started to laugh. "This is a table knife, Ursula. You couldn't have hurt me if you'd tried."

He tossed it aside and reached out with a finger to touch her collarbone. It felt like an invading parasite. Sarah went cold. She didn't know what was going to happen. She did not know what it was, so she feared it.

Even now Sarah couldn't accept he had no compassion at all, that he would do this to someone so young.

"I'm just a little girl," Sarah stammered, one hated teardrop sliding down her cheek.

"I know. That's what makes it so good."

She closed her eyes.

The noise was only *pop*, but its sheer unexpectedness, its proximity, the bright flash in the dark terrified Sarah. Something hot and wet hit her face. She opened her eyes to see Schäfer twitching as he crashed into the wall and sank, gasping, to the floor. There was a hole torn in his throat, and his blood was pumping out of it in long, vivid streaks on the cream carpet.

Elsa was at the foot of the bed, revolver still raised, a wisp of smoke curling away from the shaking barrel. Her disheveled hair was like a halo against the open door.

"Elsa."

"It *didn't* make me happy and it *didn't* make me sad when it stopped, *Dreckskerl*."

Sarah felt clearheaded, as if the noise had woken her from a daydream.

"Elsa, put the gun down—"

"What makes me sad and angry is having to bring you sacrificial lambs . . ."

Sarah ignored the unfolding wretchedness on the floor, watching only the shaking revolver barrel. She rounded the bed, stepping over the choking professor.

"Elsa, it's over . . ."

"Watching you destroy life after life, like you ruined mine . . ."

"Elsa," Sarah snapped.

Elsa flinched and her face softened. "Hey, fellow *Werwolf*," she whispered, tears welling up in her eyes. "I remembered, very late in the day, that we're supposed to protect each other.

My nanny couldn't and my mother wouldn't. I thought maybe I could do things differently."

The professor made a gurgling noise and shuddered on the carpet. Elsa tightened her grip on the butt of the gun and corrected her aim.

"Give me the gun, *Kleine*. He's gone."

"I'm sorry, Haller. I'm so sorry."

Sarah put her hands around Elsa's and looked up into her eyes, so bloodshot, so wild, so sad. Sarah couldn't imagine where Elsa had been made to go, so she didn't want to judge how she'd made her way back.

"It's all right, Elsa. Let go of the gun."

Sarah pried Elsa's fingers away from the metal. The gun was warm and the grip was sweaty. She had no idea how to make it safe, so she placed it carefully on the bed. Elsa sagged in front of her father.

"Oh, Vati, what have I done?" She sat in the spreading pool of blood and began to wail.

Now would be a good time for a plan, dumme Schlampe.
Shhhh.

Elsa grew hysterical while Sarah's fractured mind looked for connections, sought answers, solved problems. She shushed her inner voices that fizzed at her. *Fizzled . . .*

The plan arrived, fully formed. With Schäfer dead, the mission had changed. If she was quick. The Captain—Sarah stopped. There were a few loose ends.

"Elsa, who else is here apart from us?"

"What?"

"There's nobody else here, is there?" Her voice was urgent.

"No . . ."

"Right, Elsa, listen to me. Get up . . ." She had to get rid of Elsa.

"What . . ."

"Up." Sarah pulled Elsa to her feet and around to face her. "You have to get out of here. Go, get on Anneliese and ride out of here. Go to the gate, tell them there's been a terrible accident, but don't tell them anything else. Just cry. Do you understand?"

Elsa nodded frenetically.

"A terrible accident and cry, got it?"

"On my horse . . ."

"Yes, *your* horse. You've earned that horse, she's your baby and you have to take her away," Sarah soothed. "Wait for me at the gate, got it?"

"Ride away, terrible accident, wait . . ."

"Good, leave the gun and *go*."

Elsa stared down at her father, who was no longer moving, blood no longer pumping.

"What are you going to do, Haller?"

"I'm going to make it look like he killed himself, but you have to leave now. Trust me. I'm going to make it all go away."

THIRTY

———

HE ACTUALLY HAD the keys on him. The three brass keys were around Professor Schäfer's neck, under his shirt and slick with his blood. The blood was everywhere—soaked into his clothes, into the carpet, across the wall in big dripping curves, on the bed, on Sarah's hands, feet, and clothes. The room looked like an abattoir.

Sarah picked up the still-warm revolver and pointed it at the back of her neck. It was just about plausible, if unlikely. She wiped it clean of their fingerprints with her nightdress and placed it in the professor's hand. She had seen this at the cinema. She hoped that it wasn't Elsa who had loaded it, because she couldn't open it to remove any prints on the bullets.

None of this will matter if you don't get a move on.

Sarah had a window in which she could act with total impunity. What had looked impossible was now possible. If she was quick enough.

She dragged on her riding clothes but left the nightdress on, as her coat was missing and the night was a bitterly cold one. Before she left the room, she turned and looked at the grotesque ragdoll next to the bed.

She could feel that a vast caustic weight had been added to her shoulders and knew that at some point she was going to have to find a way to carry it. But not now. She dragged the feelings to the box and didn't even try to lock them away—there were just too many and they were too large.

The pill Elsa had given her had raised her thinking above the fog of confusion and sleep, making everything seem clear and precise. She ran down the corridors and stairs, trying to maintain the splintered map of the building in her head. Some of the halls were lit, some were in darkness, and several times Sarah had to feel her way to a door that she hoped was there. Twice she thought she was lost, only for a gloomy corner to reveal the way. *Trust yourself, trust yourself,* she chanted, more in hope than expectation.

Finally, she found the corridor to the greenhouse, the staggered pools of light, empty guard chair and steel door. She had no idea how long she'd been searching—or how much longer she had left to work.

If she survived this, she decided, the Captain was going to buy her a watch.

She broke the keys from the ring and worked through them, starting with the bottom lock. It all seemed to take an age to figure out, and even when she'd unlocked the door, it swung open with comical sloth. The stairs beyond it were completely dark once again, so Sarah held on to the banister and followed the machine sounds down.

What are you doing? What exactly is your plan?

I'm going to make it all go away.

Sarah quickened her pace. Was Elsa already with the guards? Were they already heading for the house? Whatever she was going to do, she needed to do it quickly.

Her foot hit the ground. The lights must be nearby, no more than a few paces from the bottom of the staircase. Where were they? As she felt her way back to the bottom step and along the wall, she examined her shattered memory of the night before. *Trust yourself, trust yourself,* she chanted over and over.

She was about to check the other side of the stairs when her fingers found a small handle. With relief she pulled it up, expecting the lights to flicker on.

The room filled with an ear-splitting ringing. The surprise made Sarah scream. Red lights came on all over the greenhouse. She had pulled the fire alarm. Above it was the light switch.

Brilliant work, dumme Schlampe. If they weren't coming for you before, they're coming now.

She tried to turn off the alarm, but it made no difference, so she left it. She'd just have to be quicker.

As she turned on the lights, she saw a glass-fronted box fixed to the wall nearby. Looking inside, she smiled, grabbing hold of the top and kicking the front out with her boot. The glass shattered into fragments and she reached in. The ax was heavy, but she could carry it, even if the weight hurt her wrist.

She looked at the machines squatting massively among the dead vegetation. Her plan revolved around one half-remembered phrase—*I've used the greenhouse's natural gas heating system to create electricity right here*—but the hundreds of pipes and cables that tangled around them looked anonymous. Daunting. Impossible.

Think. It was an old system. It must be the oldest pipework coming into the greenhouse.

Sarah skirted the edge of the glass walls, which had been whitewashed against unwanted attention. Finding dusty, empty pipe holders, she followed them, hoping she'd find the original source of the missing pipes.

You might be following them the wrong way around. Ticktock.
Trust yourself.

One huge machine looked different from the others. It was hot to the touch, smelled of burning, and rumbled. Sarah ran around it looking for the oldest pipe, the one that fed the monster. The alarm bells howled their warning about the little girl and her ax.

Out of the ground came one old, painted metal pipe that was

topped with a giant valve. Connected to this was a new and shining steel duct that snaked into the generator. There was even a whiff of gas escaping from the seal. The beautiful logic that had brought her to this place filled her with the urge to laugh.

Putting the ax on the floor, she started to undo the butterfly screws around the connection. They were well-oiled, so they slipped off easily. As each screw dropped onto the floor, the smell of gas grew stronger. Finally, the ducting came loose and the gas roared out of the valve. Sarah was nearly blown over by it and was made lightheaded. Holding her breath, she retrieved her ax and made for the lab, the starving generator shuddering behind her.

Had she had more time, she would have tried disabling the individual machines. But with the alarm summoning the guards, she would have to be more creative. She slid the heavy laboratory door to one side and turned on the lights. The bomb squatted in all its obscene majesty on its red steel throne, flaunting its inner workings. The mathematics of horror.

There will be a flash so bright and hot that anyone within a kilometer of the explosion will simply disappear. Everything within two kilometers will burst into flames . . .

Sarah did not lack for an imagination. She watched this horror unfold across the Berlin she knew, the Brandenburger Tor to Potsdamer Platz gone, and everything and everyone from the zoo to Alexanderplatz on fire. Sarah started to feel ill again. She had to make this go away.

She ran over to the workbench. The professor's notebook

sat on top of a pile of technical drawings next to his pipe and lighter. Folding up as many of the drawings as she could, she crammed them into the notebook before stuffing it into the waistband of her jodhpurs. Then she took the lighter and lit the corner of the remaining papers, watching them blacken and curl and spread. This was her matchbook and cigarette.

The bomb sat and mocked her. She assessed the design, trying to remember what Professor Schäfer had said. One fragment remained, clear as day: *If it fired now, it would . . . fizzle. Like a powerful explosive . . .*

There had to be a way of activating it, and there had to be a way of getting to safety afterward—otherwise, who would arm it? A plane would need enough time to fly away. She pictured the sparkling fuse of a movie comedy bomb as the comedian tried to get rid of it. She scanned the electrics, looking for something recognizable, seeing only an egg-noodle dish of wires.

Then she spotted the disk attached to the side of the explosives. It had tiny graduations marked into its surface, like a clock . . . like a clockwork egg timer. There was a screwdriver groove in the center. She rotated it with a fingernail and clicked it to its maximum limit. She had no way of knowing how long that would be.

What if he's finished it? What if it goes off properly?

Then it'll all be gone. Won't it?

Sarah realized that she might not make it.

She feared being captured or exposed, living as a prisoner,

hunger and pain, but death? Sarah had little, no, nothing to lose. Maybe the Captain would mourn her, but she suspected a successful mission meant more to him. She thought of the husk of a girl that Elsa Schäfer had become, and she realized, for the first time, that there were things worse than dying.

She felt lighter. The bomb, the little girl trying to detonate it, the Reich, the war, the predatory men and the vicious teachers, the innocent young soldiers, the workbench beginning to catch light behind her . . . it was all absurd. A long joke awaiting a punch line.

Give them a punch line.

She found a ribbon on the bomb that read *Remove before flight.* She pulled at it and a long pin came loose, freeing a switch, which she pressed. Then she noticed what looked like a small car battery that hadn't been connected, next to cables that ended with bare copper wire. She'd started up a car before, so she began to attach them.

The shock threw her backward, like a kick in the chest from a horse. She hit the concrete floor and lay, trembling. That would be an ignominious end, she thought. Not at all worthy of the effort she'd gone to. No, she wanted a better punch line than that. She climbed to her feet, breathless, and looked into the bomb. She nearly missed it over all the noise, but the egg timer inside the bomb was making a whirring sound. It didn't seem to be moving—or was it? She watched and watched until she was sure.

Any more reasons to stick around, dumme Schlampe? Run.

There was a flash and a wave of heat like someone had flung open an oven door. The fire from the workbench had spread to a shelf of chemicals. Each container was exploding and spreading its burning contents across the lab. It was deeply satisfying for Sarah, who couldn't have asked for a better fire, but it was definitely time to go.

She ran for the greenhouse, but as soon as she was out of the lab she was met with a thick wall of gas. Too much, too soon, too near the fire. She couldn't run through it, holding her breath. She felt a trap closing round her. *No, not like this.*

He'd have a fire escape, wouldn't he?

She looked back into the lab and spotted a small white door in a corner that she'd overlooked. She retreated into the burning lab and carefully pushed the steel door closed, expecting it to spark any second.

What if that's a cupboard, dumme Schlampe?

It says AUSGANG *on it.*

You're lucky.

The room was filling up with smoke, and as she ran to the white door, holding her breath, tears streamed from her eyes. Behind the white door was a short corridor and a second door. The air was cool and clear with a cold draft. She was nearly out. This was going to work. She had done it. Little Sarah had, against the odds, carried out her mission. She barreled down the corridor, seized on the handle, and turned it.

This door didn't open.

She rattled the handle desperately as the smell of burning slowly filled the air. Her throat caught, and she tried to swallow down the irritation. She leaned back and kicked the door. The wood splintered, but it held. Sarah coughed, a long, hacking dry heave, and it took her a few seconds to inhale. She was an animal in a trap. She wanted to howl and cry and scratch and hit things, to throw her body against the door.

Think, dumme Schlampe!

There was no key hung nearby. It wasn't in the lock on the other side, and she had nothing to pick the lock with. She couldn't go back. Looking down the corridor, she could barely see the open white door to the laboratory at the far end. Holding her breath, she ran back and slammed it shut against the smoke. Then she turned around.

The exit door was maybe a few centimeters thick. Sarah decided she wasn't going to die on this side of it. She powered into a sprint, and, closing her eyes, she crashed screaming, shoulder-first, into it.

She bounced off the wood and landed on the ground, pain surging through her shoulder. The air was clearer here, so she stayed down on the painted concrete as the black smoke rippled across the ceiling.

All her fearlessness began to ebb away like the retreating tide. Whatever Elsa had given her, its effects were drifting off, leaving a scared little girl behind.

Mutti, she thought.

What are you doing?

I don't know anymore. I thought I wasn't afraid of death . . .

Then why are you lying on the floor?

Because there's no way out.

Didn't you have an ax, darling?

Sarah sat bolt upright. *Dumme Schlampe!*

She got onto all fours, gulped down some clean air from the floor, and then, crouching, ran back to the lab.

The lab was now pitch-black and hot as a furnace. She could only keep her eyes open for a moment at a time, so she moved blindly, adjusting her direction every so often as she got off track. The pressure in her lungs grew. She was still maybe half the distance from the bomb when the urge to exhale rose, a primal need that she could barely fight.

Just get to the ax.

She allowed a little air to escape through her nose, and that seemed to placate it temporarily.

She bumped into the bomb a few seconds later, burning her arm and falling to the floor. She scoured the floor around the bomb with her hands, her eyes tightly shut. The bomb, the gas, the smoke, the guards, the fire, and now her own body—everything was conspiring against her. *There are so many ways this could end*, she thought. *Just keep putting one hand in front of the other. Commit to the move.*

The hot floor was becoming painful to the touch. *Exhale.* Sweat drenched her clothes and began to drip, sizzling, onto the concrete. The air hurt her skin. She was being cooked, like a chicken. Not much farther now. *Commit to the move.*

She touched something that was searing hot, and she snatched her arm back. *Exhale.* Casting her hand behind it, she found the wooden shaft, but it was too warm to hold. She tore at her bandage, unwrapping it from her wrist. She wound the material around her hand so when she lifted the ax it no longer hurt her fingers.

Breathe out. Her skin felt tight. Her head throbbed as pressure built up behind her nose. She rounded the bomb and opened her eyes to find the door. They stung like someone had rubbed pepper into them, so she closed them immediately. *Breathe out now.* She tried to run, but she was losing her balance. Her limbs ached. Her skin was blistering. The pressure in her chest grew until it was all she could think about, the pain that seemed to start in the very center of her head and was pushing out through her eyes . . .

She breathed out noisily and immediately inhaled.

The air seared her throat, and she choked. She fell forward . . . and through the door. She crawled the last meter and kicked it closed against the blaze. Turning on her stomach, she breathed what little fresh air there was from the centimeter above the concrete. She coughed violently but felt the clean air reach her lungs.

Made it.

No, last lap. Get up.

She pushed herself forward like a centipede, resting, breathing, recovering, before the final effort.

At the door, she took a series of sooty breaths and tried to open her eyes. They still stung, but she could make out the frame and the lock. She climbed to her feet, her lungs already screaming.

She'd never swung an ax before. The first try hit the wall and tore away a hefty section of plaster. The second hit the door in the middle and tried to eat the blade. After wrestling the ax back into her hands, Sarah knew she had maybe two strikes left before weakness or smoke overcame her. She went for accuracy rather than power and hit the lock dead center. The door splintered, cracked, and with one last kick, it swung open. Frozen fresh air poured into the corridor from the outside, and Sarah took a deep, cold, and painful breath.

Now. Now I've made it.

"Are you all right?"

Standing in front of her was Stern.

THIRTY-ONE

SARAH LEANED ON her ax, panting. Covered in sweat-caked soot, face flecked with dried blood, and hands blistered, she took a quarter of a second to decide his fate. He wasn't expecting an attack—she was just a girl. He wouldn't be able to defend himself by the time he overcame his surprise. One swing and she would be safe.

Then the thought was gone. If she couldn't kill Schäfer, she couldn't kill this boy.

Instead, she screamed and pointed back down the corridor. "He's killed himself! He tried to kill us and then he shot himself!"

"Who? The professor?" Stern's young face worked through it all.

Sarah had only a few seconds. She moved past him, the ax bumping along the ground next to her. She pointed back down the corridor. *Look there, don't look at me.* Her irritated eyes produced tears easily, but she wasn't sure whether they were real or not.

"He set fire to everything and then shot himself. It's all going to explode, we have to leave, now!" She tugged on his arm. *Look at me now.* Another tug. Sarah was now on the other side of Stern. If he tried to grab her, she could outrun him.

Then she realized: She was free. He was not.

Stern looked back down the corridor. The far end was a wall of red sparks and black smoke playing along the frame of the inner white door. He needed to see for himself, to figure it out in his own slow but sure way.

"You really have to come *now*," Sarah cried. The real feelings that she'd kept in check—she could feel them bubbling over. She allowed a small sliver of terror loose.

"If you go in there, you'll die," she yelled. "Come away—now!"

If she couldn't make him believe her, if she couldn't make him *want* to come with her right then and there, he was going to die anyway. She might as well have hit him with her ax.

Don't be the man. Don't be responsible. Be the boy. Run away.

"I have to see what happened—fight the fire."

"I *told* you what happened." She was sobbing now and pulling on his arm. "You can't stop it, all his chemicals and *things...*" Sarah pleaded with her red-rimmed eyes.

Take my hand and run away with me.

He straightened up, and Sarah's heart sank. He wasn't a boy from Dresden. He was a soldier. The enemy. The *Schutzstaffel.* The most hated of all enemies.

"I'm going in," he said, pulling a handkerchief from his pocket and covering his mouth. "You wait here. You'll be quite safe."

Sarah nodded through her tears and let him go. She swallowed the next sob, hefted the ax up over her shoulder, and ran. Now that she was an executioner, she might as well look like one.

Inside the darkened kitchen, she found what she was looking for. The coat was still on the hook. It must have been Elsa's, because it felt expensive, even if it was too big for Sarah.

She was about to leave when she spotted a shape among the shadows on the table. She grabbed the peanut butter and stuffed it into a pocket.

The stable door was wide open, and Anneliese was gone. Good—at least one life wouldn't be on her conscience. She had trouble telling the other horses apart, so she stood in the middle and called Freya's name.

The mare trotted to the gate and looked out of the stall.

You again.

Yes, me.

Sarah advanced slowly, hands up. The clock might have been ticking, but Sarah ignored it. "We have to get away, and I'm not sure you'll make it if you stay. What do you say, huh, Freya girl? Will you carry me out of here?"

The horse's ears went back as Sarah touched her muzzle, but she didn't rear or try to get away. She had no bridle, no reins. Sarah doubted now whether this would work at all, no matter how gentle the horse. Maybe she was better off just running.

She put the ax against a pillar, put her boot against the gate, and carefully climbed to its top. Freya took a step away and shook her head. Sarah kept her voice level. "No, no you don't, girl. You're the goddess of war, right? Don't get scared of me now."

Pushing the gate out, she swung a leg over the horse and reached for the mane. Her hand closed on the thick hair, and she began to haul herself onto Freya's back.

There was a flash and then an almighty bang—the sound of a million windows being blown out and glass hitting metal. A moment later the blast shook the shutters and gates. Freya reared and screamed. Sarah fell from the top of the gate but landed on the horse's sloping back, clinging on by her handfuls of mane. Freya kicked off and out of the stable at a full gallop with Sarah suspended on one side by her left leg. She watched the doorframe speeding toward her and could only close her eyes. She felt the wind of the passing wooden beam and something graze her hair.

"Easy, girl! Easy! Whoa, stop!" she howled as Freya tore through the paddock. Sarah made one final effort to pull herself onto the horse, her fingers screaming and her aching leg acting as an anchor. Finally, she leaned over Freya's neck and slid into the space between the barrel and shoulder. "Now, now we can—"

Freya leapt over the paddock fence in one graceful movement. Her neck hit Sarah in the face on the way up, and at the zenith of the jump, the girl nearly slid off. But Sarah's fingers stayed strong, and as Freya's front legs thumped into the turf, she was, more by luck than judgment, in the right position to ride the impact.

The horse didn't stop on the other side. She just kept galloping into the dark and ignoring Sarah's pleas and kicks. Sarah held on and looked back at the house, silhouetted in fire, with a jagged shape where the greenhouse had been. A column of smoke was billowing black into the cloudless indigo sky. The house itself seemed relatively undamaged. They would find Schäfer's body. She was hoping it would vanish, and not just because she doubted they'd believe the suicide story. She wanted him to disappear. Had the bomb triggered the gas explosion? Or had the gas explosion triggered the bomb? Had it gone off at all?

Freya hit the driveway and swerved. This time Sarah rode the movement and kept her balance. *It's just a floating edge, a balance beam—it's heaving, but it's three times as wide.* They were heading for the gate, which she could now see over the brow of the hill. Someone had switched on floodlights, bathing the guards and their checkpoint in cold blue light. She could make out figures staring at the plume of smoke and saw headlights speeding toward her. Freya was breathing hard, and when Sarah ordered her to slow and stop, the horse responded. Sarah summoned up her crying face and waited. Would the story hold up? If his body had been in the lab it would have been better, but they only had to believe it long enough for her to escape.

The open-topped car decelerated hard over the rise as Sarah and Freya were illuminated by its lights. The officer and guards stood up and began shouting. "What happened?" "Who are you?" "What was that noise?" No one was really in charge—they were just junior officers and even more junior men. She delivered her pre-prepared panic and tears.

"The professor set fire to the house and then—then he shot himself. I sent Elsa to get help; is she with you? There was a massive explosion . . ."

The soldiers were confused and began arguing among themselves. There were more questions, but she ignored them.

"Where's Elsa?" Sarah screamed at them. One pointed back to the gate, and, with much shouting and dispute, they drove off. No one wanted to deal with a crying girl. *Easy,* she thought with immense satisfaction. She kicked Freya into a canter.

As she approached the checkpoint, she found the few remaining guards much less bemused, much more curious, much better organized. She was brought to a halt by an officer, so Sarah kicked the horse to make it rear and fuss.

"She's scared, the noise!" she hollered.

"What happened?"

"The professor set fire to his lab—"

"Fräulein Schäfer said nothing of this—"

"She's in shock—her father just shot himself in front of her!"

"Where was this?"

This one was clearheaded, asking the right questions. Sarah couldn't read his expression against the floodlights. *Never lie when you can tell the truth.* "Upstairs in one of the bedrooms."

"His bedroom?"

"No . . ." Sarah wrestled with the memory, made it tell her story. "He came into mine with his gun, drunk, said he'd set his lab alight, that he wanted to end it all . . ."

"Where was Fräulein Schäfer?"

Careful now.

"She heard the noise, came in—we tried to calm him down. He fired the gun . . . Where is she? Is she all right?" Where *was* she?

"What did you do then?"

"She was hysterical, there was blood everywhere—I sent her to find you, then I went to check the house—"

"Why would you do that?" Curious. Perceptive. *Dangerous.*

Because his work was important. Because the house was valuable. Because . . . because . . . I'm just a girl.

"Because I left my doll in his lab. I wanted to get it," she let herself whine. "Please, where's Elsa? I want to know she's all right—please?"

"One of my men has taken her to the local doctor. She needed to be sedated."

Excuse to leave.

"I must go after her—"

"No, *Fräulein*, you must stay. You were the last person in the house, it seems."

"I passed one of your men—Stern? He insisted on going into the house . . . He must have . . . must have been there when the lab exploded."

"Regardless, you must stay here and make an official statement." That was final.

No, no, no. No official questions. No paperwork.

Sarah coaxed Freya into taking a step back. She was desperate now. "Let me go and find Elsa, she needs me!"

The door is closing.

The officer called one of his men over. Freya sensed Sarah's tension and sidestepped away from the approaching trooper.

"Please, I have to go to her!"

"No, *Fräulein*, please dismount." He was annoyed by her disobedience. She had only a few seconds.

To escape she would have to gallop around the concrete barriers blocking the gate, a feat of riding well beyond her skills. Even if Freya jumped some of it and Sarah stayed on her back, there were more guards on the other side. She might get through, but there would be a hunt, people looking for her with automobiles.

The trooper reached for Freya's muzzle. The horse reared up in protest, and the trooper shrank away. Sarah shouted for him to be careful. The officer took a step forward, and the other guards were converging. Freya backed away, farther from safety, access to the gateway blocked . . .

Everything went white.

The men in front of Sarah cried out, covered their faces, and doubled over. The light hurt Sarah's eyes, but she saw a gap and went for it, kicking the bucking Freya into action.

Then the world turned red. Freya had reached a canter half-way to the first barrier when the sound hit.

It was the crack of thunder from the creation of the world, deep as a well, dense as lead. All possible noises, all at once.

In a stab of pain, the sounds of hooves on tarmac were replaced by a high-pitched whine and muffled screams. Freya staggered, reared, and broke into a gallop, jumping over the painted barrier blocking her path.

Everything moved. The horse and its rider. The guards. The barbed wire. The grass, plants, and trees. The air. Everything was picked up by an unseen hand and thrown downwind, along with every fragment of dirt, mud, ice, and dust. Even the concrete blocks scraped across the tarmac, tearing into it.

The horse landed on her side, screaming, with Sarah thrown clear into the next barricade. The roaring died down, leaving the air filled with cries of anguish, panic, and terrified whin-nying.

The gateway was drenched by a fading red light as Sarah sat up. She was in pain all over, but she didn't feel it. She wanted to look at Freya, but she couldn't. The only thing she could focus on was the rising fireball being swallowed by the darkness above the hill, becoming a black cloud that curled into itself as it filled the sky. Fragments of brick and metal began to rain down, some still burning.

Ragnarök.

The bomb hadn't gone off at all—until now.

If that is a fraction of that power . . .

Freya scrambled to her feet, flanks bloody. Sarah approached her with her arms wide, calling her name, but her voice sounded muted in her head. The horse backed off, shaking her mane. Sarah limped away, gesturing to Freya to follow. She had to get out of there, one way or another. Freya would follow or she wouldn't. Elsa was being cared for or not. Stern had suffocated in the lab or lived. The bomb was gone or there were a hundred ready to rain down on Europe. It no longer mattered to her. *Walk. Just walk.*

The guards at the barricades were picking themselves up but weren't interested in one ragged girl when there was the end of the world to look at. Sarah just kept going, keeping her mind clear of anything that could sap her waning resolve.

As she turned away from the gates onto the road, she felt a nuzzling in her back. Freya was bumping her nose into Sarah. *Bump. Bump. Bump.*

"Hey," Sarah mumbled over her shoulder. *Bump. Bump.* "How exactly do you think I'm going to get onto you?" *Bump. Bump. Bump.*

The pair shuffled along the road, Sarah unable to run, Freya unable to leave her.

The bar was nearly empty. Most patrons had long since left, but the town's more dedicated drinkers were gathered to toast the first minutes of Christmas Day. This particular evening had been very exciting. There had been a booming noise and strange lights in the sky, which had led to an animated debate.

The door opened, triggering a bell and letting in a cold draft. The discussion petered out as, one by one, the drinkers turned to look at Sarah as she passed them. She was dressed in ripped and sooty riding gear and a stained red silk nightdress, wrong for her age. Her face was burned, and her golden hair, long since shaken loose from a long braid, was matted with dried blood. She trailed a dirty bandage from her hand across the floor. Around her neck was a sparkling necklace of clear stones so thick they must have been fake.

She approached the bar, one eye twitching. "Can I use your telephone?"

The barman wanted to ask a question, but something in the girl's expression discouraged him. He pointed to a cubbyhole in the corner. She didn't move.

"I need a pfennig."

The barman again decided that discretion was the better part of valor. He fished out a coin and proffered it. She took it and hobbled to the phone.

No one talked while she made her call, but she couldn't be overheard. When she finished, she returned to the bar.

"Do you have a dog bowl?" Sarah asked.

He was intimidated, but curiosity overcame the barman. "What do you need a dog bowl for?"

"For the horse. Unless you have a horse bowl, of course, in which case I'll have that. Except there isn't such a thing as a horse bowl, *is there*?"

"Not that I know of," he said defensively.

"So I need a dog bowl, then," she said, as if explaining something to a toddler. "Don't I?"

Sarah climbed into the front seat with some difficulty. Her body evidently didn't intend to function a second more than necessary.

The Captain pulled away from the curb. They drove in silence, away from the town, down the country lanes, merging with bigger roads and highways like a stream joins a river.

"So, that's not your blood?" he asked finally.

"No." Sarah stared ahead.

"You're wearing a nightdress."

"Stop the car."

"I just asked—"

"STOP THE *VERFLUCHTE* CAR," Sarah screamed with sudden venom.

The Captain came to a halt on the side of the road.

Sarah spun around and began swinging her fists at him in a vicious, unfocused rage. He raised his hands to fend her off, but he didn't stop her.

"You *Scheißkerl*, you *knew*, you knew, you knew what he was, you knew . . ." Tears stung her burned cheeks.

"Knew *what*? What are you talking about?" he interrupted, raising his voice over hers.

"You knew about him, that's why you sent me, why you knew I could get in there—" Her voice grew more frantic, her blows weaker.

"What about *whom*?" Sarah couldn't tell if he was actually confused or not.

"About Schäfer, that he—he liked—" Sarah lacked the vocabulary, even a grasp of the concept. She realized she didn't truly know what Schäfer would have done if Elsa hadn't intervened. If anything, the ignorance was even more terrifying. "That he liked . . . you *knew*. You *Arschloch*, you knew."

"Sarah. What. Did. I. Know?" he asked gently.

"That he . . . liked to have his daughter, who was now too old for him, invite girls to the house."

He was silent. It was too dark to see his face properly.

"No, I didn't," he said finally.

"You *liar*. You're *lying*. What did I say to you about lying? When we first started, what did I *say*?"

"I didn't—"

"What did I *say*?" she screeched.

"Never to lie to you."

"Or?"

"Withhold any information."

"Well?"

"I didn't lie to you, or withhold anything." His delivery was flat. Unreadable.

"You're *lying*," she howled. She hit him again, and again, the tears turning into sobs.

"Sarah—"

"Shut up, just shut up—"

He took hold of her hands. She tried to pull away, but her wrist hurt too much.

"Look at me. Look. At. Me."

Sarah wouldn't. He waited. Finally, she looked at him out of the corner of her eye.

"I didn't know."

In the moonlight and reflected headlights it was impossible to tell if he was lying or not. As so often, his face was like a mask. She pulled her hands free.

"Do you believe me?" he asked, and for a moment Sarah thought he might be hurt.

"Do you honestly care, one way or another?"

He started the car and concentrated on the road ahead, shutters down. "No. No, I don't."

Sarah gathered her distrust like so much fallen salt and swept it into her box of horrors, choosing to ignore what had escaped. She closed her eyes and placed her head against the window.

"Wake me when we get to Berlin."

THIRTY-TWO

THE KILOMETERS WOUND down. Sarah slept poorly, jerking awake with a miserable, sapping regularity. Now the dream dogs and bullies were joined by faceless, pawing beasts that smelled of musk. Sad-eyed boys walked into a fiery hell as she watched. But Sarah defied them all by closing her eyes and starting again.

Finally, the outskirts of Berlin rose into view in the headlights. The chocolate-box sweetness of rural Germany seeped into suburbs but vanished as absurdly theatrical National Socialist architecture crushed the city.

Sarah was nearly home. She closed her eyes again because she didn't want to see it.

The Captain gently shook Sarah's shoulder. "I can't carry you."

"Why not?" she asked.

"I'm not strong enough yet."

She looked at him as if for the first time that night. His brow was sweaty. His cheeks were still hollow, and under the street-light, his skin was the color of concrete. The hours of driving had evidently been a challenge. *What if he's never better?* Her selfishness surprised her. Then her brain went quiet again: a building in which all the lights had been shut off. She let him guide her.

The steps. The mathematically perfect path to the door.

She *was* home. It was over. Whatever else was to happen, whatever else she had to deal with following the past few months, it could wait until she'd slept.

In a soft bed with clean white sheets, in a heated apartment with a locked door, with soft white bread and garlic sausage for breakfast.

The concierge was gone, a festive tree in his place. The lift sat invitingly open, a little doorway to safety. They closed the gate against the world; its predators, bullies, and psychopaths; its zealots, victims, and onlookers. She leaned against him, as he leaned against the wall.

They rose and Sarah's spirit rose, too. Everything could wait for tomorrow.

Carpeted corridors, patterned wood. The scent of varnish and clean floors. Keys moving smoothly in a well-oiled lock.

Then into the darkness within, the space lit only by the Berlin skyline as the Captain locked the door behind her. It smelled of home and oranges.

Sarah stopped dead, her senses suddenly alive. *What? What?*

"Merry Christmas, Herr Haller. *Fräulein.*"

The Captain turned on the lights.

Sturmbannführer Klaus Foch was sitting in the Captain's armchair in his dress uniform. He was cradling a Luger pistol, which he pointed at them. "I hope you don't mind me letting myself in."

"I can only apologize that I wasn't here to meet you, Sturmbannführer . . . I'm afraid you'll have to remind me of your name." The Captain walked nonchalantly to the sideboard and lit a cigarette. "However, it's late and I'm very tired. Why are you here?"

Sarah stayed still, watching, thinking, shaking her instincts back into action. It didn't feel fair. She hadn't known or prepared. She was supposed to be safe. She had suffered enough, and with the lights on, she could see it in the window. Her reflection was so small, so brutalized, so bizarre.

"I thought you were just a typical capitalist parasite, growing fat on the work of the party. But your sudden . . . *acquisition* of such a talented ward—it piqued my curiosity."

The Captain examined his eye in a nearby mirror and adjusted his hair. *He's flanking him*, thought Sarah. *But he's not fit enough to fight.*

"I'm a businessman," said the Captain into the mirror. "When the Führer wanted a wireless set in every home, he needed someone to make that happen. It didn't happen by beating up Jews or smashing their windows. I was *happy* to leave that to people like you." It was like a public speech.

He's playing for time. Sarah took a few steps to her left as Foch glared at the Captain. She rounded an armchair as if she might sit in it. Foch fished out a notebook and read from it.

"Helmut Haller . . . seems to have appeared from nowhere just after the last war. No hometown, no family to speak of, until suddenly"—he fixed Sarah with a piercing glance—"a niece. A sister I can't find, married to someone with a strangely incomplete military file. It's all *very* coincidental, don't you think?"

Sarah swayed a few steps farther to the left, as if bored. She'd taken off the riding boots in the car, so she was able to step silently on the polished floor. She was now level with Foch. He couldn't quite watch her and the Captain at the same time.

That was when she noticed it. It was covered in a spotless dust sheet, and she had assumed it was furniture piled for cleaning, but now she had realized what it was.

"My sister and I were orphans, *Sturmbannführer*. We *did* appear from nowhere." He was dismissive, as if arguing with a bookkeeper. "She is now in a lunatic asylum, a fact you can imagine I don't share at cocktail parties. As for her poor husband, if the Luftwaffe can't do its own filing, I'm certainly not to blame. Is this how the Gestapo works now? Sending former storm troopers to do the snooping?"

"Not at all. The Gestapo have apparently missed all of this," he sneered. "Typical SS, all preening and no work."

Mistake. He's come here on his own, thought Sarah. *The Captain's going to kill him, right here. He needs a distraction.*

She pulled the dust sheet off slowly at first, but it gathered pace and dropped away to the floor with a hiss.

Foch looked at her but saw nothing untoward.

"Anyway, the most glaring mistake of all . . ." Foch replaced his notebook and leveled his gun at the Captain. Then he pointed at Sarah with his free hand. "Was *her*. Ursula Bettina Haller. Until three months ago, she didn't exist. There's a birth certificate in the name of Elsengrund, and it's an excellent fake, but you're fooling nobody. She's the weak link," he crowed.

It had a large silk ribbon and bow wrapped over its lid. It was a Christmas gift. It was *her* Christmas gift.

"So you're here to arrest me?" the Captain scoffed.

"Not at all. I'm here to put a bullet in your head and take her away." The coldness of it was shocking.

Foch stood and took aim.

The Captain was too far from the gun to do anything. For the first time since the jetty so many months ago, Sarah saw in his face a cornered animal.

Sarah was standing on the ferry again, watching the gangplank rising, but there was no lake to cross this time and no choice to make.

Sarah turned to her gift. She slammed her hands down onto the keys of the butterfly grand piano, a big two-handed C minor chord with the sustain pedal down.

Foch turned in surprise.

"Do you think Gretel would be happy with this?" Sarah interjected.

He opened his mouth to speak, but no words came out.

"With me taking her place? You think if I can play the piano for you, forever, you can pretend she's still here. But she isn't, is she?" Sarah pushed, an edge to her voice.

"Shut up," he growled. The gun wavered between Sarah and the Captain.

Under the uniform, he was fragile and weak. She had to keep him talking, keep his attention. She started to play a Satie piece.

"What are you doing? Satie is—" he complained, trying to reassert himself.

"Shush," insisted Sarah. The high notes hailed a coming darkness. Her left hand marked the sluggish marching beat. It was the sound of a black and terrible thing, emerging slowly but inevitably, just behind a door. Foch kept the gun on the Captain, but he couldn't keep his attention there. "If I'm going to be taking her place, I want to do it right, so I need to know. Who is Gretel?"

Foch seemed to curl up inside himself. He listened to the piano, but watched the Captain down the barrel of the Luger.

Sarah came to the end of the first piece and moved seamlessly into the second, more melancholy melody. Now each note pushed the piece forward with a sigh.

"What happened to her?" Sarah asked softly.

Just when Sarah thought she'd lost him, he began to talk.

"When Heydrich's men came for me, I was at home. They came for everyone at home or on holiday, when they were relaxed and vulnerable. I was in the drawing room, listening to . . . my daughter . . . playing the piano . . ."

"Gretel." Sarah nodded, bobbing her head in time with the gentle rippling of the music. The Captain watched the gun, waiting for it to move, for Foch's attention to stray.

"Gretel was . . . an imbecile. She was a small child in the body of a young woman. She couldn't read, or write, and she looked . . . but she could play. When she played the piano you couldn't tell . . . you couldn't—you wouldn't know . . ."

"If you stood behind her." A great wound had opened inside her. Sarah thought she knew what had happened but realized that she wasn't actually ready to hear it. She wanted to stop, but her pity ran as deep as her hatred, and she couldn't deny Foch the confession.

"They came in through the French doors. Gretel was frightened . . . I pleaded with them—I was a good National Socialist, I wasn't one of Röhm's lackeys. I told them they were mistaken, that I was loyal to the Führer . . . and they said . . . they said . . ."

She could see him about to crumble.

Sarah began the third piece. She wanted to stop and cover her ears, but she couldn't.

"And they said, how could I be a National Socialist and let *something like that* live?"

She could have prevented him finishing his tale, but it would still have happened. She felt the horror approaching like a distant train on a quiet night, an oncoming sense of loss and regret that she could hardly bear. *Some secrets should stay secret after all,* she thought. A tear slid down Sarah's cheek, and she tried to sniff it away.

"So they gave me a choice," he said unevenly.

Sarah's playing slowed, and the tempo drifted away.

Please don't be true, please say you didn't . . .

"I could live, but I had to make a—sacrifice for the Reich . . ." His voice began to disintegrate. "Gretel was crying, she didn't understand. They gave me a pistol . . . I asked her to play . . . and she played so well, even though she was sobbing . . . I told her she was a good girl . . ."

Sarah finished. There were no more notes to play. The gun still pointed at the Captain but shook in Foch's hand as he rocked, face wet. She didn't want to care.

"And?" Sarah said as gently as she could.

"And," he whispered, "I put the pistol to the back of her head and did my duty for the Reich."

"You shot her. While she played." Sarah said this slowly.

"I was doing my duty . . ." he whispered. The gun trembled.

Not enough . . .

"You saved your skin. What does Gretel think of you now?"

Foch straightened in his chair and took aim at the Captain.

NO—

"Vati? There are men here, they say they've come to take

you away." Sarah had no idea what Gretel sounded like, but she had once met a girl whom her mother had called a "Mongoloid." The voice came effortlessly, like she'd started up one of her mother's records. "If I play the piano, will the men go away, Vati?"

"Silence!" he screamed, now staring right at her.

Sarah began playing Beethoven, something Gretel would have played. The "*Mondscheinsonate*," the "Moonlight Sonata."

"I'm playing for you—am I playing well, Vati? Why are you angry with me? Did I do something wrong?" Sarah hated him, hated having to wade into his filth, to defile the ghost of that poor child. At the same time, allowing Gretel to use her voice opened a vein of loss and misery that she couldn't control. The words tumbled from her mouth.

"Stop." Now the gun pointed at her.

"What are you doing, Vati? Please don't. Don't kill me, Vati." With the pistol aimed at her, she realized he might kill Gretel all over again. She could feel her heart pounding in her chest, but while the thought was frightening, she was swamped by the sadness of it. Tears filled Sarah's eyes and began to gather in her throat. Betrayed and deserted by a father. By two fathers.

"Shut—*up*." The gun moved slowly away. *No—*

"Why did you kill me, Vati? Why?" She let her voice fill with her own feelings of loneliness and sadness, crying for Gretel, crying for herself.

"I didn't want to. They made me," wailed Foch, looking for support to the Captain, who had frozen mid-movement.

"You didn't want to?" She let her voice sound disappointed, offended. "That makes me sad. I'm so sad, Vati. It's so cold where I am."

"I'm sorry, Gretel." He sagged down into the armchair, holding the gun up as if it was a great weight.

Sarah closed the piano lid and walked gently toward him.

"Will you hold me one more time, Vati? I forgive you. Let me show I forgive you for what you did."

"I'm so, so sorry . . ." He looked Sarah in the face. He didn't see Gretel. He just needed forgiveness.

Sarah bent and wrapped her arms around him where he sat. "It's all right, I forgive you. Just hold me. Then it'll all be all right." Sarah felt his arms close around her and something hot, like scalding bath water, splash across her face. He jerked and there was a sucking noise.

"Shh . . ." Sarah whispered. *Hold on a minute.*

The hot liquid kept sloshing onto her face, running down her neck, soaking into her stock shirt. "Shh . . ." *Just a few more seconds. Okay. Now.*

She let go of Foch, and he collapsed in front of her. She couldn't see his body reflected in the window, but she could see the Captain, knife in hand. She could also see herself, painted top to toe in Foch's blood, as the dawn sky lightened behind.

She felt nothing at all.

Then the box of horrors disintegrated, flooding its chamber, and breaking over Sarah like a wave.

She curled up on the floor, in the blood.

She wanted to cry: for the lost like the Mouse, for the ruined like Elsa, for the dead like her mother and Gretel, as well as those she had killed like Stern or even Foch. But right now she could only cry for herself.

EPILOGUE

January 5, 1940

THE INJUSTICE WAS too much. Sarah threw her head back.

"What?" she howled in frustration. "Tell me!"

The Captain opened his hands slowly to reveal one small porcelain cup containing golden foam.

"Cappuccino," she sang, and clapped her hands together in delight, before wrapping them around it. She could feel its heat through her bandages, but she stuck her lips into the froth anyway, inhaling the sweet darkness.

"There's no rush," he said with good humor.

Sarah looked at him over the rim of the cup and made an incomprehensible noise. She slurped, letting the gentle buzzing in her cheekbones and the back of her teeth play in her head as the final drops slipped away. She felt the chill of the air on her cheeks, but she wasn't cold in her fur-lined coat. Her stomach was full and tingling.

She looked around. Copenhagen was apparently unruffled by its martial and aggressive neighbor. Here you could imagine that Europe was contemplating a holiday, not already at war. The tables outside the cafés and restaurants all along the Nyhavn were virtually empty, even in the midday winter sun. It was simply too cold. This served the Captain's purposes: they wouldn't be overheard. And Sarah wanted to sit outside because the houses and boats on the canal were painted an array of bright pastels and deep colors. They had a dollhouse quality, like something from a dream. A good dream, with no dogs.

Pretty. Fresh. Full. Warm. Comfortable. *Safe.*

Sarah allowed herself to bask in the moment. Just for a second. Then she took that moment and tidied it away for safekeeping. She now had two new boxes.

She regarded the swirly pastry in the middle of the table. "Is that for me, too?"

"Yes, it's a *wienerbrød,* a Vienna bread. I thought it would make you feel at home."

Sarah laughed. "It's a *Kopenhagener Plunder,* a *Danish* pastry, in Vienna. That's what we called it." She pursed her lips. "One of these days you'll make an error like that, something you really should know as a real German, in front of someone who realizes, and then all that"—she waggled a finger around in the air—"sophisticated cover will blow away like paper. Does that scare you, Captain Floyd?"

"Would it make you happy if it did?" he proposed.

"Not at all," she replied quickly. "But the question still stands."

"I've forgotten how to be scared. It just makes me careful."

"You like it, you mean." She grinned.

"And you, Sarah of Elsengrund, do you get scared?"

For a moment the new box of horrors popped open, and a cold shaft of memory cut through her. The predatory scientist, the rain, the monster, Rahn and the Ice Queen, the bleeding, the station, the dogs, the soldiers, the back of her mother's head . . . and then it was gone. The effect was like a static shock after walking on a thick carpet. *I know what that is, so I will not fear it.* She took a moment to recover, and then all was still.

Sarah thought about Gretel, about how no one could ever make Foch's piano clean again, about the million tiny places where the crime would remain forever. Would the owners of that piano years from now smell that something was wrong with it? Would the future Germany have any evidence of its crimes? Would it smell bad, and would people even know why?

"I want to try an espresso now," Sarah said, reaching for the pastry. "Two. With more sugar."

At that moment a woman arrived. She was dressed head to toe in black, like a widow, but with a wide white collar under her coat. Her hair was tied back sensibly, old-fashioned but oddly timeless. Her face was lined, but behind her tired eyes and the dark rings around them, Sarah could see a vivid spark. She found it impossible to tell her age.

They stood.

"Helmut," the woman said, with a thick Austrian accent.

"Professor," he said, bowing. "This is my niece, Ursula Haller."

"Really? Helmut, you've spent so long lying you've forgotten how to tell the truth," the woman complained.

"Ursula," said the Captain, ignoring her. "This is Lise Meitner."

Sarah curtseyed. The professor waved the gesture away as she sat. "I'm very pleased to meet you, whoever you are."

"I'm Sarah," she said.

The Captain rolled his eyes and replaced his hat.

"A Jew. Splendid. You've grown soft. This is your new thing? Rescuing waifs and strays like me?" She laughed. It was a curious thing. "So, you had something to show me?"

"Ursula." The Captain sat. "Would you give Professor Meitner the notebook?"

Sarah reached into her pocket and pulled out Schäfer's journal. She felt a ripple of disgust and fear as she handed it to Professor Meitner, but also a desire not to let it go. She had sacrificed and suffered so much for it. She'd nearly given up . . . something greater, something she didn't even understand properly. This book was the spoils of war, the grail, a treasure. But the contents were a mystery in a language she couldn't read. It was an affront to her intelligence.

The spots of Foch's blood on its cover had faded to a dull rust, like they might just brush away. The professor opened the notebook and began to read, not with the relaxed air of someone flicking through a magazine, but with the concentrated effort of someone meeting a challenge, succeeding, and finding the solution endlessly surprising.

"I would like a pot of tea . . . and a very large cognac. If such a thing can be found," she said without looking up.

"Espresso," chimed Sarah as the Captain stood and left the table.

A gust of wind brushed her cheeks, cool against her skin. It set the boats on the canal bobbing and creaking. She made a start on the pastry, cramming the sweet flakes into her mouth with some satisfaction.

Professor Meitner glanced at Sarah's face. "Where did you get sunburned at this time of year?" she asked as she read.

"There was a fire."

The professor made a noncommittal noise. "Where is he dropping you?"

"We're going back to Berlin," Sarah answered, chewing. "He's not dropping me anywhere."

"Why would you go back?"

Sarah swallowed. "I work for him."

Professor Meitner looked up sharply. "You 'work' for him?"

"Yes, I work for him." This was a distinction that she had earned. She didn't feel like having to justify it.

Lise held up the book. "You got this? From Hans Schäfer?" she asked. Sarah nodded. "He *sent* you to *him*?"

She *knew*. The unfinished pastry sat on the plate, now unpalatable.

"Did he know?" Sarah asked after a moment.

"I didn't mention it. Why would I? I had no idea he had children on his payroll." She was ashen. Then she added, "But that doesn't mean he didn't know."

Sarah tapped her feet on the cobblestones.

Where would you go if you left him?

"He promised me he didn't know."

"You need to be very careful, Sarah, Ursula, whatever. Very careful indeed." Professor Meitner turned the notebook over in her hands and indicated the dark stains on the cover. "Did something happen to Schäfer?"

"He's dead. His lab is destroyed. That's all that remains. I'm very thorough—and careful," Sarah added.

"I see." She opened the book again, this time with more care.

The Captain reappeared with a tray and fussed around the table, laying out cups. To Sarah's eyes, he had never looked more English. Finally, he turned a seat next to the professor and sat on it backward, leaning over the chair back.

"So?"

"So . . . it's all here. The theories, experimental data, calculations. He understood it all. This even suggests he built a diffusion plant?" The Captain nodded. "A working device?" Another nod. "*Jesus Christ.* Thank God he was so secretive."

The Captain frowned and shook his head.

"He had friends in the United States whom he worked with. There's the wreckage of his house to pick over. He had guards who are now dying of a mystery disease . . . not to mention a catatonic daughter in an asylum who . . . might have all kinds of tales to tell." He glanced at Sarah, who met his gaze with a fierce intensity. She had not done this to Elsa and knew there was nothing they could do for her. But knowing that didn't give her any absolution. He propped his chin on the chair back. "Someone will put two and two together eventually."

"But for now, this is all there is?" Professor Meitner held the notebook in the air.

The Captain put his hand on her sleeve. "Lise, let me take you to England. You can have a lab, staff, anything you need." His tone was urgent, pleading. "This is your chance to stop this war before it can start."

"At what price?" She put the book down and placed an accusing finger on it. "Do you understand what this is? Do I save the Poles by cooking German children? Do I burn cities full of innocent people? What's an acceptable number of civilian casualties? Ten thousand? A hundred thousand? The machine gun didn't end the last war, Helmut. It just made it more bloody. The ends"—she tapped the table in front of Sarah—"do not always justify the means."

"This war is going to be about more than the Poles. Britain and France have no conception about what's coming, and they aren't listening. Not to me anyway. They might listen to you." Sarah had rarely seen him so animated or expressive.

Professor Meitner laughed again. She lit a cigarette and shook her head. "Nobody listens to me. A woman? Jew or Christian? I'm ignored, despised. I could arrive in England with a working nuclear device and no one would pay any attention." The bitterness landed like rain.

"I listen to you." He put a hand on her sleeve again.

"You, Helmut, are smarter than most men." She put a hand on his for a moment, then patted it, before pulling her arms away. "But trust me, that isn't what the world wants. They hear what they want to hear, what they already know."

"And if the Nazis make the bomb before the British?" he said softly.

"You won't let that happen, will you? That's your business, isn't it? Your real business, I mean." She took a long drag on the cigarette. "They probably think they need pure carbon or heavy water—deuterium oxide—and you need to make that impossible."

The professor pulled Sarah's plate in front of her and, pushing the remains of the pastry onto the table, placed the open book on it. She poured her cognac slowly onto the pages, making the ink run.

"I could have it reconstructed, you know," the Captain began.

"But you won't," Lise said, lighting a match. "One child, maybe." She glanced at Sarah. "But thousands?" She shook her head.

Sarah wasn't certain what was happening, but she didn't want to take part in this conversation. More bombs, but for the right people? Who were the right people? The ones who had left a trail of corpses behind them and a teenager strapped to a hospital bed? *The monsters who ran the country, or the monsters who battled them?*

The professor lit a match and held it over the notebook. "I'm putting the genie back in the bottle, for now." The match dropped and ignited the cognac. The blue flame danced over the paper for a few moments until a gust of wind fanned it, and with a puff of smoke, the open pages blackened and vanished.

Sarah could feel the heat of the fire in the winter air as she swallowed the syrupy golden crema, thick with sugar and with an exciting, bitter aftertaste. It was heaven in a cup.

The book was halfway consumed.

She reached into her pocket and removed a torn, folded piece of paper. She had taken it from the notebook the night she had found the page. It was a list of girls' names, with *Ursula Haller* at the bottom. The name above that was *Ruth Mauser*.

She placed it in the fire and watched it turn to smoke.

"Professor, I would advise that you don't stay in Copenhagen any longer than you have to. I'm not sure that Denmark will be allowed to be neutral for much longer," the Captain said.

"Yet you'll take this girl back to the belly of the beast?"

"She has work to do."

"Is that right, Sarah?"

Sarah considered the question, but there wasn't any doubt.

"Yes. Yes, it is."

HISTORICAL NOTE

WHEN I WAS growing up in the UK in the 1970s, the Second World War was everywhere. In the comics and books, on the TV, in the toy shops, and even in the shoe shops, where Clarks Commandos were the school shoes of choice. The war was seen as a source of intense pride. It was still regarded as Britain's "finest hour," as Churchill had called it and, well, the children of the seventies had missed out. What could we ever do that would be as important or exciting as that?

Meanwhile, my mother's best friend was German, and we spent many summers with her family. They were gracious and loving hosts, calm and helpful friends, and almost aggressively pacifist. I couldn't play spies, spacemen, or pirates—or anything involving guns—without a lecture on the dangers of violence. This made it impossible for me to accept the idea of an evil or warlike Germany at face value.

As I got older and learned more, this dichotomy grew more confusing. The details of the Holocaust and the evils of the Nazi State were revealed in all their horror. Exactly how did these gentle, sausage-obsessed people allow this to happen? The war revealed itself to be far more complicated than we'd been taught.

Thus began a life-long, appalled fascination, trying to unpick the realities from the stories and separate the propaganda from the unpalatable truths. This book is part of that.

Almost everything in *Orphan Monster Spy*, including the fabrications and story-driven exaggerations, has some basis in fact.

While Sarah Goldstein did not exist, the idea of teenage spies, agents, and soldiers is not a fanciful one. Sarah came to life as I passed a memorial mural to the agent Violette Szabo in Stockwell, London. Part of Churchill's "secret army," she had been just twenty-one years old when she volunteered to be a Special Operations Executive agent. In fact, there were resistance couriers and partisan warriors across Europe who were barely in their teens, like Belgian Lucie Bruce, aged fifteen, or Freddie Oversteegen, a mere fourteen years old when she joined the Dutch resistance. Twelve-year-old Sima Fiterson used her blue eyes and sweet face to deflect suspicion and bluff her way through checkpoints while leading Jews out of the Minsk ghetto. All the while she had a pistol in a secret pocket so the Nazis couldn't take her alive. In Germany, teenagers as young as fourteen formed a resistance, the *Edelweißpiraten*, risking violence, imprisonment, and for six of them, death at the hands of the Gestapo in 1944. The *Leipzig Meuten* consisted of groups of children and teens that were similarly crushed by the authorities. Helmuth Hübener was just seventeen when he was executed for distributing anti-Nazi leaflets in Hamburg. There are not enough pages in this book to tell all their stories.

The *Werwolf* did exist, but not as an all-girl outfit. It was a desperate Nazi guerilla force created to cause trouble once the Allies had occupied Germany. Opinion is divided as to how organized or effective the *Werwolf* was, with some scholars arguing that it was just a scary story to spook the occupying troops. As I researched, I came across a photo of a young woman involved in one of the few *Werwolf*-related actions, the grubby murder of a mayor appointed by the Allies in 1945. In her eyes, I imagined I saw a fraction of the cold fanaticism I was writing about. I saw the Ice Queen look back at me. She told me the rest.

Even when I created elements in the service of the story, I later discovered they often had a real-world analogue. Sarah needed to go to an elite Nazi school—that was part of her tale from the very start—but before I had even written anything, I discovered that the *Nationalpolitische Erziehungsanstalten* existed and were every bit as brutal as I wanted to depict them. The Napola schools were probably better run than Rothenstadt, but the idea of Nazi efficiency and organization, still pervasive today, is a myth. The Third Reich was financial disaster, built on greed, ambition and in-fighting. Its achievements were propped up by theft and slave labor, built on a foundation of corpses. Rothenstadt is the symbol of that, a place where politics and avarice meet.

For all its power, Nazi Germany's weaknesses were often a result of its barbarity. Their nuclear weapons program was plagued by setbacks and was later revealed to have never been a serious threat. The cream of German scientific talent had been decimated by the loss of its Jewish and left-leaning colleagues, with many going on to work for the Allies, so National Socialist Germany was, in part, destroyed by its own bigotry.

One of the scientists driven out of the country was the genius Lise Meitner. When faced with experimental data that confounded the greatest minds of her age, she could picture what no one else could. In doing so, she changed physics, chemistry, and the history of the world forever. She was, in modern parlance, a badass.

However, she was also a woman and, although baptized a Christian, she was from a Jewish family. Forced to flee Germany, Meitner continued to work with her colleague Otto Hahn by mail. Her Berlin team was stumped by the data they were collecting, and it was Meitner who, in collaboration with her nephew, Otto Frisch, correctly identified nuclear fission for what it was.

Hahn got wind of their conclusions and published their joint work under his own name. He was awarded the Nobel Prize for Chemistry for the discovery of fission, omitting Meitner and Frisch's fundamental contribution to his understanding of its workings. The least Meitner should have received was the Nobel Prize for Physics, but her nomination was blocked for partly political, partly patriarchal reasons.

It's not a huge stretch to imagine that Professor Meitner could have overcome the remaining challenges to create a nuclear weapon. Robert J. Oppenheimer, the future scientific leader of the Manhattan Project—the Allied atomic bomb program—heard about Meitner and Frisch's discovery, and within a few days, he drew a plan for a crude but functional nuclear device on his blackboard. Meitner's abhorrence of the concept of nuclear weapons is not fictional, however. She refused to join the Manhattan Project, and after the bombing of Hiroshima, Meitner took a five-hour walk alone. She was under no illusions about her share of the responsibility.

Hans Schäfer is fictional, but there was a rich, independent German scientist, Manfred von Ardenne, who had set up his own laboratory working with uranium outside Berlin.

Schäfer's bomb would have been inefficient, but it would have worked. Sarah's "fizzle"—an explosion where the nuclear chain reaction does not become self-sustaining—would probably not have been anywhere as destructive as I've depicted. But anyone picking over the wreckage would have gotten very sick very quickly, and at the time no one would have known why. It was Nobel Prize winner Enrico Fermi who talked about people *simply disappearing* in a nuclear blast, but it sounded like the kind of thing Schäfer would have reveled in. I've stolen a lot of phrases like that. Apologies to the scientists involved.

The Captain's description of the bombing of Guernica is based on first-hand accounts. However, his estimate of the dead and wounded, although considered accurate at the time, was too high. Most historians now agree the dead numbered "only" around three hundred civilians. That was still 4 percent of the population. Consider 4 percent of London, New York, or Paris, or 4 percent of your town or village. Take a moment to imagine what that might have felt like.

The atrocity has been eclipsed by the war that followed, but it lives on in Picasso's painting. Picasso lived in Nazi-occupied Paris during the war. The probably apocryphal story goes that a German officer pointed to a photo of *Guernica* and asked him, "Did you do that?" Picasso replied, "No, you did."

As Sarah guessed, the Poles didn't start the war. The attack on the Gleiwitz radio station in Germany was a "false-flag operation"—it was carried out by German special forces dressed as Polish soldiers. For added reality, the SS took prisoners from Dachau concentration camp to the site and put them in Polish uniforms, before murdering and mutilating them. The SS called these prisoners the "canned goods."

It's worth noting that in the present day, Gretel would have been described as having Down syndrome, but that name didn't exist in 1934. In fact, it wasn't until 1961 that concerns were raised in the medical community about the scientifically dubious and long since pejorative term "mongoloid." The World Health Organization ceased use of the term four years later.

Sarah's mother had evidently appeared in Kurt Weill's *The Threepenny Opera* at some point, with Sarah recalling Kipling and Brecht's lyrics subconsciously. The moral of *Pirate Jenny*'s frankly terrifying tale of contempt, exploitation, and revenge, if there is one, is to always be nice to the cleaner.

I may have pushed the odd quote a month or two back and forth to fit Sarah's journey, but the specific and disturbing details are accurately retold. Old men in Vienna forced to scrub the streets—true. Jews driven out of public life—true. Marginalized Polish communities—true. The execution of the disabled—true. Kristallnacht or the *Novemberpogrome*—true. Stamped passports and the Swiss refusing Jewish refugees—true. The Night of the Long Knives—true. The changes in *We Girls Sing!*—true. Jesse Owens humiliating the Nazis in 1936—true. Langfeld's lesson plan—true.

I could keep going, but I'd fill another book. By all means, reach out to ask me for more details, or indeed, correct me where you think I've gotten something wrong.

While Sarah Goldstein did not exist, her world was all too real. Worse still, it lives on today in insidious ways.

The idea that Sarah was her mother's only caregiver sounds abusive, yet she was what is now called a *young carer*. There are about 700,000 in the UK and 1.4 million in the US, children as young as six taking responsibility for sick or disabled relatives who have no one else to turn to. Sixty-eight percent of these caregivers are bullied in school and exhibit anxiety, depression, and feelings of worthlessness. Then there are one in five children in the UK who are affected by their parents' drinking. 6.6 million children in the US live in a house with one alcoholic parent. These children can look forward to a lifetime of struggle with their own mental health.

In 2015, nineteen states in the USA still permitted corporal punishment in schools, even though to strike criminals is considered "cruel and inhuman" by the Supreme Court. Despite overwhelming medical evidence for the irreversible damage caused by caning a child's open palm, where there is no protective tissue, this is still used by some schools today.

Children have been living in relative poverty in some of the world's richest countries for decades. However, after the 2008 banking crash caused by greed and immorality in the banking sector, and the economically self-defeating austerity measures enacted by western governments, we have *hungry* children in the UK and US. In some towns, one in five children goes to school with an empty belly.

Recent years have revealed to us just how widespread the sexual abuse of children and other vulnerable people by those in positions of authority has been. This abuse was and is often institutionalized, concealed, or dismissed as trivial by churches, youth organizations, broadcasters, children's homes, schools, sporting federations, and even governments.

People often wonder how the German people allowed the Nazis to take power. They scoff at the idea that "innocent" Germans did not speak up. At some point, people say, they would have stood up, complained and protested about all those small incremental injustices that built up, until it was too late.

Right now, children care for adults, experience abuse, and go hungry. All that is required to make this stop is the will of enough people. Movements can and must start with just one person. Stand up, complain, and protest.

ACKNOWLEDGMENTS

IF IT TAKES a village to raise a child, it appears that it takes a cohort, a university, a society, and a family to write a book—let alone get it published. It's a possibility that this work could have existed without their contribution and their deadlines, but you probably wouldn't be reading it right now.

Those requiring thanks are just too numerous to be contained here, so the following is an "including, but not limited to" list. Conversely, markedly different expressions of gratitude are not abundant enough to make these acknowledgements a good read, and those that do exist are woefully inadequate.

I have to start with a tale of two Scoobies.

There is my MA cohort at Manchester Metropolitan University, aka the Scooby Gang. We met weekly online, in a watcher's library of the mind, salivating over maps, dragons, and the necessity for dead monks. We made each other better, we made each other laugh, and we messed royally with our tutors. A more supportive and talented bunch of writers it would be difficult to find, with a chemistry impossible to replicate. From the bottom of my heart, thank you to Marie Dentan, Jason E. Hill, Kim Hutson, Anna Mainwaring, Luci Nettleton, Alison Padley-Woods, Katy Simmonds, and Paula Warrington, not forgetting Dave and Jane who we lost along the way. *If there's something bad out there, we'll find, you'll slay, we'll party.* I love you all.

Thank you also to the MMU staff whose belief and tutelage turned a hack into an author—Livi Michael, Iris Feindt, Catherine Fox, N M Browne, and Ellie Byrne, with special gratitude to Sherry Ashworth for praise and validation at a critical moment.

The second set of Scoobies are the members, volunteers, and organizers of the Society of Children's Book Writers and Illustrators, or SCBWI. This is a very special organization, uniquely caring and genuinely helpful, with a real *all for one and one for all* spirit. We're not in competition. One person's success is everyone's success. Add to this free wine, tables of cake, and the best costume parties. I can't possibly name every Scooby who has touched my life, and I couldn't single out any one person for fear of neglecting someone. Look, you know who you are. See you at the next conference or retreat.

SCBWI also gave me the opportunity to meet some authors and professionals whose advice and encouragement changed my career—or at least gave me a sound bite to get me through the dark times. Being told I "could be the YA Graham Greene" is right up there with once being mistaken for Johnny Depp in a restaurant. Thank you to Elizabeth Wein, Melvin Burgess, and Lauren Fortune, to name but three.

There is, of course, nothing like someone staking their professional reputation on you and loving your work as much as you do. Enter Molly Ker Hawn at TBA, the Great Santini of editing and the kind of agent I spend every writing day trying to be worthy of. Thank you, Molly, and may your eyes be forever tiny-spider-free.

Which brings me to my editors Kendra Levin at Viking and Sarah Stewart at Usborne, whose very real connection to and empathy with the story and characters made many hard choices easy ones. Thank you for the belief and achievable deadlines. Gratitude must also go to Jody Corbett and Janet B. Pascal for keeping me on my toes.

To everyone else who expressed a preference, the deepest gratitude for your kind words and compelling stories.

I have to thank those who contributed to the story in some vital way—my Jewish consultant Deborah Goldstein, self-described "disappointing gymnast" Leila Sales, Paula and Luci for horses and Norse mythology respectively, Jo Wyton for seismic advice, and Dr. Jennifer Naparstek Klein whose counsel on childhood trauma I took (and occasionally ignored). *Danke*

& *dzięki* to Kornelia Lemberger and Jannina Broders. Thanks also to the innumerable librarians, online historians, and museum curators whose help and work have been invaluable, especially the Center for Jewish History and the United States Holocaust Memorial Museum. Miscellaneous thanks to the late great Mal Peet, SF Said, Sarwat Chadda, Kathryn Evans, Peter Bunzl, Vanessa Curtis, Clare Furniss, Non Pratt, Robin Stevens, Emma Solomon, Miriam Craig, Alexandra Boyd, Louise Palfreyman, Anna's students, and my other unnamed readers, for feedback and guidance.

Before I get to my real family, I want to express a measure of gratitude to my colleagues and friends at the company that isn't, in fact, called TLG, for their support, tutelage, and moments of invaluable humanity. Thank you Jeremy, Ali, Heidi, Greg, Janne, Lauren, and everyone in Enfield for making me part of your clan. Never forget that *det bedste er ikke for godt.*

Thank you to my big brothers, Andy and Ben, the BAM, orphans all. In particular, Andrew Killeen, a grown-up writer of thrilling and NSFW historical fiction, who has been an inspiration to me for my entire life. He was the *arbiter elegantiarum* of my teens and childhood—yes, even the Emerson, Lake & Palmer—so he gets a degree of credit (and blame) for the person I've become.

Thank you to Coco-Mojo for keeping me fit. Who's a good girl? You are. Yes, you are.

Thank you to my children, Elliott and little FH, who delight and challenge me by equal turns, delighting me as they infuriate. You are inspirational, motivational, and as close to a meaning for existence as I've found. You are wonderful people who make me proud. I love you with all my heart and with an intensity for which words are inadequate.

As for Anne-Marie, my sweetest and only . . . as a description, "muse" doesn't really do you justice. Writers are often asked, "Is your partner supportive?" by which they mean, "How do they stand you being emotionally unavailable and moody, spending all your time alone with fictional people who enrage you, and making no money in the process? Is it possible they still love you in any way?" Yes, you are supportive. You invented supportive. Thank you for helping me become myself, in every way. This book is yours.

Matt Killeen was born in Birmingham, in the UK, back when trousers were wide and everything was brown. Early instruction in his craft included being told that a drawing of a Cylon exploding isn't writing and copying out your mother's payslip isn't an essay "about my family." Several alternative careers beckoned, some involving laser guns and guitars, before he finally returned to words and attempted to make a living as an advertising copywriter and largely ignored music and sports journalist. He fulfilled a childhood ambition and became a writer for the world's best loved toy company in 2010, as it wasn't possible to be an X-wing pilot. Married to his Nuyorican soul mate, he is parent to both an unfeasibly clever teenager and a toddler who is challenging his father's anti-establishment credentials by repeatedly writing on the walls. He accidentally moved to the countryside in 2016.